# Soccer Mom In Galilee

Rachel Stackhouse

# Author's Note

This book is a work of fiction. Though every effort has been made to portray Biblical characters and events as accurately as possible, the story of Rachel and her conversations with Jesus are pure dramatization. Outside of what is also contained in the gospels, this story is merely one woman's idea of how things *might* have been.

You may read the novel straight through before taking a look at the commentary, or you may choose to read the relevant commentary after each chapter. To begin by taking a look at Dr. de Vries' introduction, please turn to page 221.

# Prologue

I have a bobble-head doll affixed to the dashboard of my car — a gag gift I received from my smart-alecky daughter on the occasion of my fortieth birthday. The doll's oversized, wrinkled white tee shirt says "All Hail Supermom." Her hair is long and straight on one side, frizzed up on the other. There is lipstick on her teeth. One arm maneuvers a floating steering wheel while the other encircles a soccer ball, a breast pump, and a copy of the Wall Street Journal. The T-shirt is pulled down over one shoulder to reveal a "little black dress" which barely peeks out below it, riding up on one thigh with static cling. Her left foot sports a sexy strappy sandal; her right, a fuzzy slipper. Her smile is ecstatic. Her eyes are glazed.

At the time, I thought it was funny. Pathetic, but funny. I used to look at it, and grin, and feel tired. When I look at it now, I still smile. I just don't feel tired anymore.

So much in my life has changed since the dream. You might not see it if you didn't know me well, at least not right away. I drive the same car, I live in the same house, and if I tell you I'll spearhead the lacrosse team's fundraising drive, I will, and I'll do a darn good job of it. But I am no longer the woman in that bobble-head doll. Her, I left back in Galilee.

I think she got eaten by wolves.

# Chapter 1

Picture a cool but sunny Thursday in spring. I had spent the morning at yet another endless meeting of the band parents, nitpicking over details of my daughter's upcoming trip to Florida. Jen Coldwell insisted that any kid who hadn't participated in either the fruit sale or the car wash should have to pay extra, and Lisa White was in a snit because neither the school nor her son took his shellfish allergy seriously enough. By the time the meeting let out I was both late and starving, giving me no choice but to resort to my favorite food group: the grease family. I ate two tacos in the car and rushed into my mammogram appointment with hot sauce on my breath, only to wait twenty minutes in one of those obnoxious cell-phone-free waiting areas before my name was called. After another ten minutes of waiting, this time in a hospital gown in a holding room air-conditioned down to fifty degrees, I at last got my turn in the vise. The technician had a funny look on her face at one point, which made me nervous. But I didn't have time to worry about it. The shop where Bekka's prom dress awaited pickup was on the other side of town, and if I didn't make a quick run by the grocery store before it was time to get Ryan, we would be eating stale cheese curls and pickles for dinner.

All of which made the day little different from any other weekday in the life of a middle-aged, middle-class, stay-at-home mother of two. I loathe the term "soccer mom," but I met every qualification. I drove a car the size of a boat with all the latest bells and whistles — my husband's choice, not mine — I had a son whose life was dominated by organized sports, a daughter whose life used to be until she learned to drive, and no particular occupation to call my own other than chauffeur, cheerleader, and personal coach. I hadn't cooked sit-down meals since the kids were in elementary school and the house was clean only when my parents came to visit, so I couldn't claim to be a chef or a housekeeper. As much as my husband traveled, even wife was a part-time gig. Still, the label bothered me.

It implied that I had no brain, no mind of my own, and as the proud holder of a B.S. degree in math, *magna cum laude*, I resented that. I had made a lucrative career for myself as an actuary once upon a time, thank you very much. When my husband and I married, I was the primary breadwinner. True, I quit work after our second child was born, but should that decision affect my very identity?

You could say I was sensitive on the topic. And deep down, I knew why. I knew that the dark, nagging sense of irritation that dogged me wasn't really about the work issue. Or the latest societal catchphrase. Or even other people's misperceptions of my character.

It was about me. And my perception of it.

But I had no time to ponder such profundities. I had learned, as all mothers do, that busying myself with a full slate of obligations provided the perfect excuse to avoid the things I *really* didn't want to do. Like clean the house, sort through all the kids' crap piling up in the attic, organize five years' worth of family pictures, and think about why, despite my claims of bliss, I spent every hour of every day feeling so shamefully mediocre.

I was doing everything a good soccer mom was supposed to do. But there was always something missing, something that made me feel — no matter where I was — like I was supposed to be someplace else. *Doing* something else. Something more. Never mind that I was packing my days with every possible life-enriching, self-actualizing, quality-parenting activity known to the suburbs. The emptiness was always there. The void. The sore spot.

I pretended like I didn't feel it.

I could do that. I was busy.

The grocery store was out of half-gallons of 1% milk and understaffed besides, forcing me to speed to get to the middle school to pick up Ryan, who had stayed late for intramurals and therefore could not take the bus home — again. I was sitting behind the wheel in the parking lot next to the field, watching him run towards me, when I felt the first inkling of what was to come.

Tiny lights, dancing at the periphery of my vision. Flashing and sparkling like reflections off water, all seated deep within the outer corners of my eyes. My heart skipped a beat. I blinked. The lights were still there.

"You're *late*, Mom," my son chastised good-naturedly, hopping into the front seat with mud-encrusted shoes. "But Brent's mom was late too, so we got to hang out for a while. It's cool."

"Good, I'm glad." I pulled out of the parking lot, willing the lights to disappear. They did not. The rippling flashes were growing by the second, reaching steadily farther toward the center of my vision. My fingers tensed on the steering wheel.

"Something wrong, Mom?"

I looked into my son's concerned eyes and smiled. Ryan was a sweet kid; I had done well with him. He had had a knack at judging my moods since toddlerhood, and even at the oblivious age of thirteen could still spot a distress signal long before my husband could. Physically, Ryan didn't resemble me at all, being fair-skinned like his father with pale eyes and a nest of wavy, light-brown hair. My own eyes and hair were dark brown, a throwback to the Greeks on my mother's side of the family.

At least my hair *had* been dark brown. My stylist would be fixing that on Tuesday.

"I think I have another migraine coming on," I answered, trying not to sound as apprehensive as I felt. I hadn't had a migraine in over a year, but the last one had flattened me for thirty-six hours, testing my prohibition on drinking to a state of stupor. I could not afford to have a migraine today. Or tomorrow.

I was busy.

Ryan mumbled some unintelligible — but I chose to believe heartfelt — words of sympathy, then extracted a dog-eared page of homework from his backpack. The drive to our house usually took twenty minutes, ample time for him to dispense with the unpleasantness of mathematics in preparation for the real business of video gaming on our family room floor. An incapacitated mother shouldn't affect those plans.

The lights in my eyes merged into prisms of color that pixilated the far edges of my vision. My heel pumped restlessly behind my toe on the pedal; at stoplights my fingers drummed upon the wheel. I turned my head this way and that with an exaggerated motion, overcompensating for the areas I couldn't see. Every minute of the drive seemed an hour. Every block stretched for miles. Mild pressure flirted with the bones of my skull, pushing on them ever so slightly, then retreating. I knew every nuance of the aura. I didn't have much time.

I pulled the gas-guzzler into our garage, careful to stop with the windshield just touching the blue ball my husband had suspended from the ceiling. The behemoth vehicle only barely fit; a few inches short on the pull-in and the automatic door would catch the bumper. I had not even turned the ignition off before Ryan and his backpack were out the door and into the house. He remembered the last time I'd had a migraine.

The pressure in my skull mounted as I walked up the basement stairs, kicking teenager debris off the steps and down onto the already cluttered floor. Weight pressed upon my facial bones as if I were six feet underwater. I opened the door to the kitchen and found my firstborn, now sixteen, snacking on a blue-green fruit roll.

"*Mom*," she entreated, her brown eyes pleading. "Where is Dad? I *have* to have his car tonight. I promised Bri and Claire I'd pick them up for dinner at Casa — you know, the pre-dance dinner — we've been planning it for *days* now."

The pain began. A sharp pinpoint of ice, driving into the back of my right eye. "What your father and I said, Bekka," I reminded, setting the bag of groceries — and her new dress — on the counter and rubbing my temple, "was that you could drive your father's car *if* he was home by tonight. But he's still in Detroit. You can take mine instead, but if this migraine doesn't let up, I'm afraid I'm going to have to ask you to take Ryan to his baseball game for me. You're welcome to go out with your friends afterward as long as you promise to pick him up on time and bring him home."

Her shoulders slumped in agony. "I can't drive Bri and Claire around in that *tank* with Ryan stinking up the place with his cleats!" Her face went into full pout. "I'd rather not go at all."

"Fine by me, Bekka."

I regretted my snappiness. I always did, but Bekka had a knack for pushing my buttons until I sounded every bit as petulant as she did, even when I did not have dozens of tiny needles pricking the back of my eyeball.

"I'm going to lie down," I explained, putting the meat away in the refrigerator. The rest of the groceries were on their own. "If you're not going out to eat, maybe you can help Ryan make some hamburger casserole later. The mix is in the bag."

"*Mom!*" she protested. "Why do *I* have to cook?"

I stumbled out of the kitchen, through the hall, and up the stairs to the master bedroom. I crossed straight to the window and lowered the shades. My vision was clearer now. The distortion always seemed to fade as the pain came on, but the photophobia was just ramping up. Every ray of light entering my pupils generated a fresh spate of pin pricks; soon, those discrete shafts of pain would coalesce into a battering ram.

I removed my shoes. I grabbed a T-shirt out of a drawer. I slid between the blanket and comforter of my king-sized bed, draped the T-shirt over my eyes, and breathed slowly. After this time, I vowed, I would see a doctor. I would not convince myself, as I had before, that this would never happen again and that it was not worth one more visit to one more medical office for one more prescription and two more copays. I would not be so short-sighted.

The battering ram took aim.

I tried to breathe as I had been taught in my childbirth classes, but my memory of the training was hazy. The days when my kids were little seemed such a blur — even as they felt like yesterday. Everything had happened so quickly, so furiously. I had tried to slow down the pace back then, to preserve each precious moment. But time had marched on, trampling me.

My thoughts spun wildly as the migraine pressed on, now a powerful, pounding pain that consumed every ounce of my strength, both physically and emotionally. I was tired... so tired. Yet my brain in token masochistic fashion had chosen this time to be intent on thinking. Despite the distraction of the pain, my gray cells wanted, with sudden manic determination, to figure everything out — to at last get me to a place where I didn't feel the ache anymore. Not the ache of the migraine but the deeper, more profound ache of knowing that life was passing me by, that no matter how much I pushed or pulled, something was still slipping away.

I was right next to what I wanted, but I couldn't touch it. I couldn't see it or hear it. I only knew it was there.

Something sharp struck against my ankle. I pulled away from it, but the pricking sensation came again. Groaning with annoyance, I groped around to investigate and discovered that the twenty-eight-hundred dollar mattress my husband and I had feuded over the purchase of last fall was no longer beneath me. I was lying on dirt.

My eyes flew open in confusion.

A chicken blinked back at me.

*Commentary for Chapter 1 begins on page 224.*

# Chapter 2

I can't write the string of words that came out of my mouth. Let's just say my kids weren't allowed to use them. I was rusty with a few myself, but the chicken got the message. It turned tail and strutted away from me across the dirt, leaving a cloud of brown dust in its wake.

I coughed. I sat up and looked around.

My heart pounded like a jackhammer.

I was not in my bedroom. I was not anywhere that even remotely resembled my bedroom. I was on the ground, inside the high stone walls of a courtyard, twenty feet or so from the door of a house.

At least I think it was a house.

I pulled unsteadily to my feet. I appeared to be in some sort of museum, like a Native American home site. The structure before me had walls built of a blackish, rough-hewn stone — a peculiar conglomerate of boxes piled high on top of each other, fusing at various levels, topped off with flat roofs and connected by wooden ladders and narrow stone stairs. The dusty courtyard surrounding it was littered with crude-looking tools and roamed by three goats and half a dozen chickens. A donkey slurped water from a stone trough. Another lay only a few feet away from me, resting in the minimal shade of a small tree, its eyes looking through me with disinterest as it twitched its ear at a fly. The air was hot as Hades and stank of smoke and manure.

My limbs began to shake.

The door flew open. A woman emerged.

She was a mature woman, at least a decade older than me, and in no way, shape, or form a Native American. She was dressed in a shapeless linen tunic that covered her body from shoulder to ankle, with another, lighter-weight cloth wrapped about her head. Her dark skin was heavily creased with age and sun, and the few wisps of hair that escaped from her headcovering were a contrast in black and gray. Her eyes alighted on me immediately, and I stood there unable to breathe, trying my best to look like anything but what I was: a confused, terrified interloper whose entire body was now trembling like a wind-up toy.

For the briefest of instants, the woman looked as confused as I was. But then the uncertainty in her face disappeared, and she bolted towards me with a confident, demanding stride that froze my feet in place.

Then we heard the scream.

It was the scream of a woman. A woman frightened, and in obvious pain. The sound shot out through the house's windows, which were little more than slits in the thick rock walls, and penetrated clear to my bone marrow. Someone was hurting. She was hurting badly.

Was I next?

The woman reached me and grabbed my arm. I wanted to shake her off, but my body wouldn't cooperate. She threw a hand around my waist and pushed and pulled me toward the door, and I followed, unresisting, my muscles as useless as a bowl of half-set gelatin.

"You're not a moment too soon!" the woman snapped. "I was thinking I'd have to do the job myself, and God knows no one wants *that*."

I stared at her, taking in a much-needed breath. Despite her tone, she did not sound like someone who was about to kill me. She also did not sound like someone who spoke English. The language coming from her mouth was all yips and yodels, punctuated with rough, unfamiliar consonant sounds. Yet I seemed able to sense her meaning, almost as if I were feeling her words rather than hearing them.

"It came on very suddenly," she continued, guiding me swiftly towards the house's open wooden door. "Everyone thought she had some weeks yet, and her mother-in-law is out. The men were frantic till Joanna and I arrived."

I studied my captor shamelessly, desperate to find some hint of goodness amidst her alien features. Her dark hazel eyes were spirited, but not unkind, and despite the waspishness of her voice, I did not sense any real malice in her.

She rolled her eyes with sudden mirth. "And they've no idea how clueless we are. I'm a businesswoman, you know. Not a—"

A man stepped up before us, blocking the doorway. He was no taller than me and not a day under 60, but the sight of his weathered, heavily scarred skin and still-muscular arms set my pulse back to pounding. His tunic was filthy with dust, stopping just below his knees to display hairy calves and bare, grotesquely callused feet. His teeth were appalling — yellowed and half rotten, and his long, stringy gray hair was pulled into a ponytail behind his neck. I had an overwhelming urge to run as far away from him — and whatever was causing that horrific screaming — as I could, but what I wanted didn't seem to matter. I was a prisoner in my own, petrified body.

"Relax, Zebedee," the woman said soothingly. "Help is here. I'll take her right up."

The older man stepped forward out of our way, staring at me with a benign, puzzled expression.

*He* was puzzled?

I fought a sudden urge to laugh. But any laughter I managed now would be hysterical, and I was not now, and never had been, a woman given to hysteria.

Heart attack or stroke, maybe. But *not* hysteria.

The woman, whose teeth were almost as bad as Zebedee's and who had an appalling lack of respect for personal space, pulled me through the doorway and on into the house.

I blinked. Compared to the near-blinding sun outside, the inside of the structure was dim, lit only by narrow strips of sunlight peeking through the high, slit-shaped windows above our heads. My eyes took time to adjust, and in the interim my ears played tricks on me. I could swear I heard the clunk of animal hooves on stone, the rustling of hay, just off to my right. But we were inside now.

The room slowly brightened. I could make out pillars of stone before me and, above my head, a ceiling made of wooden beams overlaid with branches and reeds. The floor beneath my feet was mud plaster. The clunking noise repeated itself, and I cast a wary glance to my right.

My ears had not deceived me. I was standing four feet from a full-grown cow, and another donkey was behind it. The pillars that subdivided the room had mangers stretching between them, setting off a stable area of cobbled stone. The cow pushed its nose into one of the mangers and rooted about in the hay. The donkey stood still, its eyes half closed.

I wanted to close my own. Perhaps if I did, this would all go away.

*You were lying on your bed,* I reminded myself. *What you're seeing cannot be real...*

But it wasn't only a matter of what I was seeing. I was hearing it, feeling it, smelling it. Closing my eyes couldn't make it disappear.

The scream came again.

I went rigid. But even as I was certain I could feel no greater fear, a part of my stunned mind at last began to awaken. It wasn't a woman screaming, I realized with sudden clarity. It was a girl.

A girl no older than my Bekka.

"Come on!" The woman released me and moved quickly toward a square stone pillar on the other side of the room. Waving for me to follow, she began to scramble up the series of wooden planks that protruded from the pillar's sides, using feet and hands, climbing it as if it were a spiral staircase.

I hesitated. The grabby woman with the mischievous eyes and whoever was screaming were ahead of me. The old man with the scars, the chickens, and whatever else lay beyond that courtyard wall were behind me. I could run now; take a chance on it.

The scream was followed by a moan.

*Bekka.*

I stepped forward and nearly tripped into a charcoal pit in the floor. I looked down.

I was no longer wearing my slacks and top. I was wearing a long linen tunic, a cloak about my shoulders, and a hair covering just like the other woman's. My feet were shod in horrifying leather things that looked more like torture devices than sandals, and I was pretty sure I wasn't wearing any underwear — the only thing between me and my tunic was another, lighter tunic. A cloth belt was tied around my waist, and attached to it was a heavy bag that banged against my hip.

The scream came again.

I couldn't think about clothes. Not now.

My feet started to move. I forced myself, step by step, toward the pillar, then climbed up and around it until I could thrust my head through the hole in the ceiling. The woman wasn't there. She was climbing yet another wooden ladder to a loft. I stepped into the room and stood up. The ceiling was low, but the windows on this second level allowed more light, and the plaster floor was covered with a large mat, making it seem more homelike. Crude wooden furniture and an assortment of earthenware vessels, neatly placed, lined the walls. In the far corner stood a loom.

My heart skipped another beat. This was no museum. There were no colorful explanatory signs, no soft velvet ropes cordoning off the valuables. No cleverly concealed trashcan overflowing with gum wrappers and plastic cups. This place, and these people, were real.

And so was that agonizing scream.

I waited for the woman to step off the ladder, then started up it myself. "It's all right, Leah," I heard her say, her tone gentle. "The midwife is here."

I froze on the third rung.

*Midwife?!*

"Thank goodness, Mary!" another younger female voice replied, showing equal measures of relief and continued fright. "I knew James would find her. Salome never would have gone visiting if she had known. It all came on so suddenly!"

My heart raced, even as I let out a small breath of relief. So that was it. The girl was in labor, they were expecting a midwife, and I had been mistaken for her.

All I had to do was set them straight.

I made my way up the rest of the ladder and stepped off into the loft. A single window let light into the tiny space, the ceiling of which was so low only a very short woman could stand or walk in it. The floor was covered with a thicker, more carpet-like mat, and two teenaged girls sprawled upon it; one, heavily pregnant, leaning back into the lap and arms of the other.

The laboring girl wore a long linen nightshirt, oversized and floppy, cinched loosely above her swollen belly with a soft fabric belt. Her long, dark auburn hair had been done up in a single plait, but half the wavy strands had since escaped. Her face was flushed and glistening with sweat. Her brown eyes were large and fearful.

"Where is Adah?"

The timid voice took several seconds to penetrate my scrambled mind. I looked at the second teenager, the one who had spoken. She was a bit older than the pregnant girl — slight, dark, and distinctly Arab-looking — and her words had been directed at me.

Another scream saved me from answering.

The mother-to-be curled her pain-wracked body into a ball, tensing every muscle, her breathing rapid and shallow. "Tamar," she moaned softly as the contraction subsided, "my hands are numb. And my feet..."

Tamar's large dark eyes looked up hopefully, even desperately, into mine. Discomfort rose in the pit of my stomach, and I turned from her gaze, only to find another pair of eyes also boring down on me — the eyes of Mary, the woman who had brought me here. And with no more than a moment's glance into their penetrating hazel depths, I was certain of two things. One, the older woman was no fool. She knew full well, now, that I was not the expected midwife. And number two was that neither one of these women knew a thing more about birthing than I did.

My gaze shot back to Tamar, then came to rest on Leah. The wheels in my brain — shocked numb with adrenaline — resumed a slow turn. Evidently someone had called a real midwife, and with luck "Adah" herself would soon arrive. But right now, at this moment, an ex-actuary with two children was all this poor girl had. I was no midwife; I could barely pull out my kids' splinters. But I did have a pretty good idea why Leah's hands felt numb. And I could no more sit by and do nothing to help the girl than I could watch a gerbil drown in a toilet bowl.

I cleared my throat. "I'm not Adah," I told them both. "But I can help until she comes."

At least that's what I tried to tell them. The actual sounds that came out of my mouth were gibberish.

"Thank you," Tamar replied, her lovely eyes moist with relief.

*Their* gibberish.

The thousand and one questions that revelation brought, I shrugged off onto the proverbial back burner. I was surrounded by inanity already; there was no point sweating details.

I scrambled around on the mat until my face was level with Leah's. "Your hands are numb?" I asked gently.

The girl nodded.

"Are you feeling dizzy at all?"

Another nod.

"That's all right; it's nothing to worry about, it doesn't mean anything's wrong with the baby. But you do need to breathe more slowly. Watch and breathe with me. All right?"

I maintained eye contact with the girl as best I could while stealing fleeting glances around the room. The only other thing I knew to do for hyperventilation was the paper bag trick, but there was nothing of that description in sight. There was no paper anywhere.

"You're doing wonderfully, Leah," Mary encouraged as she knelt beside us. She had in her hands a rag and a small dish of water, and as she talked, she wet the rag and placed it over Leah's sweating forehead. "I told John to put a knife on the fire," she informed me, her tone reserved. "And we have water and some linens, though not very many. My friend Joanna is around here somewhere, looking for more." She nodded her head toward a corner of the loft, where a stack of folded fabric lay, along with a large bowl and a jar. None of it looked clean.

I fought back a shudder. A knife on the fire? For what? How primitive was this place, these people? No electricity, no running water

— I got that. They appeared to be of Middle-Eastern descent. But none of that made any more sense than the museum theory.

Leah moaned. Another contraction was coming on.

"When did the pains start?" I asked Tamar.

"Only an hour ago!" Panic rose in her voice again. "I thought first babies were supposed to be slow, but one moment she was perfectly fine and the next her water broke — and she's been like this ever since! She keeps calling for her mother, but John hasn't been able to find her. And I can't imagine why James is taking so long to get the midwife. Thank goodness Mary found you!"

I shot an anxious glance at the older woman. She shot me a steely look back.

*I won't tell if you don't.*

I turned to Leah. She had allowed herself to relax for a moment, but now her lids were closed and she was tense again. Her hands clutched at Tamar's thin arms so fiercely her knuckles blanched.

"Leah," I said firmly, "you'll feel better if you try to relax with the pain, rather than tense up with it."

*Imposter!*

I gritted my teeth against my nagging conscience. True — by the medical standards of any halfway industrialized country I was a complete incompetent. But when I was pregnant with Bekka I had at least attended a class at the hospital, read scads of books on pregnancy and parenting, and watched a couple of birth videos. These people were throwing knives on fires. How much worse could I do?

I bent back down to Leah. "Breathe with me," I ordered, demanding her attention. "Slowly now, that's it..."

The poor thing tried her best, but her pain was severe. She was still hyperventilating. I grabbed my own sleeve and placed it before her mouth, trying to restrict her air flow. I had no idea if it was working.

The contraction ended and her eyes closed again.

I examined the freckles on my left wrist, but they had no idea of the time. Where *was* the real midwife? Coaching someone through contractions was one thing; delivering a baby was another.

"Who are you?"

The thin voice broke my thoughts, and I looked down into the tired, anxious face of a temporarily pain-free Leah. She was an attractive girl, in a homespun way. Her face was round and her nose large, but her skin was a smooth ivory-brown, and her thickly-lashed almond eyes were captivating even when closed.

*So like Bekka.*

My voice quavered. "Rachel," I answered hesitantly. "My name is Rachel."

The thin voice piped up again, this time barely audible. "Is the baby all right, Rachel?"

I swallowed hard. "The baby's just fine."

"Mary?" Another woman's head appeared at the top of the ladder, and my heart leapt with anticipation. The midwife!

But no.

The newcomer was, if possible, even less at ease with the situation than I was. She was a little older than me, with a plump, round face, pink cheeks, and what was probably a merry expression when she wasn't so anxious. "Here are all the clean linens we could find," she said, popping up just long enough to place a stack of dingy cloths at the edge of the loft, then beating a hasty retreat. "Do you need me up there?" she called as she fled, "Or is there something I can do down here?"

"No, stay there, Joanna," Mary answered. "You can bring us some more water, maybe. And could you check to make sure the knife's heating?"

"Will do," the voice called cheerfully.

I stared at my wrist freckles again. Leah's contractions were coming way too fast for comfort, and I couldn't deal with anything more than I was already doing. What else *could* I do? Boil water? I didn't even know the purpose of the adage. I had no instruments to sterilize, and making the questionably clean linens hot and wet would accomplish nothing.

The midwife had to come. I had to get out of here. I had no business being here in the first place.

I still didn't even know where "here" was!

"Rachel?"

The girl's small, shaky hand beckoned me closer. I lowered my ear reluctantly to her mouth.

"I think," the woman-child moaned, "I want to push."

*Commentary for Chapter 2 begins on page 226.*

# Chapter 3

NO!

I could tell Leah not to push. I could do that, and it would do about as much good as it did the labor nurse who told me the same thing right before I backhanded the interfering hussy out of my face and shot Ryan clear into tomorrow.

If the baby was coming, it was coming.

Tamar's dark eyes locked on mine. She had heard what Leah said, too, and I could tell it frightened her. But she took a breath and steeled herself, determined not to show it. "That's good," she told her friend, her voice both gentle and confident as she held the younger girl in her lap, stroking her damp hair tenderly behind her ears. "That means John will be a father in no time — and the pain will be over." She turned her gaze back to me. "Isn't that right, Rachel?"

My jaws clenched. If this "John" who had impregnated a child no older than my Bekka came within fifty feet of me, *his* pain would just be beginning.

"Absolutely," I answered, clueless. "It will all be over soon."

Mary caught my eyes. *Can you do this?*

I stared back. *No!*

Leah cried out again. Her body curled to one side; her cries melted to moans.

*Do something, Rachel! Stop being such a blasted wuss!*

I closed my eyes and took in a breath. All I could do was my best. With one swift, determined motion, I pulled up the bottom of the girl's nightshirt and looked beneath it.

The baby's head was crowning.

My breath came out with a gush. "Mary?" I said, my voice hollow, "could I have some water to wash her up? And some of those cloths?"

She nodded.

What I didn't know about childbirth could fill volumes, but I did know the importance of cleanliness. How a sanitary birth was to be accomplished in a place where every imaginable surface was coated with grime was beyond me, but I had to try. Mary handed me a bowl half full of water and a pile of folded fabric. I washed and dried my own hands, then removed the soiled linens Leah had been lying on and replaced them with a soft cushion of relatively cleaner ones. The cloths I removed were soaked with blood-tinged fluid.

I sat back, head reeling. Leah moaned again.

"If you feel like you want to push," a voice coming out of my mouth said, "Go ahead. Whatever makes you more comfortable — whatever seems right." Mary knelt in and refreshed the cloth on Leah's forehead. My own face dripped with perspiration, as did poor Tamar's. The teen's dark hair was plastered to her head and her arms were red with scratches from Leah's clinging hands.

*Please don't push, Leah*, my subconscious begged. *Wait for someone competent!*

With a sudden surge of energy, the girl hoisted herself up out of Tamar's arms. She moved her body awkwardly, but purposefully, attempting first one position, then another, before coming to settle on her hands and knees. For a moment, she rocked herself gently forward and back. Then she stopped and bore down. Hard.

My heart thudded violently against my ribs. I had no idea what she was doing or whether it was good for her or not. But her behavior seemed instinctive. And instinct had to be better than me.

I scooted up behind her and pulled up the nightshirt.

*Dear God.* The baby's head was most definitely protruding. I grabbed a clean rag and held it beneath, afraid the infant would slip out onto the floor. What else could I do?

"You're doing great, Leah," I soothed, trying my best to hide my panic as she continued to moan and push. She could *not* have the baby now, like this. She simply couldn't.

Leah shrieked.

The baby's head was out.

My own shaking hands shot forward, holding the cloth beneath her. The little blue face moved. Clear fluid spit out of its tiny mouth.

"I can see the baby!" I exclaimed. "It's moving, Leah! It's fine. Just a few—"

But I didn't have to say a thing. On the next heave the baby's head rotated to the side, and then its whole, tiny body emerged in one smooth, fluid motion — shoulders, belly, hips, and feet. The baby dropped onto the cloth in my hands and began immediately to wriggle, protesting the injustice of the process with its first, lusty cry.

"It's a boy!" I cried.

The words had barely left my mouth before a tremendous

whooping sound blasted up through the house's rafters, striking my already taut nerves like a freight train. Leah collapsed on her side, and I frantically pulled the baby clear, trying not to stretch the ominous-looking blue cord that still connected mother and infant. Mary handed me another cloth, and I wiped the infant dry. Leah rested no more than a second before scrambling to a sitting position and holding her arms out for her baby, but she was shaking so badly I was afraid to give him to her. Wordlessly, Tamar swooped in, propped Leah's torso in her lap, and supported the new mother's arms with her own.

I laid the tiny, wriggling body on his mother's chest. Fat tears rolled down Leah's cheeks.

Tamar said something. I think she told Leah he was beautiful, but even though my ear was inches from her mouth, her whispered soprano was lost in the masculine din that raged below. Bellows of joy, shouts of congratulations, and what must have been some vigorous dance steps were making the house's very walls vibrate in celebration.

"All right, all right!" a gravelly voice called from the ladder. "I'm here now. Let me through!"

I looked up into the face of a small, middle-aged woman — thin, hunched, and unhealthy looking.

*Adah.* The midwife.

For a moment — just a moment, mind you — I wished she would go away. Then my sanity returned.

I scooted away from the girls and moved to the back of the loft next to Mary. Five women were a tight fit, but I doubted I could move any farther. My muscles were jelly. I was trembling worse than Leah.

Yet another woman climbed the ladder, but had no space to enter. She was younger than me, with pretty eyes and auburn hair just beginning to gray. I assumed her to be Leah's mother.

Joanna's voice called up cheerfully from below. "Here's the knife!"

Leah's mother bent down and retrieved a wrapped bundle, then handed it off to the midwife.

I tensed. How well-trained was this woman, and what exactly did she plan to do to my baby?

I watched skeptically as the midwife removed a length of twine from a pouch on her belt and tied off the infant's umbilical cord. She then unwrapped the knife's searing blade and, grasping the still-wrapped handle firmly, cut through the cord with a single stroke.

"Oh, Leah," Tamar exclaimed, her own face glowing every bit as happily as the new mother's. "He's the most beautiful baby I've ever seen!"

Leah leaned back her shining face and kissed the older girl affectionately on the cheek. "He's your baby, too, Tamar," she said between breaths. "He'll be both of ours."

I watched as tears swelled in Tamar's eyes. She said nothing, answering only with a return kiss to both Leah and the baby.

Mary tapped my shoulder. "We should go down now."

But I couldn't move. The "we've-got-business-to-discuss" tone of Mary's voice was hardly incentive, and besides, I didn't want to leave the baby. The midwife had taken the infant from his mother and was now, for unfathomable reasons, rubbing his tender skin with salt.

Leah moaned softly, and the midwife handed the baby to Tamar. "That'll be the afterbirth," she announced. "Rise up a little."

I shook myself out of my reverie and followed Mary down the ladder. But because my legs were unsteady, my mind was racing, and the bottom rung of the ladder had been moved, my descent was less than smooth. If Mary hadn't turned and caught me I would have fallen on my face and left one leg behind.

"Easy there," she said, seeming amused despite herself, at least until her hands came into contact with the bulging bag on my waist belt. It was hidden underneath my outer tunic, but she could feel it. Judging from the startled look on her face, she could also guess what it contained — which put her a full step ahead of me.

"Rachel, come over here!" she whispered sharply, gesturing to the wall by the window. We were joined there, shoulder to shoulder, by her friend Joanna — whom I could now tell was as short as she was stout, with crooked buck teeth and a mischievous grin. Male voices continued to bellow beneath us. I wondered how many of them were down there. I wondered how good they were with knives.

Mary's gaze was harsh, penetrating. "I thought you were a bit well-dressed for a midwife," she said wryly, pitching her voice low, so as not to be overheard. "Who are you? Does Zebedee know you?"

I swallowed. A lie on that score could be easily disproved. I shook my head.

Mary's eyes narrowed. "Then what were you doing in his courtyard?"

The wheels in my brain chugged furiously. I had always prided myself on my quick wit. The skill didn't usually extend to lying, but if I couldn't believe the truth myself, how could I expect anyone else to? Sane people here lived with livestock. I didn't want to know what happened to lunatics.

"I heard that someone was looking for a midwife," I said tentatively. "I'm not, well, fully trained. But I thought maybe I could help."

Mary's discerning eyes studied me. She shot a sideways look at Joanna, who lifted an eyebrow. "That explains why you came through the gate," Mary replied, her voice clipped. "It doesn't explain who you are. Do your people live here? In Capernaum?"

My heart began to pound again. Capernaum? Never heard of it. I shot a panicked glance out the window, where from this height I could see over the courtyard wall. Beyond it stretched countless more courtyard walls, coalescing haphazardly into a sprawling town that stretched down a slope as far as I could see. An endless maze of black stone, flat plaster roofs, and dusty paths. People — dirty people — everywhere, milling about like ants. All walking, or riding on donkeys. Not a one of them wearing jeans, or even pants. No cars. No telephone poles. No asphalt.

How? No good explanation short of catastrophic memory loss could have taken me from where I thought I was and landed me in the dregs of the Middle East with knowledge of another language. Something drastic had to have happened. A significant amount of time had to have passed. Time I had no memory of.

A vacation gone wrong? A plane crash? Worldwide nuclear holocaust?

My voice caught with fright. "No. I'm not from here."

Mary put out a hand and clutched my arm.

"Then who is here with you? What man?"

My head spun. I needed a man? Were women not allowed to move as they pleased here? What would happen to them if they tried?

My arm trembled beneath Mary's hand, and she looked straight into my eyes again. Her scrutiny was piercing, yet there was something in her gaze that comforted me. I could sense her intelligence, her savvy, her strength. For all our differences, I felt, somehow, as though we thought alike.

"Rachel," she asked quietly, "Are you running away from something?"

I pulled in a breath, my lungs shuddering. Outside in the courtyard, two men walked through the gate. One was considerably bigger than me. The other was immense. Both wore short, filthy tunics with daggers tucked in their belts.

Figuring out what had happened to me, and how to get out of here, could take time. Time I might not have unless these women could be convinced to protect me.

I had no idea what explanation for my predicament might seem plausible to them, much less sympathetic. All I could do was feel my way through and hope that, perhaps, they would provide one.

"Yes," I explained, thinking in English, yet still speaking in gibberish. The effect was disconcerting, but I had no time to ponder it. "I left my home."

The women looked at each other. They seemed incredulous, which was not what I was hoping for. But when Mary turned back to me, there was a glimmer of admiration in her eyes. "Why leave? Did your husband's family mistreat you?"

I squirmed. "My home wasn't safe."

The women exchanged another glance, this one full of understanding and sympathy. *Eureka.* "So you came to Capernaum looking for other kin?" Mary pressed. "How did you get here?"

"I have no other kin here," I admitted, ignoring the second question.

Both women's eyes widened. "Are you saying you traveled to Capernaum *alone*?" Joanna asked, making clear just how moronic that idea was.

I nodded.

"But you could have been robbed, or raped, or worse!" she continued, incredulous. "I've never heard of such foolishness! From how far did you come?"

I was trembling all over again. Partly because I wasn't sure how much further such vague answers could carry me. And partly because her words were confirming the worst of my fears.

"I can't say. I don't want anyone to know where I come from... I can't risk having my husband's family find me."

Mary's eyes hardened, even as something deep within them glittered. "Oh really?" she whispered, patting the bag at my waist through my tunic. Metal clinked on metal, as if the pouch were filled with coins.

*Coins!*

"That wouldn't be because you robbed them blind, eh?"

My face suffused with heat. Lying was one thing, but I was not a thief.

"No!" I defended, facing my accuser squarely. "I did not steal this.

From anyone! Please, you have to believe me."

Neither woman had a chance to answer. Our conversation was interrupted by a voice loud enough to make all three of us jump.

"Leah's all right, isn't she? Can I come up?"

The head and shoulders of a man had popped up through the opening to the first floor. He was a young man, in his early to mid twenties, with thick auburn hair, a short beard, and a strong, square jaw. Under different circumstances, the roughness of his appearance might have spooked me. But there was no mistaking the tenderness in his voice.

"Patience, John!" Mary scolded, her good nature returned. "Your wife is fine. The midwife will be finished in a minute. You go back down, now."

*Wife?*

My anger toward the new father abated. Perhaps they married young here. This man clearly cared about both Leah and the baby. I could see it in his eyes.

The head and shoulders withdrew.

Mary turned her attention back to me.

"Well, Joanna," she continued, *sotto voce*. "If Rachel says she didn't steal the money, who are we to judge?"

Joanna looked at her friend sharply a moment, then chuckled. "Mary," she said affectionately, "You are a born troublemaker."

"No," Mary returned, "I am born visionary. And right now I'm having a vision of a very comfortably funded cause."

"We don't even know her people!" Joanna protested half-heartedly.

Mary shrugged. "I know enough."

Then, to my amazement, Mary smiled at me. "Unfortunately, Rachel, you have made a fool of me. I brought you in this house under false pretenses. I as much as told Zebedee you were a midwife."

"How does he know she's not?" Joanna offered. "Tell him she came with us... from Magdala."

Mary shot her friend a sly look. "And they say *I'm* the clever one."

Joanna smirked.

Mary threw me another appraising look. "Very well, Rachel. If anyone asks, you came with us. You only arrived a minute after we did, anyway, and Zebedee was so frazzled he won't question it. But we won't say you're from Magdala. We'll say you came down with Joanna, from Jerusalem. No one knows everyone in Jerusalem. Right, Joanna?"

*Jerusalem.*

My heart skipped a beat. I really was in the Middle East.

Mary continued to talk. "We'd best get our stories straight now. I'm a widow, like you. Been one for ages. I run a boat-building business, and run it quite well, thank you. Joanna here is married to Chuza, who manages one of Herod's estates."

Joanna swelled with pride. "And I manage Chuza."

Mary laughed. "She does, it's true. Has the man wrapped around her little finger, or she wouldn't be here with me, that's for sure. We're on a little business trip. All this excitement caught us by surprise."

Someone mounted the ladder from the loft. Mary stopped talking.

The midwife was making her way down, the now thoroughly swaddled baby tucked under a practiced arm.

"Wait!"

Leah's shout was not a request. Her small, still trembling frame leaned out over the edge of the loft, her arms outstretched toward the infant.

"Easy, child," Adah soothed. "I'm only taking him to his father."

"Oh no, you're not!" Leah insisted, her large, lovely eyes flashing with venom. "*I* gave birth to him. I will show him to my husband myself!"

After a moment of silence, Adah shrugged. Wincing at each step as if her joints ached, she climbed back up into the loft again.

Mary let out a chuckle and nudged Joanna's arm. "There's hope for that one, eh?"

She turned back to me and spoke in earnest. "Crash course, Rachel. Listen well. John is Zebedee's youngest son, and Leah, obviously, is his wife. The older son, James, is Tamar's husband."

My thoughts muddled. Thrilled as I was to have gained two protectors, the women's motivations were less than clear to me. If it was my money they were after, why cajole? They were the ones whose friends had daggers.

Mary reached out a hand to adjust my veil, which had slipped crooked in the fray. I noticed that it was black, like hers, whereas Joanna's head covering was natural-colored, with a red stripe.

"Thank you," I stammered. "For helping me. But... surely you want something in return?"

Mary's grin was pure wickedness. "Who, us? Why, we can't very well leave a fine, upstanding woman like yourself wandering around Capernaum attracting bandits, can we? A widow with no sons to inherit, nowhere safe to live, and money to spare? Why, it's *tragic.*"

"You are terrible, Mary," Joanna chided, smiling.

"No, I am devious," she answered proudly. "There's a difference."

A prickle of dread crept up my spine, but I suppressed it. Whatever plans these women had for me, they almost certainly beat the alternative. Besides which, I was beginning to like them.

"You were born devious," Joanna goaded. "My mother always told me you were a corrupting influence. I should have listened to her."

"Oh, but haven't you heard?" Mary argued, her tone all innocence. "Thanks to the rabbi, I'm a changed woman. Cured of seven demons!"

Joanna let out a snort. "I think he missed a few."

A woman swore. We turned to see the midwife nearly slip as she climbed down the ladder again. "I'm too old for this," she groused, straightening. Leah's mother was starting down the ladder behind her, and up in the loft, Tamar was poised to do the same. The midwife headed toward the steps to the first floor, gesturing for Mary, Joanna, and me to follow. The six of us descended in single file.

Three men stood waiting below, silent now. Their anxious eyes searched each of our arms in turn.

"The baby is with his mother," the midwife proclaimed, not bothering to hide her annoyance at the usurping of such a plum part of her task. "She wants to see you. You may go up now."

John, his face wet with sweat and flushed with happiness, threw a brief, triumphant look at the other men, then tackled the steps as if he were flying.

"Congratulations, Zebedee," Mary offered. "You have a fine grandson."

The older man's face crinkled into a smile. "Thank you for your assistance, Mary." He then nodded at both Joanna and me. "And thank you ladies, too. I apologize for the confusion. It's not every day we have such an event in the house, particularly not with Salome out."

"Shall I fetch her, father?"

I turned to look at the third man, who I presumed to be John's brother, James. He was slightly taller and several years older, perhaps in his late twenties. But in coloring and build, the brothers looked very much alike.

"No," Zebedee replied. "Don't bother. She should be home within the hour anyway." He smiled to himself, pulling up the edges of his salt-and-pepper beard. "And to quite a surprise."

The midwife limped toward the door. "My work here is done for the day. Tell Salome I'll return tomorrow for my fee."

Zebedee moved out after her, and my eyes were drawn to the young man remaining, whose own gaze was fixed on Tamar. She had been standing quietly at the back of the group of women, and as I cast a look at her I was surprised to see a fresh spate of tears glistening on her cheeks.

James had noticed, too. As soon as the other women began to disperse, chatting among themselves, he took a step in his wife's direction and held out a hand to her. Mary gestured to me to move outside with the others, but I hung back a second, unable to resist watching from the corner of my eye as Tamar fell into her husband's arms, burying her face in his chest.

The tunic covering his broad shoulders was spattered with muck, his shaggy hair was unkempt, and he smelled distinctly of fish. But he wrapped his arms around the girl and held her tight, dropping a soft kiss on the top of her head. Then he turned her face up to his and said something.

I was too far away to hear it.

*Commentary for Chapter 3 begins on page 229.*

# Chapter 4

You wouldn't think, given my state of mind, that the smell of cooked meat and vegetables could overwhelm the animal and human odors of the house sufficiently to set my stomach to growling. But already-overweight-woman hunger is a powerful thing, and the Zebedees didn't even begin their meal until after dark — by which time its less-than-hygienic presentation held no sway over my appetite.

I dipped my piece of bread into the bowl and sopped up some more of Salome's stew. We were reclining on the floor around a low table in another part of the second level, an area that had its own separate entrance via an outdoor staircase. It seemed to be the house's dining room.

I was still frightened, and I was still confused. But there was something about being with a family that, at the most basic of levels, comforted me. As much as was strange here, I could see that these people were no different, fundamentally, than anyone else I knew. I had always figured that people who lived more primitively must cope with near-constant death and disease by becoming desensitized. Marriages weren't expected to be love matches, so women weren't wistful. Mothers knew they might lose their babies, so they didn't get attached.

You know, like robots.

I was naive. Watching this family's reaction to the birth had been an eye-opener. Young children must die here all the time, but that hadn't stopped these people from celebrating a healthy birth. Knowing the odds, however grim, couldn't keep people from feeling.

John and James were particularly poor candidates for emotional suppression. The brothers were sailing on a serious natural high, and for most of the meal they jested with each other so boisterously that no one else could get a word in. Zebedee was flying pretty high himself, and none of the men took much notice of the three female guests sharing their table. But we didn't begrudge them their merriment. Even I, despite my still-biting angst, found their joy to be contagious.

Salome, a sturdy, good-natured woman in her forties, had been both shocked and disappointed to learn that she had missed her grandson's birth. But neither emotion had lasted more than a few seconds. A wellspring of good cheer herself, she was overjoyed with the baby, overjoyed for her son, and overjoyed with Leah's strong constitution. She even seemed overjoyed to have Mary and two women she had never met hang around her house all afternoon expecting to be fed.

The poor woman had spent hours preparing this celebratory feast with only Tamar to help her. Mary and Joanna seemed to feel no compulsion to offer assistance to their hostess, instead spending most of the afternoon resting in the shade. Doing the same felt uncouth, but I was incompetent enough in my own kitchen. In this place, I had no idea what to do and no good explanation for my ignorance.

I felt guilty. But I was hungry.

The stew, a well-seasoned mixture of lentils, beans, chickpeas, onions, and a few other things I didn't recognize, was served in one large, communal wooden bowl, with everyone taking turns sopping up their portions with bread. Not being fond of mutton, I left the small chunks of stringy meat for the others, who exclaimed over them as if any sort of meat were a delicacy.

I listened to their conversation eagerly as I ate, anxious to learn anything that could help my situation. But the bulk of the meal was devoted to family talk and reminiscing, as well as much good-natured ribbing of John and his inauguration into fatherhood. Leah's baby, I discovered, was not Zebedee and Salome's first grandchild. Their married daughter, Bernice, already had three children. But it was clear from the tenor of the family's comments that this baby held a more exalted position. He was the son of a son. A true heir. And his birth had been long awaited.

When every drop of the hearty stew had been consumed Tamar carried the empty bowl away, and Salome brought in a wooden tray of small, crumbly cakes, dried fruits, and nuts. I sampled them all shamelessly, savoring the honey-sweetened cakes and puzzling over the identities of the fruits. There were raisins, dates, and figs, some tiny things that tasted like mulberries, and one particularly odd item I suspected was pomegranate. Tamar came behind Salome offering wine from a skin, and I sipped it tentatively at first, imagining grapes stomped by dirty feet and myself inebriated. But the drink was smooth and sweet, diluted with honey. I gave in and drank a little more.

As the meal progressed, I sensed that Mary was growing antsy. She seemed to be waiting to do, or to say, something important. I waited on tenterhooks, wondering if it involved me. But only after the men had finished their meal and were reclining comfortably with their wine did Mary choose to commence her business, launching into her agenda with all the aplomb of a corporate executive.

"So, Zebedee," she began at last, leaning toward the table on one elbow, wine in hand. "How's the fishing business?"

Zebedee set down his cup and cleared his throat. "Decent, thank you. The new addition to the fleet seems to be paying off. And you? Orders holding steady?"

She nodded. "We can't seem to build boats fast enough these days. But costs are rising. Lumber has become dear, you know."

He eyed her with a wry look. "Yes, so I discovered."

Mary grinned. "I gave you a fair price."

Zebedee did not smile back, but his eyes twinkled. "You'd better have."

"Now, Father," James broke in, amused, "You know that Mary here has turned into the soul of propriety."

"True enough," Mary responded, her smile genuine. "Which brings me to the purpose of my visit." She turned to James. "I've brought two friends, each of whom commands considerable resources. I understand your rabbi wishes to travel. To reach people beyond Galilee. We would like to help."

James's eyebrows rose. His brother's reaction was similar.

"I realize the logistics are challenging," Mary continued confidently. "But if the master wishes to travel, he should, and he should be able to take as many of his disciples along with him as he chooses. With the right resources, I figure we can all travel both safely and comfortably."

John was the first to speak. "We? You mean you would like to go yourself?"

Mary chuckled softly. "My dear man, that is the whole point."

James and John exchanged a look of bewilderment, but did not seem displeased. "What about Tamar and Leah, and the other wives?" James inquired.

Mary made a sweeping gesture with her hand. "Bring them along. The children too. It will be a family affair. Much more proper that way, don't you think, Zebedee?"

The older man still seemed in shock. At last he shook his head. "Mary," he announced, "if I didn't believe in the rabbi's talents before now, this clinches it. Giving hard-earned money away? To a ministry?

You are not the same woman I used to know."

Mary's dark eyes sparkled with pleasure. "No. Indeed I'm not." With a toss of her head, she turned her attention back to James. "So, when can we see him? Is he still staying at Simon Peter's?"

A dim flicker of awareness swept through my mind, a nagging voice telling me that I knew that name, that I should know that name, that I was somehow already aware of what they were talking about. But the murkiness that separated the facts of my present from those of my increasingly distant past was thick, and instead of applying reasoning, I dismissed the odd feeling by downing the last of my wine.

"Not all the time," James responded. "He's been moving around frequently. He has to. The crowds have become merciless. We've started meeting outside the city. We'll see him tomorrow; I could ask him to come by."

Mary considered. "No, we'll go to him. I wouldn't want to risk attracting a bunch of people here, bothering Leah. Where will he be?"

"Come to the wharf mid-morning," James suggested. "He should be there by then."

"And the crowds?"

John shrugged. "You can never tell. Some days he's able to spend time alone with us, other days he's besieged from dawn to dusk. We've had people come from Tyre and Sidon, from across the Jordan, even all the way from Jerusalem. People who want to be healed, people who just want to see and hear him."

Joanna nodded. "I've come from Jerusalem," she said, speaking her first words since the meal began. "Nearly everyone has heard the rumors about Jesus. They're all quite curious."

My brain snapped to attention.

*Jesus?*

Oh, Please. They could not be talking about *the* Jesus. He could not be alive, in this place. I was alive and in this place.

*Simon Peter. James. John.*

My eyes fixed on the two young men across the table from me. They were decent enough fellows, friendly and seemingly honest, but they were both so loud, so jocular... so common. Apostles? Not hardly.

I shook my head, feeling foolish and more than a little dizzy. There was no way. Even if losing a couple thousand years' worth of time wasn't an issue, there was still no way.

"What are they saying about him in Jerusalem?" John asked with interest, sitting up.

"That not only is he a gifted healer," Joanna answered, "But that he speaks with authority. No one knows quite what to make of him. Or whether to believe all they hear. You know how such tales spread; things get embellished. The people there — as well as the authorities, mind you — would love for him to come to Jerusalem so that they can make a judgment for themselves."

"I've been telling him he should go," James said.

"He will," John argued, "When he's ready. But he's been talking of visiting Phoenicia and the Decapolis first."

I studied the brothers' faces. Whatever they were talking about, it was real to them; this was no show for my benefit. My presence had barely even been noted, and as little as I wanted to draw attention to myself now, the words in my mind came out of my mouth anyway. "Are you—" I stammered, unsure how to ask such a ridiculous question. "Are you speaking of Jesus of Nazareth?"

"Yes, of course," Mary answered, looking at me with a puzzled expression. Then suddenly, something she saw lit a fire behind her eyes. "Do you know him, Rachel? Have you met?"

My vision tunneled as her words swept through me. Perhaps it was the wine. Perhaps I was delirious. But these people certainly seemed to be talking about the man as if he were alive.

And they were asking me a question.

*Did I know him?*

Well, of course I did. Every halfway-educated person in the world did, whether they were Christian or not. I wasn't a churchgoer myself, but my parents had been half-hearted Protestants when I was growing up. Though they had only rarely attended services themselves, they had for several years hauled me and my siblings back and forth to Sunday school, making sure I always had a frilly new Easter dress and either a bathrobe or angel wings for the annual nativity play. As we grew older and complained more, their dedication to the cause had fizzled. Whatever theological platitudes I had been taught in those formative years hadn't stuck, because by the time I graduated from college I was an avowed skeptic. I respected other people's sincere devotion, but I had no stomach for religious hypocrites.

In truth, I hadn't set foot in a church for more than a decade — outside of weddings and the occasional funeral — and I had no desire to do so ever again. But my parents had not spent years stuffing me into tights and shiny shoes for nothing. Despite my now deep-seated aversion to dogma and ceremony, I did still admire the historical figure of Jesus. He, at least, seemed to have had his heart in the right place. It wasn't his fault organized religion was such a mess.

"Of course," I answered offhandedly.

Every pair of eyes at the table looked back at me with surprise. What had I just said? My face flushed with heat.

"Rachel," Mary responded, her eyebrows high, "I had no idea."

"Do you know him from Nazareth?" James inquired, narrowly beating his brother to the punch. "I thought you lived in Jerusalem."

My tongue had ceased to work. I couldn't answer. None of what was happening made any sense; I didn't know what I was thinking. I looked helplessly at Mary.

Her sharp eyes perceived my distress. "Oh, that's right," she explained glibly. "You told me you had kin in Nazareth. You must have seen Jesus's family when you visited. Have you crossed paths with him since he began his ministry?"

The purpose of Mary's words slowly dawned on me, and I let out a breath of relief, thanking her with my eyes. She thought I was from Nazareth, that it was the place I was running from, the den of my evil in-laws. She thought I had slipped, and she was trying to help me recover.

I adored the woman.

Swallowing hard, I reinterpreted her question so I wouldn't have to lie. Had I crossed paths with Jesus physically, here in... well, wherever we were? "No," I answered evenly. "No, I haven't."

James and John still watched me intently, and I was certain they were poised to ask more questions. James even got so far as to open his mouth. But Mary kept a step ahead.

"In any event," she proclaimed, diverting the men's attention back to herself, "I intend to make it possible for the rabbi to travel wherever he wants. We'll present him with the offer tomorrow. Now if you'll excuse us, it's been a long journey. I think we women are ready to retire."

Mary rose. After thanking Salome for the meal and Zebedee for the accommodations she and Joanna filed out of the room, and I followed gratefully. Despite the internal tumult my loose lips had caused, I was exhausted.

By the flickering light of the oil lamp Mary carried, we moved through a narrow doorway off the dining room into a tiny alcove that appeared to be a sleeping area, then up another ladder to a loft similar to Leah's. The space, which was separated from the room below by a thin curtain, proved exactly big enough for three grown women to lie down in.

Under other circumstances, such intimate quarters would have made me uncomfortable.

Now, I couldn't care less.

Mary set the lamp on a stand in the corner, then she and Joanna pulled their traveling cloaks over themselves as coverlets. I followed their lead. The mats underneath us could have been softer, but I had no thought of complaint. I had a safe place to sleep and two champions I didn't deserve.

"I do wish you wouldn't put words in my mouth, Mary," Joanna chastised as they settled. "I never said I would bankroll this endeavor. I said I would think about it. You know very well I insist on meeting the man first. Joanna, Wife of Chuza, is no pushover. She knows a charlatan when she sees one."

"Joanna will be charmed senseless within an hour," Mary said offhandedly, winking at me.

Joanna humphed with resentment. But she lay down and closed her eyes.

Mary's gaze held mine.

"I'm assuming, Rachel," she whispered softly, "that you've suffered a great deal at the hands of your husband and his family. If you hadn't, you wouldn't have taken such a risk to escape them."

I nodded, begging Joe's forgiveness for the slander. He was a good father and a good man, even if he was a workaholic. The latter was partly my fault; someone had to earn the money we all spent. As for my in-laws, they were nice people, but I hardly ever saw them.

All that seemed far away, now.

"Stay with us, then," she urged. "I offered you protection because I thought I could convince you to donate to the cause. I had no idea you already knew Jesus. But surely you can see the opportunity here. If you travel with us, you'll be safe. After the treatment he received on his last visit to Nazareth, he won't be returning there anytime soon. No one will know who you are."

Creaking footsteps crossed the ceiling above my head, and I heard a man's voice that sounded like Gideon, the behemoth servant/bodyguard who was accompanying Joanna. Could he and Mary's servant, Samuel, be sleeping outside... on the roof?

"I would very much like to stay with you," I answered, blinking back a moistness in my eyes. I wasn't a crier, but I was fatigued.

Physically, mentally... every way. I could see no way out except forward, and I was too tired to think, much less fight with my own aggrieved sense of logic. "Thank you. I'll help however I can. I can see how devoted you are to him."

Mary's eyes sparkled in the dim light. "He's like a son to me," she whispered, her voice barely audible over both the creaking of the roof and the still-bellowing voices of the men below. "The truth is, if he asked me, I'd give him every cent I own."

Somewhere out the window, a donkey brayed. The baby snuffled, then began to cry. I could hear John's footsteps as he crossed the eating room and barreled up the other ladder toward Leah.

Mary closed her eyes.

I wanted to join her, but my tired brain nagged at me with a few choice sound bites — pieces of a puzzle that floated and twirled in my head, begging to be fit together. *Tell him she came with us... from Magdala.*

Mary Magdalene.

The sexy prostitute?

I turned my head toward her, my pulse thudding in my ears. The woman was older than I was. She was a revered businesswoman who thought of Jesus as the son she never had.

I shut my eyes. Tight. I could take no more seeming absurdity, no more revelations, no more contradictions to what I thought I knew. Perhaps, if I slept, I would wake up tomorrow in some place that made sense again.

If so, I wouldn't see this supposed Jesus.

I reached down a hand to the purse at my belt, running my fingers over the odd-sized coins. They weren't mine; they shouldn't exist at all. And yet they were hard. Solid. Undeniable, palpable evidence of this place and this time.

My mind begin to drift. I clutched them.

*Commentary for Chapter 4 begins on page 232.*

# Chapter 5

Something stepped on me. I awoke and opened one eye, just in time for a speck of dust to dislodge from the twig-and-plaster ceiling and fall down into it.

It was morning.

Nothing had changed.

Gideon and Samuel had indeed slept on top of the house, right above us. I knew this because both of them were fidgety sleepers and because sound travels well through dried mud. So well that at some point during the restless, miserable night I had become convinced that I would never fall asleep again. Every human in the house, on top of the house, and in the houses to either side had snored. The animals below had bellowed and clopped their hooves on the cobblestones. The baby had awakened and cried. Other people's babies had awakened and cried. I had lost consciousness only in the wee hours when I had at last become too exhausted to fret over where I would regain it.

I was still exhausted. And I was still fretting.

Mary had stepped over me to reach the ladder, but Joanna hadn't quite made it. I accepted her apology, struggled to my feet, and followed them downstairs.

The house, ironically, was quieter now. The animals were outside, and the men of the family had long since left for the wharf. Leah, against her mother-in-law's advice, had descended from her loft and was tending to her baby in the room below, assisted by a doting Tamar. The industrious Salome, whom I had no doubt would have defied her own mother-in-law's advice about staying in bed postpartum, was quick to offer us a breakfast of bread and goat's milk, chatting as she did so about how anxious John had been to spread his good news.

Mary ate rapidly, rushing Joanna and me as well, offering Salome only a perfunctory thanks for breakfast before scrambling to get us all out the door. She was exhilarated. Eager. Practically manic. I obeyed her prodding on autopilot while my beleaguered, still-hazy mind struggled to get up to speed.

We were going to the wharf. Apparently the site of the family fishing business was not too far away — just outside the city gates — but Joanna insisted on riding her donkey anyway, and their two menservants were to accompany us. The quiet, hulking presence of the men unnerved me, but I kept my mouth shut. Given my ignorance of what we were journeying into, I appreciated their daggers.

The sun was bright as we stepped outside, and its heat burned off the last of the fog from my drowsy brain. The nonsensical conversations I thought I had heard last night must surely have been the effect of too much wine. I might be in some backwater at the moment, but it was still the twenty-first century. And if Capernaum was any kind of city at all, it must have some modern amenities — and methods of communication — somewhere. I had only to find them. Preferably before anything else unpleasant happened.

I stuck close to Mary as we left the safety of the courtyard and moved down the dirt alley outside. We were heading downhill, toward the city's center. I was certain things would look better there.

I was wrong.

No sooner had the tiny lanes widened into well-trampled streets than every inch of space around me teemed with smelly people, livestock, wooden carts, scampering rodents, and flies. A bazaar of shops and outdoor stalls peddled everything from dried fish and rotting fruits to large earthenware pots and tiny bottles of unknown liquids, and beggars — emaciated, barely clothed — staked out any spot where they might not be trampled. They were not just men, but women and children, too. Some blind or sick, but many seemingly able-bodied, all crying pitifully for any coin or scrap of food.

I watched them all, horrified, almost afraid to breathe. As primitive as the Zebedee family seemed, I realized now that they were at least dressed in suitable clothing, and they seemed healthy. A great many people here were not. Few had any significant fat on their bodies. Everywhere I looked I saw missing teeth. Scarred, discolored skin. Twisted limbs. Stooping backs.

Not one person was truly old.

The goat's milk in my stomach was settling poorly, and I dropped my eyes to the hem of Mary's tunic and focused on moving my feet forward. After a few minutes we emerged from the crowded bazaar at the main entrance of the city, then continued on through its gates. Outside, the crush of bodies began to dwindle, and the landscape opened up. I raised my eyes.

Before us lay a wide blue lake, its banks stretching for miles in either direction. Distant hills, mostly brown but dappled with spring green, stood tall both behind the city and across the water. Wooden boats sailed by, taking advantage of the whipping breeze that, though bringing a welcome coolness, maneuvered the omnipresent dust into every fold of my clothing.

I filled my lungs with the fresh air, then breathed out with relief. Here, surely, was a place where I could find more affluent people. People who could help me. Shielding my eyes from the sun with a hand, I surveyed the scene.

I knew what I was looking for. A distant radio tower. A paved road. Maybe even an airstrip.

I saw none of the above.

Only dirt. Rocks. Water.

More dirt.

My breathing quickened. No matter how far out in the boonies I had landed, I should be able to see *some* evidence of the rest of the world's technological progress, shouldn't I?

No trucks. No cement blocks. No soldiers in fatigues. Not a single, measly, military-issue packet of peanut butter.

I stared down at the dirt road beneath me. Smooth wheel ruts mingled with myriad imprints of sandals, hooves, and bare human feet. But there was no pattern of tire tread. Not even a rubber-soled shoe.

No aluminum cans. No plastic. Not a single scrap of paper litter.

*Twenty-first century, indeed.*

A lump rose in my throat.

"Rachel," Mary asked, eyeing me speculatively, "is something wrong?"

I held her gaze. She was incredibly perceptive. I could not lie to her indefinitely; I didn't want to lie to her at all. She was a woman after my own heart; and as much as I needed her protection, I wanted a friend. Never in my life had I felt more vulnerable. Or more alone.

But how could I tell her the truth?

"I'm a bit nervous," I confessed, trying to keep my lies as white as possible.

"About seeing Jesus?" she asked. "Why? Are you afraid he'll reprimand you for leaving your family?"

My head spun.

Pondering the metaphysics of my situation was beyond me, but even if it wasn't, I had no time. In a matter of minutes, I was going to meet Mary's Jesus. And as unsure as I was about everything else, I was quite certain I had never met this particular rabbi, in Nazareth or anywhere else.

My lies would be exposed.

Mary laughed. "Don't be ridiculous, Rachel," she chastised. "Jesus has a way of seeing the good in people. Even when they've got something to hide."

She held my gaze a moment, then gave a sly smile.

My heart skipped a beat. Did she know I was lying?

She said no more. Instead she tossed her head gaily to the side, picked up the reins of Joanna's donkey, and yanked it forward. "Come on, people!" she goaded. "We're almost there!"

The men picked up their pace, and I matched it.

My brain hurt. My stomach wasn't in the best shape either.

Up ahead I could see the wharf — a chaotic jumble of wooden posts, platforms, rope, tools, and nets. It reeked of fish and was bathed with layers of mud, dust, and every consistency of dirt in between. Men bustled about their business in and out of the water, working bare-chested and bare-legged, with loose fabric gathered between their knees and tucked into the girdles at their waists. Wooden boats moved over the choppy lake beyond, propelled by sails of varying shapes and sizes. I wondered if James and John were on one of them.

"Mobbed again," Mary lamented, staring in the opposite direction.

I turned. Across the road from the lake a large crowd was gathered, milling about on a rocky slope that swept back up into the hills.

"Let's leave the donkey here, Joanna," Mary ordered. "Gideon can take him; we'll walk up."

Joanna issued a grunt of protest, but slid off the donkey and handed him to her waiting servant.

Mary rushed up the grassy slope towards the crowd, lifting her cloak and tunic as she picked her way over the rocks. "Come on!" she urged, her voice brimming with anticipation. "It's not that far."

"All right, all right!" the heavier Joanna called back. She sounded irked, but her shining eyes looked almost as excited as Mary's. "I'm coming. But you don't have to go so blasted fast!"

I hung back with Joanna. I was desperate to look ahead at the crowd, to scan it, to search it. At the same time, the mere sight of it terrified me.

"Come *on!*" Mary called impatiently as Joanna and I fell behind. I hadn't noticed anything unusual in Joanna's posture during our short wanderings around Zebedee's courtyard, but now I could see that she held her spine stiffly as she walked.

"You want me to move uphill over rocks," she called back caustically, "You take the consequences. I'll get there when I get there. You go ahead."

Mary didn't argue. She lifted her garments higher and scrambled on up the hill without us, merging quickly with the fringes of the crowd.

I stared after her departing back, torn between sticking to her side and running away before she could hate me. Either way I couldn't face what lay ahead. A part of me still desperately wanted to believe that the present *had* to be the present... my twenty-first century present. But despite all that was good and rational and sane, I'll confess that another part of me wanted the impossible to be true. Wanted for little old me to somehow, some way be living and breathing in the first century AD. For my Mary to be the real Mary Magdalene.

For *the* Jesus to be just ahead.

My knees quaked so violently I was unable to move any faster than Joanna, but we inched ahead steadily. How large was the crowd? How far away was the object of its attentions? How many seconds before I saw the man with my own two eyes?

We reached the edge of the gathering. Still, I could see nothing but other people's backs. Taking Joanna's arm, I began weaving forward.

Then I stopped.

I could hear him.

At least, I thought it was him. The words seemed vaguely familiar. But the voice did not.

*Anyone who practices and teaches these commands will be called great...*

A flash of panic ripped through me, but I did my best to stifle it. So the voice sounded odd. How could I recognize a voice I had never heard? It was a fine voice, a deep voice, one that carried well. What else was I expecting?

I could make out only snatches of speech over the ambient noise of the crowd. Most of those gathered were silent and absorbed, but some — especially the younger children — were restless, and others murmured among themselves. We still could not see the speaker. I tugged at Joanna as a child would its mother, leading her this way and that, searching for an opening in the crowd. The slope had reached a plateau, and I moved steadily toward the hill behind, hoping to climb higher.

*First go and be reconciled to your brother, then come and offer your gift...*

"Rachel!" Joanna whispered harshly. I stopped at once, assuming I was moving too quickly for her. But one look into her eager brown eyes told me otherwise. "That boulder," she said, pointing. "I bet we could see from on top of it."

I looked in the direction she pointed. We set off.

I wanted to get a look at him. I wanted to get it over with.

*You've heard what was said long ago; do not break your oath...*

Scrambling onto the boulder was not as easy as it looked, particularly not when wearing sandals with wooden soles. I had difficulty in reaching even a ledge three feet up on its near side, and I doubted Joanna could follow me. But before I could come up with another plan, I found her stout body plastered to the rock by my side.

The ledge proved high enough by itself.

We could see him.

*Commentary for Chapter 5 begins on page 234.*

# Chapter 6

My gaze locked upon the speaker.

It wasn't the right man.

On a flat stone about thirty yards away, commanding a crowd of hundreds with his resonating, compelling voice, stood the individual these people called Jesus the Nazarene. My breath caught in my throat. My spirits plummeted.

He wasn't right. Not even close. His skin was too swarthy, his feet too dirty, his features altogether too coarse. Not that I had expected a glowing halo. I wasn't naive. What I did expect, I wasn't sure. I just knew this man wasn't it.

I forced in a breath, trying to understand the turmoil of my emotions. What *had* I wanted? Given my track record as a total religious slacker, I should be relieved to discover I wasn't missing anything.

I should not feel oddly let down.

Then I gave my head a shake, feeling silly. On what basis could I judge who was or was not the historical Jesus of Nazareth? The artwork hanging in my parents' church? I should know better. The typical facial features associated with Jesus were conceived by Europeans in the Middle Ages. By then the man had been dead for a millennium already.

Why *couldn't* this Jesus be legitimate?

I took another look.

I still wasn't impressed. The rabbi was, simply put, unremarkable. In fact, had he not been standing on the rock to speak, he would have been indistinguishable from the multitude around him. His coloring, though darker than that of James or John, was typical of most Galileans. He was of average height and build. Both his hair and beard were a medium length, and no cleaner than anyone else's. His tunic and cloak were not as fine as mine or Zebedee's, but neither were they tattered like those of the beggars in the bazaar.

He was flatly, painfully average.

I didn't know what to think. But as I watched and listened to the words he was saying, I became more certain I had heard them — or something like them — before.

*You have heard people say, 'an eye for eye, and a tooth for a tooth.' But I tell you this: don't resist an evil person. If someone strikes you on the right cheek, turn the other one to him also. And if someone wants to sue you and take your tunic, let him have your cloak as well. Give to anyone who asks you, and don't turn away from someone who wants to borrow from you.*

The man paused a moment, and the crowd emitted a low rumble. Joanna tugged at my sleeve. "Ooh, they don't like that," she said in hushed voice. "It's one thing to be generous, but he's definitely pushing it. The law doesn't say anything about letting yourself be taken advantage of. How is that justice?"

I turned toward her, once again struck by the mismatch between her words and her expression. She sounded cynical and unimpressed, but her face glowed with excitement, and her brown eyes twinkled. I wondered if she thrived on controversy.

*You've heard it said, 'Love your neighbor and hate your enemy.' But I tell you: Love your enemies and pray for those who persecute you.*

"I see what they mean," Joanna continued. "He's not just quoting the scripture; he's giving his own opinion. And not apologizing for it either." Her crow's feet deepened as her mouth crinkled into a grin. *"Scandalous."*

Joanna wasn't the only one talking; the noise level around us had risen considerably. I was watching Jesus's face, trying fruitlessly to read his lips, when I noticed a sudden change in his expression. He paused between phrases and nodded his head with a smile. I followed his eyes out into the crowd.

There, having fought her way to a prime position about ten yards from his feet, was Mary. Her face beamed as she returned the nod.

Jesus continued speaking for a few more minutes, then thanked the crowd for listening and stepped down off the rock.

"Blast," Joanna said with woe. "And it was just getting good."

A chorus of praise and pleas for more broke out as Jesus began to move away. He was quickly encircled by half a dozen men, but neither James nor John was among them. Mary had disappeared.

Disorder reigned as the crowd jostled, some people dispersing, others pressing closer to Jesus and the men as they walked down the slope toward the lake. I searched the crowd anxiously, afraid to move, until at last I caught a glimpse of Mary.

I jumped down from the boulder ledge. The action was ill-advised, since one of my wooden soles slid sideways off a rock, twisting my ankle. "Come on, Joanna," I urged, reaching up to help her descend more intelligently. "They're headed toward the lake, and Mary is going after them. We need to catch up."

Whether it was my need to stay close to Mary or an inexplicable desire to see more of this bizarro Jesus that compelled me forward, despite my smarting ankle, I wasn't sure. But Joanna seemed equally eager, moving with me as fast as she could, making no complaints about her own pain other than an occasional grimace.

"He's certainly an intriguing speaker," she mused between breaths. "Very charismatic. I can see why Mary is so taken with him. I heard The Baptist speak once, and he is a powerful presence, indeed. But my Chuza can tell you, no good will come of John's chastising Herod Antipas. That is suicide."

I scanned the slope as we walked. The nucleus of disciples was nearing the wharf. Mary was nowhere in sight.

"So what does Jesus want to accomplish, I wonder?" Joanna continued. "That was hardly a message of rebellion he just gave. It was controversial, yes, but it was peace-loving." She chuckled to herself. "A bit too peace-loving for the Zealots among us, I'll wager."

I was too distracted to follow her analysis. The fact that this Jesus did not meet my obscure expectations had done nothing to assuage the nebulous fear that had dogged me all morning. Whatever I was afraid of, I knew I didn't want to be left behind.

"He didn't heal anybody though," Joanna said with disappointment. "Mary said he healed people right and left, everywhere he went."

"He healed her, didn't he?" I commented, remembering a snippet of conversation that had made little sense to me at the time. We were back on flatter land, and I could see nothing for the throngs of people still in front of me. We were not the only ones following Jesus's path toward the lake; over half the crowd had come with us. "She said something about seven demons."

Joanna hooted with laughter. "Demons, indeed! There was never anything wrong with Mary except plain old orneriness. But she did change after she met him, there's no denying that. When she up and doubled the wages of her servants and started handing out food all over Magdala — well, the townspeople figured Jesus must have done *something* drastic!"

A roar rose from the crowd. Accolades, well wishes. Despite my own anxiety, I could feel the excitement in the air, sense the positive energy radiating around me. The collective mood rivaled the frenzied fervor of some pivotal sports event, except that the emotion here was gentler in spirit.

"He's leaving," I said, staring through a break in the crowd. "He's in a boat pushing off."

"Is Mary with him?" Joanna asked, squinting toward the lake.

"No," I answered. "I only see other men."

The words had barely left my mouth before a hand clutched my shoulder from behind. "Well?" Mary asked, her eyes dancing. "Did you see him? Did you hear what he said?"

Joanna jumped at the hand on her own shoulder. "A fine speaker," she praised. "Very impressive. But I want to hear more about this cheek-turning nonsense. Where has he gone?"

Mary pulled us close, lowering her voice. "Philip's moving him to another spot up the shore. Some of the crowd always manages to follow, but it should give him enough breathing room to meet with us."

She let go of us and looked out over the lake. "Andrew said Peter would take us in his boat, but I don't see him."

My stomach churned. As desperately as I had wanted to get a glimpse of Jesus, I had never wanted *him* to see *me*. My reasons were varied and uncomfortable to contemplate, but the most immediate among them was sufficient. I had misled Mary into believing that I knew the man already. She would expect him to recognize me as a fellow Nazarene.

"There!" Mary announced, grabbing our arms once again and propelling us toward the wharf. I looked up to see a wooden vessel cruising toward land with a large man standing on its bow shouting indecipherable orders to the workers scurrying on the shore. "I'd know that loudmouth anywhere," she finished.

"Is that Simon Peter?" Joanna asked with interest, squinting again. As the boat came closer, her lips drew into a smile. "Why, I do believe you're right, Mary. The man's vocabulary *is* as colorful as your own!"

Mary's eyes narrowed in mock annoyance. "I could outswear that lug of a fisherman any day," she protested. "I just choose not to. Right now I have to sweet-talk him into giving us a ride, so be nice. If the fish haven't been biting, he might."

The boat pulled into shore.

"Well, well!" the man thundered. "If it isn't The Magdalene! Greetings, Mary."

"The same to you, Peter," she responded politely.

I watched the interchange with breath held. Peter was older than James and John: perhaps in his mid thirties. He was also bigger, heavier, darker, and a good deal more ominous looking. Black curls hung down his back and exploded from his face in a full, thick beard. On the lake he had worn no shirt, revealing a well-exercised set of muscles, but upon recognizing Mary he had thrown on a linen cloak. The garment was technically more decent, but it was also filthy, doing nothing to soften the roughness of his appearance. When he leapt out of the boat and approached us, I'll confess I was afraid of him.

"These are my friends, Joanna and Rachel," Mary began with her best schmoozing voice. "They've come to see Jesus. I hate to impose—"

"Nah, you don't," Peter interrupted, smiling. He turned to look at Joanna and me, then granted us each a nod. His gaze met mine for only an instant, but that was sufficient to soothe my qualms. His dark eyes were both intelligent and merry, testifying to a mischievous nature that — despite his blustering — seemed wholly kind-hearted.

My muscles relaxed a little. The undercurrent of tension I perceived between him and Mary puzzled me, but I dismissed it as understandable. Two such commanding personalities were unlikely to appreciate each other's charms.

"So, what do you ladies need?" Peter continued affably.

"A ride," Mary explained. "Philip and the others have taken Jesus to someplace called Jackal's Rock. Your brother suggested you could pick us up and join them there."

Peter scanned the hillside behind us. "I thought they were staying here. Crowds get too heavy?"

Mary nodded.

"All right then," Peter agreed, turning to leap back into the boat. Its floor was covered with nets of writhing fish, their scales glinting in the sun. "Just let me unload the catch." He threw a sly look at Joanna. "Unless you'd care to ride along with them?"

Joanna raised her chin, meeting his gaze with an impish look of her own. "I prefer mine dead and pickled, thank you."


My insides knotted with discomfort. I could not enjoy the brisk lake air, nor the view of distant hills across the water. I could not even be amused by Peter's off-key singing. The wind whipped mercilessly at both the sail and our head coverings, and as the boat tossed on the waves I put my head down, holding my veil with one hand and my abdomen with the other. Mary and Joanna assumed I was seasick. I let them.

When the boat pulled up on the shore several miles north of Capernaum, the women thanked Peter and jumped out, not seeming to care that the absence of a wharf required them to slosh through muddy water on the way. I splashed out after them, not caring either.

A small crowd of twenty or so people was gathered in the shade of a grove of trees nearby, and Mary and Joanna hurried towards them. When I hung back, Mary noticed my absence and turned. "Rachel? Aren't you coming?"

"I'll catch up," I replied, sitting down on an uncomfortably rough rock. "I just need to rest a minute."

Mary's expression was skeptical, but she accepted my excuse. She and Joanna moved forward, and Peter passed me to join them.

I watched from my rock, alone.

Jesus and his friends had been sitting, but they rose as the women neared. Jesus crossed to Mary and smiled at her, saying something I couldn't hear. She gestured toward Joanna, and as Jesus turned to greet her, he reached out and touched Joanna's wrist.

The touch was light, and lasted a mere second. But I noticed it. I did so because it was the first time I had seen any man here touch a woman who wasn't his wife. Among themselves, the men were quite physical: those in Zebedee's house hugged frequently and even exchanged glancing kisses on the cheek. The women did the same. But interaction between men and women was different. The men I met had all kept a respectful distance from me, greeting with nods, never with handshakes. The embrace between Tamar and James was the only display of cross-gender affection that I had yet seen, and it wasn't intended to be public. For Jesus to touch Joanna seemed unaccountably bold.

I rose from the rock and moved closer, hoping to hear what was being said. As I came within earshot, I heard a loud peal of female laughter. "I was wondering how long it would take you to notice!" Mary cackled.

Joanna's face was flaming red. She was twisting at the waist, as if looking for something behind her. Many of the men were chuckling along with Mary. Jesus, who had stepped back from the women and was now leaning comfortably with his back against a tree, watched with a smile.

"Mercy," Joanna sputtered. "I thought I was just old!"

"You're still old," Mary taunted. "You're just not half crippled anymore, which means you can forget all those excuses about not being able to travel!"

Joanna performed a few more test contortions of her spine, then beamed with delight. "Well," she responded, her tone uncharacteristically demure, "I'm starting to think I might just enjoy a bit of traveling."

Mary laughed again, then urged Jesus to sit. The entire crowd settled onto the grass, and I positioned myself on its periphery. When Mary began to speak to Jesus in a low voice, the men near me, seeming uninterested in that conversation, began talking among themselves.

I avoided meeting the disciples' eyes, and vice versa. I was getting the idea that while the men here seemed willing to talk to respectable widows and married women — provided they were properly introduced and not alone — speaking with other females was verboten. As the men chattered on about crowd control and the relative merits of Jackal's Rock versus someplace called Catfish Bend, I looked out toward the sea and willed my limbs to stop trembling.

I was afraid.

Seeing more of the city of Capernaum, rather than offering hope for a timely rescue, had driven home the painful extent of my vulnerability. Without Mary and Joanna's protection, a woman like me — unconnected, ignorant, and unarmed — would be at real risk for bodily harm.

I wasn't used to feeling powerless. My intelligence and drive had always seen me through before; the fact that I was female hadn't really mattered. I had little need of physical strength as long as I had brains and financial resources, and at no point had anyone cared who or where my relatives were. But here, a woman's link to her kin was the cornerstone of her existence. Without family, I was wholly at the mercy of people willing to befriend me.

People I had lied to.

"Where did she go, Joanna?" I heard Mary ask, her voice too close for comfort. I froze, blood rising hot in my cheeks. I was afraid of being exposed as a fraud, of losing my protection. But I was afraid of more than that.

Seeing this alien Jesus from a distance had been disturbing enough, but the thought of meeting him face to face was too petrifying to bear. I could tell myself it didn't matter who or what he was, that I had never been in line for Christian of the year and didn't believe in hell anyway, but what I told myself and what I felt were two different things. The truth was, I didn't want to discover that the faith of my parents, and so many millions like them, was based on some monstrous error. For all my agnostic dithering, I did have some emotional investment in the issue. If I hadn't, I wouldn't have unwittingly lied to Mary about knowing him in the first place.

I didn't want any of this. I had been perfectly comfortable with my twenty-first century concept of Jesus. Never mind that it was hopelessly vague. At least it was safe; no one could disprove it. But this Jesus was not some moral abstraction I could twist and bend — or ignore — at will. He was a flesh-and-blood man. He was a couple yards away. He was a stranger to me.

And if I was a stranger to him, a whole lot of things a whole lot of people believed were just plain wrong.

My pulse throbbed.

"What's the matter with you, hiding back here?" Mary chastised upon spying me, her voice cheerful. She gestured me forward with an arm. "Come on up!"

My stomach lurched. I could not respond. But when the men around me rose to their feet, I did the same.

"Oh, Jesus," I heard Mary say. "Come here. I've brought someone else to see you."

The men around me parted. Blood drained from my face. He stood by Mary now, not five feet away. I wanted to run, to hide, to escape anywhere, any way. But my feet wouldn't move.

"Someone I believe you already know," Mary continued.

There was nowhere to run. I turned toward him and looked up.

His eyes met mine.

His unfamiliar face smiled.

"Hello, Rachel."

*Commentary for Chapter 6 begins on page 237.*

# Chapter 7

I stared into his eyes like a deer caught in headlights. I wanted to see divinity. I wanted to settle it. I wanted neon signs to flash, fireworks to gleam. I wanted to see the Jesus that my parents and everyone else thought they knew, and satisfy myself that they hadn't been wasting their time.

I couldn't do that.

I didn't even know what I was looking for.

What I saw was a man whose expression was kind, whose eyes showed a keen intelligence. But there was nothing awe-inspiring about him. No extraordinary power emanated from his person. Charisma, yes. Warmth, yes. Magical glowing rays of supernatural force? Unequivocally, no.

A queer sadness swept through me. I had not seen much to remark on from a distance, true, but I had hoped that a closer view would show me more. As leery as I was of acknowledging the supernatural, I'll confess that I wanted to encounter it. I wanted to see the Jesus of my childhood, the one with the soft brown hair and luminous blue eyes, the omnipotent, all-knowing one.

The one whom I had secretly been hoping would take one look at me, wave his arm in a shower of purple sparks, and spirit me home.

Now I felt like a fool.

Yet oddly, I was no longer afraid. If there was nothing awesome about Jesus's bearing, neither was there anything threatening in it. He simply stood, studying me as I studied him. Like the unabashed stare of a small child, his dark eyes seemed to pierce right through me, laying bare my every flaw and strength without apology. Ordinarily such blatant scrutiny would make me squirm, but Jesus's gaze held no judgment. Whatever discernment he applied was not only unprejudiced but coupled with a heavy dose of empathy, the significance of both being overshadowed by evidence of an emotion for which I was wholly unprepared.

Amusement.

His smile was subtle, but his brown eyes twinkled.

"Hello," I answered at last, my voice a croak. Despite the

disappointment, my mind still spun, searching for answers. This man might not be divine; but he was definitely intriguing. I could not take my eyes off him.

"Rachel told me she hasn't seen you in a while," Mary interjected into the silence. "But I'm glad you remember her. I've been hoping to convince her to support your cause."

My heart thudded with panic, but Jesus said nothing. His expression didn't alter.

Mary flashed me a conspiratorial look, then spoke again. "She's certainly shown herself to be a fearless traveler. I was thinking of keeping her around."

I swallowed, trying to ground myself, to think clearly. His knowing my name was explainable — Mary or Joanna must have mentioned it. But unless he was even worse with faces than my husband, he had to know we hadn't met before. Why perpetuate my fraud?

He cast a glance at Mary, then turned back to me with a nod. "Please," he said politely, still with the same unflappable, subtle smile. "Join us."

*Join us.*

I felt myself nod back.

He turned away. Mary put out a hand and squeezed my arm. *I told you it would be fine*, her smug smile proclaimed. *Trust me!*

She turned her back and walked after Jesus, whose attention was being diverted by the newly arrived James and John. The brothers' loud voices wafted over the crowd as they launched into some humorous tale of John's having announced his son's birth to the fish. Amidst the chorus of responses, one voice stood out, ringing through the air with an almost palpable warmth, cheering me even as its distinctly mortal nature disturbed me further.

Jesus was laughing.

We stayed with the disciples all day. In the late afternoon the boats returned us to the wharf, where Mary and Joanna met up with their servants and Joanna proudly insisted on walking rather than remounting her waiting donkey. Jesus had been invited to dinner at the home of a Pharisee in Capernaum, and the disciples were escorting him on his passage through the city. Mary, Joanna, and I were not a necessary part of the procession, but we walked with the men anyway.

Mary was so gay she practically skipped. Jesus had accepted her offer of financial assistance with enthusiasm, and his disciples all seemed to be looking forward to the journey. The consensus was that it would take a week or so to prepare. Tents and supplies must be purchased. John's son must be duly circumcised. Leah must be well enough to travel.

I drifted along like a stick in a river.

My brain was mush. All day, as I had alternately rested and moved with the group, sharing bread, fruit, and some bizarre partially fermented grape juice for lunch, I had kept one eye on the sky, half expecting a plane to fly overhead. I could not accept that I was stuck here. Could not believe that two days and a night had passed already, and that another night was coming on. All day I had studied Jesus, looking for some sign that I had been wrong about him, waiting for something amazingly dramatic to happen.

Nothing did. No magical trans-millennial transport occurred. No sudden harmonization of whatever it was that I was experiencing with the reality I thought I knew.

Now, the cacophony of noises and smells in the crowded streets once again threatened to overwhelm me. I had felt claustrophobic on my first trip through the city; accompanying a celebrity was an unadulterated nightmare. Bodies were everywhere. I was treading water in a writhing sea of heads, shoulders, and arms, and I could scarcely move without getting touched by someone. And though I was getting used to the smell of manure and fish, body odor still got to me. After two days without a shower I was less than fresh myself, but the pungency of the milling crowd was unspeakable, and I was queasy enough just from nerves.

"Are you all right, Rachel?" Mary asked with concern. "You look a little green."

I forced a smile. Mary was on cloud nine; I didn't want to spoil things for her. Nor did I want to appear weak. "I'm fine."

I had had no more opportunities to speak with Jesus. With everyone around him constantly vying for his attention, he was never alone. But even if I could talk to him again, I didn't know what I would say. I was far too confused to be coherent.

The ambient noise of the crowd swelled, and the people in front of me stopped moving. Mary and I looked up. At the top of the hill ahead of us was the first figure I had yet to see who stood out from the masses. First off, because he was seated on a full-sized horse, the only example of that species I had seen. Second, because he wore a bright red cloak and something that looked halfway like trousers.

I watched him with fascination. Here, at last, was the Capernaum equivalent of the country club set.

"What is it?" Joanna asked Mary, squinting. She was too short to see over the immediate crowd, even if her vision was better. At five feet seven, however, I was taller than many of the men, and Mary was only an inch shorter than I.

"A centurion," Mary answered.

"Well, what's he doing?"

Mary shook her head in puzzlement. "Nothing. Just sitting there staring at Jesus."

"Rabbi!" a voice proclaimed ahead of us. A trio of men approached Jesus with haste, and the crowd parted before them as they came. They weren't dressed as nicely as the horseman, but they were clearly VIPs. Their cloaks were relatively clean and decorated with brightly colored threads, and their bearing was that of men who demanded respect.

"This man needs your assistance," one of the three explained. His hair and beard were pure white and thoroughly groomed, hanging below his waist. "He has a servant he values very highly who is sick and about to die."

A second, who shared the same fastidious appearance, stepped forward. "The Roman is a good man," he said earnestly. "He has been very accommodating to our people; he has even built us a synagogue. But he doesn't consider himself worthy to ask you for help."

One of the younger disciples standing behind me let out a low growl. "He shouldn't do it."

Another replied quietly, "But he will."

"You think?"

"Half a shekel."

The first snorted. "No deal."

The disciples' muttering drowned out Jesus's reply, but as the emissaries — whom I presumed to be high-ranking religious leaders — turned with relieved smiles and began to lead our procession up the hill toward the centurion, the gist of Jesus's response was obvious.

"Told you."

"Did I argue? I said that he *shouldn't* do it, not that he wouldn't."

"Don't be ridiculous, Simon," came a third, much deeper voice. "Of course he should."

As the group moved forward I dropped back, giving myself a

better view of the speakers. Call me nosy, but having something to focus on seemed to help the nausea, and none of the men took the least notice of me. Mary forged ahead.

The Simon who had started the conversation was a thin young man of twenty-one or twenty-two, with olive skin and straight, jet-black hair. His dark eyes glittered as he debated. "Helping a Roman without asking anything in return could be seen as condoning the occupation. I'm not saying he should let the servant suffer, but he could at least bargain with the man first. Elicit a donation. Free a slave."

"That's not the way he works. You know that," his companion answered. The second youth was of a similar age and build, though lighter in coloring. His bushy brown locks were so thick as to give him a wild look, but his gentle smile and unusually straight teeth tempered the effect. "He sees all people as equals."

"Well, so do I," Simon replied, frustrated. "But that's not the point. How can social justice ever be achieved if no one is held accountable?"

"But agreeing to help one centurion doesn't mean Jesus won't stand up to the Romans when the time is right. He's just—"

"You never do see the big picture, Thaddeus," Simon interrupted. "One exception here, one there, and pretty soon you've got nothing. What this movement needs is focus. Constant, unwavering insistence on the elimination of injustice."

The corners of my mouth twitched. I almost smiled. These guys, at least, were not all that alien. With a little imagination I could be in a college pub, listening to some particularly earnest political science majors.

"Would it be justice for Jesus to let this centurion's servant die just to make a point?" Thaddeus fired back. "How is the occupation his fault?"

"I didn't—" Simon bit his lip, then let out another growl. "All right. Fine."

Thaddeus smiled slyly. "Three to two."

"Two even!" Simon insisted, his dark eyes blazing.

"Three to two," Thaddeus repeated calmly. "You forget the unfortunate altercation with Uzzi this morning."

Simon's spirits dampened. "Oh. Right."

"You should both stay away from Uzzi."

I turned to look at the disciple from whom the deeper voice had come. He was taller than me, but not very muscular, with fine, dark hair prematurely streaked with gray. From his face and skin I would judge him to be in his late twenties, but his low, gentle voice and keen brown eyes showed a wisdom beyond his years. "Uzzi is a smooth talker, and I know you *think* he has Israel's best interest at heart, but surely you can see the man is dangerous."

Simon scoffed. "You think all Zealots are dangerous."

The tall man's eyebrows rose. "That's because they are."

"Dangerous to the Romans, maybe," Thaddeus argued.

"Dangerous to themselves," came the answer. "Jesus told Uzzi as much. I hope he listened."

Simon sighed. Mention of Jesus's conversation with Uzzi, whatever it had entailed, obviously disturbed him. He said nothing else, but as I watched him walk, his expression fluctuated from intent to concerned, as if he were internalizing the battle.

I was fairly certain that the Zealots were a sect of Jews who had tried to overthrow the Romans by force — a fact that I had picked up, I think, from a miniseries on cable. I was also fairly certain that they had failed, which made me appreciate the good sense of the prematurely gray disciple. Yet when I looked at the young Simon, I couldn't help but be reminded of myself at his age. I, too, had been an idealist once, certain that I had all the answers — and that with the help of a few like-minded friends, I could change the world. I wasn't surprised that these two would feel passionately about the freedom of Israel. But I could also see that, despite their relish for debate, there wasn't a bellicose bone in their bodies.

Our procession slowed. "Oh, look there," Thaddeus remarked, pointing ahead. "He's gotten bogged down again. Looks like they need us up front."

Simon looked up, his expression cheering. He stretched out his arms, locked his hands, and extended his fingers. "Ah, yes. Crowd control. Our specialty. Coming through!"

I looked toward Jesus and saw that his progress had, indeed, been slowed to a halt by the pressing crowd. The half-dozen disciples immediately encircling him were doing their best to keep his path clear, but the Jewish officials at the front of the group seemed both frustrated with Jesus's slow progress and flustered by the ardor of those struggling to see the popular rabbi. The officials were responding to the people with agitation, which had the interesting effect of slowing Jesus down further. The townspeople who stopped and smiled at him were favored with a smile in return; those who reached out a hand —

particularly the children — received a touch of his own. I did not see any mature women request such a touch, but among the children, Jesus did not discriminate. He seemed neither hurried nor uncomfortable; in fact, though the idea was unfathomable to me, he seemed to be enjoying himself.

Looking up the hill, I could see Simon and Thaddeus taking their places at the front of the group with practiced efficiency. Sandwiching the grousing officials between them, they cut through the crowd with arms outstretched. "Stand still and let Jesus pass, please," they ordered, their young voices surprisingly polite. "Don't push. Everyone will see him."

My thoughts turned bittersweet. I could still remember how it felt — that youthful, burning enthusiasm for a cause. Having a mission, a dream that consumed you. In my own case, it had been social work. But the phase hadn't lasted long; I had gotten turned off by low pay rates in the field before I even finished college. Being shrewd enough to realize that I was good at mathematics — and not so good at doing without the finer things in life — I had done what any forward-thinking, practical young person would do. I had decided to leverage the better-paying talent, assuring myself I could still do community volunteer work on the side.

I never did, of course.

I was busy.

I shook my head to clear the memory. Watching these two young men beam with pleasure at their chosen vocation had taken me back to a place I had forgotten. Intentionally.

I preferred to forget it again.

Under Simon and Thaddeus's skillful guidance, the group resumed its forward motion. But as Jesus neared the spot where the centurion's horse stood, the Roman surprised the crowd by dismounting. A tall and leggy man, he walked toward Jesus with long strides, then greeted him with a nod that was surprising in its deference.

"Rabbi," he said, his manner self-conscious, "don't trouble yourself to walk any farther; I don't deserve to have you under my roof. I'm a man under authority, with soldiers under me, and I know that if I tell one to do something, he'll do it. So if you'll only say the word, I know my servant will be healed."

The crowd murmured. Jesus's face broke into a smile. He cast a glance at the officials, or perhaps at Simon and Thaddeus, then answered in the form of an announcement. "I tell you the truth; I haven't found anyone in Israel with such great faith. Go home now. It will be done just as you believed it would."

The centurion's face shone with pleasure, but he didn't tarry to bask in Jesus's praise. He merely thanked him and departed, walking his horse away up the hill.

"Can he really do that?" a tenor voice asked behind me as the procession began to move again.

I turned my head. The speaker was another of the younger, twenty-something disciples. I had noticed him earlier at the lake because of his pale eyes — a rare trait here. His hair was a nondescript brown, but his long face and thoughtful expression gave him a high-born, noble visage that made him seem out of place amidst his rougher, more earthy cohorts.

He was speaking to the prematurely gray disciple, the one who had warned Thaddeus and Simon off the Zealots. "Do what?" the other man responded, his deep voice amused. "Heal people?"

"No!" the pale-eyed disciple insisted. "I know he can heal. I just mean, well... I thought he had to touch the person."

The other grinned. "Perhaps you should create a rule book for him, Thomas. Then we'd know what to expect."

Thomas rolled his eyes with a sigh. "Oh, stop. You know what I mean. In all this time he's never healed anyone without touching them."

"He just said he's never encountered such faith before," the other disciple suggested practically. "Perhaps that's the difference."

Thomas seemed to consider. "Perhaps."

*Doubting Thomas.*

I wished for a moment that I could simply shut off my brain, blocking out all incoming data until I could process what already smothered me. So much of what was happening seemed familiar, and somehow right. But just as much of it seemed wrong. Ever since I had first laid eyes on Jesus, a war had been waging — a war between the facts I thought I knew and the reality that insisted on playing out before me, mercilessly, constantly, and in excruciating detail. I wanted to believe my brain over my senses; I felt safer that way. But with every dusty step I took and every putrid smell that wafted under my nose, my confidence in my little gray cells eroded.

We had gone no more than fifty yards before another commotion developed. I left the disciples with whom I had been walking and caught up to Mary. "What is it?" I asked. "What's happening?"

She grinned. "The centurion's servant is healed, of course. He hadn't even gotten home before his servants ran out to tell him."

I looked out over the crowd. The townspeople were smiling and laughing, celebrating *en masse* as if the healed servant had been a personal friend to each. Thaddeus and Simon, evidently on cue from Jesus, had stopped trying to move forward and instead paused a moment as the rabbi took extra time to interact with the frenzied crowd. The officials slipped away.

"I can't see!" a little voice piped up to my left, frustrated to the point of tears. "I can't see!"

I looked over to discover a boy of no more than four or five, hanging onto the hand of a young teenager. The older boy was watching Jesus with delight, completely ignoring the plaintive wails of his much shorter sibling. I was about to break decorum and insist he help his little brother when a quick movement startled me.

"How's this?" a familiar deep voice asked. The graying disciple, whose name I still didn't know, had swept up the lad and hoisted him onto his own shoulder.

"Ohh..." the lad cooed. "Is that him? The rabbi? The one stretching out his hand?"

"That's him," the disciple replied. "That's Jesus. Amazing fellow, eh?"

The little boy could only nod, eyes wide.

"We should go, Kish," the older brother said, looking embarrassed.

The man put the child down, and the two boys scurried off.

I looked back at the disciple with fondness. He was a young man after my own heart: level-headed and non-violent, with both a sense of humor and a soft spot for children. As had happened upon my first meeting with Mary, I sensed a natural simpatico between us, and the prospect of a friendship. I offered a warm smile, forgetting to consider whether it would be appropriate.

I gathered it was not. Though he returned the gesture politely, he seemed uncomfortable, and he moved away from me without speaking.

Curious, I caught up to Mary. "What is that man's name?" I asked her in a whisper, wondering if it were one I knew.

Mary's eyes followed my surreptitiously pointed finger to the apostle in question. "That's Judas," she answered.

My stomach lurched. "What did you say?"

"Judas," she repeated. "The Iscariot. Nice man, and learned. He's well-traveled too, which will come in handy on the road."

"You like him?" I stammered.

Mary raised an eyebrow. "Why wouldn't I? He's very kind, and he's intelligent. A bit of a fussbudget sometimes, but we all have our faults." She smirked. "Well, except me, of course."

I looked back at Judas, and my knees weakened with another gut-blow of contradiction. Common wisdom in the twenty-first century — not to mention all twenty centuries before it — condemned the man as history's ultimate back-stabber. He was known the world over as selfish, heartless, avaricious scum.

Who was I to disagree?

*A darn good judge of character, that's who.*

My jaws clenched with frustration. I could always spot a scam artist, even as a child. I knew perfectly well that the storybook lady on TV wasn't smiling specifically at me, and that the fifth-grader next door wasn't really making millions selling rocks. As a single woman I had warned countless girlfriends off of obvious operators; as a mother, I could tell which kid's parents were in debt up to their eyeballs, having marital problems, or tipping the bottle. I wasn't clairvoyant; I simply noticed things others didn't see. I knew how to read people.

The disciples I had met were a far cry from the serious, noble types I had always envisioned, true. But I could tell that they were all good men, with good hearts.

And Judas Iscariot was, too.

Another sharp burst of nausea reared within me, making the sea of people around me pitch like a wave. I was treading on dangerous ground, and I knew it. But was it so impossible that my instincts could be right? What were a bunch of two-thousand-year-old stories written in quill pen anyway, compared to my own eyes and ears? However this insanity of misplacement had come about, I was here now, and I perceived what I perceived.

I looked back at Judas. He was walking alongside Thomas, whose hand rested affectionately on his friend's shoulder as they talked. They were smiling. Laughing together.

I turned my head away.

*Hang history.*

I was on my own.

*Commentary for Chapter 7 begins on page 240.*

# Chapter 8

I stared into the flames, exhausted. Every muscle in my body was tired, and my feet were killing me. Next time I saw sandals with leather soles for sale, I was going to buy them, no matter who said they didn't wear well. I had no intention of being around long enough to wear a hole in anything.

*You go, Rachel. Just keep saying that.*

I shook the pesky voice out of my head. Determination had gotten me nowhere in the last, long couple of weeks, but then neither had sarcasm. The truth was it didn't matter what I did, how I thought, or what I wished for. The sun kept rising and it kept setting, and every blasted cycle found my butt in exactly the same place.

"Do you have a blister?" Tamar asked sympathetically, kneeling beside me. "I've seen you limping. Some of this oil should help. Here."

I dipped a finger in the jar she held, then rubbed on the yellowish-green lubricant. They used oil for everything here. But it did help a little.

I thanked her, and she smiled at me.

She was excited, as everyone was. It was our first night of camping along the caravan trail, and exhilaration hung in the air like dew.

We had set out from Capernaum this morning at the crack of dawn: Jesus and the men, several wives and children, and the benefactors: Mary, Joanna, and me. We brought with us an inventory of pack animals, provisions, and camping gear, including a donkey cart for Leah and the baby to ride in. The cart had plenty of room for the other children and anyone else who needed a rest, but today everyone was so anxious to be off that few had taken advantage of it. Even Leah had insisted on getting out and walking a bit, with the baby nestled in a linen sling tied over her shoulder.

By the time we reached our stopping point I was more than ready for a nap, but the other women had all hustled to fetch water, build a fire, chop vegetables, cook the stew, and serve the menfolk — as if such tasks were a treat rather than the same tedious chores they performed in their own homes *ad nauseum*. Even Mary and Joanna, who normally held themselves above such menial work, had chipped in for the sheer camaraderie of it.

I felt obligated to hustle right along with the rest of them, and the exertion had left me ravenous. Then again, I was always ravenous. Portion sizes here — even those taken by the men — were miniscule, and I had to constantly restrain myself from eating more than anyone else. I had gotten so hungry by mid-morning that I was tempted to pluck stalks of grain from the roadside and gnaw on them like a rabbit.

The evening meal had been good while it lasted, but now every crumb had been consumed. The few dishes and utensils involved had been cleaned, the children had been settled into their tents for the night, and the men were drinking wine around their campfire. The women had gathered to socialize at the cooking fire, and the faces reflected in its orange glow all beamed bright with anticipation. Traveling itself was not a huge novelty to these women, as most had made a pilgrimage to Jerusalem at one time or another. What excited them was their illustrious company, and the prospect of participating in a mission in which anything — quite possibly something amazing — could happen.

The thrill hadn't quite reached me.

The baby squalled, and I looked up to see Leah put him to her breast. Born at six pounds, tops, the infant Jesse seemed a small baby, at least relative to my own. But he had a good appetite and was healing remarkably well from his circumcision. Leah carried him with her everywhere and nursed him on demand, so his crying was unusual. But since nightfall he had seemed particularly fussy.

"Is he swelling?" Tamar asked with concern, leaving my side to sit by her sister-in-law, pull back the baby's swaddles, and examine his wound.

"No," Leah answered. "That looks better every day. I think he's just out of sorts from the trip."

Baby Jesse was not the only one. Despite all I had done to help prepare for the excursion, I had never really expected it to happen. Being out here now, in an even more primitive and challenging environment, was yet another rude awakening.

Faking competence at the Galilean-woman thing had been taking every ounce of energy I possessed, both physical and mental. With everyone here assuming I already knew how to milk a goat, bake bread in a rock oven, and trim a hangnail with a four-inch blade, I was forced to spend every waking moment watching, listening, and imitating just to maintain the illusion. Such heroics, along with the general chaos of the trip preparation, had been sufficiently arduous to prevent my having the time to feel sorry for myself. But now, with the day's work largely done and a mesmerizing flicker of flame before my eyes, I could not stop thinking about my family.

I missed them. I worried about them as well, though not as much as I might have, had I not flatly refused to believe that they were also missing me. I preferred to imagine that they were all hanging in some funky plane of suspended animation, where they would remain — safe and sound — until I made my way back to them.

Tonight I missed my husband in particular. Which was somewhat ironic, given how little time we ordinarily spent together. His business travels often took him away for weeks at a time, and even when he was home he was distracted, trying his best to spend quality time with the kids without coming across to his superiors as undedicated. His boss, better known in our household as "The Man," was a childless divorcee who believed that the Company, with a capital C, came First, with a capital F, and that since he himself had nothing better to do than work, then none of his underlings did either. Pretending to agree with such a philosophy created a stressful juggling act for Joe, but he wasn't by nature a complainer. He made good money. The job was okay. He could deal with it.

At least he said he could.

Baby Jesse let out an angry sound, eliciting a ripple of sympathetic tension from the women ringed around the fire. The nursing idea wasn't working. He seemed to be getting increasingly uncomfortable.

Bernice, who was Zebedee and Salome's daughter, looked up from the load of brush she was placing strategically on the flames. "Walk him around a little," she suggested. "Give him a bounce. Milk's probably not settling."

A strong, plain-looking woman, Bernice showed all the healthy spunk of her brothers, but lacked their jocular humor. She had been married for many years to Philip, also a fisherman, who worked for her father. The couple had brought their children along on the journey, and Bernice quickly proved herself to be a natural leader, a hard worker, and an effective parent. She was often brusque in her dealings with the other women, but I tried not to hold the latter against her. Mothers of three were allowed some slack.

Leah didn't answer her sister-in-law, whose tone had been more overbearing than suggestive. But she did rise with the baby and start to walk.

"He usually drops right off to sleep after he nurses," Tamar whispered anxiously, once Leah was out of earshot. "And she just changed his linens. What could make him so fussy?"

Joanna answered with a gentle laugh. "Babies don't need a reason to be fussy, my dear. It's perfectly ordinary."

"I hope so," Tamar replied. But she could not take her eyes off Leah, who was pacing with the baby in wide circles around the fire. When Jesse began to howl even louder, Tamar rose with a jerk and walked toward them.

"I still can't believe those girls are old enough to be mothers," I thought out loud. My Bekka didn't even like to baby-sit. She said that the sound of crying gave her a headache.

"They're plenty old enough!" Mary responded in surprise.

I swallowed, not realizing I had spoken where she could hear me. But Mary didn't miss much.

"With all the girls that get married off at eleven and twelve?" she continued defensively. "Our daughters are lucky we know better. It's just common sense that girls should be allowed to finish growing first. All you have to do is look at how many babies die when the mother's twelve. The girls die, too. They're just not big enough. No self-respecting father should let his daughter marry till she's sixteen; that's what my mother always said, and thank goodness people are listening now."

"It is better," Joanna agreed. "Better to have a healthy baby at sixteen than die trying before you get there. I hear that in Egypt, they'll marry them at ten. Ten! Never mind the odds against the girl living to twenty. The fathers just want them out of the house."

Jesse was screaming now. The women watched as Tamar extended her arms and took a turn, but though the change of hands startled the baby temporarily, he soon resumed his fit.

"What's wrong with him, Bernie?" John had appeared by his sister's side, his expression troubled. "Did something happen?"

"Of course not," Bernice retorted. Though most women used a deferential tone when speaking with a man in public, Bernice often spoke to both James and John as if they were mildly annoying pests, making me wonder if brothers were an exception. Her next words, however, were softer. "Babies cry, John. I'm sure he's fine. Go back to your fire. We'll take care of him."

John didn't move for several seconds. He stood still, debating. Then with a frustrated huff he moved back toward the men.

Mary chuckled. "I thought for a moment he was going to try and calm the little tyke himself."

"Now that would be something to see!" Joanna agreed. "A strapping fisherman tending to an infant. He'd never live it down."

Bernice smiled wryly. "John can surprise you sometimes."

Their words confused me. I would have given anything for Joe to take a shift when our own babies were fussy. He had tried to a few times, but he was nervous with newborns; he hadn't gotten completely comfortable with the kids until they were older. Besides, he had always needed the sleep more than I did, since he was the one working.

The baby screamed louder. Leah and Tamar returned to the fire, both their eyes frightened and moist.

"Let me try," Mary said confidently, rising. "My oldest daughter used to scream her head off in the evenings. Nearly drove me mad. But she was healthy as a horse, despite it."

Leah handed the infant to Mary, her relief evident. Mary flipped him over with his belly on her arm so that he could rest face-out, viewing the world like an airplane. Or, as Mary must have thought, like a bird. Supporting his tiny head with her hand, she bounced him gently as they toured around the fire, and the new position seemed to appease him, at least momentarily.

The other women seemed highly amused.

"She's not at all what I expected," whispered a small, mousy woman to my left. "She's so kind!"

"She is now," Bernice responded, her tone flat. "You never met her before, did you, Naomi?"

Naomi shook her head. She had a nervous manner, not just now, when speaking about someone who could possibly overhear, but all the time. On the road she had been jumpy as a cat. "I only heard about her. The richest woman in Magdala, Bartholomew said — maybe all of Galilee. And a *terror*. He said grown men were scared of her."

Joanna chortled.

"I doubt that," Bernice said cynically.

"Oh, but Bartholomew wouldn't lie," Naomi defended, albeit meekly. "He heard that some of the townspeople begged Jesus to come to Magdala so that he could drive the demons out of her. And that when he did come, she locked herself in her house and started throwing stones out—"

"My dear," Joanna broke in, giggling as she talked, "I'm sure your husband is the soul of integrity, but he was obviously misinformed.

The Magdalenes are famous for scandal. They love nothing better than a good story."

Naomi stared at Joanna, her eyes growing wide with alarm. She looked immature and frail as a butterfly, but she was actually in her mid twenties, the mother of two rambunctious boys who were attending a synagogue school in Cana with their cousins. The antithesis of her larger-than-life, liberal-minded husband, she had so far acted helpful, quiet, and diffident. This was the first I'd heard her speak.

She appeared to regret it.

"I didn't mean any disrespect," she answered, her voice quavering. "Mary just seems so much more likeable than I'd heard. I mean, I knew she was intelligent for a woman, but it's just—" Naomi stumbled for the right words. The woman was so uptight she made *me* nervous. "Well, I mean, after meeting her myself I can see why Jesus is so fond of her."

The baby was screaming again. Mary returned to the fire with a look of annoyance, which I knew to be directed at her own failure, not the unhappy newborn. "I'm sorry, Leah," she said humbly, handing him back. "I tried. Maybe if you nurse him again."

Leah made another attempt, but Jesse would have none of it. He curled his reddened little body into a ball, clenching his tiny fists tight and alternating his screams with gasps for air. Bernice took a turn holding him. So did Joanna. I laid him on a cloth on the ground and took off some of his swaddling clothes in case he was hot. But nothing seemed to help. And despite all of the older women's assurances that even healthy babies cried, Leah was frightened and so was Tamar. I was getting anxious myself. The baby seemed too young for colic. I wasn't sure what else could be wrong.

I had just given him back to Tamar when John returned. "Can't you do *anything* for him?" he asked his wife shortly, exasperated.

Leah looked up at him with irritation — the first direct affront I had seen from her. She was a headstrong girl, and whether wives were supposed to defer to their husbands or not, I had a feeling she would mature to hold her own. Fortunately for John, she was still acting compliant, primarily because she was giddy in love with him.

"I'm doing everything I can think of," she answered, working hard to keep her voice controlled. "We all are. He just won't stop crying."

John started to say something else, but bit his lip. As his son continued to scream, he paced a few steps, his angst showing clearly on his face. Then abruptly, he stopped by Leah's side and reached for the baby. "Let me have him, then," he ordered. "I can't do any worse, can I?"

The women stared. Joanna's jaw dropped. Naomi gasped.

"Oh, John, for heaven's sake!" Bernice chastised mildly, shaking her head. No one else said a word.

Leah handed the baby over to his father. John juggled the baby awkwardly, but ultimately got him into a safe cradle position inside one strong arm. The baby quieted a little, and John began to walk away with him, smiling.

I was smiling, too, but I was the only one. Judging by the other women's expressions, a man who lowered himself to tend to an infant was anything but "cool." As much as all the men had celebrated over and admired little Jesse from a distance, I had only seen John hold his son once before, and Zebedee and James rarely even touched him. Taking care of babies was women's work.

Obviously, John was confident enough in his masculinity that he was willing to accept a little ridicule for the sake of his son, and I was so proud of the guy that I could have jumped up and flung my arms around his neck. But as far as the other women were concerned, he might as well have braided his hair and worn face paint.

When the men at the campfire noticed the spectacle, they began to hound the young father with chuckles and good-natured barbs. But to John's further credit, he ignored them, concentrating on the baby. Unfortunately, Jesse's temporary stunning at the novelty of being held by a man could not hold off his cries for long. Soon he was screaming so loud that even the men at the campfire had to shout to hear themselves.

"Are you going to feed him too, John?"

"Now, *that* I've got to see!"

Just when I was sure I could no longer restrain myself from shushing the heckling apostles with some very unladylike words, John gave up. He returned to the women and handed the baby back to its mother, his expression more worried than abashed. "I can't do anything with him either," he said miserably. "What could be wrong?"

None of the women had an answer. I wanted to reassure Leah and John, but I didn't know what to say. Jesse appeared healthy. He was alert, responsive, and an excellent eater. He had even gained a little baby fat already. But I had no idea what maladies could befall babies in an environment such as this, and the more his anguished screams continued, the more distressed I became.

Leah's tears overflowed as she clamped the baby possessively against her chest. Not caring to be held so tightly, he protested even louder, but she seemed too distraught to notice.

Another man appeared from out of the shadows and stepped up to Leah's side. "May I hold him?"

Leah whipped her head around, her eyes wide. Jesus stood beside her with his arms outstretched.

For a long moment, she seemed too shocked to respond. Evidently, a father humiliating himself over an infant was one thing, but for an unrelated rabbi to do the same was preposterous. Leah's lips moved, but no sound came out.

"Of course," John answered for her, though he was barely composed himself.

Jesus's brown eyes twinkled at them, as if he found their reaction amusing. He accepted the baby from Leah and held him out at arm's length for a moment, taking a good look at him.

"What's this now, Jesse?" he asked.

The baby, true to form, responded to the change of hands with another temporary cease-fire. His screams diminished to snuffles as he looked back at the strange, bearded man, attempting in that typical, comical newborn way to focus his crossed eyes on the face before him.

"You mustn't upset your mother so," Jesus chastised gently, as if speaking to a wayward — but well-meaning — adult. "Or your father."

The infant's brow knitted in concentration. I wasn't sure if he could actually see Jesus clearly or not, but regardless, he seemed fascinated. After a few seconds he let out another wail, but when Jesus tucked him under an elbow in a football hold, the infant became still again. Then, without another word, Jesus took the baby and walked away, heading back toward the men's campfire. John followed eagerly, and though we could hear an occasional squeal from Jesse echoing back to us as they walked, the baby was the only male making noise. The once-heckling apostles had fallen silent.

Leah sank down by the fire. "Well," she said breathlessly. "I guess Jesse's all right."

Mary chuckled. "Of course he is. He could hardly have better company, could he?"

Joanna shook her head in disbelief. "A grown man talking to a baby," she muttered, then added, with a laugh to herself, "and some say he's not a rebel!"

The women had little more to say. They seemed stymied

somewhere between respect for a man who could solve a tough female problem and disappointment in one who had acted "silly." I felt my cheeks flush with indignation. Their idea of what was appropriate was so stifling they couldn't begin to appreciate what Jesus had just done. Or John either, for that matter.

I wanted to shake them.

But I kept my mouth shut.

Another figure approached the cooking fire, and for a moment I thought it was John, returning the baby. But it was James. He said nothing to any of the women, but crept up quietly toward Tamar, attempting to catch her eye. Her gaze was absorbed by the fire, however, and only when he stepped up and touched her lightly on the shoulder did she notice him. She rose immediately, her face alight with a shy smile.

I felt a twinge of jealousy.

None of the women here could be called lovely. Respectable females didn't wear makeup and nobody had shampoo, which left them at a hopeless disadvantage compared to the blow-dried, plasticized women of my acquaintance. But despite crooked teeth and a preponderance of pimples, some women did stand out as attractive, and Tamar was one of them. Even though the loose tunics concealed everyone's degree of curvature, Tamar had a natural grace that reflexively drew the eye. Her hair was a fetching shade of black-brown, her dark eyes large and expressive, her cheeks rosy, her bone structure delicate. She emitted confidence without arrogance, beauty without vanity, intelligence without guile. The sum total was a rampant sex appeal of which she seemed wholly unaware.

The same could not be said for James. He took his wife's hand and guided her away from the fire and toward their waiting tent, and as I watched them walk away together, my melancholy returned.

I would be crawling into a tent with Mary and Joanna tonight, and under the circumstances I should be grateful for any amount of safe sleeping space. But it would be nice to have a husband by my side, someone I could count on to be there, night after night.

I hadn't had that for years now. Somebody had to pay for the twenty-eight-hundred-dollar mattress.

I stood up and stepped back from the flames. Self-pity was getting me nowhere. And this ridiculous situation could not go on forever. Somewhere, the proverbial ruby slippers had to be waiting. All I had to do was find them and click my heels.

But where were they?

The evening was cool, but not cold, and the night air felt refreshing. Low rumbles of laughter drifted over from the men's campfire, and on impulse I walked toward the sound, stepping close enough to see their faces in their flickering light, yet keeping myself in the shadows.

"And then," Peter was saying, his face alive with drama, "the guy says to me, 'well, you fixed the net already, didn't you?'"

The men erupted in guffaws. Thomas accidentally spit out some wine. Thaddeus rolled on his side, consumed with laughter. Simon let out an undignified snort, and Judas's face was red as a beet. Jesus was laughing too, I noticed, and without a trace of self-consciousness. Despite their frivolity, none of the men appeared to be drunk; probably because the near-constant intake of fermented beverages pushed everyone's tolerance for alcohol sky high. They were simply in a festive mood, enjoying the night and each other's company.

I looked in Jesus's arms for the baby, but Jesse was with his father again, nestled comfortably in John's lap, even as the fisherman's whole body vibrated with laughter. The newborn's eyes were closed tight. He was sound asleep.

I stood still for a long while, lurking, listening. I wanted to hear Jesus speak again, to hear him say something profound. He still didn't look or sound right to me, but his actions just now, at least, had seemed oddly on target. Hadn't Sunday-school Jesus loved babies?

But as Peter launched into his fourth fish tale, I realized my waiting was in vain.

This was not Sunday-school Jesus. This Jesus had greasy hair, ragged toenails, and a stain on the hem of his tunic. He was leaning back on his elbows, facing the fire, laughing at the storyteller along with the rest of the men. He would not be interrupting the joviality here with some sober screed on deportment or piety.

He was relaxing. He was enjoying himself.

He was acting pretty darned mortal.

I turned around and walked back toward my tent.

*Commentary for Chapter 8 begins on page 243.*

# Chapter 9

It was morning, some days later. I stretched my arms in the sunshine that beat down on the dew-sodden road and recited my promise not to obsess over how grubby I felt, but to accept the fact that I was as clean as anyone else — and to be grateful I was still healthy.

At least there was no more goat's milk for breakfast. I hated to turn down any form of sustenance, but now that the yellow-white sludge was unavailable, I was off the hook. The hard cheese made from it was much easier on my stomach, and along with a little bread and water it made a decent enough breakfast. The last few days had been strenuous ones, fraught with hilly travel, but last night I had slept well.

I was trying to accentuate the positive.

Mary, Joanna, and I were accompanying Jesus and most of the men on the short walk from the camp we had set up last night to the village that was our next destination. Our role was to purchase supplies. Jesus and the men would visit the synagogue to meet with the clergy, and those left behind would either rest or complete the process of making the camp livable for a two- to three-day visit. At least this was the plan. But with Jesus, plans had a way of changing.

We had no idea whether anyone in the village was expecting us. Sometimes the rabbi would announce the next stop on his agenda; sometimes he wouldn't. Often, when people knew where he was headed, an ardent youth or two would run ahead and announce him. But here in the hills, villages were fewer and farther between, and so were people. The latter delighted me.

It wasn't that I disliked people. I just disliked having droves of them within inches of my person 24/7, a pet peeve which set me apart here. Everyone else preferred the cramped "luxury" of staying in supporter's homes to camping in the open, but to my surprise, I had come to favor the outdoors. Camp had its share of pesky insects and dirt, but so did a lot of houses; at least when we were camping I had some illusion of fresh air and breathing room. Last night, I had gotten lucky. No one seemed to know anyone in the village of Nain, and since Mary and Joanna viewed the place like a resident of Malibu might view Chickenfactorytown, Mississippi, the decision had been made to camp.

Nain, apparently, was close to Jesus's hometown of Nazareth in terms of both geography and squalor. It was hilly and isolated, and most of its people were very poor, eking out a meager living with cattle, vineyards, and olive groves. Seeing Jesus, the disciples remarked, would be the highlight of these people's year.

We had not yet reached the village when we saw a crowd heading toward us on the road. My first thought was that it was a welcoming committee, but the commotion accompanying it — a disturbing combination of drumbeats and high-pitched wails — proved me wrong.

"It's a funeral," Mary announced to the squinting Joanna. "We should stand aside."

Sobered, our party moved to the road's shoulder and waited for the procession to pass.

In front was a single drummer, a boy of ten or eleven. Behind him was a crowd of women, clapping their hands in rhythm and uttering cries of grief. One woman stood out as she wailed at the top of her lungs, clutched her belly, and sporadically fell to her knees.

I watched the group, puzzled. All of the women were doleful, but the display of the loudest was of a different nature, a nature wholly insincere. It was as if I was watching an overzealous actress in a second-rate stage production.

"Dreadful," Joanna muttered beside me. "I could do a better job myself. The deceased obviously hadn't a cent to spare. Not a single flutist, even!" She clucked her tongue sadly. "The elders really ought to help with this sort of thing."

I began to understand. The loud woman was a professional mourner. She might not even have known the person she was mourning. But I could tell from the sorrow on their faces that most of these women did, and their sadness was both genuine and contagious.

We stood in silence as behind the women came a group of men and young teens, all of them dirty and poorly clad. At the back of the group came a simple bier, which the strongest of the men supported on their shoulders with wooden poles. On top of it, resting inside a low-sided, open coffin, I saw the body of a boy.

I drew in a sharp breath. He looked fourteen, maybe fifteen. Not much older than Ryan. His eyes were closed, and his skin was as pale as naturally dark skin could look. But his sweet, nearly cherubic face and thin but muscular form seemed somehow too vibrant still, as if death had come by cheating.

My heart sank. I could all too easily put my own son's face upon the body. The grief of those who had loved him enveloped me, seeping to my bones like ice.

Mary uttered a gasp herself, and as I looked around at the disciples nearby, I could see that all were similarly moved. All, that is, except Jesus, who stared at the bier with a look that made no sense to me, that I could only describe as frustration.

I didn't ponder his reaction for long, as behind the bier came a woman whom I knew immediately to be the boy's mother. She was so aggrieved she could not have walked without the support of the two women on either side of her. Her tunic was tattered, her cloak torn nearly in two. Her black veil announced her as a widow as well.

"My baby," she moaned repeatedly. "My only child."

Her lament bore no relation to that of the hired mourner up front. This woman's anguish was not for show. It was consuming her. I knew that a poor widow without a son had only the bleakest of futures, but in her eyes I could see a depth of pain far beyond any concern for food or shelter. The boy had meant everything to this woman; one precious child had been her entire world. I could not look at her without seeing the gaping hole in her heart, without feeling her pain slicing through my own chest.

But there was nothing I could do.

I turned my eyes away.

It was then I noticed that Jesus's gaze was riveted on the woman just as my own had been. The fact that he was seeing — and feeling — the same pain was written clearly in his face. Unlike me, however, he did not turn away. Instead, he stepped forward.

He walked straight into the women's path. The two supporting the boy's mother stopped, startled. Jesus leaned down to catch the mother's eye. "Don't cry," he commanded.

The woman stared back at him as if in a daze. Then slowly, still watching him, she silenced herself and straightened.

Jesus stepped forward and put his hand on the coffin. The men carrying it, who had only just noticed the interfering stranger, stopped moving at once and squared their shoulders in defense. But Andrew, Peter's younger brother, was quick to reach Jesus's side and explain. I had become fond of Andrew. Though he lacked his brother's charisma, he was perhaps the boldest of the lot — never afraid to forge ahead, always looking for a better way. He was also an excellent diplomat. "Peace," he proclaimed, using his best conciliatory tone, "This man is

Jesus. Jesus of Nazareth!"

There was no question of the men's knowing that name. Their mouths dropped open as they stared first at Andrew, then at Jesus. Wordlessly, they set the coffin on the ground and stepped back.

It happened so fast we all doubted our eyes. There was no incantation, no swell of background music. No buildup, no dramatic pause. Jesus simply bent down next to the coffin and told the dead boy to get up. The boy's eyes opened, and he turned his head from side to side, disoriented. "Is my mother here?" he asked, sounding much younger than he looked.

Jesus offered him a hand, helped him out of the coffin, and pointed him in the direction of his mother, who stared wide-eyed, unable to move until the boy came close enough to touch her. She fell on her knees then, embracing him.

No words came from her mouth. No words came from any of us. The others seemed to feel, in those first few moments, just as I did. They assumed they must have missed something.

What had happened wasn't believable. It was too quick. It was too anticlimactic. It seemed too much like a hoax.

I couldn't help but wonder if the boy had truly been dead.

Jesus stood still only briefly, watching the emotional reunion with another expression I couldn't decipher. He seemed pleased at the mother's joy. That much was obvious from his smile. But there was something else in his eyes, a queer, unsettled sentiment, rather like resignation. And as he left the still-stunned, still-speechless crowd and turned away, alone, to continue walking toward the city, I got the bizarre feeling that in his view, what had just happened was nothing to be fussed over. That he didn't view it as the show of strength it seemed; but rather, unfathomably, as a show of weakness.

After a few seconds' worth of shock, the disciples hastened to follow him. But they, like me, were more stupefied than excited. Mary's face had paled, and as we walked she kept her gaze riveted on Jesus's back, almost as if she were afraid of him.

My voice returned at last. "Has he ever done that before?" I whispered.

Without looking at me, she shook her head slowly. The ordinarily saucy Joanna was equally pale and equally mute.

It was not long before several of the men from the funeral passed us at a run and bounded up on the road beside Jesus. "You are a prophet!" one shouted. "One of the greatest prophets ever, right here in Nain!"

Others ran up with them. The chorus increased.

*It's a sign! At last, God is going to help us!*

*Yes, at last!*

*A real, live prophet!*

Jesus said nothing. He regarded the men with patient smiles and kept on walking.

As we neared the town, the frenzy increased. The entire funeral procession had turned around, and many of them had run ahead of us. By the time our party reached the first of the unimpressive stone buildings that marked the outskirts of Nain — there were no city gates — the townspeople were already swamping the streets, waiting.

As we entered, their cries echoed from every direction, even from the roofs above. *It's Jesus of Nazareth! He raised Ahira from the dead!*

*Look there! It's Ahira! He's alive!*

*God be praised!*

My heart pounded as I attached myself to Mary's side. The people of Nain were excited, happy, delirious with joy. But all I could feel was apprehension. I had experienced crowds before, but this one was different. The people were quickly becoming crazed, almost out of control. They surrounded us on every side, pushing, pressing closer to the object of their adoration. They were yelling with joy, but still, they were yelling. They wanted to thank Jesus, but they were shoving each other to do it.

I took in a breath and tried not to panic. Simon and Thaddeus had taken the lead, and though I couldn't see them in the seething crowd, I was sure they were doing their best to keep us moving toward the synagogue as planned. But James, Andrew, Peter, and the other disciples were having a hard time carving out enough space for Jesus to breathe. The women, as usual, brought up the rear, with me plastered to Mary's one side and Joanna to the other. Mary's servant Samuel, bless him, walked behind us, attempting a buffer from the crowd in that direction, but as the space around us continued to shrink I wished heartily that the immense Gideon, whom Joanna had left at camp to help repair a cracked cart wheel, was with us as well.

When a particularly aggressive man pushed in front of us and elbowed his way forward, we had no choice but to stop. When another followed, slipping into the gap he had created, it was like a dam had broken. All at once a flood of frenetic villagers divided us from the rest of the apostles. Mary and Joanna and I looked at each other with alarm.

Which way had Jesus gone? We could no longer see any of them.

Panic threatened. I wanted to scream. I wanted to sharpen my fingernails, clench my fists, and start clawing and punching — whatever it took to get out of this nightmare. The people around me were sweating and filthy. The stench of mingled bodies, manure, and garbage in the streets was overwhelming. The whole village seemed no more than an incorporated slum, its occupants raving lunatics. I knew that the people were excited rather than angry, joyful rather than desperate, but neither of those things made me feel any less vulnerable to being trampled to death. Where were the disciples? Were they abandoning us?

"Mary! Rachel! Where are you? Samuel!"

The voice was barely audible over the road of the crowd, but its deep pitch helped it carry. "Judas!" I shouted, throwing decorum to the wind, waving my arm high in the air. "We're here!"

In a second I saw them. Judas and Thomas pushed their way back to either side of Joanna and me, then with Samuel's help from behind, they held back the crowd as we all pushed forward until we were once again within sight of the rest of the disciples — most notably the towering, curly black head of Simon Peter.

I breathed a sigh of relief, fighting a highly inappropriate urge to give the valiant young Judas, who remained protectively at my left side, a heartfelt hug of thanks. Instead I tried to focus on forward motion, and soon I was relieved to see the looming of a tall stone structure that was almost certainly the synagogue. I could only hope that it was surrounded by a sturdy wall with heavy, solid gates.

My wish was granted. The courtyard wall was not only sturdy, but guarded zealously by several bright-robed men I took to be church officials. I was still hopelessly confused by the various designations for clergy, but these men clearly had clout with the townspeople. Their fierce orders quieted those within earshot, and when at last we reached the gates we were able to walk through them unimpeded. At least unimpeded by the townspeople. One of the officials looked askance at Mary, Joanna, and me, and I suspect was about to ask us to wait outside, but Thomas boldly informed him that we were with Jesus and ushered us in without awaiting permission.

The gates closed behind us.

My knees were trembling. Clammy sweat coated my skin. I wanted to sink down on the ground and collapse, but since no one else was resting, my stubborn female pride prevented me.

Mary and Joanna did not look nearly so traumatized as I was. If anything, they looked elated. I glanced around to discover that despite the harrowing nature of our entry into town and the hard work the disciples had just performed, not one of them seemed unduly drained. On the contrary, they were upbeat, galvanized.

They were celebrating. Celebrating — as they had been too surprised to do at the time — the amazing feat that Jesus had performed on the road. They were not only impressed, they were ecstatic. They knew their master was a gifted healer, but bringing the dead back to life had not been in the playbook. Jesus had raised his game. They were backing a winner.

The only near-death experience I had been thinking of was my own.

Thoroughly embarrassed, not to mention feeling like a hopeless weakling, I took a deep breath and bucked up my traitorous knees. The courtyard was filled with people, but — I assured myself — it wasn't crowded. My standards for the term had lowered so much now that if I could stretch out one arm without smacking someone, I was content. Compared to the streets outside, this was bliss.

I looked around. The synagogue itself was a modest one, tall and rectangular, with an entry consisting of stone steps and the obligatory colonnade, presumably facing towards Jerusalem. The building was not at all ornate; it didn't even have a proper women's court. Female worshipers were always cordoned off from the men by some means. In the Capernaum synagogue, we had had to watch from behind a screen. But here, there seemed no place at all for women to gather besides out in the courtyard, an oversight that added insult to injury. The women of Nain would be lucky if they could even hear the speakers.

I couldn't hear anything myself. Jesus had chosen to sit on the stone steps of the synagogue, rather than going all the way inside it, but the officials and select townspeople who had been let in were clustered so tightly around him I couldn't understand what any of them were saying.

"Let's rest here a while until the crowd settles," Mary suggested. "Then we'll take Samuel and head for the market."

My pulse quickened. I could only hope she was joking. I wasn't setting one foot outside this sanctuary until at least two-thirds of the population were asleep.

"We should ask one of the other men, too," Joanna added, mopping her sweating brow. "Not that we'll be mobbed again if Jesus isn't with us, but really, what a wretched little town!"

Joanna's complaints didn't pack nearly the punch they would have if she hadn't looked so delighted while delivering them. "I can still scarcely believe it," she beamed. "Raising a boy from the dead! Mary, did you have any idea?"

Mary shook her head. "I was surprised myself," she admitted. "But I won't be anymore."

"Do you think the boy was really dead?"

The words were out of my mouth before I could stop them. And as the women's eyes narrowed at me, I wished fervently that I could shrink down and disappear into the dust.

"What do you mean, *really* dead?" Mary asked sharply. "Either you're dead, or you're not!"

I scrambled to redeem myself. "I just mean, well, sometimes a person falls into a deep sleep before they die."

Why I felt the need to quibble, I didn't know. As a child I had had no trouble believing stories that defied the laws of physics. So God rained frogs on the Egyptians? Fine. If he created the world, he should have administrator access, right? My adult view of an intelligent creator was less anthropomorphic, but it was also more nebulous. Grown-up Rachel, truth be told, hadn't given the issue a whole heck of a lot of thought.

Did I believe in miracles now? Maybe. Probably not. I had a healthy respect for the laws of physics. Then again, there was a strong appeal in nothing being impossible, and — cynic or no — I wasn't willing to rule out the possibility of any miracle happening ever.

I just wasn't sold on this one.

Perhaps because this particular trick hadn't been performed by some mystical, theoretical Jesus who had lived in some alternative universe an incomprehensibly long time ago. This one had come from a man of average height who liked his stew heavy on the onion, who laughed out loud at fish jokes, and who teased Matthew about his snoring.

This Jesus was way too normal to have that kind of power. And I was way too inconsequential to witness it.

"I don't know what I'm saying," I stammered.

"I understand, Rachel," Joanna said in a motherly tone. "It was a shock to us all. Just goes to show we have no idea what he's capable of." She looked out toward the gates. "He'll certainly be besieged by the sick now, won't he?"

Mary watched me for a long moment, and I perceived her shrewd eyes saw more than I wanted them too. But she chose, thankfully, to let it go.

Jesus's voice reached our ears, and we turned toward the steps. The initial furor of discussion over the incident on the road had subsided enough for the disciples to get all the men seated, and Jesus had begun to field the usual clergy FAQs. We moved to the edges of the crowd and listened as he talked, though more and more I found such interviews painful to observe. The officials always greeted Jesus with respect, but once they had him within their clutches they frequently turned passive-aggressive, peppering him with questions that were accusatory, even snide. Jesus was not quick to anger; with most people, he was the soul of patience. But when something did rile him, he made no attempt to hide the fact. His approach to conflict was always direct and fearless, though to date it had been well controlled. I had yet to see him lose his temper.

This morning he seemed as unflappable as ever, answering questions about his dubious observance of the Sabbath with no trace of defensiveness. He seemed relaxed, perhaps even a little melancholy. As I watched his gaze stray occasionally to the synagogue wall, over which drifted cries of praise and pleas for help from the townspeople, I perceived that he wished to be someplace else.

If I didn't know better, I would think he wanted to be back outside.

But the man was not insane.

By now, as Joanna had said, every sick, lame, and undernourished — not to mention potentially contagious — person in the village was likely to be squatting just beyond the courtyard gates. And judging by the rampant poverty we had witnessed, there would be many more of them here than in a place like Capernaum. The crush of humanity we had experienced on the way in was nothing compared to what Jesus would face on his way back out. We might very well have to fetch more of the men from camp to bring him home safely.

My attention was drawn to two relatively well-dressed onlookers, both in their twenties, who were snapping at each other as Jesus talked. Impatient from the beginning, they were becoming increasingly agitated, and just as I was certain they would come to blows, one of them shouted out to Jesus, interrupting him.

"Teacher! Will you please tell my *brother*, here, to split his inheritance with me?"

The man's voice was full of venom. His brother swore at him.

Peter grumbled, shifting his significant weight. He was not above swearing himself, but he had no tolerance for anyone who disrespected Jesus. Nor did he share his master's even temper.

Jesus put a swift hand on Peter's arm. He looked back at the young man who had asked him the question and smiled — a benevolent, but aggrieved, smile. The same sort of smile, I fancied, that a mother would give a six-year-old who had captured her a frog as a present, tracking mud in the kitchen in the process. "Who made me a judge or a mediator between the two of you?" he responded. "You should be on your guard when it comes to greed. A man's life doesn't consist in the abundance of his possessions."

"Well, no," the younger brother acknowledged stiffly. "But there's no shame in being comfortable, is there?"

"Of course not," one of the officials piped up. "There is the question of deserving."

Jesus's gaze turned on the speaker. "Yes," he agreed mildly, "there is." His eyes held a playful twinkle, but I doubt the official caught it. Several of the disciples, however, hid sly smiles as Jesus launched into a parable.

It sounded like a new one, and I moved closer to listen myself. Jesus was a good storyteller. Remarkably good. His facial expressions and inflections were wholly animated; his sense of timing, perfect. He even used different voices for different characters. This one was about a farmer who reaped so much grain he didn't have enough room to store it, so he tore down his existing barns and built bigger ones. After he had put everything he had in the new barns, he realized he had stored up enough to last him for years, so he resolved to kick back, relax, and be merry.

"However," Jesus explained, rising and moving adroitly through the still-seated crowd as he talked, "the man didn't know something. What he didn't know was that that very night, *he would die.*"

There was a dramatic pause. Jesus reached the edge of the gathering and turned around. "So," he asked casually, "who do you think ended up with the goods?"

The officials looked at each other. They were bright enough to realize that the question was rhetorical. But they didn't seem to care for the message.

"Are you saying it's a crime to be wealthy?" the older of the bickering brothers asked, annoyed. "That the man *deserved* to lose everything?"

Jesus's gaze drifted toward the synagogue wall again. The townspeople had not given up their cries. If anything, they had become louder.

*Jesus, prophet! Please, help me!*

*My mother is ill! Please, come outside!*

*Let us see him! Let us see the man who raised Ahira!*

Jesus turned toward the brother. "The man who stored up things for himself might have been rich, but he wasn't rich toward God. You can't serve both God and money."

The officials grumbled. But none of them disagreed.

"Thanks for listening," Jesus said. "I'll come again soon."

The disciples sprang to their feet, surprised. They had expected Jesus to stay in the synagogue most of the morning. But he was already heading toward the gate.

Judas, who had been standing near the edge of the crowd, was first to reach him. "Rabbi," he asked nervously, looking back at the disgruntled clergymen. "Do you have to leave so soon?"

"Can't you hear them?" Jesus answered. "They need me."

Judas didn't ask whom he was talking about, or what he meant. He merely sighed, threw a conciliatory wave back to the officials, and stepped up to help Jesus open the gate.

The other disciples rushed to join them.

My heart began to race. The crowd outside sounded larger than ever. That Jesus would voluntarily dive back into such a mob amazed me, but the thought that I might be forced to as well was sheer horror. I looked around for Mary, but she was busy talking to some of the men. "Are we leaving now, too?" I asked Joanna, my tone frantic.

She shook her head. "No, we'll wait. It will take all the disciples' efforts just to protect Jesus. Mary's seeing if another of the men will stay with us and Samuel. Then as soon as the crowd calms, we'll get the supplies. In the meantime," she said wryly, "we'll hang with the privileged."

I watched as all the disciples except Matthew, our portly, forever jovial ex-tax-collector, filed through the gate. The five of us who were left returned to the stone steps of the synagogue and sat down. Mary and Joanna began to speak eagerly about the further fame Jesus was sure to accrue now, and what it would mean for all our futures, but I couldn't concentrate on the discussion. My attention was drawn to the courtyard's other occupants.

By their dress, I guessed that two groups were represented: the clergy and the well-to-do. By Mary's standards, probably no one in a village like Nain was upper-crust. But among the townspeople, these were the elite: the ones who had been let through the gates while the others were barred.

*We'll hang with the privileged.*

Outside, the crowd roared with excitement. Inside, the officials bickered. Jesus had impressed some and irked others; they didn't know what to make of him. What exactly was his point about wealth?

I felt a coldness in the pit of my stomach. These people thought of themselves as affluent. They had no idea, looking at me, that their entire synagogue could fit in half my house. That my dresser drawers held gold and jewels. That my bed could sleep five people. That clean, hot water ran from faucets in my private bath; that every room was climate-controlled. They could only imagine the splendor in which Herod himself lived, and I bet — precious metals excluded — that not even his living room could compare to mine. Yet among my own people, I was average. So average I wanted more.

I took in a deep breath. My limbs were still trembling. But it was all right; I was safe now. I was exactly where I needed to be, sheltered by the courtyard, away from the rabble. Communing with those of semi-equal ilk. Enjoying a privilege to which I was entitled.

I looked out at the high stone walls. I thought of Jesus on the other side, smiling at people, touching them, healing them. The gnawing in my middle deepened.

He was where he wanted to be.

So was I.

*Commentary for Chapter 9 begins on page 246.*

# Chapter 10

We were in the courtyard at the home of a Pharisee. Word of Jesus's raising the widow's son at Nain had spread like wildfire, and in every town we entered now, the local officials were champing at the bit to question him. Rumors about other things Jesus had done, both true and untrue, preceded us at every turn, and on our trips to the markets for supplies, we women made a point of picking up as much of this scuttlebutt as we could. It seemed that Jesus's willingness to rub elbows with sinners and outcasts was attracting more and more attention, of two different sorts. The common people thought it was fabulous. The clergy smelled scandal.

How many days and nights I had spent here I could no longer count, nor did I want to. Time had long since lost its meaning. Whole days could fly by with my having only the vaguest notion of their passing, while single minutes could seem interminable. Yet it was my past, and not my present, that had begun to feel surreal — to the point where I was forced to entertain a new and horrifying idea: that what I was experiencing now was all there was.

What if I had come to be lost in Capernaum because of an injury? An injury that had left me clueless of my real past, replacing it with some delusional fantasy of machines that could fly and children that were never born? Perhaps I only *thought* I possessed prior knowledge of the people I'd met here, when in reality it was all some twisted sense of déjà vu — a trick of brain chemicals and misfiring synapses?

The prospect made me sick inside, and I fought off the nagging thoughts with a vengeance. Whether the theory held some hint of logic or practicality didn't matter — I refused to accept that the family I loved had never existed. Not even when my thoughts turned darker still, and I began to doubt my own sanity.

My only recourse was not to think at all. To concentrate solely on the present. Second by excruciating second.

Right now, I was concentrating on dinner.

Our host for the evening was a Pharisee named Simon, a man of obvious high standing in the community whom I had disliked immediately. Many of the Pharisees were decent, kind men who were only trying to do their jobs — which, it seemed to my uneducated eye — consisted of regulating the people's daily lives to the point of lunacy. The Jews were expected to follow hundreds of commandments, prohibitions, and injunctions, many of which must be performed in Jerusalem, a trip which few had the resources to make on any kind of regular basis. I had no idea what these laws actually were, but once aware of their existence, I tried hard to mimic the other women's actions and think before I did anything that could be illegal — which was difficult, given that one could break the law by something as simple as using the wrong type of utensil on the wrong type of food.

Fortunately for me, Galileans in general and the common folk in particular tended to be lax on a great number of these rules, no matter how much the Pharisees fussed. The result was an us-versus-them mentality which left the legalists beating their heads against the walls and the populace viewing their clergy more as jailers than as shepherds. Jesus made no secret of his sympathies being with the little guy, and because of that the legalists couldn't help but see him as an irritant, no matter how much they wanted his power and influence in their corner.

This particular Pharisee, Simon, was one of the most pompous I had yet encountered, and pompousness was a trait I had zero tolerance for. He spoke with his chin up and his chest out, no matter to whom he was speaking, and with his servants he was caustic. The disciples didn't like him either, and would have preferred for Jesus to reject his invitation. But Jesus wasn't one to reject an invitation anywhere.

As usual, the women were not invited to the dinner itself. None of the houses had enough room inside for everyone, so the women typically ate in the courtyard, along with whatever male tagalongs could also not fit into the upper rooms. Sometimes the host's wife would bring food out to us; but because of our numbers we generally brought provisions and cooked for ourselves. Tonight, we were eating well. On impulse, I had splurged and bought chicken meat.

The gesture was entirely selfish. I made an irritable vegetarian, and if I was forced to eat one more dinner of the salty dried fish Mary was so fond of purchasing, I would scream.

"Oh, my," twittered Naomi nervously, as was her custom. "Look there!"

We turned our heads in the direction she pointed to see a small woman slipping furtively through Simon's front gates, right under the nose of the two menservants who argued with each other just outside it. The woman's long black hair flowed freely down her back, except for two braids in front that were looped upon her head like a crown and tied with red ribbon. Her face was painted. Her tunic was cut wide and low, exposing one bare shoulder, and she wore no cloak. She clutched a small jar to her breast with both hands.

The women watched in silent surprise as she proceeded boldly to the stone staircase leading up to Simon's dining room. Without a backward glance, she slipped up the steps and moved through the upstairs house door.

Joanna chuckled. "A prostitute in a Pharisee's house. Now that's rich. What will happen, do you suppose?"

"The question is," Mary posed thoughtfully, her expression devilish, "whom did she come to see? Jesus... or Simon?"

"Well," Leah broke in, her cheeks flaring red, "All I have to say is, John had better not see *her.*"

"Leah!" Tamar protested lightly. She was holding the sleeping Jesse, as she often did. "Don't say such things. You know better."

I hid a smile. Leah was a sweetheart most of the time, but there was a fire in her that no amount of societal subjugation could douse. John pretended that such spirit in a woman vexed him, but he was obviously attracted by it. Leah's brown eyes scanned the circle of women as if evaluating something; I was surprised when her gaze stopped on me. "Rachel," she said, her voice full of mischief, "Come with me. Let's go see."

Mary chuckled. "Yes, Rachel. Why don't you? We'll expect a full report."

"We can climb the staircase and look through the windows," Leah cajoled. "No one will see us. Come on!"

It was a foolish lark, and I knew it. But with a stomach full of chicken meat, I was feeling unusually feisty. Furthermore, I was curious. The "morally depraved" frequently came to hear Jesus speak, but they were rarely so bold as to approach him. For a prostitute to follow him into a private home was beyond the pale. Such women were considered unclean, and no self-respecting Jewish man — much less a prominent Pharisee — was allowed anything to do with one.

This could be good.

Leah took me by the hand and led me up the same staircase the prostitute had climbed. But after looking through the window, she turned around. "They're on the other side," she whispered. We walked around to another staircase out of view of the rest of the women, but the windows on that wall were too high to see in from the steps. This did not stop Leah. She put one foot on a protruding wooden rafter, hoisted herself up, grabbed onto a window ledge, and peeked through. After a second's hesitation, I climbed up on the next rafter over.

"How did you get in here?!"

Simon's angry voice startled me so much I nearly lost my footing, but I soon realized he wasn't yelling at me. He had discovered the prostitute.

The Pharisee's dining room was the finest I had seen, relatively large and decorated with wall-hangings and ornate metal trinkets. The men — a dozen of Jesus's disciples along with several other Pharisees — were packed into the room, reclining on fine cushions with their heads clustered around a well-spread table just off the floor. The prostitute had sneaked in behind Simon's back and was standing unobtrusively against the wall, but once her presence was noted all the Pharisees rose up in outrage.

"How dare you come into my house! Out with you!" Simon thundered, raising his arm in a threatening gesture.

The woman, who looked as though she were in her late twenties or early thirties, looked terrified, but she nevertheless stuck her chin out defiantly. "I only want to see Jesus!" she cried. She was a pretty woman, or at least she had been once. Her cheekbones were high and her eyes expressive, but her skin bore the ravages of too much sun and too little food, and her brow was etched with the scars of a lifetime of peril and ill treatment.

"Get her out of here!" Simon raged at a manservant, who cringed as he passed his master to move toward her. "When I find out who—"

"Simon," Jesus said quietly, his calm tone deflating the Pharisee in mid-rant. "It's all right." He put down the bread he was holding and sat up. He looked the woman in the eyes.

Her face brightened. The tight set of her shoulders relaxed.

I knew what she was feeling. She was sensing the same thing I had upon my own first meeting with him — that his eyes could see right through her, perceiving her every flaw. Yet he would appear to pass no judgment. In his gaze she would see an acceptance that was unconditional, an affection that was genuine.

It would shock her. Much more so than it had me. The woman had doubtless been scorned, abused, and mistreated for most of her life. She was probably not used to any sort of kindness, particularly from church officials, who could be as cruel as — or ever crueler than — anyone. Yet here was a rabbi, and perhaps even a prophet, who knew full well that she slept with men for money and yet didn't hate her for it. He even seemed to see the good in her.

It must hardly seem possible.

Her eyes glistened with tears. "It's true," she murmured. "What they say about you. That you love the sinners."

Simon let out a groan. "Oh, please! Rabbi, you can't—"

Jesus put up a hand to still him. "What is it you want from me?" he asked the woman.

Tears spilled onto her cheeks, and she choked up, sputtering. "Nothing, Rabbi. I don't want anything from you. I just wanted—"

She lurched toward him then, falling at his feet in a crying heap. As soon as it looked as though she would actually try and touch him, several of the disciples made moves to intervene. But they weren't concerned with his safety so much as with propriety, and it took only a subtle gesture on Jesus's part to dissuade them. When the woman realized that no one was stopping her, she cried all the harder, her tears falling freely over his bare, dusty feet.

I heard Leah breathe in sharply.

Simon's eyes nearly bugged from his head. He let out a groan of disgust, then turned to the Pharisee next to him, his snide voice loud enough for everyone to hear, "And they say this man is a *prophet?* I daresay a prophet would know what kind of woman was touching him!"

Leah squelched a shriek as she lost her footing on the beam and slipped down to the steps below. I jumped off to help her, but not only was she fine, she was desperate to get back up to her place again. After concluding that no one had heard her fall, I climbed back up to my own spot.

The prostitute had opened the bottle she carried, and was now dousing Jesus's feet with what appeared to be perfume. It smelled strongly, even through the window, and I could only guess at the cost of the gesture. Mary and Joanna each carried perfume, but they used only drops at a time on themselves. This woman had poured out her whole jar.

The Pharisees grumbled. Even the disciples shifted uncomfortably on their cushions. That Jesus seemed to be enjoying the spectacle only added to its impropriety. But no one had the nerve to intervene.

"Simon," Jesus said calmly, after the woman had ceased the worst of her sobbing and had begun to dry his feet with her hair, "when I came into your house you didn't give me any water to clean my feet, but she wet them with her tears. You didn't give me any oil for my head, either, but she poured out all her perfume. And—"

He paused. The woman had started crying again, and now she was actually kissing his feet. The disciples turned their heads in embarrassment. The Pharisees stared in horror. "Nor did you offer me a kiss," Jesus continued with a grin. "But she has."

He put a hand to her chin, raising it gently to stop her. "You're right," he announced, presumably to Simon, though he was still looking at the prostitute. "This woman has sinned. She's sinned quite a lot, actually. But she also loves. She loves much and she loves deeply. So her sins are forgiven."

"But *you* can't say—" one of the other Pharisees began, flustered.

"Rabbi!" Simon protested, interrupting. "You can't mean that. The best among us don't sin in the first place. Why should she—"

"He who hasn't been forgiven of much, doesn't love much," Jesus said offhandedly, standing and pulling the woman to her feet.

He then let go of her, stepped back, and smiled. "Your faith has saved you. Go in peace."

"Oh, for the love of—" Simon never finished the thought. Or if he did, I didn't hear it. Leah was tugging on my sleeve.

"We have to get back around to the fire," she whispered. "They may follow her out!"

The Pharisees' not-so-subtle grumbling wafted out the window as I reluctantly stepped down off my perch and followed Leah. We were not quick enough, and nearly collided with the prostitute as she flew down the other staircase and out the gate into the street. But because none of the men had followed her, Leah and I were able to return to our places unnoticed.

"*Well?*" Joanna questioned, her eyes bright with excitement. "What happened? Did they throw her out?"

"Not hardly," Leah said breathlessly, her voice hard. The tone of it surprised me, and I turned to study her face. She was livid. "You would not *believe* what that woman did! What Jesus let her do!"

The women listened with bated breath as Leah recounted the story, and from a perspective wholly different from my own. "And *then,*" she finished, her youthful skin glowing with perspiration, "she kissed his feet!"

One could count the gasps. The only woman who didn't gasp was Mary, whose cool-as-a-cat demeanor forbade her gasping at anything.

"She *kissed* him?" Tamar demanded, incredulous.

"Right there in front of everybody!" Leah answered.

"What did Jesus do?" Bernice asked.

"Nothing!" Leah insisted. "He was smiling at her!"

"Oh, dear," Joanna said tragically, as her eyes danced. "What did the disciples say?"

"What could they say?" Bernice cut in, her voice irritable. "Jesus does whatever he wants."

"Well," Leah fumed, "if John ever let some prostitute kiss his feet like that, I'd—" She broke off.

"You'd do what?" Mary prompted.

"I'd pull her hair out!" Leah finished, her small fists clenched.

"But why would a prostitute act like that?" Tamar asked, confused. "Why was she crying in the first place?"

"Because she's mentally defective," Bernice answered curtly. "There's no other excuse for it. She should have known she would make him unclean."

I should have kept my mouth shut. I knew that. My sole goal was to fit in, not to seem different, not to make waves. I was safest acting like a bump on a log, helping quietly, providing the occasional coin as needed. But these women were ticking me off.

Especially Bernice. Bernice thought she knew everything, when she actually knew nothing, because she never listened to what anybody else had to say. She had her opinion, and it was fact.

I knew women like Bernice. There were sixteen of her in the PTA.

Tonight, she was going down.

"And why do you suppose she *became* a prostitute?" I asked. "Do you think she woke up one morning and said, 'I could get married to a nice man who'll take care of me. But what the heck, I think I'll become a prostitute instead?'"

Most of the women blinked at me dumbly. I thought I caught Mary with a grin. "If she was forced into prostitution because she had no protection and no other way to survive, how can we blame her? Would it have been better if she starved to death?"

Bernice's eyes narrowed. "People make their own beds, one way or the other."

"People are born into a variety of circumstances," I fired back. "Some manage better than others. The point is, Jesus didn't automatically dismiss this woman as worthless just because she was a prostitute."

I looked at Tamar. "She was crying because Jesus, unlike every other man she's probably ever known, treated her with respect. It overwhelmed her. She couldn't believe it. She was so touched she wanted to do something for him, anything to show him how much she appreciated his looking at her as a worthwhile person."

Tamar's eyes moistened. She got it. I could tell.

Bernice was another matter.

"Be that as it may," she said curtly, "It was hypocritical of him to allow her such latitude, when she hadn't earned the right by her actions. We're the women who support him most. If anyone's allowed to kiss the rabbi's feet, it should be one of us."

My cheeks flared with heat. I knew I should shut up. Making an enemy of Bernice could make my future journeying much, much less pleasant. But I was on a roll.

"What would be hypocritical," I snapped, "would be for him to go around telling thousands of people that he who is least will be greatest, and then snub the very people who need him the most."

Bernice stared. She didn't answer.

*Swish.*

For a long moment, no one said anything.

"Rachel's right," Joanna announced finally. "One reason everyone loves Jesus is that he treats people the same, whether they're lepers or priests." She chuckled to herself. "Well actually, he treats the lepers a bit better, doesn't he? What happened doesn't really matter; he isn't married. It obviously meant a lot to the woman, and there's no one to be made jealous by it."

"I suppose," Leah agreed. Her voice still held a note of irritation, but I suspected she wasn't annoyed with Jesus so much as at the continued thought of another woman kissing John's feet.

Naomi, always the peacemaker, began speaking of some particular fruit she had seen in the market, and the conversation drifted mercifully away. Bernice busied herself with wiping down the utensils. My face still felt hot.

Mary stealthily crept around the fire until she stood at my elbow. I was surprised that she had not said a word during my rant, even though I was fairly certain she agreed with me. "Just out of curiosity, Rachel," she whispered, her dark eyes sparkling. "What would you do if a husband of *yours* let a prostitute kiss his feet?"

I didn't even think about my cover story. Instead my imagination flashed a picture of Joe, ensconced in a deluxe hotel room in Chicago, some scantily clad hussy slobbering over his insteps.

My fists clenched.

"I'd pull *his* hair out," I muttered.

*Commentary for Chapter 10 begins on page 248.*

# Chapter 11

The surface of the Sea of Galilee was choppy, but the sky was clear and the sun beat down with its usual brutal intensity. Mary, Naomi, and I climbed into a boat with Bartholomew, settled our supplies on its floor, and took our places on its weathered wooden benches. Tamar was with us, too, but she was traveling on her husband's boat. The rest of the women had stayed in Magdala.

*Beautiful, wonderful Magdala.*

A thriving harbor town of boat-building and fish pickling, Mary's hometown was like a resort compared to all the squalid little villages — like Nain — that Jesus went out of his way to visit. Such prosperity had brought the port of Magdala a hard-core reputation for debauchery, which it doubtless deserved. But I loved the place, because Mary's house was there.

At Mary's house, we benefactors lived like queens. We slept on soft mattresses, ate fresh unsalted fish, and — most incredible of all — were able to take baths. Slipping into the tepid and none-too-sparkling water in Mary's tub last night had been absolute heaven. I had almost forgotten what it felt like to be clean.

But I wouldn't stay clean for long, because Jesus wanted to keep moving. He preached in Magdala as he did everywhere else, but though word of Mary's transformation and other miracles drew many people to see him out of sheer inquisitiveness, his presence did not draw the same doting, enthusiastic crowds it drew elsewhere. Fortunately, Mary's offer to lend a slew of boats, which the disciples could use to transport our group for short trips to other lakeshore communities, was accepted, ensuring Magdala as our base of operations for at least a week or so.

Today we were traveling southeast to the region of Gadarenes, which was fine by me. As long as I knew that I would lay my head in Magdala again shortly, I was more than willing to tag along and help the men out with their meals. I had gotten better at the task, though I suspected — as evidenced by the telling lift of Mary's left eyebrow — that I did occasionally break some unknown rule or other. She never said a word to me about it, however; and neither did anyone else.

It felt good to be sailing, away from crowds and out on the open water, and my spirits were relatively high. My internal angst would never cease completely, but as with most types of constant stress, my mind had eventually begun to numb to it, and I was better able to go long stretches without dwelling on what I had lost.

Today was a good example. The wind was whipping my freshly cleaned hair, my clothes had been laundered, and I had not spent the previous night sleeping on rocks. The view from the boat was sweeping and majestic. Temporarily, at least, I was content.

I didn't notice the clouds. Not until Bartholomew grew silent.

Naomi's husband was a chatty fellow. An intellectual ahead of his time, he was by far the most liberal of the disciples in terms of his attitude about women. He seemed genuinely interested in the female perspective, and would frequently engage Mary and me in discussions of a sociopolitical nature, even as the other disciples — who viewed such discourse with women as both inappropriate and a waste of time — shook their heads at him, perplexed. Everyone respected Mary, but as for why Bartholomew sought me out, I flattered myself that he appreciated my intelligence and quick wit. There were certainly never any rousing debates or clever banter between him and his skittish wife.

Today he was once again dissing the Essenes, a sect whose grim asceticism was anathema to his own open-minded, merry-making soul. Jesus had the right idea, Bartholomew insisted; the rabbi knew how to enjoy life. There was nothing wrong with eating, drinking, and basking in the simple pleasures. God never intended for people to be miserable. The Essenes were radicals. They were nuts.

Bartholomew stopped ranting suddenly, his eyes fixed southward. Unnerved, I followed his gaze.

A cluster of dark gray clouds had appeared from nowhere, rolling up onto the horizon with visible speed. I tensed as I watched his brow crease. Bartholomew was an experienced fisherman, as were all the disciples piloting our boats. I had the utmost confidence in his instincts, but at this point, that was more disturbing than soothing. He exchanged a hard look with James, who was sailing the boat nearest us, and both adjusted their sails. I got the feeling they were heading for the closest shore. I got the feeling they were worried.

The wind bucked our boat with a sudden, rude gust. The clouds continued to roll toward us. The sun disappeared.

All of our boats were speeding toward the nearest stretch of land. But even I could see we would never make it. Sheets of gray rain were visible to the south now, pummeling the water, churning its surface to a misty haze. The waves at the storm's edge grew. First, swells. Then whitecaps.

The women didn't speak. There was nothing anyone could say. We hunkered lower in the center of the boat, pulling our cloaks tightly around us, waiting. I could see Tamar in the next boat huddling near her husband's feet and was grateful Leah and the baby had stayed behind. It would be terrifying to have an infant out in such a storm. What if they both went overboard?

The wind picked up still further, and my heart pounded. Could any of the women swim? I feared I knew the answer. There were no swimming pools in Galilee, nor even swimming holes. Streams and creeks were dry most of the time; the Jordan river was shallow enough to wade through. The fishermen would have learned to swim as part of their trade, and perhaps children living around the shore might master the art. But women who had grown up in the cities, bathed in three layers of linen reaching to their toes?

The waves hit first. Then the rain. The boat rocked violently, its center quickly sopped with lake water. Mary had a bucket in hand, and as more water sloshed in, she tried to bail. But she could not keep her balance well enough to be effective; it was difficult enough just staying in the boat.

The pelting rain was everywhere. Opening my eyes was painful, but even when I did, there was nothing to see. I could make out only the dimmest outline of the boat next to us and nothing of the others. Bartholomew stood bravely at the sail, shifting his weight to meet the impossible thrusts of the waves, yelling indecipherable words to the other sailors.

The left side of the boat tipped skyward. Naomi screamed. With instinct, because I had no cogent thoughts, Mary and I both shifted our weight at the same time, lunging to the left and banging our shoulders against the heaving floor. Bartholomew did likewise, and with a thump the boat righted. But I had no illusions of safety. The storm was all around us. The sky was dark. We might or might not be anywhere near the shore.

Maybe this was it. Maybe this was where I died.

My eyes stayed closed. Bartholomew and James continued trying to shout to each other over the roar of the storm. Mary had stopped trying to bail and sat still. Naomi whimpered like an animal. Then she shrieked again.

I opened my eyes just in time to see James's boat lurch. Tamar's small form pitched violently sideways, and my heart leapt into my throat. Surely the girl couldn't swim. What would happen if she went overboard? How could James leave his post at the sail without sacrificing the other passengers?

I was a good swimmer. Somewhere in my attic I still had the blue ribbon: first place in the breaststroke, regionals, ages eight to ten. But I had never had official lifeguard training. Too boring, too much time in the sun. If Tamar did go overboard, did I have any chance of being able to save her myself? Or would I just as likely drown us both?

I watched in horror, my every muscle taut. There was no doubt in my mind that if Tamar fell into the water, I would go in after her. Call it stupidity. Call it mother instinct. Call it whatever you want, but the fact was that I could swim and that Tamar could be Bekka.

Tamar recovered from the tumble on her own and settled back into the center of the boat with the men. I let out a breath of relief. James and Bartholomew continued to yell, and all at once I realized what they were yelling.

*Jesus.* They were begging the rabbi for help.

A grim feeling of dread pierced through me. I had seen this Jesus heal people, yes. But I had also seen innumerable faith healers, illusionists, and psychics demonstrate just how much control the mind has over the body. I was still not certain what had happened to the boy in Nain. But I did believe in the laws of physics, and I believed in the forces of nature — a nature that was no different here than in my own backyard. Insects bit. Rain fell. Corpses rotted. This place might be foreign to me, but it was no never-never land where the sky turned purple and rivers ran uphill. It was ordinary. It was natural.

It could be deadly.

The disciples' continued pleas swamped me with sudden pity for the man they were calling. What they were asking wasn't reasonable, and it wasn't fair. If this Jesus really could command the weather, wouldn't he have done so already? Wouldn't he have done something on that miserable night early on when it rained unexpectedly, soaking the sleeping mats and putting out all our campfires? Or on the day on the road when we ran low on water and it was so hot that Joanna nearly fainted? I was sure that Jesus would *want* to do something. I didn't doubt for one second that he would dive into these wretched swells himself to save any one of us. But to have his friends beg him for the impossible? It must be like a dagger through his heart.

*Dive in himself.*

My blood chilled. Jesus had grown up in Nazareth, in the hills. He probably couldn't swim either.

I rose up in the boat, stretching my neck to see.

Despite all the time I had spent in the rabbi's company, I had not spoken directly to him since our first meeting at Jackal's Rock. Nor had he spoken specifically to me. He was always surrounded by other people, and I didn't mind that. I had been content with the occasional smile, the deliberate meeting of the eyes that seemed to say, "Thank you for helping, Rachel. I haven't forgotten you." Yet for all the seeming miracles of healing I had watched him perform, I still had not perceived a single hint of omniscience, no evidence he had a clue as to my true situation, much less was able to help me with it.

This Jesus was a truly kind and wonderful man. I was not convinced he was anything more, whether the past I remembered was real or not. But I didn't care about that now. I didn't care how history had embellished his biography, or even if history had ever recorded it to begin with. What bothered me was that he couldn't swim.

I scanned the surface of the water. I could make out several boats now, despite the rain. Peter's large form was obvious at the helm of one, and behind him, I was reasonably certain, stood Jesus. *Stood* Jesus. I raised myself up further in the boat. I could barely keep my balance, yet Jesus was standing. Was Peter insane letting him do that, when one good swell could knock him overboard?

I put a hand on the side of the boat, clenching it tightly. If Jesus did go over, I would get him back on that wretched boat myself, or die trying. What other purpose did I have here, anyway?

"Rachel!" Mary squawked through the wind. "Get back down!"

I continued watching Jesus. He wasn't doing anything except standing calmly, moving with the rocking of the vessel. I could see all the other boats now, and though all were still rocking, none threatened to tip.

The storm was passing. The sky to the south showed a band of brightness. The clouds above us were moving quickly, drifting to the north as hurriedly as they had come. Both the rain and wind were slowing everywhere. The storm was spent.

Bartholomew let out a whoop, and within seconds all the disciples were cheering. All the boats had stayed afloat. Not one, and no one, had been lost.

Tamar reached up and clung to her husband's waist, her face pale with fright. Mary sat up and started bailing again. Bartholomew bent down to the still-huddled Naomi, assuring her that everything was all right. She latched onto him like a magnet and held him, her face pressed tightly against his knees.

The rain stopped. The disciples cheered anew as hot rays of sun peeked out from behind the fleeing clouds. The boats' sails were set back toward the southeast. We resumed our travel toward the Gadarenes.

Everyone was relieved. And joyful. Everyone, that is, except two of us. I was shaky, and I was annoyed with myself. Not because I hadn't believed Jesus could help. But because I still wasn't sure whether he had.

As for Jesus, he simply looked sad.


You would think that such an experience would make our group a wee bit hesitant about further lake travel. But no. Only I seemed to give it a second thought. Even Naomi hopped willingly into the boat when we left the Gadarenes, though this time she settled even closer to her husband. Tamar appeared to have the utmost confidence in James, and Mary was always unflappable.

Once again I bit my tongue and went with the flow, hoping we would at least head straight back to Magdala. When it became apparent we were heading to a shore near Capernaum instead, I wanted to scream. I had nothing against Capernaum itself, and truly enjoyed Salome's company. But Jesus could get no peace there. So many people knew our group by sight now that he could move nowhere near the city without attracting a mob.

No sooner had our boats pulled close to shore than people traveling on the road along it began to point at him and cry out, and within minutes a swarm of needy, cloth-wrapped people were storming the seaside, ready to engulf us.

I sighed.

*Moment by moment, Rachel. Don't look ahead.*

No one seemed to have any idea why Jesus wanted to come here. He routinely made spur-of-the-moment decisions and changes to plan, a trait which drove several of the disciples, most notably Judas and Thomas, to distraction. They wanted to schedule him, to route his travels efficiently and make better plans for food and supplies. But Jesus would not be scheduled. And I would not be getting another bath tonight.

To my relief, however, we did not disembark. Instead Peter anchored Jesus's boat a little ways offshore, and the other fisherman followed his lead. The people who gathered at the water's edge asked Jesus to speak, and he obliged, his voice carrying easily over the gentle lap of the waves. The audience was peaceable, and for a while I began to hope that we might leave here soon enough to get back to Magdala by dinnertime.

We did not. A well-dressed man, whom Tamar recognized as a synagogue ruler named Jairus, approached the boats with his chest heaving. He had heard of Jesus's unexpected arrival, he explained, and had run the entire way from his house in town. The man was flushed with exertion, his eyes red and puffy from crying. One look into his desperate, earnest face, and I found my heart going out to him, hoping that Jesus would help him whether I got a bath or not.

Jesus asked Peter to bring in his boat, then stepped out to meet the man. I could not hear their conversation, but when it became clear that the man's request required going on into the city, I steeled myself wearily. I could deal with another mob. Really, I could. How much worse did it have to be for Jesus, with people constantly shoving their grubby hands at him, begging for the slightest touch?

The disciples secured the boats onshore and dispatched several men to watch them. The rest of us headed toward town.

The mobbing began. We all took our usual positions, with Simon and Thaddeus leading, Jesus's core of disciples protecting him, and the women behind. But today we had neither Samuel nor Gideon to bring up the rear. Gideon had stayed with Joanna, and Mary had given Samuel some time off in Magdala, which was his hometown, too. We hadn't missed them until now.

When three of the disciples peeled off from the others and came to walk behind us, I breathed a sigh of relief. One, of course, was Judas. Though I still couldn't get the man to speak to me, he was always aware of the women's presence and was eminently considerate. With him came James — not Tamar's James, but Matthew's younger brother — and Peter's oldest son, a youth of fourteen. Like his father, Aaron was strongly built and big for his age. Unlike Peter, however, he was shy and unassuming.

The crowd was hideous, and Jesus was jostled unmercifully. When he stopped, suddenly, and began looking around him in confusion, the crowd pressed in all the more, and several of the disciples grew irritated. "We really need to keep moving," Andrew suggested tactfully, holding off several exuberant youths with his broad back.

"Someone touched my cloak," Jesus answered.

"A hundred people have touched your cloak!" Peter responded, wincing as an older man in rags inadvertently poked an elbow in his ribs.

Jesus lifted his gaze over the crowd. "Who touched me?" he asked. "I felt it. Who was it?"

Peter and his brother exchanged a look of exasperation. But when the people in the crowd realized Jesus was talking, they quieted. He repeated the question.

After a moment's silence, I heard a squeak to my left. "It was me."

I looked over to see a woman of about my own age, emaciated and pale, stagger forward. The disciples parted and let her through to Jesus, and when she reached him, she fell at his feet, trembling. She looked terrified.

"I've been bleeding for years," she explained, her voice quavering. "No one has been able to cure me. I only wanted to touch your clothing. I knew it would make me well."

A hand clutched my arm. It was Tamar. She was watching the exchange with rapt fascination, her dark eyes wide. I don't believe she even realized she had grabbed me.

Jesus asked the woman if she was cured, and with a smile she answered that she was. He told her that her faith that healed her — a comment he made frequently — and told her to go in peace. She sprang up without another word and disappeared into the crowd, and Jesus resumed walking. Tamar released my arm and scuttled forward.

"Bleeding for years," Mary muttered in my ear. "It's a wonder she wasn't dead already. She had plenty of color in her cheeks when she left, though, didn't she?"

I mumbled an answer, but my eyes were on Tamar as she moved stealthily forward through the men. Such boldness was unusual for her. I had noticed that, whenever possible, she kept herself at a distance even greater than necessary from any man other than James. Now she was practically elbowing John and Philip out of her way.

Neither took much notice of her. They were too busy holding off people they didn't know. Eventually Tamar positioned herself close to Jesus, and in the chaos of a sea of reaching hands, she extended her own. After two near misses she managed to swipe the end of his sleeve with her fingertips, and upon doing so, immediately dropped back out of the fray.

I looked around me. No one else had noticed. Mary's eyes were watching the crowd. Jesus kept moving.

Tamar faced away from me, and at first I could not read her expression. But as her pace slowed, she gradually fell back into step with Mary and me.

Her shoulders were slumped. Moistness rimmed her eyes.

"Tamar," I said, as softly as I could in the roar of the crowd. "Are you all right?"

She jumped at my voice, her eyes wide. "Of course," she answered, making a valiant — but ineffective — attempt to smile. "Why wouldn't I be?"

I made a quick decision not to press her. At least not here, and not now. Whatever was wrong with her, she obviously didn't want anyone to know about it.

The mob's onslaught continued unabated until at last, after what seemed an hour, we reached the house of Jairus. We followed the ruler through the gates to his courtyard only to find another crowd gathered inside. A chill swept down my spine as I heard the now-familiar wailing, accompanied by the haunting tones of wooden flutes. I knew what the sounds meant. Either someone was dying, or they were already dead.

A tall man approached from the house's doorway, his own eyes reddened and puffy. "I'm sorry," he said sincerely, laying a hand on Jairus's shoulder. "But your daughter is dead. We needn't trouble the rabbi any further."

Jairus turned toward Jesus with a frantic look, but Jesus was already in motion, heading for the house. "You don't need to do that," he insisted to the mourners at the door as he passed. "She isn't dead. Only asleep."

Jairus jumped to follow Jesus into the house, along with Peter, James, and John. The rest of us remained outside.

The sounds of mourning changed to those of confused chatter. Some of the people even snickered behind their hands. Jesus's claim was preposterous, they muttered. Even insulting to the girl's relatives. What idiot couldn't tell death from sleep?

I used to think that I could. After Nain, I wasn't so sure. I still had not settled in my own mind exactly what had happened there, particularly not when we had seen death so many times since. In the large cities, there were funerals almost every day. Why had Jesus not resurrected those people? What had made the boy in Nain so different, so special?

I had yet to get used to death. In my experience life's end was neatly and sanitarily tucked away from sight, then prettied up for public viewing. Here, it was visible. It was ubiquitous. It was unavoidable.

Just days ago, on our way into Magdala, we had encountered a human body lying just off the caravan trail, tossed in a heap like so much roadkill. It was a woman, and not a decently clothed one. She had obviously been dead for days, and though I was hardly an expert on such matters and couldn't look at her too closely without feeling nauseous, it appeared her death had been a violent one. The disciples had reacted to the sight the same as I did. After the briefest of glances, they walked hurriedly past.

But when Jesus saw her, he stopped. I don't believe that anyone expected him to revive a corpse in such an advanced state of decomposition. But what he did do was almost as disconcerting. He announced that we should bury it.

The disciples had been mortified, insisting that the woman's body was unclean, and that having anything to do with it was unlawful. Jesus hadn't argued with them. He had just fetched a shovel off one of the pack donkeys and started to dig.

He did things like that. I realized now that I had grown up envisioning the Bible's Jesus as a bit of a pansy, walking around with a cloud of sycophants seeing to his every whim. Not this Jesus. He was strong, he was handy with tools, and he was used to hard work. He pitched in around camp as much as anyone; to the disciples' utter horror, he even took his turn digging the latrines. They used to argue with him about the propriety of a rabbi performing such menial labor, as did Mary herself — and vehemently, believe me — but they had all long since given up. Jesus could not be talked out of doing anything he thought was right.

We all knew he would not be talked out of this, either. If someone offered help, he would accept it, but lack of assistance wouldn't deter him. If he had to bury the wretched woman's body all by himself, he would. No matter how long it took.

Peter had cursed fluently, then fetched the other shovel. The rest of the men had grabbed rocks and began to dig with those. I thought of making a cross for the grave, and even went so far as to collect two sticks before realizing the depth of my stupidity.

We women had gathered wildflowers instead.

After much sweat, exertion, and aggravation on the part of the men, the body had been buried, and we had all marched on. No one had spoken a word of it since. I had a feeling no one would.

Asking why some deaths were reversible and others not seemed a loaded question.

Now, as we waited to see what would become of Jairus's daughter, I watched Tamar carefully. Her mood was deteriorating. She had moved away from Mary and me to rest her back against the courtyard wall. Her expression was dreary, her eyes far away.

I could stand it no longer. I told Mary how I had seen Tamar touch Jesus's sleeve, and how she had seemed disappointed after. Mary listened. She did not appear surprised.

"Tamar fears she is barren," Mary explained in a hushed tone, as if airing a sensitive secret. "She and James have been married for over three years now, and she hasn't gotten pregnant. She wouldn't be brazen enough to ask for help with such a problem, but seeing that other woman be cured by just a touch must have given her hope."

Mary studied Tamar over my shoulder, her eyes heavy with empathy. "It's no small matter for her. Not when she could be divorced."

I blinked. Surely I had misheard. "Divorced? But they haven't been married all that long yet, and it's obvious James adores her. Surely she isn't really worried."

Mary's eyes remained on Tamar. "Look at her, Rachel."

I did. The teen was fighting tears.

"But James is a good man," I protested, determined that Tamar was overreacting. "And he *loves* her."

Mary's gaze swept back to me. Her expression hardened. "Good men do what's expected of them," she said dryly. "And that kind of love can be more trouble than it's worth."

I didn't get the chance to reply. The front door of Jairus' house swung open. Its owner stood on the threshold, beaming, his hands lying protectively on the shoulders of a young girl. She looked out at the crowd with wide, nervous eyes. She smiled a shy smile.

The courtyard erupted in cheers.

My chest tightened. So, another person had escaped death. One more had been inexplicably chosen. Unaccountably spared.

Two women had been healed today. But not three.

I looked back at Tamar.

Her tears fell.

*Commentary for Chapter 11 begins on page 251.*

# Chapter 12

I could not stop thinking about Tamar. As much as these women's placid acceptance of gender discrimination still irked me, I had come to believe that at heart, our similarities outweighed our differences. I had even come to believe that I could drag someone like Mary back to the suburbs with me, and that after a brief adjustment period we could be drinking fuzzy navels on my deck, complaining about the price of gas or dishonest contractors.

Now I wasn't so sure. The idea that a young woman like Tamar could be tossed aside for some "failure" she had no control over and that no one, not even her female friends, would think less of her husband for it, set my blood to boiling. Divorcees didn't just suffer dishonor here. They could be left homeless. They could starve.

Sexism was one thing; even I could deal with a little second-class treatment when I had to. Hadn't some people or other been doing so in every culture since time immemorial? But for a man to abandon a loving, loyal wife because of barrenness was heartless and cruel in any millennium, and I didn't want to believe James capable of it, no matter what Mary said.

So I stewed.

I stewed when we returned the boats to Magdala and set out on foot again, and I stewed even more when I realized we were heading back into the hills. After a brutal day of travel we stopped outside a medium-sized village in an olive grove near a spring, an unusually pleasant resting spot frequented by shepherds and other caravaners. The grove itself was shady and green, the hills nearby were dotted with sheep, and the lilting melodies the shepherd boys played on their flutes drifted to us on the breeze. Even those of our group who most disliked "roughing it" were content to set up camp here rather than look for lodging in the village. The ambience should have improved my mood.

It did not.

Jesus and most of the men headed straight for the town synagogue as usual, while a few men and most of the women stayed behind to set up camp. I typically stuck with Mary, who went wherever Jesus went. But after seeing that Tamar was going with James, I decided to stay back. I wanted to talk to Leah alone.

I joined the teen mother as she rested with her back against an olive tree, nursing the contented and rapidly growing baby Jesse. She was munching on a handful of tiny, dried salted fish as she did so. I tried to ignore that.

We chit-chatted a while about babies and breast feeding, which was a challenge, given my tendency to veer off into debate over orthodontic pacifiers, collapsible bottles, and electronic pumps. But I managed to stick to the basics, eventually working the conversation over to Tamar, and how unhappy she seemed recently.

Leah nodded, then sighed. "She tries to keep her spirits up. But every month that passes with no sign of a baby, she gets more afraid. I only wish there was something I could do for her. It's tragic, really. No one would make a better mother."

I chose my words carefully. "But she's happy in her marriage. I mean, she seems happy. With James."

Leah's brown eyes looked at me with an expression I had come to know all too well. It was the how-can-you-seem-so-intelligent-and-still-be-so-clueless look. "Are you kidding?" she responded. "She's madly in love with the man, and he adores her. He's adored her since she was twelve. When his first wife died—"

My eyebrows lifted. "He was married before?"

"Well, he was betrothed," Leah corrected, "but there never was any wedding. She died a few weeks before it was to happen. James could have gotten betrothed again right after, but he didn't. By then he had noticed Tamar, and he was determined to wait for her."

Leah's eyes turned wistful, her tone half-dreamy. "They got married about five minutes after she turned sixteen. She worried the whole time that he would choose someone else, and she begged her father to let her marry early, but he wouldn't. One of Tamar's sisters had already died in childbirth, and the way Tamar looks, her father knew there would be no shortage of men interested in her when the time came. James was willing to wait. He waited four years, much to his own father's annoyance. But she was worth it to him."

The way Leah was speaking, almost as if describing the plot of a romance novel, made her — for once — seem like the ordinary teenage girl she might have been. I let myself mull the image: she and my Bekka hanging out, listening to music, meeting friends at the mall. They would squeal and laugh and talk about boys, clothes, music, and boys again. Marriage and babies would come up about as often as theoretical physics.

*Hmm.*

I hated to admit it, but as horrified as I was at the thought of Bekka being a teenage mother, I rather liked Leah the way she was. Why, I preferred not to contemplate.

I could never in a million years condone arranged marriage. But I was beginning to understand it better. My previous images of resigned, emotionless girls being shipped off to wed complete strangers was a stereotype. To be sure, there were brides and grooms in many cultures who had no choice in the matter. But at least in this tight-knit tribal community, nothing prevented the young people from surveying the available field and making their wishes known. Boys and girls might not be able to talk to each other after puberty, but they could hardly spend their entire lives in such close quarters without taking notice of one another. Parents, of course, could be sensitive to their children's wishes or not. Zebedee had obviously been indulgent with James. It all came down to personalities. Cultural norms might differ, but people were people and love was love.

Or was it? Reminded of my mission, my blood began to simmer again. "So," I began, trying to keep my voice even, "is Tamar just sad about not getting pregnant? Or is she afraid of something else?" I didn't want to make the suggestion myself. I wanted to hear it straight from Leah. I wanted Mary to be wrong.

The seventeen-year-old gave me "the look" again. "Of course she is. She could be divorced."

The words hit me like a punch in the belly.

"And she knows what would happen then," Leah continued, her tone grim. "Her father would take her back, of course, but he's old, he won't live more than another year at most. And once it's known that she's barren, no one else will marry her. She would be at the mercy of her older brother, and he's a jerk. He wouldn't throw her out, but he'd let her know she was dead weight, believe me. She'd end up treated no better than a servant, spending the rest of her days waiting on her shrew of a sister-in-law."

"But that's so unfair!" I protested, my face flushing with anger. "How could James even *think* of doing that to her?"

Leah's voice turned sober, philosophical. "He wouldn't want to. But it would be expected. A man needs children."

*And what about what a woman needs?* The retort was a silent scream. Leah didn't like the status quo, but she obviously accepted it. She might rebel against the lesser indignities of womanhood, but she bore no hope of changing society. And it was society she blamed for Tamar's dilemma, not James.

I was far less understanding.

The baby stopped nursing and began to cry, and Leah adjusted her tunic — which interestingly, had a convenient slit much like my own maternity dresses — and moved him to her shoulder. Then she stood and began the walk-and-bounce.

I sat in place, ruminating. The baby quieted, and Leah came back. She stood still a moment, studying me with a look that was almost fearful.

I studied her in turn. What was she thinking?

"Rachel?" she asked tentatively, a tremor in her voice.

"What?" I replied, confused. For all the alarm in her expression, I could have morphed into a vampire.

But whatever she had been about to confront me with, she didn't.

"Never mind," she said, averting her eyes. "I need to change Jesse." She whirled on her feet and headed back toward the supplies.

I watched her go.

My heart beat fast.


Hours passed. Long, uncomfortable hours in which Leah seemed uneasy around me, and in which I caught her conversing in hushed tones with Bernice whenever they thought I wasn't looking.

Perhaps I was being paranoid. Perhaps I hadn't seen Bernice whispering to Naomi, and Naomi stealing horrified looks at me out of the corners of her eyes. Perhaps the odd-girl-out sensation I kept feeling, reminiscent of a bad day in junior high, was due to nothing more than a killer case of PMS.

Or perhaps my house of cards was tumbling.

If so, Tamar's fate would be bliss compared to mine.

I stood alone, half-paralyzed with foreboding, staring at Bernice's children as they played. Danger was all around me here; I could never seem to get away from it. But this scene, at least — this tiny, trifling pocket of human activity — was blessedly normal. And comforting.

The children laughed and shrieked at each other, delighting in some rough-and-tumble game they had devised with a crop of climbing-sized boulders. I hadn't heard them play so loudly before; perhaps because I hadn't been in camp when most of the men were gone. On the road, the children were so quiet and well mannered I had begun to wonder if they were normal.

Bernice was busy building up the cooking fire. Every few moments she glanced up to see where the children were, but otherwise, she seemed unconcerned. At least unconcerned with them. Toward me she threw withering looks.

I breathed slowly and focused on the children.

My Bekka and Ryan hadn't played on rocks. We did have some big ones in our front yard, but the kids had never spent much time outside at home. When they were little I used to drive them to amusement places with climbing tunnels and ball rooms for play dates with their friends. As soon as they were old enough I had taken them to gymnastics and karate lessons, T-ball and soccer games. Piano, dance, orchestra, clogging. Bekka had been on an art binge for a while. Ryan had tried fencing. I encouraged them to do whatever they wanted, drove them wherever the lessons were. It wasn't fun for me, but I hadn't complained. I was a mom.

Bernice's little girl fell down at full speed and flopped face-first onto the dirt. She scrambled back up and kept playing, ignoring the red-brown earth plastered into her hair. I started to walk over and dust her off, but then I stopped. Such a move would only make this child, too, think I was crazy. Mothers here loved their offspring, yes, but their idea of parenting was far removed from the modern tenets I adhered to. As important as their children were to them, as fervently as births were celebrated and deaths mourned, none of these parents made their children's day-to-day activities the focus of their attention, much less anyone else's. Bernice's daughter was considered plenty old enough to dust off her own hair, if she cared. She would find my doing so strange indeed.

Such hands-off parenting was, of course, bound to be detrimental to the children in some way; and whenever Bernice annoyed me, I subconsciously began looking for the damage. So far, I hadn't found any. The truth was that Bernice's children were not only obedient, but almost unnervingly content. They accepted age-appropriate chores as a part of life, but when opportunity availed, they were more than capable of making their own fun. Knowing how much these children lacked relative to my own kids made me sad. But I doubted I could explain such a feeling to them, given that they expected so little. Their satisfaction seemed dependent on nothing more than the security of their family; if they felt safe and loved and had enough to eat, they were happy.

I supposed their ignorance was a blessing. Making Ryan and Bekka magically ignorant of online gaming and gift cards, respectively, could save me a fortune. But it was tough to go backward. In my neighborhood, any boy who didn't have a reasonably up-to-date gaming system was considered neglected. A girl who didn't have the right clothes would be scarred for life. Every self-respecting mother at the elementary school bus stop knew exactly how well everyone else's children were doing at school, what span of enrichment activities they were engaged in, and how much effort had gone into their last birthday party. The latter, of course, was the quintessential measure of maternal devotion. I myself had once stayed up all night hand-painting seahorses, clown fish, and clamshells on seventeen matching aquamarine plastic plates, cups, and party hats. Bekka's preschool friends hadn't really appreciated them, but I made darn sure the bus-stop moms were aware.

I bit my lip. Even in my own rambling thoughts, my competitive streak shone through. The kids had their sports, and I had mine. Competitive mothering was the centerpiece of the suburban Olympics, and my eye had always been on the gold. And why not? It was, after all, for the kids.

A hand touched my shoulder. I jumped a foot.

"Sorry. Didn't mean to startle you," Mary apologized.

I released a pent-up breath. Mary and Joanna had returned from town, along with their servants. I had been so lost in thought I didn't notice. Now Joanna and Bernice were talking quietly together, throwing frequent glances my direction.

Frantically, I searched Mary's wrinkled face for some sign of what was happening, dreading that I would see in her eyes the same awkward, sudden fear that had come up in Leah's. But all I saw was a bemused sort of sympathy.

"Let's sit a minute," she suggested.

My legs trembled as I folded them beneath me. "So what did I do?" I asked. "Why are they all upset with me?"

It took forever for her to answer. She just kept looking at me with those intense dark-hazel eyes of hers. Eyes that seemed able to see through me almost as well as Jesus's could.

"Are you a Gentile, Rachel?"

I blinked. Some moments passed before I understood what she was asking. Gentiles were people other than Jews. In many cases, they were pagans. Some people spoke of them as if they were a different species. Jews wouldn't go into Gentile houses. Mary and Joanna wouldn't buy meat from their shops, nor even cooking utensils, because they would have to be purified first. Everything about Gentiles was associated with that dreaded, omnipresent word: *unclean*.

Mary was asking me if I was a Gentile. Why?

I couldn't answer.

"You don't know the law from beans," she stated matter-of-factly. "I could tell that the day I met you. But you dressed like a Jew and spoke like a Jew, so who was I to judge? I supposed you were flustered. Or sheltered. Or something."

I swallowed. All those times I had made little gaffes in my actions, all those times I had asked stupid questions — she had noticed. But she had held her tongue about it.

Now Leah had the same suspicion. And she had confronted the other women with it.

"I've been covering for you, you know," Mary continued. "The others wouldn't allow you to travel with us if they knew. The disciples would be horrified." She grinned. "Well, some of them would be. I doubt Jesus would care."

I managed to stammer, "Did he say something about me?"

"No," she replied. "But I know how he feels. Haven't you heard his story about the helpful Samaritan? He doesn't tell those marvelous little stories just for entertainment value, you know. He's trying to send a message. I don't know if all the others got it, but I did."

My hands were shaking. I sat on them. "But you were protecting me before that, even. Why?"

She looked at me speculatively, her crow's feet crinkling. "I don't really know. I suppose because I like you."

I let out a nervous chuckle. My eyes moistened. "Well, thank you. But I don't know why you would. I'm worthless around camp; all I do is get into trouble."

Mary smiled. "Why, some of my best friends are troublemakers. Your boldness is what I like. I've never met anybody — with the exception of myself, of course — who's as bold with men as you are, Rachel. It's terribly refreshing."

My eyes widened. Me, bold? I had been trying my hardest to be demure!

"I find it strange to see such boldness in a woman who's been mistreated," Mary said smoothly. "Most end up like Naomi, cowering and anxious."

I let her words sink in. "Naomi?" I repeated, bewildered. "But Bartholomew would never hurt her! He's the most level-headed, tolerant—"

"Not Bartholomew," Mary interrupted. "Her father. And her oaf of a brother. Bartholomew lived next door to them. He married her to get her out of there. He treats her like a queen, now, but she's still not over it. You've seen her. You know how she is."

"Yes," I muttered, embarrassed not to have suspected as much.

"Yet *you*, Rachel," she continued, her voice growing intent, "challenge every man you meet with your eyes. You look at them levelly; you talk to them as if you're their equal. A rather odd reaction to abuse, wouldn't you say?"

My heart thudded against my breastbone so loudly I was sure she could hear it. So that was it. I had noticed that other women lowered their eyes when speaking with men, but I could never quite manage it. Now I was paying the price. Mary was fishing; she knew I was lying about my past. Even if she didn't mind my being a Gentile, she had to resent me for deceiving her.

I wanted so badly to tell her the truth about my life — everything I remembered, from my first memory of my grandfather taking me on a merry-go-round to the day I had paid $650 for the formal gown Bekka would only wear once. But Mary couldn't and wouldn't believe a word of it. Nothing I did in the course of an ordinary day would make the least bit of sense to her, and the technology and plethora of manufactured goods I lived with wouldn't be the only source of her confusion.

Mary the Magdalene was nothing like me. She would never sit on my deck and drink a fuzzy navel — not unless she had finished doing something that actually meant something first. The woman had spent every day of the last few decades working her tail off to build a business that would give her rare power as a female, not to mention show men everywhere what women in general were capable of. Granted, in the beginning, she had probably been driven by greed. But when she recognized Jesus's potential to transform lives, had she not left her hard-won comforts behind in order to help him? Her goals for herself were higher, loftier. Resting on laurels was not her style.

I practically lived on mine.

I cleared my throat, stalling. If she didn't believe that I had left my family because of abuse, what justification could I have for being on my own with so much money? There wasn't a single scenario I could conjure that could explain my situation satisfactorily, including the truth. There was no reason why she should tolerate my pathetic, lying butt one second longer. There was no reason why anyone should.

Yet Jesus had.

Hadn't he?

The rabbi himself had asked me to come along. And he had known darn well I wasn't from Nazareth when he did.

Hope flared. My back straightened. Jesus's motives were no clearer to me now than they had been then, but under the circumstances, they were of secondary importance. What mattered was that this whole traveling shebang was *his* show. Not even Mary could argue with that.

I turned and faced her squarely. "Mary, you know me. You know what kind of person I am. Jesus himself asked me to join you. He must have had his reasons." I paused and lowered my voice. "Can't that be enough?"

Mary's eyes narrowed. She raised a hand to her chin and strummed her fingers along her jawbone. After a few seconds, her lips curved into a smile.

"You're a clever one," she said slyly. "I knew *that* the day I met you, too."

My eyes fell closed with relief. When I opened them again, Mary was getting to her feet. I hastened up with her.

"We'll have to tell them you're a Jew. No way around that," she instructed. "But we can be vague about the rest of it. Just tell me this. Is anyone likely to pop around looking for that bag of money? *Do* you have a family somewhere, missing you?"

Joe's face conjured itself in my mind, and a wave of emotion raised hot tears behind my eyes. I had come perilously close, just now, to being the next lone, unprotected woman whose corpse would rot beside the road. I wanted to go home. I wanted to be with my husband again, with my kids. Short of one-upping the bus stop crowd, I might not have accomplished much in my old life, but I wasn't accomplishing anything here either. Of what use was I to these people? I thought I had come to understand them; I had even begun to care for them. But if Leah would back away from me just because she thought I was a Gentile, and if one of Jesus's best friends would dump his wife for infertility, maybe they weren't the people I thought they were.

"No," I lied again, my voice cracking. "There's no one."

To my surprise, Mary took my hands in her own. "Rachel," she said quietly. "Don't worry. I'll tell the others you were ill before — that you have spells where you get confused and can't remember things. Joanna will go along; she's busy defending you even as we speak. And the rest will accept you if we do."

The olive trees behind her moved. I steadied my feet. "Thank you," I stammered.

"No problem," she said brightly, dusting off the seat of her tunic as idly as if we had been discussing the weather. "You're doing a good thing, Rachel, in supporting Jesus. You'll see. If people listen to him, one day there'll be no more women abused."

*If people listen.* My eyes watered, and I swiped at them. She was wrong. Jesus's words hadn't kept people from mistreating each other. People didn't listen.

"What we're doing is important, Rachel," she reiterated. "And you're right. If your being here wasn't important, Jesus wouldn't have asked you to come."

An image flashed of myself and Mary Magdalene, equal figures in the annals of history, and it was all I could do not to laugh. Mary had made enough of her life that a girl born two thousand years later on the other side of the earth had grown up knowing her name. What meaning had my own life had? I was raising two great kids, true, but they were independent, thinking people, not just feathers in my cap. What else had *I* done? What would I accomplish once Bekka and Ryan were grown and out of the house?

"We both know my money's more useful than I am," I responded, cutting off my own, discomfiting thoughts. "I just carry the pouch around."

"That's not true," Mary countered. "You're a brave woman, Rachel. Were you not ready to dive into the lake in the middle of that storm to save poor, helpless Jesus from an untimely death?"

I stared at her, astonished.

She laughed out loud. "I can swim, too," she explained with a wink. "But I figured the rabbi could handle it."

*Commentary for Chapter 12 begins on page 255.*

# Chapter 13

Mary was true to her word. Whatever she and Joanna told the other women to convince them that I was Jewish did appease them. Leah and Naomi even seemed apologetic afterward. But no one said anything to me directly.

I was still feeling a bit shell-shocked when I headed into the village the next morning, but oddly, I had acquired a new sense of self-confidence. I was not doing all *that* badly. Mary and Joanna might have taken me under their wing because of my money, but they had genuinely come to care for me. The realization was both touching and sobering. They had gone out on a limb for me more than once. I was determined not to disappoint them.

I was tired of living in fear. Almost as tired as I was of waiting for something spectacular to happen — expecting every other stiff breeze, loud noise, and flicker of flame to be the magical catalyst that would send me back to the future.

I was stuck here.

I might as well accomplish something.

The money in my bag was down by a third already. I had been watching Mary when she purchased things, taking note of relative costs, but I still wasn't sure how much I was worth. I offered Mary as much as she wanted for supplies, but she always spent more of her own money than she took from Joanna or me. She had purchased nearly all the camping gear herself, half the pack animals were her own, and she delighted in playing Santa Claus. When Thaddeus's sandal wore a hole, she slipped a new pair onto his mat when he was sleeping and got up early just to watch his expression when he found them. She loved every minute of her "mission"; and her joy was contagious.

I wanted to do more, too.

This morning I had insisted that she stay in camp while Joanna and I made a supply run of our own. It wasn't a difficult sell, since Jesus planned to preach in the countryside, and Mary always preferred to stay near him. Shopping away from her watchful eye, I figured I could buy her a little gift. I could also indulge in more chicken meat.

We were a party of four. Gideon had come with Joanna, and Mary had sent Samuel with me. On our way into the village we passed scores of townspeople heading toward the spring to see Jesus; by the time we reached the bazaar, it was blissfully uncrowded.

It was also devoid of chicken meat.

I bought some pomegranates for Mary, which were her favorite. But I could not bring myself to purchase any of the fly-covered strips of mutton that were all the small market had to offer. We were about to leave when one of the vendors informed Samuel that if we were set on purchasing chicken, we would have to see the bird woman.

The referral was made with obvious disdain. My eyes narrowed.

Female business owners were uncommon. Rich and successful ones like Mary were exceptionally rare, which is how she had come to be such a celebrity even before meeting Jesus. Husbands, fathers, brothers, and sons controlled wealth; a woman only got the chance to be financially independent if she was widowed with none of the above — and if she had been left with adequate resources to support and protect herself. Even then, it took guts of steel to push the cultural barriers, demand respect as a businesswoman, and put up with the deflating, derogatory crap men like these shopkeepers constantly dished out.

I squared my shoulders. Only one of the vendors had even bothered to mention the "bird woman," which could mean that her business was a squalid embarrassment to the village.

Or that it was a smashing success.

I asked where we could find her, but even the shopkeeper who had mentioned her seemed reluctant to give directions. They all hated my staring them in the face, but I was done trying to compromise on that issue. Stupid men could get over it or get out of my way.

"Just listen for the squawking," he said dismissively.

Annoyed, Joanna and I moved to the periphery of the market, straining our ears for any sounds of crowing or clucking that might rise over the general din. But before we could hear much of anything, I felt a sharp tap on my shoulder.

"You with Jesus?"

I whirled to face the chest of a very tall, lanky woman who towered over me by nearly half a foot. Her frayed tunic was speckled with the clinging husks of a thousand tiny, cracked seeds, and she smelled pungently of a chicken coop. Her hair was oily and unkempt, her arms long and gangly. Her brown eyes, though small, were keenly observant, but her overlong, crooked nose and equally crooked buck teeth so dominated her homely face that her eyes were scarcely noticeable. She stood before us with a severe look, holding a broad, shallow basket filled to its brim with yellow, brown, and peach-colored eggs of varying sizes.

"You with Jesus?" she repeated impatiently.

Her speech wasn't clear. I could understand her, as I could the others, but I had heard enough of the language to recognize that the sound of hers was different. Her consonants were slurred rather than sharp. Her vowel sounds were harsh and husky.

"Yes, we're with Jesus," I answered. "But he's outside the city now. On the hillside by the spring."

The woman seemed to relax a little. "I don't need to go there. I saw him speak at the synagogue yesterday. Would you take him this?" She extended the basket.

Joanna and I gazed into it with awe. It was unusual to see so many eggs gathered into one place, even in a market. Eggs were a prized commodity, and they spoiled quickly. If these were fresh, they had come from a great many birds.

"Thank you," Joanna said, accepting the basket with grace. "Jesus will be most appreciative."

The woman's eyes darted from me to Joanna, then back again. She seemed to be making a concerted effort to speak clearly, but her words still came out mushy, not unlike those of a drunk. "Tell him he is welcome."

Like a soldier called to about-face, she whirled on the ball of one foot and left us, marching away down the lane with an almost comical gait, her back humped, her shoulders slouched. Given the briskness of her movement, I did not think she was lame. My guess was that the posture had developed from a fruitless effort to hide her height.

"Thank you! Can we tell him your name?" I called after her, feeling guilty at accepting such a lavish gift from such a pitiable figure, even if it was for Jesus. But the woman did not stop or turn around. She did not acknowledge me at all.

"A half-wit," Joanna said sympathetically, picking up a yellow egg and sniffing it with relish. "But a generous one."

The light dawned in my brain just as the spindly figure moved out of view. "She's not a half-wit," I corrected, chastising myself for thinking the same, merely because she talked funny. I could remember hearing the same slurred speech, albeit in a different language, from the father of a childhood friend of mine. A man whose telephone had a light on it.

"She's deaf," I proclaimed, stepping away from Joanna and looking down the lane after her. "She must also be a very good lip reader."

Joanna clucked her tongue in pity. "Well if she's deaf," she asked, "why wouldn't she want to deliver such a gift herself, so she could meet Jesus and ask for his help? He could heal her."

My feet itched beneath me. People with impediments were ubiquitous here, but for some reason, this one's plight affected me. Perhaps it was her vague resemblance to my sweet and towering third grade teacher, who had jokingly referred to herself as "Ichabod Jane." Perhaps it was the fact that she had gone out of her way to offer Jesus a gift without asking anything from him in return. Or maybe it was the way she had looked at me when I had addressed her as an equal. She had seemed surprised.

"I don't know," I answered, puzzled. "But I'm going to find out."

I started after her. I heard footsteps behind me, and knew that Samuel was following. Good old Samuel. He was a nice sort of chap, for a hired goon. I would have to buy him some fruit, too.

I reached the spot where the woman had disappeared and spotted her awkward form several courtyard gates away. I started to call out, then realized it would be pointless. I increased my speed instead.

When at last I caught up with her, I was out of breath. Her long legs gave her a powerful stride, and she appeared to be in a hurry. I intended to jog past her to get her attention, but she sensed my presence when I was still behind her, no doubt from the beating of my feet on the ground. She whirled immediately to face me, her posture defensive.

"What do you want?" she asked, her guard lowering at the sight of me. Still, as Samuel approached calmly from behind, she kept a wary eye on him.

For a moment I could think of nothing to say. "Are you the bird woman?" I asked finally, hoping the term was not an insult. "We were looking for chicken meat." We didn't really need chicken now that we had the eggs, but it was as good an excuse for chasing the woman as I was likely to come up with.

She smiled a little. "I've got anything you want. Chicken, guinea fowl, duck. Even pheasant. You ever try blackbird?"

My mouth watered. Call me uncouth, but the nursery rhyme popped front and center into my fat-starved brain. Blackbird pie. A warm, flaky crust. Chunks of juicy meat, bathed in a thick cream sauce...

*Knock it off.*

I swallowed, trying my best to ignore my growling stomach. The sound of it, at least, couldn't be heard, because the courtyard we were now walking alongside was exploding with noise. Screeches, clucks, squawks, caws... every imaginable bird sound rang out from within. The tops of wooden cages were visible over the wall, and the house beyond looked very large indeed, certainly the largest on the street.

I smiled. It couldn't be easy for any deaf person to run a successful business. But this strange-looking *woman* was doing just that.

When I didn't answer, her gaze became suspicious again. "Is this for Jesus?" she asked.

"It's for all of us," I explained. "His disciples, their families, and the women who support him, like Joanna and me."

Her eyebrows rose. "He has need of women's help? As benefactors?"

The slurring of the woman's words no longer fooled me. She was far from a half-wit. I could see her intelligence in her eyes, her strength in the care-worn lines of her face. But before I could respond, a shower of gravel pelted her backside, some if it striking my own feet.

"*Witch!*" yelled a boy of eight or nine as he ran, retreating, around a corner. Another boy of even younger age ran with him, chanting, "Dumb witchy birdy witch!"

In a flash the woman turned, pulled a rock from a pouch on her tunic, and hoisted it into the air. So aggressive was her action that I found myself flinching, but the gesture, I soon realized, was for show. Though she had plenty of time to zing the little pests before they made their escape, she contented herself with a few rude words, then returned the weapon to its holster.

"Disrespectful brats," she muttered, making a futile effort to dust off her husk-covered tunic. "They didn't hurt you, did they?"

I shook my head, then looked in consternation to a point further down the lane, where a half-dozen more youngsters had gathered to watch the melee with delight, pointing and grinning.

My face grew hot. Not only had this woman's success in business set her up for resentment by her fellow vendors, but her disability and unattractive appearance had made her an object of public ridicule. I could only imagine how often children sneaked up on her, pelted her with gravel and dirt, and yelled insults she couldn't hear, purely for sport. Kids could be cruel. So could their parents.

"Jesus heals people," I blurted, overcome with the desire to avenge this woman's rotten luck, preferably by some means other than my first instinct, which was to chase down the rock-wielding little beasts myself and inflict some good old-fashioned corporal punishment. I had to remind myself to take into account the harshness of their own lot; they truly might not know any better.

"Why don't you come with us and ask him for help?" I urged.

The woman's expression, which had a moment before been sympathetic to me, became defensive again. "I don't need any help. I do just fine. Do you want to buy some meat, or not?"

I caught her eyes, certain that I could imagine what she was thinking. She had overcome incredible odds to be where she was, which despite the ill treatment I had just witnessed, was a relatively good place to be. She was strong; she was capable; she was a success. Asking for help would mean proclaiming there was something wrong with her, after she had worked long and hard to prove that there was not.

"I know you don't *need* help," I agreed, my voice low. "But Jesus would help you anyway. He would want to."

*Like I want to.*

I didn't say the last part. I didn't want to scare her away. I could hardly explain that a few minutes in her presence had convinced me she was a woman after my own heart: proud, determined, and competitive. She was defensive of her situation, but she wasn't bitter. Given a more even playing field, who knew what her chutzpah could accomplish?

I didn't doubt for a second that if she went to Jesus, he would do everything he could for her. The man's compassion knew no bounds. I was less certain of his medical abilities, though I tried not to dwell on the uncomfortable skepticism that continued to plague me, no matter how many apparent healings I witnessed. The fact was, I wanted him to heal this woman.

Could he do it? She must have been able to hear once, or else she wouldn't be able to talk so well. But even that ability was bound to deteriorate over time, isolating her further.

I wanted her to hear again.

I wanted to be the one to make it happen.

Me. The superfluous female with the money bag.

Maddeningly, the deaf woman shook her head. "Your Jesus has

enough to do," she said softly, so softly I could barely understand her. "Other people are sick. They're poor. They're dying. They need him more than I do. I'm fine."

She turned and walked to her gate. I sprung after her, laying a hand on her arm so she would look at me. "Please," I begged. "You saw him speak. You collected all those eggs. You must have liked what he had to say."

Her face softened. "Of course I did."

I smiled. I couldn't remember Jesus's official bio mentioning the immense popularity of his message with women, but I suppose I could have missed that part.

No one here had. Women adored Jesus. He was kind, he was respectful, and he didn't look or talk down to them, regardless of their social status. He did the same for men, of course, but that hardly detracted from the gesture. When Jesus spoke in the synagogues, the women's courts were always crammed to bursting. But he didn't just speak in the synagogues; he also made a point of speaking in the open, where the genders were not segregated, and where the village women came to him in droves, children in tow, chores left undone. I had heard Andrew comment more than once that women were over-represented in the crowds that Jesus drew relative to those of John the Baptist, whom Andrew had also followed. The difference in demographics puzzled him. It didn't puzzle any of us.

Jesus knew how to speak to women, both in his manner and his message. The political turbulence that marked the time made the gentler, more peaceable kingdom he spoke of a tantalizing vision for either gender. But it was in his emphasis on individual character that women — who were largely left out of the political realm — most felt Jesus's favor. To have a loving nature was a strength; compassion, peacemaking, and humility were virtues. Actions were more important than rhetoric, and the actions of every person, no matter how small or insignificant she might seem to others, mattered.

I could tell from the look in the bird woman's eyes that Jesus's speech yesterday had moved her. It had moved her so much that she had gone out of her way to do something nice for him.

"Come with us and talk to him," I cajoled. "The rabbi could use a woman like you in his corner."

If she thought I was after her money, I didn't care. Whatever appeal brought her to camp was worth trying. Strong women didn't like asking for help, but they had a hard time refusing to give it. When it came to the workings of the professional female ego, I could write a thesis, and I knew that all I had to do was introduce her to Jesus and he would do the rest.

But it wasn't going to happen. Her eyes flickered with temptation for only a second, then she put her hand out and opened her gate. "If he needs anything else, come back and tell me."

"Wait!" I ordered, frustrated. I grabbed her arm again. "At least give me your name, so that I can tell him who sent the eggs."

"It's Susanna," she answered, "But—"

She broke off, her gaze darting downward. An immense rooster had wedged himself through the crack in the gate and was making a break for freedom. He succeeded, but instead of heading into the street, the beast ruffled his feathers, issued a rude noise, and began pecking viciously at Susanna's ankles.

With one quick swoop of her hand — and a few choice words — she snagged the cock by the neck and tucked his struggling body beneath a sinewy arm. When her eyes returned to me, they lit up a little. "Here!" she insisted, extending the rooster by his feet. "You wanted chicken, you got it. This one's been asking for it for a while. No charge. Tell Jesus to enjoy."

I stared at the bird helplessly, fighting the urge to step back. I knew that my incompetence was showing, but I had no idea how to deal with the sharp beak of a live, ornery rooster. I didn't even buy whole carcasses at the grocery store. Not having to cut up your own chicken was, after all, the whole point of discretionary income.

Samuel stepped up and took the rooster like a pro, grabbing its legs and neck and pinning it swiftly beneath an elbow. I resolved again to buy him something nice.

I turned to thank Susanna for the gift, but cut myself off.

I was talking to a closed gate.


Jesus was back in camp. It was dusk, my favorite time of day, when all but the most stubborn remnants of the crowd had returned to their homes to attend to the business of dinner and sleep. Many of them would return at first light tomorrow. But until then, our band was relatively alone. The spring water was cool; the falling temperature, refreshing.

I clutched the basket of eggs. Bernice's eye had been on it for hours; Joanna was practically drooling. But I didn't want them to begin cooking just yet. I wanted to show the basket to Jesus, whole and intact. I wanted him to know from whom it came.

He was standing near the fire, talking with Judas. Matthew and his brother looked on, patiently waiting their turns. Peter, James, and John were reclining a little distance from the fire, their eyes closed. Most of the disciples were sitting or lying down. Apparently, the village crowd had been beyond enthusiastic. The rabbi's protectors had had another grueling day.

I caught myself shiver. I was uptight, and I was ashamed of it. I had no business being afraid. Fear was understandable when I thought Jesus was some kind of cosmic magician, but now I knew better. So why did I hesitate to approach him?

He was hardly a frightening person. His astute brown eyes could be intimidating, but their twinkling revealed the tenderest of hearts, and his smile could warm one to the core. I hadn't been avoiding him because I feared he would say something upsetting to me. I had been avoiding him because I felt out of place.

I had no business being here, no right to chew up his time. The life I had already lived was almost as good as the heaven these people dreamed about. I didn't need anything. I had already had it once.

What had I done with it?

I tightened my hold on the basket and looked around. The tax-collector and his brother were talking to each other now, and Judas was by the fire. Jesus was gone.

I sighed. The man had an uncanny ability to disappear when one wasn't watching. He often managed to slip away through crowds even when people *were* watching. Peter once joked that Jesus must be able to make himself invisible. Not everyone was certain he was joking.

I found the rabbi standing over by the trees where the donkeys were tied, jesting with Samuel and Gideon. The farther we traveled, the less the two servants seemed like hired help and the more they seemed like disciples. They still stuck by Mary and Joanna whenever the women needed protection, but around camp they had begun to mingle more and more with the other men. At first the apostles had treated the servants differently, paying them little attention. But such lines of status had become blurred, no doubt because Jesus himself disregarded them. Customs involving distinctions of class were among the rabbi's favorite rules to break.

I took in a breath and started walking. Samuel was graciously sharing the mulberries I had bought him. Jesus was relaxed and essentially unoccupied. Now was as good a time as any.

"Jesus?" The name caught in my throat, and I fought to keep the redness from my face. It was no use. When he turned around and looked at me I flushed from head to foot.

*This isn't about you, Rachel. Get a grip.*

I held out the basket toward him. I could see it shaking in my hands. "A woman in the village gave you this as a gift," I forced out, my voice still raspy. I cleared my throat and continued. "She heard you speak yesterday, and she wanted to do something for you. She gave us a rooster, too. But I wanted to tell you—"

He was looking directly at me. Involuntarily, I averted my eyes. I didn't want him to look too close. Didn't want my thoughts exposed. All at once I was glad Gideon and Samuel were watching. Surely their presence would prevent Jesus from saying anything particularly personal to me... if he *had* anything personal to say to me.

I glanced at his eyes for just a second, then pulled my gaze away again. "Susanna is deaf. She's compensated beautifully, but her life would be so much better if she could hear. I tried to convince her to come see you, but she wouldn't; she's too proud. She feels awkward asking for help when she knows so many people are worse off than she is. But if you could help her, it would—"

My babbling stopped short. Blood drained from my face.

*Oh, no.*

I had said "if."

No one said "if" to Jesus. "If" was an insult. Faith was what he valued. The very faith I was so obviously, blatantly lacking in.

My intercession on behalf of Susanna was worse than no help at all. People showing faith was what mattered most to him. Faith and—

"Susanna," Jesus repeated thoughtfully, picking up an egg. He didn't sniff of it to see if it was fresh, as Joanna had done. He merely held it, brushing his thumb across its smooth, speckled surface. Then he looked at me.

His gaze was searching. There was a sadness to it, but also a glimmer of expectation. At least, I thought I saw such a glimmer, before my own eyes turned away again. I couldn't stand to feel so exposed.

My face was flushed to steaming. I wanted to drop the basket and run. What was I doing? All this time I hadn't said a word to him, and when I finally did I had messed everything up.

"Out of the overflow of the heart," he said quietly, "the mouth speaks."

My eyes flew back to his. What did *that* mean?

But he had turned to Samuel and Gideon. "We shall have a fine dinner tonight!" he said cheerfully, holding up the egg. Then he replaced it in the basket, nodded at me politely, and walked back toward the campfire.


Dinner was exceptional. Bernice had scrambled the eggs to perfection, adding cucumber, onions, and parched barley to make something not too far from an omelet. But I was unable to enjoy it. Jesus's enigmatic statement rang in my ears.

I didn't know what he meant. I didn't even know whether I'd been admonished or complimented.

The rabbi could be frustrating that way. He could take the most complicated issues and points of law and illustrate them so that they seemed simple. Yet when you expected a simple answer, you got some bizarre phrase or quotation out of left field. If you asked him nicely to explain, he would, but in my case that wouldn't be happening. My traitorous mouth was shut for the duration.

I wasn't cut out to be anyone's hero.

The men were finishing up their meal and the women beginning to clean the dishes when all conversation was silenced by the disturbing wail of an animal. At least it sounded like an animal. It was a thin, unearthly cry whose pitch raised and lowered at random. As it drew closer, the sound became more human, like the yodel of a lunatic. The disciples sprang to their feet, staring into the darkness, waiting. The women huddled close to the cooking fire. Several stiffened with fear, as if expecting a demon.

The sound stopped, but footsteps pounded. Someone was running on the road out of the city, heading toward us.

"*Jesus!*"

The voice was unmistakably female. The disciples' defensive postures relaxed. "What's a woman doing out here alone?" Bartholomew asked out loud. We were all thinking the same thing, but no one answered. Such a woman must be mad. No sane woman, not even a widow with Mary's aplomb, walked alone after dark on a country road — much less ran screaming down one without a torch.

The footsteps came closer, then slowed down.

"Jesus?"

A figure became visible in the shadows.

"Stop there!" Simon ordered. He and Thaddeus were closest, and they turned toward the stranger, straightening to their full height. The other disciples closed in silently behind them, alert and ready.

I was on my feet as well. The woman's last word had struck a chord in my brain, and I ran forward around the edge of the men to get a look at her myself.

The woman stood in darkness, but her silhouette was unmistakable.

"I want to see Jesus," she explained with a haughty air, not cowed in the least by the dozen or so strong men who stood glaring at her. "Take it easy. I'm not going to hurt you."

I smothered a laugh. Most of the disciples continued staring at the woman in surprise, but I recognized Judas's deep rumble beside me. "Well, we appreciate that," he chuckled.

The woman turned and looked right at him. And at me.

A wave of warm satisfaction rocked me to my heels.

She had heard him.

*She could hear.*

"This is Susanna," I announced, my heart thudding against my breastbone. "She's the birder who gave us the eggs."

With a quick nod toward me, Susanna moved forward, brushing aside the chastened figures of Simon and Thaddeus, pushing through the rest of the unresisting disciples till she caught sight of Jesus on the other side of the fire. He was sitting calmly, finishing his serving of eggs.

"Jesus," she said again.

He looked up at her.

Her face was shining with sweat. Her eyes glowed with excitement in the firelight. "I know you did this, Rabbi," she said slowly, breathlessly. "Now I want to hear your voice. Please, say something. Say anything!"

Jesus's eyes sparkled at her with amusement. He smiled. "Anything."

*Commentary for Chapter 13 begins on page 258.*

# Chapter 14

More days. More nights. More healings, more crowds. The days passed in a flurry of heat, work, and excitement. Jesus's popularity continued to grow; our band was more rarely alone. There were more people to feed, but with the addition of Susanna to the fold, there seemed less work to do.

The woman was a powerhouse.

She had walked into camp the morning we were leaving with a pack over her shoulder and a purse on her belt, ready to contribute. Mary, whose savings I suspected must be getting stretched, was delighted to have her, and so was everyone else. Perpetually energetic, and always humming to herself now that she could hear, Susanna took on any job that needed to be done as well as many that didn't. Idleness was a foreign concept to her, and if she had lived where I lived I had no doubt she'd be the CEO of something.

Susanna, like virtually every other mature Jewish woman who wasn't married, was a widow. According to her, the only man in the village who would have her when she came of age was an elderly birder who had already buried two wives and several children. He was short and cross and had little skill for the family business, but after Susanna showed a natural talent for it, the two of them got along fine. He had lived for years as an invalid while Susanna wheeled and dealed with other birders in the area and built up her own prized stock. By the time her husband died, Susanna had garnered considerable wealth and made a name for herself and the business all over the region. But to the people of her own village, she was still just an ugly, uppity deaf woman.

Jesus's issues with Nazareth, she could relate to.

Susanna had not been with us for long before Jesus made the tactical decision to begin sending the disciples out on their own. The men had been apprehensive at first, unsure whether the clamoring masses would welcome them in their rabbi's stead. But Jesus lacked nothing as a motivational speaker, and in short order we had developed a new routine of splitting up and reforming, covering a wider area and reaching more of the small, scattered hamlets that might otherwise be missed.

Throughout the process the women stayed together, protected by whatever portion of the men happened to be resting with us between excursions. James and John were particularly protective of their wives, carefully alternating their own trips so that one of them was always nearby. I had not forgotten my disturbing conversation with Leah, but the more I witnessed James's behavior with Tamar, the more determined I became to discount both Leah and Mary's comments. Other men might divorce a barren wife, but I still could not believe that James would. He was assertive, brawny, and loud, true. Jesus hadn't nicknamed James and John "sons of thunder" for nothing. But I was sure the rabbi did so with a sense of humor, seeing beneath their machismo exactly what I saw: two unusually soft hearts.

Up to now, everyone's spirits had stayed high. It seemed impossible to feel otherwise with Jesus around. With thousands of people now walking for miles and waiting for hours for a mere glimpse of the miraculous healer, we all felt privileged. There was something magnetic about him, something that made people not only desire his company, but want to be important to him. I knew the feeling, as I found myself wishing I could have just a few moments alone with him myself — to try and get some straight answers to the myriad questions spinning in my head. But it was just as well he stayed otherwise occupied, because I didn't have the guts to ask him anything. As fascinated as I was with the man, I wasn't ready for another confrontation. Were he to present me with some incontrovertible evidence of divine omniscience now, I would be thoroughly spooked. And if he didn't?

Watching from a distance was safer.

The traveling disciples were preaching east of the Jordan now, while Jesus and our group were staying west of it, in Samaria. As buoyed as we all were by the rabbi's steady warmth and enthusiasm, the last few days of travel had been especially grueling, and the strain was beginning to show. The advantage of being in Samaria was that the Samaritans, not being Jews, couldn't care less about Jesus and left us alone. The disadvantage of being in Samaria was that the Samaritans, despising Jews, couldn't care less about being hospitable. Testimony about Jesus's importance did nothing to mitigate their rudeness to his emissaries, which infuriated the valorous James and John, especially, to no end. But Jesus himself raised no contention over the issue. When a village refused to sell us supplies, we simply moved on. Now, after several such refusals in a row — even with the trade-savvy Mary and

Susanna as our ambassadors — our stores had begun to run low. To make matters worse, the weather was unbearably hot, and news of Herod's barbaric execution of John the Baptist had taken a heavy emotional toll. No one spoke of the possible implications for Jesus, but for the first time, tempers around camp seemed to be running short, and nerves began to fray.

We were resting in a miniscule patch of shade on a hillside near the road when Jesus disappeared again. It was noon, and it was hot. Mary and Susanna had gone with a few of the disciples into town, to try once more to purchase food, and the remaining men had fallen asleep in the shade. But the rabbi was nowhere to be seen. Mother-hen Bernice, who took it as her personal duty to keep track of everyone's whereabouts at all times, began looking for him, grumbling to herself. We were out of fruit altogether and had barely enough vegetables for one more meal, she groused. If this village was a bust, we would be living on nothing but bread.

She spotted the rabbi some ways off at the bottom of the hill. He was heading for the well just outside the village, where we had all stopped earlier, and as she watched, she let out an exasperated sigh.

"Why is he going there?" she said to me as I watched with her. "We brought up plenty of water already. Besides, he has nothing to draw with."

"Maybe he just wants to be alone," I suggested.

I could sympathize. Jesus was an extrovert of the first order, but even extroverts needed some solitude. Despite my own growing dislike of the heat and the inhospitable nature of Samaria in general, I wasn't altogether unhappy to be away from the constant crowds. It might be miserable here, but at least it was a peaceful misery.

"Well, he won't *be* alone for long," Bernice said with annoyance. I followed her eyes to the road, where emerging from around the bend of another hill a woman walked slowly, carrying a water jar.

"Samaritans!" Joanna, who had joined us, clucked her tongue. "Really. A woman going to the well by herself, and at this hour?"

"A disreputable woman, no doubt," Bernice proclaimed. She turned to her middle child, a son of around eight, and held out a small water jar. "Mark," she instructed. "Take this down to Jesus. He'll need something to drink out of." She turned back to us with a huff. "The rabbi certainly can't ask her."

The youngster, who was ordinarily obedient to a fault, bristled. "I can't carry a water jar, mother!" he protested, crossing his skinny arms over his chest. "I'm a man!"

I grinned. The child had a point; carrying water jars fell strictly within a woman's purview. The feminist in me wanted to rail against such firm divisions of household labor, but since I hadn't mowed a lawn since I married Joe, I really had no right to talk. Besides, the situation unfolding intrigued me. I knew that no self-respecting Jewish man would ever talk to a Samaritan woman; they barely talked to Jewish women. Not to mention that winding up alone with a female was pure scandal, even if it did happen accidentally.

Call me a voyeur. But I was curious.

"I'll carry the jar," I told the boy, taking it from his mother. "But I'll need a man to go with me."

Little Mark threw his chest out proudly. "I can escort you, ma'am."


We were still some distance from the well when the Samaritan woman reached it. She was easily identifiable as a non-Jew by her hat, which was woven of straw and had a wide brim that shaded her face. What the Jews had against hats I had no idea. Personally, I would love to wear one. But I wouldn't dare, no matter how sunburned my nose got. My "Gentile" behavior had raised enough eyebrows already.

The Samaritans and the Jews had common ancestors, but at some point the Samaritans had gone their own direction, refusing to have anything to do with the temple in Jerusalem and setting up their own center of worship at someplace called Mount Gerizim. They hated it when Jews from Galilee came through their territory on pilgrimages to *the* temple, and could be quite hostile to them, which is why many Jews stayed East of the Jordan the whole trip. The differences between the people seemed petty to me, but many a war had been fought over less.

Jesus was resting in the shade of a group of trees near the well. The woman came up, took one look at him, and then faced away. I was still getting used to the fact that what seemed like rudeness to me was expected behavior. Men and women who weren't allowed to interact were supposed to behave as if they weren't aware of each other, and the Samaritan woman was doing her part. She dipped her water jar in the well and went about her business, ignoring Jesus completely.

The boy beside me took in a sharp breath. "Look at that tunic!" he whispered. "It's cut far too low. For shame!"

The child's mimic of his straight-laced mother was so dead-on, even to the derisive tone of voice, that I couldn't help chuckling.

"The rabbi shouldn't sit so near her," the boy continued. "Someone might see. Samaritans are bad. He shouldn't be around them at all."

My smile faded. There was nothing amusing about bigotry. I had always despised the tendency of some people to label others as good or evil, depending on variables as arbitrary as the country into which they had been born. Mary had been right in thinking that Jesus's parable about the good Samaritan had fallen on deaf ears. What people took from it was the concept that an occasional Samaritan could be nice; the idea that the hearts and minds of all humans were essentially alike hadn't registered. Not with these people. Nor with many of my own.

I watched Jesus as he sat leaning with his back against the tree trunk.

*Go talk to her.*

My footsteps slowed as the precocious Mark prattled on about how his mother said that Jesus needed to be more careful with whom he associated. Not that Jesus would ever act immorally, of course, but the point was that other people could get the wrong idea...

*Go on*, my mind begged. *Show them. Show them you think she's as important as anyone else, even if she was born female and Gentile.*

Jesus got to his feet.

I beamed.

"What is he doing?" Mark protested, stopping in his tracks.

Jesus crossed to the well and walked to within a few feet of the woman before settling comfortably on a nearby stone. We couldn't hear him, but we could see his lips move. The woman's head turned toward him with a jerk.

"He's talking to her!" the boy whispered hoarsely, his eyes wide. "He can't do that!"

"It appears he can," I said cheerfully.

"But he can't be alone with her!" the boy protested, indignant. "I'd better go."

I reached out a hand to stop him, but he had already charged ahead. I expected him to barge right into the conversation, perhaps pulling on the rabbi's hand to distract him. But I was thinking of my own kids. Bernice and Philip's son ran forward just far enough to where both adults could see him, then stood solemnly, several feet away, his eyes on the ground.

Neither figure took much notice. They continued to talk, and the conversation was lengthy. Judging by the looks on both their faces, it seemed also to be intense.

A queer surge of jealousy passed through me as I realized that this woman had talked more with Jesus in five minutes than I had in... well, however long I had been here. With the exception of Mary, none of the women in camp ever spoke with him privately. Yet this woman was receiving his complete focus — and for a protracted period of time.

So what made her so special?

I wanted to hear what they were saying, but didn't dare go close enough to intrude. After what seemed an eternity, the woman put down her water jar by the well, turned away, and hurried off toward the village at a jog.

I looked over my shoulder toward the group on the hill, wondering if Bernice had seen. There she was, staring down, her hands planted on her hips.

At least half the camp was staring down with her.


Jesus returned as if nothing unusual had happened. The disciples, though clearly taken aback, said nothing to him — as if they wouldn't know where to begin.

Their reaction struck me as drastic. They knew that Jesus didn't shrink from the company of sinners. Had they not watched the prostitute at Simon's house kiss his feet? They also knew how he felt about Gentiles, or at least they should have from the sermons he gave and the parables he told. In treating a disreputable Samaritan woman like a human being, the rabbi had done nothing more than practice what he preached.

Yet still, they seemed surprised.

Could the fact that he had been alone with a woman be even more scandalous than the fact that she was a Gentile? I had a difficult time believing that. The two were in sight of our camp the whole time, everyone knew he never laid a hand on her, and there was no one else around to testify to anything different.

No, impropriety was not the issue. The issue was racism.

"Blasted Samaritans," Mary muttered to the women, who scrambled to serve a meager lunch in the heat. "I had the one woman ready to sell, and then her husband stopped her. Not a one of the rest of them would even talk to us. As if our money wasn't as good as any!"

"We've got to get back over the Jordan," Bernice insisted. "Better to have crowds and eat well than starve to death in this place." She took a bite of the food she was serving, then made a face. "This is the worst bread I've ever made!"

No one could disagree with her. The loaf *was* the worst she had ever made. The Jewish women along our routes were always generous in loaning the use of their bread ovens, but in Samaria we had had to make do with stacking rocks atop the fire. A well-constructed stone oven distributed the heat evenly, but a makeshift one could leave parts of the dough burnt or raw. My piece seemed to have suffered both fates.

"What did he say to her?" Leah asked boldly, unconcerned about the change of subject. We all knew exactly what she meant.

Bernice looked over her shoulder to where the men were eating. I looked, too. Their quiet conversation was out of earshot, but I perceived their mood as tense. Jesus was sitting a little ways off by himself, looking out toward the village road. He wasn't eating any bread. As I watched, James offered him a piece, but he refused it.

I looked back at Bernice. She had noticed, too, unfortunately. I felt a surge of sympathy for her wounded chef's pride. We had never known Jesus to be a picky eater. Perhaps he had something else on his mind.

Bernice turned back to Leah. "According to what Mark told his father, Jesus started out by lecturing the woman about living water. But then he told her all about herself — how she had had five husbands, and wasn't married to the man she was living with now."

Leah's young eyes widened. "And what did Jesus say about *that?*"

"Well, he didn't reprove her," Bernice answered, her mouth twisting in disapproval. "But his knowing her history did convince her that he was a prophet. Then she started debating with him about Mount Gerizim, like they always do, but he told her a time was coming when it wouldn't matter where you worshiped."

The women were silent. I tried to remember if Jesus had said something to that effect before, but I wasn't sure. Even if he had, the fact that he was saying it to someone besides a Jew was notable.

"Apparently this woman was still skeptical of him, and she insisted that only the most holy and anointed of men could explain such things and know what they were talking about."

Tamar — whose docile nature precluded questioning the authority of her own husband, much less Jesus — took in a breath, aghast. "How did he answer her?"

"He told her that *he* was exactly what *her* people had been waiting for," Bernice responded dryly. "At which point she dropped her jar and ran off."

"Jesus, instruct the Samaritans?" Joanna asked with amazement. She had looked limp as a noodle all day, with beads of sweat adorning her forehead like raindrops. But nothing perked her up faster than a little scandal, particularly a righteous one. "But no Jew can tell them anything! They won't listen."

I watched for Mary's reaction, but she showed none. The heat and sub-par food was getting to her, like the rest of us, but I expected her to spring to Jesus's defense eventually. Despite her mutterings about Samaritans, I knew that she had long since taken the rabbi's message of tolerance to heart. She might be cranky, but she wasn't racist. And unlike so many of the others, she seemed to see the connection between what Jesus said and what he did. Namely, that there was one.

Could I say the same for myself? I had always considered myself tolerant, but the issue of racism rarely came up. There weren't any minority families in my neighborhood; there were only a few in the school district. Things were different closer to the city, but I didn't get down there much. I didn't have any reason to.

"I can't imagine what Jesus would preach to them even if they would listen," Bernice agreed with Joanna. "Their customs are so different; he can't very well preach the law."

"He doesn't preach the law to Jews, either," Mary noted.

I caught her eyes and grinned. "Perhaps his message is more universal," I suggested.

"Perhaps," said Tamar thoughtfully, "he brought us all over here *because* he wanted to preach to them."

"Well he didn't do it for the cuisine!" Bernice snapped, pinching a burnt end off her scrap of bread and flicking it into the dirt.

I cast another glance at Jesus. His eyes were still on the road, as if he were waiting for something.

"I'm used to dealing with Samaritans," Susanna announced. Her voice, which had always had a tone of authority to it, grew clearer every day now. "They have the best peacock stock anywhere around. Very astute breeders. These people here—" she waved a hand toward the village, "they're right on the pilgrimage trail to Jerusalem, so they're a little sensitive. But most Samaritans are all right."

The other women stared at Susanna with awe. None of them, I realized, had spent much time in Samaritan territory before now, much less actually entered a Samaritan town. They would only have seen those Samaritans who came into the Jewish areas to trade. But Susanna had met the Samaritans on their own turf and done business with them. Her perspective was unusual.

Leah threw up her hands. "Well, I suppose there's no reason he *shouldn't* preach to them. But they don't seem very receptive. I mean, the woman ran away, didn't she? What kind of woman can spend any amount of time with Jesus and not be totally taken with him?"

My brow furrowed. Leah had a point. This darker, coarser Jesus might not be the cinnamon-haired, blue-eyed softie I had envisioned as a child, but the man had charm. No conversation with him could ever be dull. He was too good at commanding one's attention, too skilled at forging an instant, intimate connection with nothing more than a glance. You might not know what he was thinking, but he could certainly make you wonder. His very presence emanated a cryptic sort of warmth that was both potent and addictive; no one who had experienced even the briefest of brushes with it could walk away without wanting more.

So why had the woman run off?

Jesus stood up.

I followed his eyes to the horizon and saw thirty people, maybe more, heading toward us on the road. All of them were Samaritans.

Everyone rose to their feet in nervous silence. We were outnumbered already, and still more people were coming. If the Samaritans wanted to make trouble...

"Look there, Bernice," Jesus said with a smile, pointing into the distance as he walked by her. "I think someone has brought us some fruit."

Bernice's jaw dropped. Indeed, a woman near the front of the group was carrying a wide basket filled with what looked like grapes and figs — maybe even some nuts.

"Well, what do you know?" Mary exclaimed. "She didn't run away after all, did she? She only wanted to spread the word."

Looking into Jesus's face as he walked past, I realized that Tamar had been right. He hadn't been content just to sit in Jewish territory and talk about tolerance. He had uprooted every one of us from our comfort zone and brought us to where the Samaritans lived. He had treated the least of them with respect. He had made plain that he would like to help them, too.

Now they were accepting his offer.

I smiled to myself. The man did know how to work people. I studied the faces of those around me, eager to gauge their reactions. Most had been so certain that Jesus's interests lay with their own kind that his actions now made little sense, and their expressions showed it.

But I got it.

For once, I was ahead of the curve.

I watched as Jesus walked out alone to meet the band of hatted, colorfully clad Samaritans.

I sat back down and finished my bread.

*Commentary for Chapter 14 begins on page 261.*

# Chapter 15

Coming together again in Galilee was like a party. The disciples' attempts to preach and heal on their own had been successful, and their self-confidence soared. They had grown closer to each other during their travels, and with their return our whole group began to feel a new and invigorating cohesiveness. Increasingly, the men seemed less hampered by their old attitudes about social customs and the law and were more influenced by Jesus's own behavior. Case in point: Twice now, I had gotten Judas to talk to me.

It had not been easy. I had practically had to court the man. But like a preteen at a middle school dance, all I really wanted was to engage his interest, to get to know him better, to become his friend. My affinity for him had only grown in the time we had spent on the road, and I felt a curious compulsion to try and connect with him intellectually. I would not admit, even to myself, why that might be.

Our covert, piecemeal return to Capernaum had been both effective and enjoyable, allowing a few precious days in which Andrew and Peter could be quietly reunited with their wives and children, and in which young Thomas could marry his betrothed. But Jesus himself could fly under the radar for only so long, and when news of his return leaked out, we were forced to move north into the countryside to give him some breathing room.

Today we were gathered in the middle of nowhere, somewhere between Capernaum and another lakeside town called Bethsaida. We had hoped to reach Bethsaida by nightfall, but the crowd that had followed Jesus out of Capernaum was immense, numbering in the thousands, and instead of turning around for home after a mile or so, they had kept on walking with us. The rabbi's fans were obviously unwilling to give him up so soon, and Jesus had responded to their devotion by pausing in this halfway shady, grassy area to preach.

It was a good crowd, as crowds went. There were no questioning Pharisees and no local elders jockeying for Jesus's favor. There wasn't even much pushing or shoving. The people had sufficient room to spread out, and Jesus's voice carried well over the still, dry air. Only those who were truly dedicated to the rabbi had made the effort to come so far, and their respectfulness showed.

Mary, Joanna, and Susanna had taken their servants and the ever-willing Matthew — who was still in withdrawal from the wheeling-and-dealing rush of his old tax-collecting job — and ridden ahead into Bethsaida to buy food. It had become clear that we would be camping tonight, and we weren't carrying enough with us for a decent supper.

I had stayed behind intentionally to talk to Judas, and as soon as the shopping party departed I began to look for him. Opportunities for meaningful discourse with the man were rare. He wouldn't talk when there was a chance of anyone overhearing us; nor would he allow himself to be alone with me.

I found him standing by himself on the hill behind Jesus, isolated, but in plain sight.

*Perfect.*

I walked toward him. He was surveying the crowd with obvious unease; his young face lined with worry, every muscle in his body tense. I stopped my approach five feet short of him and looked where he was looking, but the scene below looked wonderfully peaceful. "What do you see?" I asked, confused. "What's so alarming?"

Judas was, as Mary had said, "a bit of a fussbudget." But I didn't hold his anal-retentive streak against him. The "go with the flow" vibe that dominated our travels was all well and good, but every team needed some detail-oriented person to keep his feet on the ground and his ears open, and when it came to subtle moves of strategy and negotiation — particularly with white-bearded synagogue types — Judas was our go-to man. He had appointed himself the political watchdog of the group, and he continued his vigilance in that quarter despite the good-natured mocking of his more laissez-faire comrades.

I admired him immensely for that.

He turned and looked at me, his dark eyes transparent in their assessment of whether responding to me would be prudent. I tried hard not to smile, knowing that if anything would make him pull back, that would. He was unmarried, having lost a wife in childbirth shortly before he met Jesus, and even though he was considerably younger than me, I didn't want to give the wrong impression. And I *could*, thank you very much. For someone old enough to be a grandmother, I didn't look that bad.

At least, I didn't think I did. Then again, I hadn't seen a mirror since Magdala.

His eyes left mine. He sighed and looked out over the crowd

again. "What do you see, Rachel?"

My eyebrows rose. I scanned the crowd, but still saw nothing unexpected. "I see a huge number of people who are extremely fond of Jesus."

He nodded. "That's what I see, too. But do you know what Herod sees?"

My heart skipped a beat. I had long since decided to discount whatever Bible stories I still remembered. Too much of what I had been taught as a child was different from what I was experiencing here. Too much of the rest of it, I didn't like.

*All that stuff was wrong.*

"Herod should see a peaceable man with a peaceable message, who poses no threat to either him or the Romans," I said stubbornly.

Judas's gaze slid sideways toward me. His deep voice softened. "You're an intelligent woman, Rachel. You know better."

*No*, my mind screamed, *I don't*.

"Anyone who can command this kind of following among the common people is a threat to Herod," Judas continued gravely. "It doesn't matter what Jesus's message is. He's amassing power and influence. That's all that matters. The last thing Herod wants is another Ezekias or Judah on his hands. That's why he killed the Baptist."

I suppressed a shiver. As much as I wanted to believe that the people around me were as peace-loving as my own neighbors, and that wars would always be something that happened someplace other than where I was, I could not escape the dire reality of Judas's words. I knew that he was referring to peasant revolts that had brought unspeakable bloodshed to Galilee. I had heard them mentioned before. I knew far more about them than I wanted to.

"But it would all be a misunderstanding," I insisted, aware of how naive I sounded, but unable to stop myself. "Executing the Baptist made the people hate Herod even more than they already did. Surely he can see that. If he understands that Jesus isn't preaching rebellion, he should realize the benefits of turning a blind eye to him. Now more than ever."

Judas shook his head. "You talk like Herod is a reasonable man. You give him too much credit. Our esteemed tetrarch has the maturity and intellectual acumen of a ten-year-old." He breathed out heavily. "A ten-year-old with a very big stick."

I stiffened. I was aware that nepotism, as opposed to stellar leadership skills, had put Herod in power, but still I had hoped for the best. I should have known better. "There must be something we can do," I asserted.

He nodded. "I believe there is, yes."

I looked at him hopefully.

"Jesus has to start cooperating with the Jewish leadership. Rome tolerates them as a matter of policy; if he stayed firmly under their auspices, he might be safe. But if he continues to distance himself from the establishment, the Romans will consider him out of control, and a threat."

"But Jesus—" I began, and stopped myself. Judas knew full well how Jesus felt about "the establishment." That's why he looked so worried in the first place. "Have you talked to him?"

"All the time, Rachel," he answered ruefully. "All the time."

A sick feeling welled up in my middle, and with no further words I turned and walked back down the hillside toward the disciples' wives, eager to surround myself with more positive energy. The specter Judas had raised was too grim for words, and I refused to contemplate it. Particularly not now, when everything was going so well. I would discuss the issue with Mary, and she would reassure me. Judas was overreacting. That was all.

I knew nothing.

I arrived to find Bernice in a tizzy.

"Jesus said *what?*" she demanded of her husband, who had reached the women's resting spot just before me.

"He wants us to feed them," Philip repeated. His calm, peaceable demeanor was the perfect complement to his wife's control-freakishness. But when push came to shove, he was no doormat, either.

Bernice's eyes widened with disbelief. "*All* of them? But there are thousands of people here! Does he have any idea how much that would cost?"

"About eight month's wages, I figure," Philip replied smoothly. "And yes, I told him that."

"But Mary isn't even here!" Bernice protested, "She's already gone to town, and Joanna and Susanna went with her." She looked at me. "Perhaps if we sent Rachel after them—"

Philip shook his head. "Jesus doesn't want us to buy food. He said to just look and see what we have."

Bernice's face turned reddish-purple. "What we *have?* We don't even have enough for ourselves! That's why they went to town in the first place!"

"He asked for what we have," Philip countered, his voice firm. "Let's just give it to him, shall we?"

Bernice bit her lip. She began to inspect the baskets and bags we had unloaded from the donkeys earlier, flipping open lids and untying knots, muttering to herself as she went. "Why couldn't people have brought their own food? It should be their own responsibility to think about that before they go traipsing off into the countryside... Rachel, check that basket Mary left, will you? And what about their own money? We sent someone ahead to buy food; they could do the same if they used their heads. It's called *planning*, people. *Planning!*"

I helped the other women scramble to sift through the supplies, even the meager personal ones some of the group had left with the donkeys. But most of what was brought had been consumed at lunchtime, and I found only one small loaf of bread. It appeared to be a secret stash of Joanna's, and I begged her forgiveness as I lifted it, knowing she would do the same if Jesus asked. The rabbi had a way of making you *want* to please him.

"If he'd given us even an hour's notice," Bernice continued to mutter, "I could have tried to do some baking. I've got flour, but they can't eat that..."

As much as Bernice's brusque, superior manner annoyed me, I could sympathize. Her strength was competent management. She was organized, efficient, and always prepared. I knew that she wasn't really upset about the inconvenience of having to scrounge for food. What bothered her was her own inability to deliver what the rabbi had asked for. Failing was an insult to her pride. Never mind that no one else blamed her; she was her own harshest critic.

The women reconvened, and Bernice consolidated all our findings into one basket, which she gave to her son. "Here," she said miserably, pushing the boy out towards his waiting father. "It's all we've got."

Philip looked down into the basket. "Barley loaves," he proclaimed soberly. "Didn't we have some fish?"

"They're on the bottom," Bernice snapped. "We ate the bigger ones."

Andrew approached us with haste, his wife Shua close on his heels. The two were a horribly mismatched couple. Shua was as unimaginative and inert as Andrew was bold and adventuresome, and their lackluster relationship was almost painful to behold. It was exactly what I had expected most arranged marriages to be; yet I had noticed that the two were more accommodating to each other than a lot of "happy" couples I knew.

"How much do we have?" Andrew asked anxiously, eyeing the little boy's basket.

"Not enough," Philip answered, steering his son forward. "But we brought everything we had."

Shua looked down into the basket herself. "I'm sure Jesus will think of something," she said lightly.

Both men looked at her. Then, saying nothing, they turned and started off toward Jesus. She followed.

The other women settled back down in the shade, and I joined them.

"I hope Shua stays with us this time," Tamar said idly. "I do believe she really missed Andrew."

"I told her to go!" exclaimed Peter's wife, Helah. Helah spent as much time with us as she could whenever we were close to Capernaum, and I liked her immensely, even though she, like her overbearing husband, had scared me to death on our first meeting. If Andrew and Shua were opposites, she and Peter were twins. She was huge for a woman, not as tall as Susanna, but with twice the brawn. Like her husband, she was loud, passionate, opinionated, and prone to impulse. But she was also outgoing, good-natured, and loyal to the bone. They were closer in age than most couples, which meant either that Peter had married young for a man or that he had married an "old maid" in her early twenties. However it had happened, they were clearly a love match; both wore their devotion to each other and to their children on their sleeves.

Under different circumstances, the intrepid Helah would have loved traveling with Jesus herself, whether Peter came along or not. But she was responsible for a large and needy household which included her own brood of offspring, several orphaned nieces and nephews, Peter and Andrew's elderly parents, and a frail great aunt. Shua, who lived under the same roof, shared some of that burden. But either Helah didn't find her sister-in-law much help or she genuinely wanted the younger woman to be happier.

"She needs to spend more time with her husband," Helah continued. "I keep telling her that. She should realize by now that Andrew's never going to stay home. First it was the Baptist, then Jesus. The man was born to roam. If she wants another baby, I told her, she's got to go where he goes. The little tykes don't pop out of pomegranates."

Leah chuckled. Naomi smiled. Even Bernice offered a smirk. Bernice's ten-year-old daughter Elizabeth, who was tending to her preschool-age sister Eglah, hid a knowing look that disturbed me. Tamar gazed off into the distance, her lovely doe eyes melancholy.

Watching the heartsick teen coddle her little nephew made my chest ache. I knew how empty Tamar must feel. How guilty. How concerned.

James would *not* divorce her.

If he tried, I would personally skewer him.

"What do you think Jesus will do with the food?" Leah asked, changing the subject in deference to her sister-in-law. "I mean, how will he decide who to give it to?"

"It'll be a mess," Bernice proclaimed, becoming flustered all over again. "He can't pick favorites, and there isn't enough to go around, no matter how small he tries to break the pieces. I don't see why he bothered to take any at all. If he could have just waited until we sent someone to town..."

I stood up, walked several yards away, and leaned my back against a tree. My tolerance for Bernice came and went, and at the moment it was gone. I didn't really care what Jesus did with the food. It hardly seemed important when Tamar was worried about being abandoned and Judas was worrying about Herod. I could not dispel the sense of foreboding Judas's words had put into my head, and Bernice's prattle only aggravated me further. Why did the woman have to obsess over every little detail of our existence? Didn't we all have more important things to worry about?

*Hypocrite.*

My teeth gritted.

Okay, fine. So I was a worrier, too. But my situation was different. If I had lost sleep when the elementary school announced it was cutting five minutes off recess, it was because I cared. And if I had led campaigns to have the middle school tennis courts refurbished and the vending machines removed from the high school cafeteria, it was because I saw a need. *Someone* had to battle against unimaginative class parties, the exposed springs in the bus seats, the unfairness of the vetting process for the gifted program, overzealous soccer coaches, under-zealous soccer coaches, the inequitable distribution of homework, burned-out tenured teachers, poorly timed in-service days, the lousy catering at the volunteer luncheons, those awful flickering lights in the high school chemistry lab, the clashing color scheme of the new auditorium, the ridiculous schedule for eighth-grade band camp, the off-brand hot dogs at the baseball concession stand, and those obnoxious slacker "working" parents who made people like me do all the work.

Right?

I was doing it for my kids, after all. I wanted them to have the best. Not materially speaking — necessarily — but in terms of their experience growing up. It was my job as a parent to make that happen. It was the most important job I had.

Was that so wrong?

My eyes returned to Bernice. She had fetched her needle while she talked and was mending a hole in little Eglah's tunic. Four-year-old Eglah, who could already pound dough, pluck a chicken, and clean dishes. Her older sister chopped vegetables, carried water, wove baskets, and could make goat cheese.

Ryan still couldn't run a load of laundry.

*Stop that!*

These were different times; I could not compare. Put Bernice in my neighborhood and she would be complaining about the mailman throwing his cigarette butts on the lawn every bit as vehemently as I did. And her kids would be just as whiny and incapable.

I winced. I hadn't meant to think that.

Things were different for Bernice; her priorities were different. She loved her children, but encouraging them to do more for themselves was what good parenting meant to her, and to all these mothers. It was a necessity of their survival. Even the most hyperactive and anxiety-ridden among these women had too many subsistence-related issues to dwell on to even consider obsessing over the minutiae of their children's lives.

And that was too bad.

Peter and Helah's teenaged son approached me quietly, holding out a basket. I looked down at the salted fish and bread, took out a small barley loaf that looked like the one I'd taken from Joanna, broke it in half, and put the other half back. "Thank you, Aaron," I replied absently. The shy boy turned and left me without a word, then offered the basket to a cluster of young men standing just downhill.

I bit into the bread. It was unusually tasty.

*Jesus will think of something.*

I was in mid swallow when the light dawned. I pulled the bread away from my face and looked around.

Everyone was eating. As far as the eye could see, the disciples were wandering around with baskets, offering people the same fish and bread that Aaron had just offered to me. The crowd was all smiles. Many of them were cheering.

It all seemed eerily familiar.

I stared suspiciously at the hunk of bread in my hand, breathed out with a huff, and took another bite.

At some point — I'm not even sure when — I had given up trying to figure out *how* Jesus did what he did. The mechanisms no longer mattered. Whether he had broken a basic law of physics by creating matter, or whether he had tapped into some existing food source no one else was aware of, the result was the same. The crowd had gotten food. The boy in Nain was alive.

The people were paying attention.

When I was growing up, I had envisioned Jesus as a sort of touring shaman, wowing people with magic and bolts of lightning, perhaps throwing in a message from his sponsor during the breaks. But what I had seen here was nothing like that. First off, the "miracles" lacked mood music. Without the backdrop of a swelling orchestra, one was never sure exactly when something sensational was happening. Furthermore, for all his brilliance as a motivational speaker, Jesus was a lousy showman. When bizarre things happened not only was he reluctant to take credit for them, he didn't even like to talk about them. His script was all sponsor, all the time. The theatrics just boosted the ratings.

If Jesus himself didn't dwell on the mechanics, why should I?

I finished my bread. The rabbi was preaching again. Sitting behind him, I couldn't hear every word he said. But by now I knew the themes, and I was in no mood to appreciate the irony of the fact that today he had chosen — once again — to address the evils of worry.

*Look at the birds of the air...*

I sighed. I had heard this one before, and though he used various examples at different times, the gist of it was always the same. *Don't sweat the small stuff.* Unfortunately, what he considered "small stuff" in this day and age was pretty much the sum total of my affairs.

*Where your treasure is, your heart will be also...*

My heart was with my treasures. I suppose that was true. My heart, and my mind, were necessarily consumed with the complicated trappings of modern life. But that was hardly my fault. These people couldn't begin to understand how much more complex life was for me, how many more issues I battled every day, how much more I *had* to worry just to keep up with it all.

"Rachel?" Bernice whispered as she came upon me. "Could you help us? We need to hang a screen for a latrine. There's no cover anywhere around here."

I grimaced. "Sure."

Bernice prattled on as we walked. "All these women out here — no thought as to what they would do. All spindly little trees, no bushes anywhere. Not that the men aren't just as much of a problem. This many people out here with no holes dug! I've always thought that not burying waste led to illness, and I'm not taking any chances on the young ones picking up something out here. Too many die from the diarrhea, you know. Although I suppose now, Jesus could help..."

I tried to shut my ears. Okay, so Bernice's worries might be more weighty than mine, but I was still in no mood to hear them.

"The way he's fed everybody is amazing, isn't it?" she continued. "But you know, the big piece of linen we've been using for the screen is getting really frayed. No one's complained, but it bothers me. I've had Elizabeth mend it twice, but we could really use a new one. I've half a mind to ask Mary about it. Then we could take the old one and use it for rags, because even our supply of those is running thin, and you can't buy scraps at a decent price anywhere..."

A smile tugged at my lips. More weighty worries, indeed. Multiplying bread and fish was a neat trick, but curing perfectionists like Bernice and me of fretting for the sheer sport of it? Now *that* would be a miracle.

The noise of the crowd swelled. Understanding of what had transpired had been slow to spread, but as it did, excitement grew. When Jesus's voice could no longer be heard above the clamor, he wrapped up his sermon and moved to regroup with the disciples. I watched as Judas hung back, reluctant to leave his post. Amidst the thousands of happy faces around me, his visage stuck out — troubled, almost sorrowful. His head turned in my direction. His gaze caught mine.

*This is just what I was talking about,* his expression conveyed, sailing over the jubilating masses to strike me like a cold wind. *It will only make things worse.*

I averted my eyes, staring down at my sandals.

Sweet, thoughtful Judas was a worrier, too.

If only his fears were as trivial.

*Commentary for Chapter 15 begins on page 264.*

# Chapter 16

I could not get Judas's words out of my mind. With every step we took, with every new and doting crowd that gathered around Jesus, the sick feeling in my stomach only grew. I kept assuring myself that I had no real foreknowledge, that nothing I thought I knew could be trusted to be accurate. Like what Jesus looked like. Like how he had traveled around Israel in one neat circular path with exactly twelve all-male disciples whom he had demanded abandon their wives and children. Like how Mary Magdalene was a young, sexy prostitute who had a thing for him (and possibly vice versa), and how Judas was some shifty-eyed, avaricious villain whom all the other disciples had been too naive to see through.

I had been wrong about all those things. I could be wrong about the rest of it. Was it so inconceivable that someone somewhere had made a mistake about how Jesus had died? Dramatized? Embellished? Fabricated altogether?

I was not ashamed to hope. I didn't care one whit about the world's salvation or whatever abstract theological concepts such stark brutality was supposed to have accomplished. Jesus wasn't some cartoon character. He was a man I happened to be very fond of, and I didn't want him to get hurt. I would be upset if he so much as stubbed his toe — the horrifying images that flooded my mind every time I looked at him now were intolerable.

I refused to believe it. It didn't *have* to happen.

Judas was working on it.

I pushed a needle through the thick leather strap I was attempting to mend and tried to ignore the festering pain in my middle. I had had an ulcer in college, and I had survived it without prescription drugs. I would get through this one, too. Even if we were headed to Jerusalem.

*Jerusalem.*

"Are you all right, Rachel?" Mary asked, eyeing me critically. "You look a little green."

"Just a sour stomach," I answered. "Nothing serious."

"Well, I hope it isn't catching," she responded. "Bernice has been looking a little off, too."

I glanced up at Bernice, who had indeed been quieter than usual the last few days. But she looked well enough at the moment.

"We'll be fine," I murmured. *It's not our health that's in jeopardy.*

I fussed with the strap from one of the donkeys' saddles, which was close to wearing through and needed reinforcing. I hadn't volunteered to do any mending before, but the task hadn't looked that difficult, and I had become desperate to keep myself busy. Naturally the job was much harder than it looked, and I had already expended three times the effort that Tamar or Bernice would have. But the point was not to finish quickly, or to impress anyone. Naomi might not be the brightest bulb in the chandelier, but none of the women were idiots. They already knew full well that I was incompetent with manual skills. Never mind that I was great at using a minimum bias approach to determine the rate relativities for a multiple rating variables class plan. That didn't mean squat.

We were visiting a town along the pilgrimage trail. Jesus was in its synagogue; the women were waiting outside. This particular synagogue had an unusually large outdoor courtyard, well-planted with shade trees, and we had enjoyed our visit here once before. But this time the mood was different.

The townspeople had greeted Jesus as enthusiastically as ever — in fact, more so. Since our last visit we had traveled northeast of Capernaum all the way up to Tyre, on the Mediterranean Sea. Jesus had preached to crowds in Phoenicia and Caesarea Philippi to the north, and throughout the area of the Decapolis to the east. Rumors of his feeding the crowds, calming storms, and walking on water had spread throughout all of Palestine. The people loved him.

The establishment did not.

At the moment, he was facing the latter. A group of officials had met him at the city gates and ushered him through the streets and straight to the synagogue, where other Pharisees and church elders waited inside. The disciples stuck close by him; to a one, visibly agitated. Even Jesus seemed unusually solemn.

I sat under a tree and churned out stomach acid.

The grillings by the Pharisees were getting worse. More frequent, more intense, more combative. Judas had told me about them in some detail; ironically, I seemed to have become his chief confidant. The other disciples, disconcerted by his doom-and-gloom attitude, were beginning to view him more as a detractor to the cause than a defender of Jesus, and their lack of cooperation distressed him greatly. Knowing that Judas was breaking any number of mores by unburdening his concerns to me, I tried to be supportive. I listened, I sympathized, I encouraged. But when it came to convincing Jesus not to make things worse for himself, Judas was clearly getting nowhere.

Hypocrisy in religious leaders was something the rabbi couldn't stand, and he wouldn't let it slide, no matter how uncomfortable or inconvenient the alternative. We could all see his point. The further up in the religious hierarchy an individual was, the more likely he seemed to act with intolerance and even cruelty. To many of these men, upholding the law was more important than exhibiting compassion and love, and Jesus had pointed out the error in such thinking over and over, in various ways and with countless examples, but only rarely did any of them get it. Personally, I figured they didn't want to. They were too comfortable with what they had and where they were, and they had no intention of letting some charismatic peasant screw up a good thing — whether he was right or not.

But Jesus continued to call a spade a spade, continued to insist that people were more important than the law, and thus continued to tick off virtually every religious official he came into contact with. So the pattern was set: the hypocrites got their well-deserved upbraidings, the people and the disciples watched with admiration and delight, and Judas chewed his lip until it bled.

Today's session did not appear to be going well. I could hear Jesus's raised voice ringing from inside the synagogue, speaking beautiful words about how the greatest commandment was for people to love both God and each other. But I knew that it was falling on deaf ears when Judas popped out and stared at me, hard. He was frustrated near to tears.

My stomach burned. I had tried to share Judas's concerns with Mary, but she would hear nothing about Jesus's not knowing best. She was as exasperated by Judas's negativity as any of them, and our conversation was fruitless. I had not brought it up again.

A shrill scream from the street made me puncture myself with the needle. Quickly, I squeezed my thumb to make it bleed. The last thing I needed now was tetanus.

The scream came again. The women stood up, watching the courtyard gates. "What was that?"

"It sounded like a woman."

"A woman in pain!"

"Or frightened."

The courtyard gates burst open, kicking up a cloud of dust on the dry ground. Several men burst through, and I recognized them. They were some of the elders who had whisked Jesus into the synagogue earlier. Not all the officials had stayed to hear Jesus preach; many had left right after delivering him.

They were up to something.

Judas turned to the newcomers, squaring his shoulders. He said something to them I couldn't hear, but whatever it was, it made no impression. One of them shoved by him and barged on into the synagogue.

"Stop it! Leave me alone!"

The unseen woman's cries sent a sharp chill down my spine, and I dropped the strap and sewing needle at my feet. Through the gates, more men were coming, more of the same well-dressed official types. They were dragging a woman with them by the arms, and as she struggled and cried one of the men caught her hair in his fist to propel her. They forced her into the courtyard and shoved her onto the ground beside the synagogue steps, slamming the gates on the clamoring townspeople behind them.

"Oh no," whispered Susanna, standing beside me.

"What is it?" I demanded, frightened. "What's going on?"

The woman's forehead was bleeding. Trails of blood wound their way back into her hair, over her ear, and down one hollow cheek. She was young, perhaps in her early twenties, and pitifully thin. Her tunic appeared to have been torn in the struggle, baring one bruised shoulder. She was a strikingly pretty woman, with high cheekbones, large dark eyes, and a long, thin nose. But she also seemed unnaturally frail, as if poor nutrition or illness had left her a shell of herself. As she lay on the ground, bleeding into the dirt, her small chest heaving for breath, she reminded me of a China doll, tottering on a high shelf, moving helplessly closer to the edge as an earthquake rumbled around her.

The men were holding something. Amorphous blobs were in their hands; whole groups, baseball-sized or larger, were cradled in their arms.

*Rocks.*

"She must have committed a crime," Susanna answered, her own voice uneven. "Something punishable by stoning."

A strong heat flickered up my veins, displacing the previous chill. *A stoning?* No. That wasn't possible. Only a sadist would hurl a rock at a helpless female who lay crying on the ground. These men weren't Roman soldiers, or even common rabble. They were church leaders.

"They can't do that!" I croaked, not caring who heard me.

Mary did. She stepped up to my other side. "No, they can't," she answered, her voice deadly calm. "Not unless they want trouble. Only the Romans can carry out executions."

"Then what are they doing?" I pressed.

Other men began to pour out of the synagogue. We could not see its entrance, as we were behind it and to the side, but we could see Jesus as he walked down the corner of the steps near us and sat down on the ground, a few feet away from the woman, not looking at her. The disciples were either still in the synagogue or standing farther back on the steps; but the officials were amassing in the open courtyard, several of them scanning the ground for more ammunition.

*No.* It couldn't happen.

"This *woman*," announced one of the Pharisees, his voice dripping with derision as he clutched a sharp-edged, grapefruit-sized stone in his hand, "was caught in the act of adultery." He kicked up a cloud of dust in her direction, then turned fiery eyes on Jesus. "So, teacher, what do you say?"

Mary swore softly.

"What?" I begged.

"They've set a trap," she murmured. "If Jesus condones the stoning, he'll be breaking Roman law. But if he condemns it, they'll say he has turned his back on the laws of Moses. That he is disloyal to his own nation."

My face flushed with heat. Anger pulsed through me.

"So what do we do?"

Mary's head gave a little shake. "I don't think there's anything we can do. If she was caught in the act, there must be witnesses..."

"You don't see the *man*, do you?" Susanna hissed. Her fists, like mine, were clenched with fury. "It takes two to commit adultery! I bet those jackals let him go."

"I can't watch this!" Leah exclaimed miserably. She turned, with baby Jesse in his sling, and walked back into the grove of trees. Several of the other women followed her.

All of the officials had rocks in their hands now. The woman had turned her face to the ground, sobbing. Peter stepped up behind Jesus, ready, I was sure, for anything. Jesus merely sat, not looking at any of them, not saying a word. He scratched in the dirt with his finger.

I felt as though I would explode.

"He *can't* let them do it!" I insisted.

Mary's voice turned defensive. Defensive of Jesus. "He can't stop them, Rachel. The law is clear."

"She has to be punished!" one of the men shouted.

Others rumbled their agreement. "She is an adulteress!"

"It is the law!"

My mind roiled. I saw torture chambers, racks. Spears and bludgeons. Sawed-off shotguns, assault rifles. Train cars headed to Auschwitz. Missiles. Bombs.

If love was ageless, so was hate. Sadism and cruelty survived in every age. Didn't stonings still happen in some parts of the world, even in my own time? Perhaps where I had come from such acts of brutality were less common, less accepted, less *visible*. But the motivations behind it were the same. Hostility, raw and biting. Hostility born of frustration, or anger, or oppression, or hunger, or hopelessness, or even boredom. Hostility that was almost always, somehow, conveniently clothed as justice.

But it was *wrong*. It was always wrong. And I didn't care who was poised to accept it, including Mary. I didn't care if this woman had cheated on her husband. I didn't care if she had killed her husband. She didn't deserve to be pelted with rocks by a mob of angry, heartless men; she didn't deserve to die a slow, agonizing death through blunt trauma and loss of blood.

And I would *not* stand by and watch it happen.

My eyes rested on Jesus with such intensity I was sure they could bore through the back of his head. I could not see his expression. I could not tell what he was writing in the dirt. But as I watched him, sitting there, ignoring the cacophony around him with his usual unflappable calm, I began to feel a flicker of hope.

"Stone her!" an angry voice yelled.

"Yes, stone her!"

"Are you going to answer or not, Rabbi?"

Jesus raised his head. I held my breath. I had no idea what I could possibly do if the stoning began, other than go down with her. But I had to do something. And that was *me*, Rachel. The woman who had stiffed the neighborhood charity drive this year because she wanted a time share at Hilton Head. The woman who had once blocked a handicapped spot at the mall because her feet hurt and she was too lazy to move the shopping cart out of the way so that her SUV could fit in the next slot over. Truth time: I was nobody's angel. But right here, right now, the gloves were off. And if I felt this strongly, no one with as much natural compassion as Jesus could possibly stand by and do nothing. Maybe the others were blinded by what they viewed as normal, or by what they viewed as just punishment for an especially grievous sin. But divine or not, a man of Jesus's intelligence should see right through such cultural blinders. He had to.

He would.

Jesus straightened and faced the officials. "If any one of you has never sinned," he said plainly, refusing to rush, "he should be the first to throw a stone at her."

*Yes!*

A warm jolt of victory rushed through my limbs; hot tears sprang behind my eyes. I felt a bit sheepish at the deja vu his words touched off. The scenario was a familiar one; I should have remembered it.

I hadn't. But I had still believed the best of him, hadn't I?

Even when Mary wasn't sure.

Jesus sat back down and resumed scratching in the dirt. The officials stared at him. Then they scowled. A few started to speak, then stopped themselves.

"Dear God, he's brilliant," Mary whispered with adoration.

I smiled.

The men grumbled amongst themselves, their faces hot with fury. Finally, an elderly man with long white hair threw down his rock in disgust. The gray-haired Pharisee beside him did also. One by one, more followed, casting their rocks to the ground with vehemence, a few coming close to — but never actually hitting — the woman on the ground. Before long every one of the men had thrown down his rock and left, either through the gates or back into the synagogue itself. I could not see any of the disciples. The woman lifted her head, slowly, and scanned the courtyard. Only Jesus was anywhere near her.

He stood and came closer. He offered her his hand.

The woman looked up at him, bewildered. Her chest still rocked with every breath; the bloodied side of her face was caked with dirt. Her eyes met his. She stretched out her hand.

Jesus helped her to feet, speaking to her softly as he did so. I could not hear his words, but they seemed to both calm and baffle her at the same time. She answered something back.

Jesus responded with more words and a smile. Then he let go of her hand and retreated to the synagogue steps, moving out of sight.

The woman stood where she was for several seconds, staring after him, and I could see her small frame shivering. Finally, she took a deep breath and turned. With dizzy, staggering steps she moved toward the courtyard gate. She opened it a fraction and looked out.

Her whole body trembled.

"Poor thing," Susanna murmured beside me. "It'll be no better for her out there."

My head swiveled to the birder. "They won't still stone her!"

"No," Susanna agreed. "But she's been labeled as an adulteress now. No one will take her in. If she has no money—"

I was already walking.

I was sick of it. Sick of this whole, annoying sexist society. Men could cheat on their wives with abandon; cheating wives *were* abandoned. Jesus's quick thinking had saved this girl from a slow agonizing death, but what now? What exactly was she supposed to do with herself? Prostitute? Beg? Die an even slower death from starvation or exposure?

My feet pounded on the dirt. *Lousy, insensitive, stupid men... And where are her women friends? Why can't any of them stand up for her? If I owned a house in this town...*

I had a tent, didn't I?

*Ha!*

I was almost out of breath myself when I reached her, and my face was still flushed with anger. I drew in a lungful of air and tried to calm myself.

"Wait! Don't go out there," I told her, trying my best to sound sympathetic and friendly, despite my desire to pound something.

The girl jumped a foot. When she turned and saw me, she relaxed a little, but her eyes were still fraught with terror. "I don't have any choice," she whispered, her voice still ragged from crying.

Looking at her closer, I could see that she was younger than I thought. Twenty. Perhaps even eighteen or nineteen. Her skin was soft and unblemished. Her thick, perfectly formed eyebrows reminded me of Bekka's.

I put a hand to her face, brushing the dirt and clotting blood from her temple. "You don't have anywhere to go, do you?"

She shook her head, then winced, as if the action itself was painful. "My father won't... take me back," she answered in halting phrases. "My husband... if he sees me... he'll kill me himself."

"And not be prosecuted, most likely," came a sharp voice over my shoulder. Susanna was standing behind me. For a tall woman, she could move like a cat. "You can't go back out there, honey," she added, her voice softer.

The girl let out another sob. "He told me not to sin anymore. He saved my life. But what... what will I..."

We didn't need to ask who "he" was. Susanna stepped forward and laid a comforting hand on the girl's arm. "It's not possible," she said in her direct, no-nonsense manner. "Not out there. No girl without family or funds can survive within the law. You'd have to steal or sell yourself to eat."

The girl's eyes spilled over with fresh tears. "But he said—"

Frustration reddened my cheeks again. Susanna had a point. Why had Jesus told the girl such a thing and then walked off? Where were the disciples? How could they all be so blasted shortsighted?

"What I'm sure he *meant,*" I interrupted, "was that you should stay with us. We can help you get to another town. Jerusalem, maybe. Nobody knows everybody there," I quoted from Mary, thinking fast. "We could find someone to take you in, someone who wouldn't have to know your past. I have money. We'll work something out. Jesus has friends all over who would be happy to do us a favor."

"Absolutely," Susanna agreed, showing her buck teeth in a smile.

The girl's back straightened a little. She looked from Susanna to me as if we were fairies, fluttering about her with pixie dust. "You would do that for me?"

We nodded. Tiny sparkles of joy illuminated the depths of her eyes. *Just like Bekka's.*

"I can work," she insisted, her voice bucking up. "I mean, I don't mind working for someone else. As long as I'm away from here, and safe..."

"You'll be safe," Susanna assured.

But even as the words came out of her mouth, a grim worry churned my stomach again. We could hardly protect the woman ourselves, if her husband demanded her return. The disciples would have to help us. They would have to agree to leave town promptly, and quietly, without calling attention to her, and if worse came to worst...

Morbid thoughts spun in my head. Would the disciples even care? How much sympathy would they feel for a pretty young wife who had cuckolded her husband? Jesus was above all that; he had stopped the stoning. But then where had he gone? How could he just leave the poor girl with no one to help—

I glanced over my shoulder. Jesus was standing on the synagogue steps, watching us. The disciples were all there, too, right behind him. None of them had said a word, but they were close enough to overhear.

Jesus hadn't gone anywhere. He had only stepped out of the way.

"Thank you," I heard the girl gush, her voice shaking with sobs again. "I don't know how to thank you."

I couldn't answer her, because Jesus had caught my eye. He was smiling at me.

At *me*.

*Good job, Rachel.*

My heart thudded like a jackhammer. Jesus's eyes moved to Susanna, and he smiled at her, too. But the first one had been mine.

Maybe I wasn't completely worthless after all. I might be lousy with a needle, or bread baking, or a live rooster, or with just about anything else that mattered to basic survival. But I had done *something* right. Jesus had said so.

He was proud of me.

"Come along," I said brightly, circling the girl's waist with an arm. "We'll get you cleaned up. That cut looks pretty nasty. What's your name, by the way?"

"Mahlah," she answered.

The other disciples watched in silence, their faces neither approving nor disapproving, as we marched the girl around the corner of the synagogue and back to where the other women waited among the trees.

I had been anticipating some amount of prejudice on the part of the men. But I was not prepared to encounter it from the women.

Leah, Bernice, and Naomi stood squarely in front as we approached, their faces drawn tight with concern. Joanna stood to the side, munching on dried fish and failing to hide the amusement in her eyes. Tamar and Priscilla, Thomas's new wife, hung back where we couldn't see them. Mary was leaning against a tree, facing away.

"This is Mahlah," Susanna announced, her voice not without a touch of threat. "Jesus has saved her life, and we have offered to take her out of town with us, to help her get set up someplace else."

None of the women said anything.

My face grew hot again. "Jesus wants us to welcome her," I added, with emphasis on the name.

Bernice cleared her throat. "We are all glad that he stopped the stoning," she said without expression. "But the fact remains that this woman is an adulteress."

Mahlah wilted beside me. Susanna put an arm around her shoulders.

I left them and stepped up to Leah. Bernice's persnickety version of piety was a given, and Naomi thought whatever anyone else told her to think. But Leah ought to know better. Leah was a feminist in the making; she just didn't know it.

"Leah," I said in a low voice, hoping Mahlah would not overhear. "She is a girl just like you, who happened to make a mistake."

Leah's eyes widened in surprise. "A mistake?" she said incredulously. "Eating pork is a mistake! She willingly betrayed her own husband, in the worst possible way! She's not like us, Rachel. She is a *criminal.*"

I stared at her a moment, trying hard to understand. My own society could certainly go overboard when it came to making excuses for bad behavior, and being a believer in personal accountability, I found the tendency frustrating. But the opposite approach was no better. This was accountability taken too far and applied too rigidly. Extenuating circumstances *could* exist. Besides, there was also a lot to be said for clean slates and second chances.

"But why did she do it?" I whispered, holding Leah's gaze. "You don't know what her life was like. Her husband could have been horribly cruel. Or, for all we know, the other man could have forced her. Just look at her, Leah. She's broken, and she's terrified. Criminal or not, she's no threat to any of us. She's just a desperate young woman who needs our help. And our kindness."

Leah's brown eyes moistened. "I don't know, Rachel," she whispered miserably.

But we both knew she did.

I looked behind her, and caught Tamar's eyes as well. Sweet, gentle Tamar would never hurt a fly. But did she have the courage to stand up to Bernice?

She blinked back at me, willing, but weak.

"Mary," Susanna called, her gruff voice demanding. "Tell them what Jesus would want."

All eyes turned toward the Magdalene. My pulse began to throb again. We all knew that Susanna had little respect for authority of any kind. But nobody, short of Jesus, told Mary what to do. She was our unquestioned leader; she was Jesus's own confidant. He talked to her as much as he talked to any of his disciples, a point which no one, particularly Peter, failed to notice. Mary had tolerated Susanna's audacity with good humor thus far. But now was hardly the time to push. If Mary refused to welcome Mahlah, there was no way the girl could stay and camp with us.

"Please, Mary," I added solicitously.

Mary straightened and turned toward us. She walked slowly to where Mahlah stood, huddled against Susanna's towering frame, still trembling. The cut on the girl's temple was starting to bleed again.

The look on Mary's face was inscrutable, and as she reached the frightened girl I suffered a panic of doubt. Surely, Mary would accept her. Mary knew Jesus well. She understood.

Didn't she?

Mary reached out a wrinkled hand and touched Mahlah's trembling chin. "Did Jesus forgive you?" she asked.

Mahlah swallowed. Then she nodded. "He... he said that if none of the men condemned me, then neither would he."

I watched, my heart warming, as a smile crossed Mary's face. "Well then, none of us will condemn you, either. Will we, Bernice?"

Bernice stiffened. But to her credit, she didn't look all that upset. She might even have looked a little relieved. "Of course not," she said shortly. "Welcome, Mahlah."

"Welcome, Mahlah," the other women responded. Leah smiled and gave the other girl's hand a squeeze. Joanna offered a hug. Tamar was the last to speak to her, only because she was busy wetting a clean rag to wash the wound. I watched the other women take charge with a surge of pure pleasure.

They were good people. All of them.

Even me.

*Commentary for Chapter 16 begins on page 267.*

# Chapter 17

We were camping in Judea, across the Jordan. Dusk had fallen, and dinner had been served.

Mahlah was sitting quietly by herself a little ways behind the women's fire, struggling in the dim light to mend her only tunic at the same time she was wearing it.

I spied an opportunity. I went and sat down beside her.

Mahlah wasn't much of a talker. I had tried several times to get her to open up to me about her past and her problems, but the girl was as timorous as a fawn. She acted as if she considered herself our slave rather than our friend, a view which I noticed that few of the women actively discouraged. Not that they were mean to her; everyone was quite friendly. But there seemed to be an unspoken assumption that Mahlah was different. She worked very hard around camp, almost as much as the unstoppable Susanna, yet it was understood that Susanna — as one of Jesus's benefactors — wasn't expected to do menial labor in the first place. Mahlah, who didn't have a dime to her name, evidently was.

I still had not gotten used to the whole concept of master and servant, and I was certain I never would. The Jews didn't have "slaves" in the sense that whole castes or races of people were born into lifelong servitude. But their "servants" were viewed as a form of property, just like their animals or — for that matter — their wives. A servant might be working for a specific amount of time to pay off a debt, but more often he or she worked purely for room, board, and protection, with no end in sight. Most servants were treated well, and no less humanely than were many wives and children. But what bothered me about the system was the same thing that bothered me about attitudes toward British house maids, migrant farm workers, and night-shift janitors — the idea that one group of humans was, because of their occupation or station in life, inherently better than another.

In that sentiment, however, I was alone.

Almost. Jesus treated "underlings" with the same respect he gave everyone else, and sometimes more. But the disciples seemed to find this tendency of his more amusing than enlightening, as if it were a mere quirk of his personality. Cute, but hardly practical.

Tonight, as we gathered around the cooking fire waiting for the Pharisees — who had rudely ambushed Jesus in the middle of our camp — to finish their interrogation and go home, I was determined I would finally get through to Mahlah. I wanted to know exactly what sequence of events had brought her to that synagogue with her forehead sliced open and her life on the line. I also wanted, perhaps naively, to help make up for some of that ill treatment.

"You're a pretty good seamstress," I praised, keeping my voice low, fearing she wouldn't speak if the other women could overhear. "Personally, I stink at mending things. I stink at pretty much all housework, in case you haven't noticed."

The girl's dark eyes turned on me with a puzzled expression. The concept of self-deprecating humor was lost on her. "I'm sure you're very talented," she said cautiously.

I laughed. "You're too kind. We both know I shouldn't be allowed within a mile of the stewpot. But I am good at one thing."

Her eyebrows rose, but she didn't speak.

"I'm a good listener. And I enjoy hearing about people's lives. I've been traveling with all these other women for a while now, though, so their stories are old news. I'd love to hear more about you."

She studied me for a second. "There's not much to tell," she demurred.

"Let's start with your family," I pressed, undeterred. "What sort of business is your father in?"

Her eyes turned oddly wistful. "He's a beekeeper."

At last, we were getting somewhere. "And you have brothers and sisters?"

"Three brothers. I'm the oldest."

"And the man you married? What business is he in?"

Her jaw muscles tightened beneath her smooth, flawless skin. "He's a merchant."

Our conversation progressed as such, with me cajoling and her responding with answers that were short, to the point, and emotionally guarded. But eventually, I got it all out of her.

I did have my talents.

Mahlah was "given in marriage" to a man almost three times her age whom she had not met until the betrothal. Her father was a self-absorbed materialistic jerk (my interpretation, not hers) who had always been indifferent to his female offspring and was only too happy to accept an offer from the highest bidder at the earliest decent opportunity. Her intended was a wealthy businessman who had divorced two wives already because neither had given him a child. As old as he was, he was starting to get desperate, and Mahlah, being young and healthy and coming from stock that had produced three male children in the last generation, was the perfect candidate.

Simply put, she had been sold as a brood mare. Unfortunately for her, the stallion on which she was depending might as well have been a gelding. Reading between the lines of Mahlah's tactful story, which included the information that neither of his previous wives had ever had so much as a miscarriage, I gathered that her husband was probably sterile, which made her situation at best hopeless and at worst dire. After three years with no baby she had been given an ultimatum. One more year, and then she, too, would be divorced.

Mahlah had known that going home in disgrace was not an option. Her father had made clear that he considered her nonrefundable. He had enough mouths to feed already. If she screwed up, she was on her own. When her time had all but run out, she allowed some of the household servants to convince her that the services of a younger, more virile stud were the only thing likely to save her from the streets. The servants, who had seen two wives cast out already, seemed genuine in their desire to help. But it had only taken one of them to betray her. She was set up and caught in the act. The strapping shepherd who had been recruited for the task managed to escape, albeit with a price on his head. Mahlah had been taken before the elders for punishment.

I was the first person who had even asked why she did it.

Adultery wasn't uncommon, but stonings were, and I surmised that the village elders might not have been nearly so brutish with her if they hadn't known Jesus was coming. They had seen an opportunity to trap the troublesome rabbi into defying Roman law, and they had seized it.

Poor Mahlah had been nothing but a pawn.

A heaviness settled in my gut. I was a free woman here, and I had my own money. But there was only so much even I could do for someone like Mahlah, other than making her a personal assistant. And how could I take responsibility for someone else when I had no guarantee of my own future? The money I had left wouldn't last forever, and I had fewer marketable skills than she did.

I needed help.

"Come with me," I ordered the girl. "We're going to talk to the others."

Her eyes widened with alarm. But she obeyed.

Within a few minutes I had unapologetically imparted the gist of Mahlah's story to the other women, and I was gratified when they reacted with empathy. But on the question of what she could do to provide for herself, sound ideas were scarce. Bernice suggested that Mahlah could offer herself as a servant to one of Jesus's wealthier supporters, and this was generally agreed to be her best option. Though Mahlah's husband would almost certainly divorce her, her prospects for making another marriage — without her father to arrange it and with the stain of adultery on her resume — were negligible.

Mahlah accepted this advice with stalwart gratitude, and had I been more with the times, I would have too. But I wasn't with the times, and the injustice of it burned me.

"There's Mary and Martha," Joanna suggested. "We should be stopping by there soon, shouldn't we? Or maybe Judith. Either of them could probably take on another servant."

Mary nodded in agreement. It was uncommon for a Jewish household to be headed by a woman, particularly a prosperous one, but among such self-made matriarchs as there were, support for Jesus's ministry was almost unanimous.

"Do they—" Mahlah's light, hesitant voice was barely audible, but everyone was so surprised to hear it that they quieted and leaned in. "Do you know anyone who keeps bees? I can do any kind of housework, but— I mean, I'd be happy to do anything, but I'm especially good with bees."

Mary and Joanna looked at each other. "I don't think I know any beekeepers," Mary replied. "At least not any that would be good candidates to take you in."

Joanna shook her head. "Mary and Martha love their honey, for sure, but they don't keep a hive."

Mahlah's back straightened. Her dark eyes danced. "I could make one. I know how to bake them from clay. And I can attract the bees, too. As long as there are flowers around…"

Mary studied the girl critically. "It's not that easy to keep a hive going, you know," she cautioned. "I've had servants try it a couple times."

"Oh, but you have to know what you're doing!" exclaimed Mahlah, forgetting herself. "Most people either don't remove the bad comb, or else they disturb the bees too much. You have to make sure you have a healthy queen, and that the hives have just the right amount of sun…"

Mary turned to Joanna with a grin. "A woman beekeeper! Think those two would go for it?"

Joanna chuckled. "I don't know why they wouldn't. They'd do anything Jesus asked."

My moment of triumph was rudely shortened. A loud, unfamiliar voice rang from the men's campfire, indignant and combative.

"That is *not* the law!"

The women tensed. Jesus's altercations with the Pharisees were no longer amusing. He did have supporters in the establishment, but those men were in the minority. More and more we encountered Pharisees and Sadducees who made clear from the get-go that they saw Jesus as a nuisance and a troublemaker — though most were still reluctant to display this attitude publicly, given his enormous grass-roots support. Gone were the days when scores of curious officials would attend Jesus's friendly informational sessions in the countryside, or compete among themselves for the privilege of inviting him into their homes. Now they confronted Jesus behind the closed gates of synagogues or, like tonight, in secret after dark. They weren't confronting him with good-faith questions, either. They were confronting him with traps.

"Oh, please just let them go back to the city!" Leah fretted, throwing a pebble into the fire. Leah was always throwing things. I could take her home and put her on a softball team. Senior varsity.

Jesse squalled for his feeding, and she tucked him expertly into her tunic.

Maybe not.

"Something bad is happening," Leah continued. "Or it's going to happen. Tamar and I have both seen a change in the men, and we're not imagining things. John and James won't talk about it, but we can tell they're upset."

The gnawing pain in my stomach resumed. Judas and I weren't alone anymore. Everyone in camp felt it now. The lighter moments among us had become fewer and farther between. Tonight, apprehension hovered in the air, thick and choking.

Not knowing what was going on with the disciples was especially frustrating for the women. As much as Mary spoke with Jesus, she was not always privy to the secrets shared among the men. Or at least she claimed not to be. It was usually Leah, by virtue of the fact that both she and John were natural-born talkers, who was our prime source of information. Bernice claimed Philip was no help at all, and though Bartholomew would tell Naomi anything if she dared to ask him, he wasn't a member of the inner circle and wasn't always in the know himself. Neither, of course, was Judas. James did share information with Tamar, but she was less likely than Leah to divulge things. When she did, however, she was also less likely to embellish them.

The women's gazes moved from Leah to her sister-in-law.

"Is that true, Tamar?" Mary asked softly. "You've noticed something?"

Tamar gave a nervous nod. "Yes. For some time now. James is worried, but he won't explain."

"When did this start?" Mary asked, her brow creased.

"Mount Hermon," Leah answered. "Remember when Jesus took Peter and our husbands on a walk with him — no one else? When John came back he was shaking like a leaf. He's never told me why. He won't, no matter what I do. But ever since then, he's been anxious. And it's only getting worse. I think..."

Her voice tapered off, and her face reddened. She shook her head.

"Tell us, Leah," Mary ordered.

Leah drew in an uncomfortable breath. "John didn't say this. But I think that Jesus told them something horrible is going to happen to him."

Silence fell. Rumblings of an argument drifted over from the men's campfire. Coldness stung deep in my marrow.

"I agree," said Bernice quietly. "Philip has been worried, too." She turned to Mary. "Has Jesus said anything to you?"

Mary's jaws clenched. Her dark eyes were moist. "Not specifically, no," she answered. But watching her closely, I wasn't so sure. She had not seemed herself either, in the last few days. Something was gone from her — the sparkle, the zest. She seemed, all at once, years older.

*Jesus did tell her something*, I thought to myself. But she would die before she betrayed his confidence.

"I suspect the men think they're protecting us," she offered.

Naomi looked close to fainting. Joanna didn't look so good herself. Thomas's new bride, Priscilla, was the first to speak. "It's Jerusalem, I think," she said, her young voice crisp and bold.

Priscilla was only sixteen and a half, but like Leah, the girl was all moxie. I could easily picture her and Bekka parasailing or rock climbing... at least until Bekka got bored and reached for her cell phone. An adventurous soul by nature, Priscilla had been hounding her father for months to convince Thomas to marry her right away so that she, too, could travel with Jesus on the road. The clueless Thomas had been reluctant to "inconvenience" his young bride.

We had bought them a new tent for a wedding present.

"Whatever Thomas is afraid of is going to happen in Jerusalem," she repeated. "He doesn't want Jesus to go there, but he won't tell me why."

Mary, who had been sitting, rose with a jerk. "There's no use in us worrying about it," she announced, her tone brooking no dissent. "Jesus knows what he's doing. None of us should doubt that." She turned to the fire. "We'll need more wood soon."

"I'll get it," said Bernice, her voice oddly clipped. I watched as she grabbed a torch and moved off toward the thicket of brush behind us.

Plenty more wood was already stacked by the supper blanket. Bernice knew that. She had stacked it there herself.

As I watched her stumble away in haste, minus her usual self-possessed carriage, I felt an odd inkling that something wasn't right with her. Then I felt an even odder inkling that I should do something about it.

"I'll help," I murmured, rising.


I found Bernice hiding in the brush near the latrine, vomiting her dinner in near, practiced silence. I stood at a respectful distance, waiting, until she was done.

I waited quite a while before at last she emerged — face green, eyes watering, limbs shaking.

"Bernice?" I whispered, announcing my presence. She hadn't noticed me before. Now, in the flickering torch light, her eyes betrayed just how much my presence startled her, irritated her, and then — strangely — comforted her.

"You needn't worry about me," she insisted, with no trace of her usual bravado. "I'm fine."

I lifted an eyebrow. "Obviously."

"No," she assured. "Really. I'm not sick. I'm—"

I knew before she said it.

"Pregnant," she finished. "I know they say that each one's easier, but I seem to be the exception. I felt perfectly fine with Elizabeth. Mark and Eglah were worse. This time, I can't seem to keep anything down."

With guilt, I remembered how often I had noticed her looking unwell lately, and how I had never asked her about it. She had been working as hard as ever.

"You should tell everyone," I suggested. "No one will mind if you take it easy for a while. They'll be happy for you."

Her eyes caught mine, and I saw something in them I hadn't before.

Compassion.

"I know they'll find out sometime," she said softly. "I'm already showing. I just— Well... it will feel so awkward to celebrate. I have three healthy children already. And you know how much..."

Her voice trailed off.

I felt a catch in my throat. So, Bernice did have a heart. She loved Tamar as much as the rest of us, and as happy as she was about expanding her family, she knew that a fourth, by-all-standards gratuitous pregnancy would be salt in her sister-in-law's wound.

I reached out a hand and touched her arm. "I understand. I do. It will be hard for Tamar. But she'll be happy for you, too. You know she will. That's just the way she is."

Bernice smiled. "She's one of the most genuinely kind people I know. It's no wonder James loves her so much." To my surprise, she looked straight at me. "You have a kind heart yourself, Rachel."

I blinked. I reminded myself that Bernice had never caught me pretending not to see the tip can at the ice cream stand, or saving an extra lounge chair at the pool so I could spread my stuff out. What she had seen of me here was hardly representative.

"Thank you," I answered sheepishly. "So do you."

I asked the next question without giving myself a chance to second-guess. I had been wanting to ask it for a while, but I hadn't collected the nerve.

"Do you think your brother would divorce Tamar?" I blurted. "I mean, could he *do* that?"

Bernice lowered her eyes. She stalled before answering. "I want to say no. But I can't, not absolutely. I can't think of a single other man in the tribe who has stayed married to a wife who was barren. Not forever. Not when he's young and has no children. A rich man might take a second wife, but James couldn't. Even then, it's not about being able to provide, it's about obligation. Continuation of the line. There's so much pressure — and not just from our father. James is a first-born son. With John, it would be easier, but..." She stopped and took a breath. "I just keep hoping that James will play the rebel. That he can accept the fact that he may never have children and then stand up to the grief. But it wouldn't be easy for him. There are some things a man's ego just can't take."

A low roar of voices issued from the men's campfire. We turned toward the sound. The glow of a half-dozen torches illuminated the retreating forms of the Pharisees as they headed back toward town. Around the fire, the disciples had risen to their feet and were conversing among themselves — heatedly, it seemed, yet not loud enough to be overheard by either us or the Pharisees.

"More trouble," Bernice murmured. "I'd better get that wood." She moved past me and back toward the cooking fire, but stopped when she noticed I wasn't following.

"Aren't you coming Rachel?" she asked. "You don't have a torch."

I stayed where I was — feet rooted to the ground, watching the disciples' frenzied gestures to each other, trying to understand their tense, hushed speech.

I didn't need a torch.

My stomach was on fire.

*Commentary for Chapter 17 begins on page 271.*

# Chapter 18

I stood there in the dark a long while, my heart pounding as I watched the men gradually break off into smaller groups, huddling and debating. I had told Bernice I didn't mind finding my way back to the cooking fire in the dark. I hadn't counted on needing to get to the latrine.

Looping by the cooking fire to get a torch would take too long. I was in a hurry, and since the moon was nearly full I figured I could manage. I assessed the lay of the land, the line of brush as it deepened farther from the road, and began walking.

I could not imagine being pregnant under such conditions. Cooking, seasoning, and working with smelly fish while nauseated were like cruel and unusual punishment. Of course, I could not imagine how Bernice managed to get pregnant in the first place, with all three of the couple's children sleeping in the family tent.

Well, I *could* imagine it, but I preferred not to. There were some aspects of these people's lives I could never get used to.

Lack of toilet paper was another one.

I found the latrine without difficulty, did my business as hygienically as possible, and then, without conscious thought, found myself moving back toward the men's campfire. Not very long ago I would have been terrified to be on the fringes of camp by myself, without so much as a torch for protection. Our caravan had never been a target of bandits because of our size. But still, the specter of the unknown had always loomed large, particularly after dark. Tonight, I had more concrete worries. I wanted to know what was going on.

*Jerusalem.*

I crept back to my previous spot as furtively as I could, unabashed by my blatant eavesdropping. Something had happened — just now, tonight. Jesus had not only made the Pharisees furious, but he had flustered the disciples as well. What on earth had he said? How bad was the damage?

The danger?

My knees trembled. I hated showing such weakness, but consoled myself that it was brought on by frustration as much as fear. I felt as if I had been dumped into the middle of a raging river that was pulling me and everyone else helplessly downstream, and all I could do was cling to whatever wreckage happened to float up next to me. I couldn't get out. I couldn't save myself, much less anybody else I cared about. I couldn't do a blasted thing.

And the water kept on flowing.

Brush crackled off to my left; the light of a torch drifted behind the trees. I froze where I stood, my back to a sturdy sapling. I probably should have said something to whoever it was. But I didn't. Odds were it was one of the men on the way to the latrine, in which case I would much rather he pass by me unaware than grill me on why I was standing alone in the dark. But the torch didn't pass by. Instead, the sound of footsteps stopped a few yards away, just beyond one of the smaller tents.

Mary and the rest of us had purchased enough tent space for everyone, in case of inclement weather. But most of the men preferred to sleep outdoors around the fire. Only the ones whose wives were traveling with them bothered to set up the tents each night. Even then, they sometimes left their wives inside and went out to sleep by the fire.

All of them except James. And it was James whose voice I heard now, hushed, but with poorly controlled excitement, speaking to a smaller shadow I was certain was Tamar.

"You won't believe this," he told her, his hands grasping her upper arms as they stood outside their tent, the torch planted in the ground beside them. "You won't believe what the rabbi just said!"

I should have announced my presence. But of course I didn't.

"What?" Tamar prompted, her silvery voice distressed.

"The Pharisees were trying to trip him up, like they always do. But he's too smart for them. These particular fellows, I think, were trying to catch him in some statement that would anger women, because they know how much support he has among them."

"The Pharisees care what women think?"

James chuckled. "Well, no. Not really. But they care what women *do*, and when they see huge crowds of women supporting Jesus and encouraging their husbands and sons to do likewise, they see a threat to their own leadership."

"I see," Tamar murmured.

"What they wanted," James continued, "was to get him on record as agreeing with the divorce law. They know perfectly well that Rabbi Hillel's interpretation serves the interest of men, at women's expense, and they figured if Jesus openly endorsed it, he would be bound to alienate some of his female followers. Preferably some of the ones who are bankrolling him."

I stood still as a stone, waiting. I knew more than I cared to about the nation's inane divorce law, and about Rabbi Hillel, who had several generations ago interpreted some convoluted passage in Deuteronomy to mean that a man could divorce his wife for any reason — like, say, burning his dinner — and from then on had no responsibility toward her. From the man's perspective, it wasn't too far off from the no-fault divorce laws I was used to. But the woman's perspective was different. First off, only the husband could initiate the divorce; the wife had no such option. Second, divorce left the woman high and dry, without financial support or physical protection, because unless she was lucky enough to have inherited her own money somewhere along the line, marriage was a woman's only respectable, non-indentured means of support. Divorced women were allowed to remarry, but because other men's castoffs were not prime pickings, a divorced woman without a sympathetic family could easily find herself both homeless and hopeless.

No disrespect to a famous rabbi, but after having seen any number of mature women without widow's scarves begging in the streets, I was no fan of the great Hillel. And I didn't believe Jesus was either — not under the circumstances. It was one thing for couples to divorce freely when both parties were free and independent and able to support themselves. But the law as these people knew it was absurd.

And cruel.

"Did he agree with Hillel?" Tamar asked, her voice barely above a whisper.

"No," James's voice carried easily to my ears, triumphant and filled with electricity. "He agreed with Shammai!"

"Shammai?" Tamar repeated slowly, "Didn't he say—"

"That divorce is only permissible in the case of adultery," James finished.

Tamar was silent for a second, letting it sink in. "Did Jesus say specifically—"

"He said that any man who divorces his wife for any reason other than marital unfaithfulness, then marries another, commits adultery."

She gasped. "He didn't!"

"He did."

I watched their silhouettes as James pulled his wife to him. His voice lowered to a rough whisper, but I could still understand him.

Barely.

"I would never have divorced you, Tamar. No matter if we never have children. I know you haven't believed me when I've said that before, but I swear to you, it's true."

Tamar seemed to be stifling a sob. "I wouldn't have blamed you..."

"Well, you should have!" he responded, pulling back a bit. "Jesus is right about this, like he's right about everything. A wife deserves her husband's loyalty. She deserves to know she's protected. And now that Jesus has agreed with Shammai, no one could possibly fault one of Jesus's own disciples for hanging onto a wife he loves, can they?" He brought her closer again. "Child or no child."

I would have given anything to see Tamar's expression at those words, but her face was hidden in shadow. All I could see was her standing on her tiptoes and flinging her arms around his neck.

"Unless..." James began.

Her head sprang back. "Unless what?"

"Well," he began, the mirth in his voice plain. "You weren't planning on being unfaithful to me, were you?"

Tamar let out a sound so uncharacteristic that at first I wasn't sure it was her. It was a growl. She emitted it just as one of the slender hands she had wrapped around her husband's neck struck him lightly on the shoulder. "Don't ever say that," she admonished, her voice breaking. "You know you're all I've ever wanted."

He touched his forehead to hers. "And you know I feel the same. So will you stop worrying now?"

Tamar took a moment to answer. "Yes," she said, slowly, deliberately. "But I still want a baby."

James didn't respond to that. At least not in words. What he did do was let go of Tamar just long enough to open the tent flap, then take her hand and pull her inside.

I moved away as quietly as I could. My eavesdropping was unforgivable, but I didn't regret it. My gut instincts about James had been vindicated.

And my instincts about Jesus?

I crept closer to the men's fire, scanning the shadowed figures for his profile. He wasn't there.

The problem with gut instincts, I had discovered, was the fact that the gut controlled them. And on the question of who this Jesus really was, my insides, as of late, had been frustratingly silent.

The other women seemed to know exactly who he was. He was a

healer, a teacher, a spiritual leader, and a visionary who was destined to elevate their people and their society — to change life as they knew it for the better. Not just the life of the nation, but *their* lives. How individuals acted, how they treated each other, how they lived, how they died. Everything could be transformed. And perhaps the same could happen in other countries, too. Who knew?

Not everyone agreed with such a warm and fuzzy interpretation of Jesus's mission. The Zealots still wanted him as a military leader. Anyone who viewed Israel's primary problem as being Roman domination naturally wanted him to address the issue. But Jesus's message was not, and never had been, political, and he had declined at every turn to embroil himself in that battle. Which left many people shaking their heads in confusion.

Attitudes about who Jesus was and why he was doing what he was doing were as varied and innumerable as the rocks under all our feet. But with the possible exception of those disciples who weren't talking, I had not heard a single soul assess Jesus's mission in terms even remotely close to those I had grown up with. Unlike the Greeks, these people's worldview had no precedent for the commingling of humans with deities, and even with a track record of miracle-making that grew increasingly impressive at every stop, no one here considered Jesus of Nazareth to be superhuman. A prophet, certainly. Some skeptics called him a magician. Many people wanted to believe he was some *other* human — like Moses or one of the other big names in Judaism — risen from the dead. The point of that angle was lost on me, since I considered that Moses and the others had done their thing already, and that Jesus deserved his own limelight. But everyone seemed to want to make *something* of him. Something other than a very nice, unusually intelligent man who got a kick out of wandering about performing random acts of kindness.

That wasn't enough for any of them. They wanted more.

And so, I acknowledged as I searched the milling silhouettes, did I.

Jesus was nowhere to be seen, but I did notice that the men's campfire had burned down very low, which offered a convenient excuse for my hanging about in the brush. Evidently, while the Pharisees were here, none of the disciples had wanted to leave the conversation long enough to get wood. Now they were so consumed with their discussions on the divorce edict that they didn't notice how much the flames had dwindled.

Gathering firewood, luckily, was one of the few things I could do with competence. Large pieces of wood were rare along the roadsides, where travelers regularly hunted for fuel. But I had learned what types of brush could serve as a fair substitute, and I had become skillful enough at it to manage even in the moonlight.

I began to rummage in the thicket, breaking and twisting the appropriate branches.

I was happy for Tamar. What Jesus had said, if followed, would be a stroke of victory for all these women. They could not be cast aside; their husbands were stuck with them. Maybe that would make some men less likely to marry in the first place, but I doubted it. They all wanted children. Voluntary celibacy was neither fashionable nor laudable. Jesus's own unmarried state was an oddity for a man his age, but since no one had ever mentioned this as a problem, I gathered that he, like John the Baptist before him, was considered above the convention.

I scratched my arm on a branch I didn't see. I swore softly, feeling suddenly irritated, and kept gathering.

*He agreed with Shammai.*

What was it about James's description of Jesus's announcement that bothered me? Jesus had said the right thing. I would hardly have felt better if he had agreed with the other rabbi, allowing wives to be tossed aside as so much garbage. So what was my problem?

My jaws clenched. I knew what my problem was. Jesus might have given the right answer for these people, but he hadn't given the right answer for me. I knew several women who had left unhappy marriages, remarried, and were better off for it. Rabbi Shammai's rules, rather than helping them, would have consigned them to a lifetime of unhappiness.

I stopped and stood a moment in the darkness, considering. What if a women here was abused by her husband? Was Shammai's way better for her?

Probably.

I let out my breath in a huff. Despite the point I wanted to make, I knew that an abused wife here still *was* better off married than she would be abandoned on the street, where she would be vulnerable to the same abuse and more — only now from any man. At least as a married woman, she retained the respect of her family and the community, which did have some ability to intervene in the case of mistreatment.

Poor divorce law was hardly the sum total of these women's

problems.

So why couldn't Jesus have said that women should be allowed to divorce their husbands, too? Didn't some women in Rome and other areas nearby have that privilege already? Better yet, why couldn't he have made a sweeping statement that would last through the centuries to my time, about how divorce was okay if it was mutual and thoroughly considered and both parties were fairly provided for in the settlement? For that matter, why couldn't he have come straight out and said that women were equal to men?

Why couldn't he have *been* a woman?

"Who's there? Rachel, is that you?"

Thomas's voice broke my reverie. He was standing a few feet away. Someone, I was guessing the younger James, was with him.

"Yes, it's me," I answered. "I'm just getting some firewood. The campfire's dwindling."

"Why don't you have a torch? Did yours go out?"

"I haven't got one. I can see all right, though. I'm almost done."

"Shall I give her this one?"

The voice was indeed that of James "the lesser," as he was sometimes called, not as an insult, but to distinguish him from the taller, older, and more influential son of Zebedee. But his question was not directed at me, even though he stood no farther from me than Thomas did. His comment had been directed to the man beside him, because he — like about a third of the disciples — still did not feel comfortable talking to a woman.

"Keep your torch, James," I said sharply, far more sharply than I meant to. I knew he meant no disrespect, but that didn't stop his attitude from bothering me.

*Chill, Rachel. It's not his fault.*

"Thank you both," I forced out, fighting to sound conciliatory. "But I'm fine. I'll bring this load to the fire in a minute."

The men dropped back without another word.

I snapped the next branches with a vengeance. What did women have to *do* here to earn society's respect? It wasn't a matter of the men not liking me personally, or not being friendly. James was happy enough to run and get a torch. Yet talking to me was inappropriate. Why? Because such an exchange might be misconstrued as intimate, since if it *wasn't* intimate, what point could it have? It wasn't as though, outside of the reproductive arena, any female had anything important to say.

I scratched my shin on a thorn. I swore again.

I could have the wisdom of Solomon — which come to think of it, I *did*, and 99% of the male population here wouldn't lower themselves to partake of it. I could explain how diseases were caused by bacteria and how engines could run on steam — no one would take me seriously. Even if I wasn't spouting science fiction, even if I was doing exactly what Jesus had done, duplicating every miracle and every sermon, not half the women and probably none of the men would listen to me. I would be dismissed as an uppity screwball or indicted as some kind of witch. I wouldn't live long enough to travel.

Which is why Jesus wasn't a woman.

*Duh.*

I growled to myself. Anger still boiled within me, and I was in no mood for reason. I had gotten through to some of these men, at least. Bartholomew had been born liberal, but Thomas, who hadn't, was becoming more so every day, thanks to Mary and me. Judas had been tougher to modernize, but I had worn him down too, eventually, and I was proud to think that his view of women might have improved somewhat through his knowing me. But the men Jesus collected around himself were hardly representative of the general public. Heart and soul, they were cream of the crop, and their minds had broadened further under his influence.

The unenlightened masses would never take seriously any claim that women were equal to men. The idea would be every bit as preposterous to them as that of sailing a hot-air balloon, even though both, practically and materially, were within their grasp. It was too much change, too fast. They weren't capable of assimilating it, no matter who delivered the news.

A sharp rock grazed my ankle, and the scrape stung. Annoyance was making me careless, and I knew I was asking to injure myself. Subconsciously, I had some idea that the pain would make me feel better.

It didn't.

I had heard all the rhetoric before, the excuses for why Sunday-school Jesus *hadn't* said this or that. Prudence dictated that he work within the current cultural climate, navigating its waters with due respect for what the people could and could not absorb... yada, yada, yada.

I sighed. Perhaps Jesus's curriculum *was* best under the circumstances. He had chosen to emphasize the great commandment, that people should love God and one another, and more sweeping societal attitudes had evolved from that over time. Perhaps he had planned it that way from the beginning.

Or perhaps he was a mortal product of his time who meant everything he said at face value and who saw nothing wrong with treating women and servants like property.

A branch poked me in the eye. I swore out loud — some syllable I didn't even know — and dropped my load squarely on top of my feet.

I swore again. I had stacked a ridiculous number of sticks into my arms, making the pile so high that an unnoticed offshoot had nearly impaled my cornea. Now I had battered my insteps as well.

And I was still mad.

I squatted down and began to pick up the load.

Another hand appeared in the dark.

I jerked to attention, lifting my head and staring at the man who crouched before me, gathering the sticks into his own arms.

"Let me help you with that," Jesus said pleasantly.

I watched in embarrassed silence as he retrieved the load from the ground, then stood. My head spun. How much of my profane mutterings had he heard? And how *did* he manage to slip around so blasted quietly?

I stood up with him, managing a breathy "Thank you."

Fortunately, the darkness hid the redness of my face. I had no idea what expression might be on his. Why *was* it that on the few occasions I was actually face to face with the man, I had to act like a such a dolt?

I swore internally. I had gathered too big of a load because in some twisted part of my psyche, I was trying to prove I could carry as much as a man could. Which was so hypocritical — given that I always made Joe take out the trash when he was home and never felt the least compulsion to better my biceps in any way other than lifting a chocolate bar — it was downright pathetic. I was no he-woman; never had been, never would be. But when intellect didn't count for beans, I had to get my self-respect somehow, didn't I?

"You're welcome," Jesus responded. He arranged the sticks he had picked up into a more manageable bundle. Then, without a word, he dumped the entire load back into my arms and walked off toward the fire.

For a moment, I stood speechless. Then offense gave way to a chuckle. Mindreading, or coincidence?

Regardless, it amused me. I followed him.

Having Jesus's solitary company was like nectar. The effect was no different, perhaps, than a teenager meeting a rock star, or a young gymnast meeting a gold-medal Olympian. I couldn't tell how much of my pleasure in his company came from respect, and how much was due to genuine liking. All I knew was that being around him made me feel good.

When he reached the nearly extinguished campfire he turned and took the wood from me, then laid it down next to the fire and began placing sticks carefully upon the flames. Good fire-building was an important skill here. I had improved, but Jesus had always been an expert at it. It was one of the many tasks around camp he didn't have to do, but did anyway.

Sunday-school Jesus hadn't built fires. At least not in the portraits. He was more likely to be seen sitting around with babies on his lap and lambs at his feet and doves flying around his head. I had seen this Jesus hold many a baby, but I was pretty sure the doves would have annoyed him. Watching him build up the fire, pausing now and then to push a lock of greasy hair over his shoulder, one saw little fodder for artistic froufrou.

But some things were in the eye of the beholder.

"There he is. Let's ask him."

I turned at the voice, and my heart sank a little. Simon had spied Jesus, and the group of disciples with whom he was talking started toward us.

My time was about up.

"Jesus?" I asked hesitantly.

He put down the stick he was holding and looked up at me.

My heart pounded against my ribs, but the approaching men goaded me into action. I wanted to ask him. I had to ask him. For all I knew, this could be my last chance.

His brown eyes sparkled in the firelight. His expression was attentive, open. I wasn't afraid of him anymore. But I was scared to death of his answer.

Sometimes, when he looked at me, I was certain that he *knew*. Knew everything about me, where I had come from, whom I was married to, how much I loved my kids, and how confused I was about what the heck I was doing here. I was certain that he had, somehow, engineered the whole thing, and that he alone held the power to send me back.

Other times that seemed like nonsense. As much as I wanted to believe he was some fantastic supernatural being, as much as that would both explain things and give a fairy-tale ending to my current plight, I was still unable, intellectually, to swallow it. The man was just too normal. Too human. Every single "miracle" I had seen could have some alternative explanation. History could have developed, just as it had and with all the consequences to world religions, even if he weren't divine. His message could still have withstood the test of time. His life would still have had an impact.

And wasn't that in itself a credit to him?

Whether he was what I had grown up thinking he was or not, the fact remained that I liked the man I knew. I admired and respected him more than any person I had ever known. I cared deeply about what happened to him. And — for various and selfish reasons — I wanted desperately for him to like me.

I also wanted desperately for him to help me.

I just wasn't sure he could.

He was still waiting for me to say something. The men were coming closer. I took a quick breath and found my voice. "Do you know who I am?"

I blurted the question unevenly, hot blood rushing full-force into my face.

There, I had said it.

It would all be over soon.

Whatever his credentials, I knew he wouldn't lie to me. If he was more than just a man, he would know exactly what I was talking about. If he wasn't, he would think I was a nut.

If he wasn't, he already did.

I studied his eyes in panicked silence. The beating of my heart was audible.

He shifted position, resting more comfortably on his heels. His brown eyes locked on mine, penetrating, yet giving away nothing of his own feelings. "If I asked you the same question," he replied, "could you answer me?"

My composure crumpled. Stomach acid surged; my knees quivered. I wanted to swear again, and at the same time I wanted to cry.

He had done it again, hadn't he? Just like with the Pharisees. Turning tables was his forte.

But his question wasn't a trick. I knew, as I looked at him, that if I answered his question honestly, he would do the same with mine. All I had to do was come clean. All I had to do was make up my mind.

*Who was he?*

I gritted my teeth. My eyes turned away. The other men were coming closer. His question was still on the table.

Itchy Easter dresses. Long, boring sermons. Dogma. Ritual. Salvation from a fiery hell. Sacraments. Theology 101. It all seemed so distant, so bizarre, so irrelevant. Could the man before me really be *that* Jesus?

Did I even want him to be?

I liked the man I knew, whether he could help me or not. Even as a human, he was amazing. Plus, he was scientifically plausible.

And in a couple weeks or days, he would die a horrible death in Jerusalem. And that would be the end of him.

Or not.

A groan escaped my lips as I turned my eyes back to his. He was still waiting for an answer. Patiently.

Hopefully?

"No," I whispered, my voice breaking on every word. "I can't answer."

*I'm sorry.*

His eyes held mine for only an instant. Disappointed. But not surprised. He turned to place another stick on the fire.

"Then neither can I answer your question," he said quietly.

It wasn't a reprimand. But that didn't stop me from feeling terrible.

"Rabbi," Thaddeus exclaimed, reaching us first. "Could we ask you a question? About the divorce law?"

The other men encircled us. Philip knelt down beside Jesus and began to help with the fire-building. Jesus looked up at Thaddeus. "Of course," he answered.

My feet carried me backward. Between the men and behind them, back into the dark. My moment was over.

I had blown it again.

Hot tears welled up behind my eyes, and I stumbled toward my own tent in a haze. I hoped no one was there yet. I hoped the other women were still at the cooking fire, perhaps toasting Bernice's good fortune with a round of honeyed wine.

I wanted to be alone, so I could cry in peace.

I didn't cry often. When I did it tended to be a cumulative effect — building up a little at a time, some aggravation here, something sad there, throw in a hormonal surge, and eventually the lid blew off the pot. I had been working toward a good cry for ages now.

I found the tent empty. I crawled inside.

It was hot and stuffy. It smelled of BO.

I laid down on my mat and bawled like a baby. I wanted to blame the eruption on the loss of yet another hope of getting back home. But what really bothered me was something else. Behind my closed eyes burned an image I couldn't erase. An image of Jesus's face, looking at me with disappointment.

I had hurt him.

*Me.*

*Commentary for Chapter 18 begins on page 275.*

# Chapter 19

Mary's age-spotted hands clutched at the wooden handle of the millstone. She turned the heavy disc slowly, deliberately. Her eyes followed its movement. Her thoughts seemed far away.

I had been miserable enough these last few days worrying about Jesus and myself. Now I was worried about Mary, too.

My rock was crumbling.

We were in the courtyard of a private home in Jericho. Mary, Joanna, Susanna, and I were being put up for the night by one of the neighbors of Zacchaeus, a local tax collector who had been so thoroughly impressed by Jesus that he had offered accommodations for everyone. The four of us were slated to sleep in an upper room even smaller than the tent we were used to, but no one complained. We were all too tense to bother.

Jericho itself was a pleasant place, situated on a hill overlooking a valley whose spring made it refreshingly green and humid. But our party could take no joy in the city's beauty, nor even in the generous hospitality of its residents. We were all too aware of its proximity to our next stop.

Jerusalem.

What had begun as a nagging worry on the part of James's and John's perceptive wives had now escalated to grim common knowledge. Jesus had told all of the disciples the same thing. In Jerusalem, he would die.

He was going there anyway.

My ulcer had settled into a steady state of aching any time I wasn't eating, which was almost always. Every time anyone said anything about Jerusalem, I got a little extra kick of acid. Whenever Jesus angered a Pharisee or a teacher of the law, I felt like doubling over.

No one wanted to accept what Jesus had said. Despite their faith in the rabbi's wisdom and their allegiance to his authority, none of the disciples could bear the thought of losing him so soon.

Neither, evidently, could Mary.

Though she frequently waived her unspoken exemption from menial labor when in camp, I had never seen her lift a finger in the villages. The disciples' wives assisted our hostesses with their chores; Mary and Joanna bought gifts instead. Yet now Mary was sitting and grinding. Grinding as if every kernel of uncracked grain was her mortal enemy.

I sat down opposite her. My hand joined hers on the handle, and together we rotated the heavy stone wheel around in its basin, pulverizing the grain sandwiched beneath. It was a loathsome, boring, tiring job.

For some reason, it felt good.

"You've been quiet this afternoon, Mary," I said, unable to stand another moment of her grim silence. Like everyone else, she had been thoughtful, preoccupied, and depressed ever since Jesus had made his unthinkable announcement. But in the last few hours, she had seemed suddenly worse.

Her brow creased. "I don't like being away from him like this," she muttered. "I might miss something."

I smiled at her, sadly. Jesus frequently took meals at houses where the women were not invited; our group being separated for a few hours, or even a day, was hardly unusual. But I knew what she meant. Her remaining time with the rabbi could be limited. She wished to savor it. "What is it you're afraid you might miss?"

"Anything," she replied. "There's no telling what he'll say. He's been acting different, lately. Have you noticed?"

I nodded. We had all noticed. Jesus had never been afraid to tell hypocrites the truth about themselves before, but in the past few weeks his criticism of the establishment had become increasingly brazen. The beleaguered Judas had gone so far as to accuse him of intentionally picking fights, which was not strictly true. But with all the disciples now acutely sensitive to the danger that loomed, Judas was no longer alone in his concern. Jesus had always insisted that the law was made for people, rather than the reverse, but his acts of civil disobedience along those lines — everything from failing to perform the ritual washing before a meal to healing people on the Sabbath — had become more blatant. Though he still healed, and preached, and took time to interact with the townsfolk, the Powers-That-Be had become focused on his rule-breaking. He was not supporting the establishment. But the people still supported him.

It could not continue.

"He seems very determined," I said vaguely.

"Yes," she replied. "Determined to say everything that needs to be said, whether people want to hear it or not."

I studied her eyes. Even buried in the midst of a desert of crow's feet and sagging, sun-ravaged skin, they were beautiful eyes. Yet they were miserable. "He said something new?" I asked, beginning to understand. "Today?"

She shook her head. "Nothing new. More like something old that the stubborn ones among us keep ignoring."

I had an urge to reach across the mill and shake her. For all her beating around the bush, I knew the distress signal of a guilty conscience when I saw it. I radiated guilt vibes on an hourly basis, but as Mary wasn't the self-conscious sort, I knew that something was really eating at her. Something other than the same concern over Jesus's fate that had all of us strung up in knots.

"What is it you think you've done wrong?" I asked, skipping over several steps of conversation.

Mary's hand on the mill slowed. She looked up at me with surprise, then lowered her eyes. "I've been doing wrong my whole life," she said wryly.

Mary wasn't bad at the art of conversational evasion, but she was messing with a master. I shook my head. "You're worried about something specific. Something that's come up again recently. What is it?"

Her gaze drifted over the courtyard wall. She was a silent for a long time. I waited longer.

"The tax collector, Zacchaeus," she offered finally. "Did you hear what he told Jesus he would do?"

I had. Our host for the day was a rather pathetic specimen of a man. He was one of the richest individuals in the city, thanks to his line of work, which provided handsomely in proportion to one's crookedness. But he was ridiculously short, shorter even than Leah, which along with his general lack of attractiveness must have left him with an inferiority complex. He had been incredibly anxious to see Jesus when we arrived; but, convinced he would receive no consideration from the taller people who blocked his view, and lacking any concern over how ridiculous he might look, he resolved his problem by shimmying up a sycamore tree and dangling precariously over all our heads. Jesus had found the man's antics so touching he had invited himself over, sending the little outcast into paroxysms of pleasure.

"Zacchaeus told Jesus he would give half of everything he owned to the poor," I answered Mary, "and that he would pay back four-fold any amount he had cheated anybody. What of it? He was deliriously happy when Jesus called him out of the crowd. I got the feeling he would have said anything."

"He probably would have," Mary agreed. "But that isn't the point. The point is that what he did say seemed to please Jesus very much. Didn't you notice that?"

I grasped for the piece I was missing. People often gave money to the poor in honor of Jesus. He was always happy about that, particularly when the gift proved to be a real sacrifice for them. But I failed to see the connection with Mary's own track record. She had given more of herself than anybody — her time *and* her money.

I didn't answer. I stalled by using my free hand to dribble more grain down the center hole of the millstone. My silence proved advantageous.

"He said it was easier for a camel to go through the eye of a needle than for a rich man to enter the kingdom of God," Mary continued soberly. "You didn't hear that, I bet. It was on the road the other day, when the ruler stopped us. Jesse was fussing, and you were walking him around. I didn't think you caught it."

My eyebrows rose. She was right; I had overheard little of that conversation. Both Jesse and his mother had been tired and cranky, and I had been feeling motherly. But now the phrase about the camel evoked the same annoying sense of deja vu I had had so many times before, and which had consistently proved useless. "What exactly did Jesus say?"

Mary's speed on the grindstone increased. "The ruler asked what he needed to do to have eternal life, and Jesus told him to keep the commandments. But when the ruler said he was already doing that, Jesus suggested he also sell his possessions, give the money to the poor, and follow him."

She frowned. "But of course, the ruler couldn't do that, so he went away looking like a ten-ton weight had been dumped on his shoulders."

I caught her eyes. The feeling she was describing was her own.

I sighed. What *was* it with women and guilt?

"Mary," I began, treading carefully. "You've given Jesus everything he's asked for and more. You've made all this possible. You've given money, time, used your business connections with other tribes. You've lived in a tent for months. You're sitting here in the dirt grinding grain with the likes of me. What more could Jesus want from you?"

Her expression turned hard, determined. "You've seen my house, Rachel. Have you ever been anywhere nicer?"

I couldn't answer the question literally. The twenty-two-year-old who cut my hair lived better. So did the guy who delivered my paper. Even inner-city public housing had more amenities. But here? Now?

"Herod lives better," I quipped, attempting to lighten her mood.

I failed.

"I have everything I need, and then double that," she admitted bitterly. "I bought stuff I didn't even want, just to have it. Trinkets, really. Because I needed to *feel* rich. Because I wanted people to know how well I could run the business... how much better I could run it than any of the men I inherited it from."

"Believe me," I responded, "people know. Men respect you. You don't need trinkets to prove that."

"Well it's a good thing," she responded soberly. "Because they're pretty much gone now. I've sold them all. This venture has been a bit more expensive than I anticipated."

I shook my head in confusion. The woman was talking in circles. "Then what are you blaming yourself for? You've already done what the ruler couldn't!"

Mary's dark eyes looked at me sharply, the depths behind them wracked with pain. She stopped grinding abruptly and stood up. I followed her as she crossed to the cistern by the back wall of the house and brought a ladle of water to her lips. We had been out of earshot of the other women before; now we were out of sight as well.

"Tell me what's bothering you, Mary," I begged.

She swallowed. "I didn't need any of the things I sold. They were excess to begin with. I'll hardly miss them. Other people look at what I've spent, and maybe they're impressed, but they don't know the truth."

She set down the ladle and leaned her back against the wall of mud bricks. "What Jesus asked of the ruler... I couldn't do it, either. I couldn't even go as far as Zacchaeus promised. Selling half of what I own would mean sacrificing the business."

Her voice broke. Her steady, strong eyes were, for the first time I had ever seen, moistening. "I can't do that, Rachel. I just can't."

My brain spun. Spun immediately and without mercy to a view of my basement, a room half as big as Mary's house that I used for little except storage. All the kids' sports equipment, outdated electronics, out-of-favor furniture and decorations, boxes of books. I cleaned it out every once in a while and hauled things off to charity, but the room was like a hole in the sand at low tide. It always filled back up. Even if I did dispense with everything in it, the kids would still have all the stuff in their rooms, in the family room, and in the garage. I wouldn't lose any clothes; my jewelry was upstairs, and the kids' baby pictures were in the attic.

The attic! When was the last time I'd even looked up there?

My stomach threatened another spasm, but I shrugged it off. We weren't talking about me.

"Jesus wouldn't expect you to give up your business," I said firmly. "That wasn't what he meant."

"Oh?" Mary responded, her voice intentionally dull. "And what *did* he mean?"

I almost smiled. For once, I did have the benefit of some wisdom — the collective wisdom of two-thousand years' worth of determined Christians scrambling to justify their preferred lifestyle in the face of clear instruction to the contrary. The struggle had always amused me. I had heard everything from "God wants Christians to appear successful" to "it's not how much you have, it's how you *feel* about it," to my personal favorite — which came from my own, multiple-gold-ring-wearing, sports-car-driving, yacht-sailing, summer-home-owning, corporate executive uncle — "Jesus was talking to an individual in a particular situation; that advice wasn't meant for everyone."

Personally, what I knew about the Bible's dictates against the accumulation of wealth seemed straightforward enough. But I had never felt personally obligated by them, because I wasn't rich.

An image of Joe's and my extensive collection of entertainment media, stacked on glass shelves in the living room around the six-foot wide, state-of-the-art television monitor we had gotten each other last Christmas, forced its way into my mind.

I shook my head to dislodge it.

"Mary," I began, "You have no reason to believe that Jesus isn't happy with your contribution, and every reason to believe that he is. Zacchaeus didn't give *all* his belongings to the poor, did he? He only promised half, and as you said yourself, Jesus seemed thrilled with that."

She looked at me skeptically. "You've heard all the other things he's said... about how foolish it is to store up treasure on earth. He talks about it all the time. It's one of his favorite topics. Just because he hasn't singled me out for criticism doesn't mean the message doesn't apply."

I bit my lip, acknowledging that even my dear old uncle would have trouble debating a woman as sharp and knowledgeable of Jesus's words as Mary. And she wanted *me* to be right.

"I've tried to reason it out a hundred ways," she continued, her voice tired. "But it always comes back to one thing. Power."

She lifted her chin and inhaled. "I could do without the comforts. I've been perfectly content out here, as long as I'm with him. Nothing else matters. If he told me he wanted to travel like this forever, I would dump the business in a minute and stay with him till I died."

She released the breath in a huff. "But he's not saying that, is he? He's telling us this won't last forever, that we're going to have to manage without him. But I don't have anything without him. Nothing except the business. And if I give that up now, where will I be?"

She swiped at a single, brimming tear. "You know how it is, Rachel. For a woman, money is everything. It means freedom. It means respect. My business is the only thing separating me from the widows begging at the bazaar who are lucky to get back and forth from their hovels without being molested. If I didn't have money, no one could care less what I thought, no matter how brilliant I am. Even these men, Jesus's own disciples, who have come to respect me now, wouldn't have given the time of day to a *poor* widow with big ideas. Not before Jesus came. And maybe not after."

Her eyes locked on mine. "But Jesus saw it. He took one look at me and he knew. He knew I had a brain, and a good one. And he wanted me to use it. He wanted other people — men — to see and acknowledge what he saw."

She paused a moment, then smiled wryly. "He saw all the bitterness and frivolousness in me, too, but he was willing to overlook that. And I figured if he could, I could. Why not use my evil genius to do some good for a change?"

Her gaze drifted away again. "But no matter how devoted I've acted, I've always kept an insurance plan. The business has always been there, just in case. Ready for me to resume my old life should anything happen to sabotage this one."

"But you're not the same person," I interrupted, irritated. If Mary Magdalene was hiding a black heart that was unsalvageable, mine was petrified sludge that had no business beating. "There's nothing wrong with working hard to make a living. And if you're talented enough or lucky enough to have made a comfortable life for yourself, there's no shame in that either."

*There*, I thought with satisfaction. My uncle would be proud.

"The fact that you're planning for any contingency, keeping the business going while you're away, is a very prudent thing to do," I finished.

Her lips pursed. "Prudent, or faithless?"

I growled beneath my breath. Jesus's talk of not worrying, about feeding and clothing the birds and the lilies and such, was difficult to square with the reality of everyday living. Especially for me. What could I say to a woman who felt guilty about not giving up the one thing that maintained her status as a thinking, independent individual and quite literally could keep her from starving to death? What kind of argument could I make, when I was reluctant to sell my cross-country skis on the off-chance Joe and I might actually vacation somewhere we could use them again, when I had skied with them only twice in the last ten years and when anywhere we might go we could probably rent others?

I didn't know what to say. I wasn't so blind that I couldn't see the self-serving nature of my uncle's arguments, and the flaws therein. But I couldn't accept Mary's interpretation, either. Despite Jesus's copious attention to the subject of wealth hoarding, he had never expressed dissatisfaction with anyone's attempt to earn a living. He just liked for people to share. Mary was asking too much of herself... too much of anybody.

I tried again.

"You're a good teacher, Mary," I began, inspiration striking. "You understand things the rest of us don't, and you can explain them almost as well as Jesus can. Not many people have that kind of insight. It's a talent I expect Jesus wants you to use. But how are you going to make good use of it if you lose your livelihood? With the business, you'll be free to go where you want and teach people — even if it is only other women — what Jesus has taught you. Without the business, you'd be scratching and clawing just to keep yourself fed. How would that help anyone? You don't have to live like a queen. If you want to sell your mirrors and your baubles and live more simply, then fine... do it. But the business hasn't been holding you back from doing what you need to do. If anything, it's enabled you."

Her hazel eyes brightened. A ghost of a smile dawned. "Good point," she agreed.

"Why, thank you."

"I suppose it's easier to see things clearly when you don't have twenty years' worth of efforts to impress the neighbors hanging around your neck like a millstone," she added.

I swallowed. I told my inner voice to shut up. We were talking about Mary. Not me.

"But you're right," she continued. "There is a difference, isn't there? Between what enables a person... and what holds them back."

*Four cellphones. The exercise bike. The housecleaning service — but only twice, in spring and fall. Boxes of albums from the eighties. Three video gaming systems. Dues at the club. Lightning-speed internet and premium programming. The riding mower we hadn't used since we hired the lawn service. Bekka's photography studio. Joe's weight set. My treadmill. A half-dozen computers...*

*SHUT UP!*

"Still," Mary continued, mercifully interrupting my raving mind, "I'm not sure Jesus didn't mean every word he said, exactly as he said it. The question is, if I went to him tomorrow and told him I had given up everything — and I mean *everything* — would he be pleased?"

I sucked in a breath. Maybe that was the question. I certainly couldn't answer it for her. But Mary, unlike me and everyone like me, didn't *have* to sit around wondering and debating the issue. She had an option few people did.

"Why don't you talk to him?" I suggested. "Tell him you're confused; ask him to explain. Surely he'll tell you what he really wants you to do."

Mary's sharp eyes locked on mine. "I could do that," she replied. "But to be perfectly honest with you, Rachel..."

Her voice trailed off.

"Yes?"

The muscles in her jaw tightened.

"I'm too afraid of his answer."

*Commentary for Chapter 19 begins on page 278.*

# Chapter 20

I tried not to shiver. If anyone noticed, they wouldn't understand. By all superficial accounts, it was a glorious moment. The people of Jerusalem — more people than I had ever seen congregated in any one place at one time — were ecstatic about Jesus's arrival in the city. The news that he had resurrected a man four-days-dead in the tomb, right next door in Bethany, had raised excitement over his long-awaited visit to a fever pitch, and the townspeople poured into the streets like flowing water, streaming out of every courtyard gate and every alley while scores more watched and cheered from the flanking rooftops.

I was fighting with everything in me to believe that what I *thought* I knew was wrong. But the familiarity of the scene unfolding before me was dead-on accurate.

Jesus was riding on a donkey. The people waiting for him in the streets were taking the cloaks off their backs and laying them down on the filthy, dusty road for us to walk over. Others had broken branches from trees and were waving them high above their heads as Jesus passed by. Many of them were chanting. It was an exuberant, joyous, frenetic celebration.

It made my blood run cold.

I walked close to Judas. Of all the disciples I felt sure that he would understand, that he would feel the same chilling undercurrent of danger that made my teeth chatter in my jaws.

He did.

"I haven't heard people chanting like that before," I commented, my voice stilted. I didn't dare look directly at him. As freely as he now spoke with me at camp, he was still leery of being obvious about our relationship in public. But I could tell from the taut set of his muscles and the quick, alert movements of his eyes that he was as uptight as I was. And as in need of a confidant. "What does it mean?"

I had to wait several seconds for his answer. His voice was hushed, but its deep tone carried, even through the roar of the crowd. "Psalms. They are greeting him as they would royalty."

My already raw stomach churned. I didn't need to ask him how the establishment would respond to such a twist in the public's perception of Jesus. The priesthood and aristocracy had felt threatened enough by the rabbi's irreverent attitude when his followers saw him only as a healer and a teacher. To call him a prophet was pushing it. The title "king" would be acceptable to no one. Not the Jewish theocracy, and most definitely not the Romans.

"What can we do?"

Judas's eyes flickered briefly toward mine. They were careworn. Bordering on desperate. His tone was dry and lifeless. "He could save himself. But he won't. He won't listen to me. The others know I'm right, but they do whatever he tells them, whether it makes sense or not. So now we're all walking off a cliff."

I shivered. Even in the heat, I could not suppress the urge. The coldness in my gut would not abate. I knew perfectly well what degree of irony — or perhaps idiocy — could be attached to the fact that, at this critical juncture, I was voluntarily aligning myself with a man named Judas Iscariot. But even as my conscience badgered me with the absurdity, I had no power to ignore what I was experiencing. I could not flip a switch and override the people and the heat and the disease and the anguish on the basis of a bunch of stories I still couldn't rule out as being the creations of my own mind. I had no doubt, at any level, that Judas loved Jesus like a brother. All he wanted was to save his friend's life.

He just didn't know how to do it.

Neither did I.

History alleged that whatever Judas had done, it had turned out badly — for both of them. The thought of either of these strong, wonderfully kind young men meeting a premature death sickened me, and the helplessness I felt now, here in the face of it, was too painful for words. I didn't know how to stop what was happening. Even if I did, it seemed impossible that I could.

If learning how to live in a foreign environment had taught me one thing, it was just how insignificant I really was. In my world, people gained a sense of self-importance by sitting in front of their televisions pretending superiority to idiotic talk show guests or spewing their personal views anonymously across the internet. Safe in our cyber cocoons, we could fool ourselves into believing we knew better than everyone else, that we had real influence, real power. We were sure we could call the shots in the flesh-and-blood world, too — if we wanted.

But we couldn't.

I was only one small cog in an infinitely large machine whose master switch was beyond my reach. I could do my job, turn the next wheel or not, but I couldn't stop all the others. And I could run ahead of our procession right now and jump up and down and scream that the establishment was plotting to execute Jesus, and that the only way for the people to save him was to rise up and physically defend him 24/7 against their own leaders, or else stop following him at all.

But it wouldn't work. Whether or not such interference would unravel some theoretical time-space continuum was not even worth contemplating. The fact was that absolutely no one would pay the least attention to the ravings of a practically elderly female, no matter if she was traveling with Jesus or not.

I had no ability to change the course of history.

But that didn't mean I could stand around and do nothing, either.

I braved a look at Judas. "Jesus doesn't trust the establishment," I asserted, heart pounding. "Perhaps you shouldn't either."

Judas's eyes flashed with indignation. It was the first sign of temper I had seen from him, but it didn't frighten me. What it showed was a man at the end of his rope, cracking under the strain. "But the establishment is all we've got!" he responded, forgetting not to meet my eyes. "I happen to know that many of the officials are sympathetic to Jesus, even if they're afraid to say so openly. There's still a chance they can sway the others, if Jesus will only meet them halfway. If he doesn't, there is no hope. The Romans will step in. And they won't wait much longer to do it."

I stepped back slightly and dropped my eyes. Judas's voice was rising, and it wouldn't do for his words to be overheard. As fond as the other disciples were of Judas as a man and a friend, they were having a hard enough time cooperating with what Jesus wanted without Judas's far more logical-sounding words ringing in their ears, and tempers had been running short all around.

No one seemed to have overheard, perhaps because we were spread out more than usual. Unlike the mobs in past cities, this crowd stood back a respectful distance from our procession.

*They're treating him like royalty.*

"But surely these people would turn against anyone who hurt Jesus," I insisted, trying to be encouraged, rather than saddened, by the myriad shining faces, the chanting children, the waving palms.

Judas did not turn his head, and I noticed in profile the deep creases in his brow. They hadn't always been there. "The people already hate the Romans," he said, his voice low again. "It's our leadership that's afraid to risk alienating its own nation. That's why if Jesus would just cooperate with those in power, meet with the Sanhedrin... I believe he could work something out. There are some corrupt individuals there, yes, but there are also plenty of decent ones." His eyes blazed with frustration. "If he would only work within the blasted system!"

I swallowed. The creeping realization that this man could *be* me became stark. Not only did I understand how he felt, I knew I would act the same way under the same circumstances. Logic before emotion. Systems, processes. It was the way I operated, the way I had earned money. There was nothing wrong with it. It was just the way I was. Judas was immensely fond of Jesus, but ultimately, he would put his faith in the system. It was the only practical, logical, and responsible thing to do.

It would also kill them both.

I had to try something. Anything. Even if it meant arguing against what would have been my own best instincts, too. "Judas," I said earnestly, "you know that Jesus is intelligent. He's no fool when it comes to reading people, and he's said this is what he wants. Maybe he *does* know what he's doing. Maybe he's seeing a bigger picture. Perhaps you should trust his judgment."

Judas didn't look at me. What he did was huff out a breath. His eyes half rolled.

I knew what he was thinking. He was thinking I was as every bit as naive and romantic as the rest of them, trusting blindly in whatever Jesus said, oblivious to the obvious, living in a dream world of denial. *He* was the only sensible one. It was his job to keep the rest of them grounded. To keep them safe from themselves.

He knew better than Jesus did.

He sure as heck wasn't going to listen to me.

I watched, my heart heavy, as Judas rushed his steps and pulled ahead, cutting off our conversation. He respected me — to an extent. But I was still just a woman.

I dipped my chin, concentrating on keeping my eyes dry. All around me, the disciples' wives seemed energized by the crowd's adoration of Jesus. They were blissfully unaware of its dark side, and I felt no need to educate them. None of them could change what was to happen either, but their ignorance, at least, kept them from feeling it. This biting, piercing sense of powerlessness was all mine.

I was used to getting what I wanted. I had been raised to believe that I could be anything I wanted to be; that if I wanted something badly enough and worked hard enough for it, it could be mine. I wanted to grab that same brass ring now. I wanted to take charge and set everything right — Supermom to the rescue. But even if I were to look down and find myself wearing superhero tights and a cape, I wouldn't know where to begin to fix this. I didn't know what was right.

The intentions of my acid-scourged gut were clear enough. My gut wanted to airlift both Jesus and Judas from the middle of this hideous, portentous display and set them safely down hundreds — maybe even thousands — of miles away. They would both live full lives. They would stay friends. The disciples left behind would be a bit bewildered, but eventually they would regroup and continue the ministry. Jesus had showed them the transforming power of love, and they believed in it now, heart and soul. His commandment was more than rhetoric to them. It was the whole meaning of life.

But my gut couldn't airlift anybody anywhere, and my brain knew that. My brain also knew that if Jesus's life had ended differently, countless historic dominoes would be displaced, affecting future societies in a way that was impossible to predict. Who was I to mess with all that? What right did I have, when I wasn't even supposed to be here? And if I did interfere, would I not be making the exact same, self-important, ill-fated judgment call that Judas was about to make?

I dared a glance upward at the object of the crowd's attention. Jesus's expression was solemn. He usually enjoyed the people's veneration, responding to it with genuine appreciation and affection. Perhaps he knew that this time, it wouldn't last.

I put a hand to my stomach.

My brain might be calling the shots. But my gut wasn't going down easy.


I had no desire for any of the food in front of me. The skinned body of the sacrificial lamb had been roasted whole over an open fire, twisted on a wooden spit. The smell of meat, which ordinarily affected my fat-starved metabolism like one of Pavlov's dogs, now only wracked me with nausea.

We were gathered for the Passover celebration at a private home in Jerusalem. There were so many people buzzing about I wasn't even sure whose home it was. But it didn't matter.

Everyone's euphoria over Jesus's dramatic welcome into the city had dissipated days ago. The rabbi had wasted no time in causing a scene at the temple, then clashing repeatedly with the hostile officials who lay in wait for him at every turn. The establishment had begun an all-out effort to discredit Jesus with the people, and rumors of plots against his life were rife.

The disciples, with the exception of Judas, were still determined to toe whatever line their master wanted them to toe. But to accept the situation with equanimity was not within them. They were tense, and they were watchful. Not one of them had slept soundly in days. When we had at last reached the house where the men were to eat their Passover meal, they had climbed the steps to the upper room like zombies.

The women, as usual, waited outside.

Our numbers had grown. We had left a contented and optimistic Mahlah with Mary and Martha in Bethany, but we had been joined in Jerusalem for the Passover by several other Galilean pilgrims, including Zebedee and Salome, Andrew's wife Shua, and the mother of the younger disciple James. A group of Jesus's relatives from Nazareth, including his mother, was expected soon. Food was plentiful, and hands to help in its preparation had been abundant.

But no one felt festive.

Leah, Tamar, and Priscilla picked at their meat with puffy eyes and reddened noses, evidence of the misery they made no effort to hide. They knew that Jesus was in mortal danger now, and they knew that their husbands were prepared to die in his defense. Naomi, Bernice, and Shua, though displaying the reserve one might expect from relatively more mature women, were equally disturbed. The plump, wisecracking Joanna had become silent and sallow, and our tough-as-nails Susanna, to the surprise of all, showed cheeks as tear-stained as those of the teens.

Then there was Mary. Quiet, withdrawn, exceptionally weary. Her bright eyes, always so ready with a sparkle — or an impudent gleam — appeared glassy and unseeing. She seemed to walk in an imaginary cloud of her own making, not interacting, not comprehending, just thinking, feeling, and breathing in a space that was all her own. She would not talk to me, or to any of the women. Yet every moment she had the chance, she stuck tight to Jesus's side.

Even now, as the other women huddled in loose groups to eat, chatting in hushed, awkward tones of anything but the fear that chilled us, Mary stood by herself without eating, her gaze locked on the house of our host, studying the door Jesus had walked through as if by willpower she could dissolve it.

I moved to stand beside her.

No words of comfort would be adequate. Even if I could somehow convince her, as well as myself, that all those lovely resurrection stories were true, it still would not take away the horror that was yet to come. But I could not witness her pain now and do nothing.

I put my arm around her shoulders. She leaned into me limply, resting her head against mine.

"I found more than a son in him, Rachel," she said quietly, though her voice remained steady. "Did you know that? Ever since I was a little girl, I've had this itch — more of a compulsion, really — to do something important. Something more than just making a good marriage and raising children. My whole life I've worked hard to *be* more, to *have* more than anyone else. But I was never satisfied. I wanted to build something sturdier than a bunch of fishing boats. I wanted to build something that would *last*. And when I met Jesus, I found it. A purpose I could be proud of. Helping him made my life *mean* something, Rachel. Finally. But the price—" Her voice faltered at last, and her shoulders shuddered beneath my arm. She stifled a sob. "Dear God, the price is high. Why does it have to hurt so much?"

I held her tighter. "Because you love him," I answered. "We all do."

Her words were brimming with larger issues, but all I could focus on was her pain. Perhaps, in a former life, such talk of love for a younger male friend would seem strange. But spending time in the company of a man like Jesus changed one's perception. For him, showing love to relatives, friends, neighbors, and enemies alike was as ordinary as breathing. Even the hypocrites he harangued could easily have perceived it, had they lowered their defenses enough to feel. He wasn't ashamed to act loving toward people, no matter what anyone thought. Giving and receiving love was his greatest joy, and the trait was rampantly contagious.

Mary forced in a few deep breaths. Then she lifted her head and straightened. "It's time, Rachel," she said after a moment, her voice stronger now, full of resolve. "I have something to tell everyone."

She left me and gathered the women of our party together to stand as we had so often stood before, in a circle around the cooking fire. Her eyes were steely, and her manner was composed. The moment of weakness I had just witnessed was over. Mary was as human as any of us; but she was made of stern stuff.

"I'll keep this short and to the point," she began. "You all know that Jesus has told his disciples he will die. Here. In Jerusalem. He has also said that he will rise again. There has been a lot of talk about what that means, and I can't claim to understand it myself. What I do understand is this. He told me himself that these things must happen. And as much as I hate it, I have promised to abide by his wishes."

No one said a word. Mary swallowed and went on.

"He also told me this. He wants no one to die with him. He wants the disciples to carry on with his work, not to sacrifice their lives in some pointless skirmish. We all know any of them would die for him, as would we. But he won't allow them to. He insists they save themselves."

Leah, across from me, stood ashen faced. I could imagine the relief felt by all the wives at Mary's words, but I could also understand the peculiarity of the request — and its burden. Dying for a just cause was the stuff of heroes. Running away to save one's self was a disgrace.

Jesus's challenge, once again, had come with a twist. Abandoning him would not be easy for any of the disciples, for they, like innumerable soldiers before and after them, would rather die than be thought a coward. But I was confident they would do it. They would do it because he asked them to.

I caught the movement out of the corner of my eye, a slight movement of a dark head and a cloak that, in the crowded, dimly lit courtyard, should have no reason to attract me. But it did. And when I turned my gaze to the courtyard gate just in time to see Judas slipping out of it, my feet went so far as to rise and shuffle a step.

*No, Judas! Don't!*

But my feet went nowhere. He had taken off at a jog; I could not catch him. Even if I could, I wouldn't be able to change his mind. I had tried already. He was convinced that Jesus's last hope lay with the Sanhedrin, and he was committed to arranging a meeting, whether Jesus consented to it or not.

It was for the rabbi's own good.

My insides felt as though they had been gouged. The gate swung closed. Judas was gone.

"I'm telling you this," Mary continued, her voice still strong, "so you can be prepared for what *we* have to do. The men cannot stay with Jesus, or they will be arrested. But no one will take notice of a few harmless women. I myself intend to stay by Jesus's side no matter what happens—" her voice quavered only slightly, "till the bitter end. And I was hoping some of you would join me."

"I will," said Salome immediately, straightening to her full, diminutive height. "No one will pester an old woman like me. I'm not worth their effort. If my sons can't be there for Jesus, I'll stand by him myself."

Other women began to speak at once, promising their support, just as the courtyard gates opened to a flurry of activity. More pilgrims had arrived. Mary Magdalene left the circle and approached the visitors, going immediately to a small woman about her own age, embracing her tenderly.

The newcomer drew back, looking up into Mary's face expectantly. I heard no words pass between them, but Mary's expression must have answered what was left unspoken. The other woman buried her head on Mary's shoulder and began to sob.

*Jesus's mother.*

I looked away, then turned on my heel. I wish I could say that my desire to avoid Jesus's kin from Nazareth was based on the fear that my ruse about knowing his family would be debunked, but I had forgotten all that. The truth was that I couldn't stand by another second watching these noble women — who already stood to lose everything — pledge to give even more.

They were going to stay with Jesus. They would force themselves to watch the whole, grisly, horrible thing. They seemed to think it would help him, that it was the least they could do.

It was more than I could do.

Maybe they didn't realize how bad things would get. Maybe having grown up here, they were more inured to suffering and torture. I had witnessed my share of onscreen violence, but this was not a screen, and the person suffering was not an actor. It would be bad enough to watch such horrors perpetrated on a stranger. But to stand by and do nothing while it was happening to someone so empathetic and kind, who would go out of his way to spare anyone else any sort of pain...

I couldn't do it. I couldn't stand it. My sense of powerlessness would be intolerable. Whether I wept and wailed from a safe distance, ran forward and beat the soldiers with my fists, or threw myself in front of the executioners would make no difference to the outcome for Jesus. I couldn't save him; I couldn't even lessen his pain. And if I could do nothing, I couldn't bear to be there at all.

I just couldn't.

So what good was I?

The words pummeled my brain as I walked away from the women, aimlessly, desperate to be alone. What was the point of my being here at all? Of all places, among all times, why now?

And why me? Maybe somebody else would have done better. Maybe somebody else, given such a fantastic and unexpected opportunity, would have turned all this mess around and pulled out a happy ending.

But not me. Not Rachel. Supermom hadn't accomplished jack. She had worked up the nerve to talk to Jesus exactly three times and had screwed up every one of them. She had started off by letting him know he didn't meet requirements — nothing personal, he just didn't look right. Then she had asked him to heal somebody... but only *if* he could. Nice vote of confidence, there. And then, as her grand finale, she had refused to commit herself to believing he was anything more than a particularly nice man who happened to have a way with bread, fish, and psychosomatic illnesses.

All in all, it had been a stellar performance.

*Stellar.*

With only the light cast off from scattered torches to guide me, I felt my way around the back of the house and climbed a ladder. I didn't care where the ladder led, as long as it took me out of sight. I found myself on a narrow span of roof just above the level of the courtyard wall and planted myself on it, resting my back against the dried mud.

I had felt like a failure before. I had had a miscarriage once, before Bekka. The doctors insisted it wasn't my fault, and rationally I knew they were right, but I still couldn't rid the guilt from my system. I couldn't stop wondering if it were the cough medicine I took, or all the junk food I had been eating, or the fact that before I knew I was pregnant I had sprayed ant killer all over the house. I would never know why, but I would always, no matter what anyone told me, feel like I had failed my child.

I had been determined not to fail the other ones. Maybe that was what had turned me into such a rabid mothering machine. But then, I had been determined not to have a failed marriage either, and I had been letting that one slide. Joe and I spent way too little time together and expended way too little effort trying to change that. It was a bad sign I had been ignoring, but seeing so many women trapped in loveless marriages for the sake of security had given me pause. Being able to marry for love was a privilege, and I had no business taking that fact, or my husband, for granted.

I had failed my family, all around. I had neglected my marriage in favor of micromanaging our children to the point of making them incapable.

Supermom, indeed.

So what good was I? All my youthful dreams of changing the world had seemed silly once I got mired in diapers and a mortgage. What little time I had for volunteer work I had shifted from charitable organizations to helping with my own kids' schools and activities. Just six months ago my conscience had nagged me into offering to help out a friend at a soup kitchen, but every time she had called, I had had something more important to do.

Mary had wanted her life to mean something, something beyond the expected, the mundane. And she *had* made it mean something. Much more than she knew. When she expressed that ambition to me I understood, because once upon a time, I had felt the same. Only at some point, I had given up. And I never even realized it had happened.

I picked up a stone from the roof and tossed it over the courtyard wall into the alley. I had never been one to sit around feeling sorry for myself, and I didn't want to start now. I wanted to act. I wanted to pour myself into the problem at hand with everything that was in me, to fight until I was weary, to attack the sense of failure that dragged me down and beat it back into oblivion.

I wanted the nightmare that was Jerusalem to end without bloodshed, without pain. And I wanted another chance to talk to Jesus. One I didn't screw up.

A chance to make things right.

I jumped as a door swung open beside me.

*Commentary for Chapter 20 begins on page 281.*

# Chapter 21

Embarrassed to be caught lurking where I was, I rose to my feet and flattened myself against the wall. The door opened only partway, allowing the dim glow of the lamps inside to spill out into the darkness. I could hear the rumble of many male voices from within, but the female figure who stood lodged in the doorway now, half in and half out, was pausing to listen to the barked instructions of another woman just inside. "Throw it in the alley. Not straight down!"

Protected from view by the door, I slipped on around the corner of the house. I heard a whooshing sound as some unidentified substance was flung over the courtyard wall, then the solid thump of the door reclosing. Breathing a relieved sigh, I decided to stay where I was. The roof on this side was no more than a ledge. But I did have benefit of a window.

I felt no compunction as I crept silently across the roof to the narrow, slit-shaped hole that allowed a modicum of air into the house's stifling upper floors. Such windows barred both rain and burglars, but they were worthless against peeping Toms. I stood up on my tiptoes and looked inside.

The room within was large for a house of this size, but it was still crowded. The men reclined around the standard low table, some closer to it and some farther away, as space allowed. The slit-hole gave only a limited view from any angle, and I moved my head this way and that, looking for Jesus. I didn't see him.

The men appeared to be somewhere in the middle of their meal. But rather than talking casually among themselves, or listening to the rabbi, they were quiet. They seemed focused, oddly, on one of the servants.

Where was Jesus? He could not possibly have left the house alone. Not tonight. The disciples wouldn't have let him. If he had exited through either the front door or side staircase the women would have seen him, and I myself had been by the back door for a while now.

I continued to maneuver my head to different angles, searching the depths of the room. I could not see all of everyone. Perhaps I had missed him. The men were having their feet washed, which was odd in the middle of a meal, but everything about tonight was odd. The Passover celebration was supposed to be festive, but the tension in the crowded room was so thick it seemed to ooze out the slit like smoke. Tension... and sorrow.

The servant stood up and walked with his basin of water toward the next man's feet. As soon as he rose, I could see that it was Jesus. He had removed his cloak and was bare to the waist. He had a towel tied around his middle.

I turned away from the window. My knees felt wobbly, and I wanted to sit down, but the ledge was too narrow for comfort. I moved back around the corner and plopped down on the smooth-rolled mud where I had been before, my back against the bricks.

I didn't want to see Jesus washing his disciples' feet. Every detail that jibed with my memory only made the rest of it — the worst of it — seem more inevitable. That he would lower himself to such a menial task didn't surprise me, not knowing his nature as I did now. I doubted that the disciples were surprised either, though it obviously made them uncomfortable. Jesus had a real genius about him when it came to illustrating a point. I hadn't even been in the room with them, and I got it. He would be handing over the mantle soon; the disciples would be in charge. He wanted them to understand that the best leaders considered nothing beneath them. That humility was their best defense against the corruptive influence of power — the power that gave birth to hypocrites.

My eyes closed. All at once, I was tired. Tired of being hit in the face with my own inadequacies. I could see now, looking at the disciples, exactly why Jesus had chosen them. Peter was loud and irreverent and human and funny, but he was indeed a rock. His strength of character went deep, far deeper than any casual observer would guess. The same was true of James and John, who underneath all their showy machismo and bluster were exceptionally good and kind-hearted men. All the disciples were, by their very natures, loving people. They expressed it in different ways, and each had his own unique talents and faults, but they were and always had been on the same page.

Internally, they were strong. They might not have known that when they met Jesus, but they all knew it now. They had learned where their abilities fit into the mix, and like Simon and Thaddeus and their penchant for crowd control, each had been proud to do his part. Jesus had let none of the men, however surprised they were to be included in his company in the first place, waste time and effort bemoaning their shortcomings. Instead he had encouraged them to look inside, find their strengths, and get to work. *Pronto.*

But it wasn't just the disciples, was it? Jesus had the same effect on most everyone he met. Mary Magdalene, by all accounts, had been a total ogress, but the ambition that lay beneath her selfish behavior had turned to gold when she was given the right challenge. Leah and Bernice had joined the group with deeply ingrained sanctimonious attitudes about class and race, and they still paid lip service to what they saw as "fittin'." But I could tell they didn't believe the rhetoric anymore. If push came to shove they would always, now, put people above the picayunish. Joanna had gone from pampered to pampering, and Susanna's self-defensiveness had turned to advocacy. Tamar... well, Tamar had been practically perfect to begin with. But she did seem more confident now. Both in her husband and herself.

And then there was me.

I took in a deep breath, then released it with a shudder.

I had to have strengths. Even if they weren't what I used to think they were. Maybe they weren't so obvious, but I couldn't be a total loss. Mary liked me, didn't she?

I smiled to myself. That was something. Despite her devotion to the cause, Mary was not the sort of woman who liked everybody. But she saw something in me. What? She had said that she admired my boldness, particularly with men. But was that truly a trait of mine, or just a reflection of another culture?

I considered, and my smile widened. No, Mary was right. I knew plenty of women in my own day and age who would do anything to avoid making waves, who could never bring themselves to stand up for anything unpopular. I wasn't one of those women. Not in my daily life, and not when I had worked for a corporation. People didn't scare me; I had always been difficult to intimidate. Okay, granted — men with daggers scared me. But smart-alecky MBAs in suits? Forget it. I had always defended myself when I needed to, and other people when they couldn't or wouldn't defend themselves. I had never thought of the tendency as a talent; it had seemed more like an attitude. An attitude which had, on many an occasion, gotten me into trouble.

Still, it was fun. I had always liked being a crusader. But as my desire to change the world had morphed into a desire to make my own life perfect, I had begun to crusade for different things. Things which, once won, had made for increasingly hollow victories. My foot had remained on the pedal, but my wheels weren't on the road anymore. They were spinning in the clear blue air.

I was a crusader without a cause.

I grimaced. My earnest, idealistic teenaged self wouldn't know me anymore. She would plant her hands on her hips and remind me, with dropped jaw, that *my* mother would have made me pick up my own stupid prom dress.

She would have made me pay for it, too.

So who was I? What part of that naive but well-intentioned girl was still inside? What exactly did I have to do to find her again?

*Out of the overflow of the heart, the mouth speaks.*

Jesus's cryptic comment flooded my brainwaves, pestering me as it had repeatedly ever since the day he had spoken those words — the day he had healed Susanna. I had yet to understand them. They had come on the heels of my colossal blunder in asking him *if* he could heal her, and I had assumed that he was either accusing me of blabbering — which, though accurate, would be out of character — or that he was pointing out a Freudian slip. My heart had doubts. My mouth had just proved it.

But what if he wasn't accusing me of anything? What if he had meant the words as a compliment?

I thought back to the context — how nervous I felt at approaching him, but how determined I was to see Susanna healed. I understood what an obstacle her pride had become, how hard it was for her to ask for help when she was quite certain she could do without it. I felt for her, and I wanted to help her.

*Out of the overflow of the heart, the mouth speaks.*

My lips drew into a smile. I was such an idiot. He hadn't been talking about the "if." He was big enough to ignore that. He had been talking about the rest of it. He had been praising what was in my heart.

Compassion.

It was something I assumed almost everyone had. Something feminine, something sweet, something... well, *weak*. But everyone wasn't like me. Everyone hadn't gone wobbly in the knees watching the mourning of the widow in Nain. But her pain had affected me deeply, just as it had Jesus. I had been tortured by the fact that I couldn't do anything, but he could, and he did, whether he was supposed to or not. Perhaps he couldn't stand it, either.

And what of Mahlah? How many of the women had stood there, content to do nothing, while a bunch of thugs threatened to throw rocks at her until she died? Jesus hadn't let that happen, and I wouldn't have either, whatever it took. And after she was saved and left to fend for herself, to walk out the gate into an even slower, but still-certain death, who had stepped forward to help her? Not Mary. Not Bernice. Not even Tamar.

*I* had. With Susanna right there behind me. And Jesus waiting and watching, thanking me with his eyes.

*Good job, Rachel. I knew you'd come through.*

I did have talents, blast it all! I was bold, I was brave, and most of all, I was compassionate. I had never thought of the latter as a strength before. But that was because I was an idiot.

I had a bleeding heart, and I should be proud of it. My attraction to social work had been no accident. It was inevitable. My more practical side had taken me on a different course, but I wasn't going to bemoan any of that now. I had two kids and a husband I loved, and I would never regret any decision that had brought me to that place. But that didn't mean my future was set in stone. Logic and practicality had their place, but so did my crazy, beautiful bleeding heart, and I would never consider it a weakness again.

It was a strength. *My* strength. And from now on, I was going to use it.

The wooden door scraped open across the mud roof. Light spilled out over the courtyard wall. I stood.

My pulse pounded, but this time, I didn't run away. Someone was coming out.

"You can put the ladder across to the wall," an unfamiliar male voice whispered, "then drop down into the alley. No one will see."

The man was followed closely by Peter, then Andrew. Just as the three of them reached down and began to pull up the ladder, Jesus himself stepped through the door.

They were leaving. Now, in the darkness. To steal away from the crowds out front. To go to the quiet place where Jesus would ultimately be arrested. This was it. I wouldn't see him again.

"Jesus?"

The word came out of my mouth as an impulse, but I didn't want to pull it back. Not even after the other men jumped a foot, then fixed me with a scowl. They had not expected to find a stray woman eavesdropping on the roof. It was hardly a pleasant surprise. They had more important concerns.

Yet Jesus stepped around the door to face me. "Yes?"

We were standing in shadow. One of the men had a torch, and the orange glow of oil lamps spilled out the door from inside. Jesus's face was half-hidden in the flickering light, but I could see him well enough.

I didn't want to waste his time. But I did, desperately, want to help him. I was certain now that there must be something I could do. And if that meant walking every step of the way with those beastly Roman soldiers, I would do it. I would do anything, whatever he wanted. He knew my strengths. I would let him choose.

"What do you want me to do?" I asked evenly. Clearly. My chin held high.

He regarded me for a moment, his expression unchanging. "Stay here," he answered. "And pray for me."

A part of my composure crumpled. Warm waves of relief seemed to gel my every muscle, even as the fiber of me stood firm. I would not have to stand by and watch him be tortured. He didn't want me to. Perhaps he felt there would be enough torture already.

I was grateful beyond words. I was so touched, I wanted to cry. But I wasn't done yet. Not nearly. The ladder had been laid across from the roof to the courtyard wall, and the other disciples were already filing out the door and walking across it. I didn't have much time.

I swallowed, and met his eyes. This time, my voice betrayed me. I was frightened. Frightened of what was to happen — both to him, and to me. But I had to know the next step.

"And after?" I asked.

His head tilted a little, as if he were trying to see me better in the dimness. He didn't smile, but the familiar sparkle was back in his eyes. The sparkle that conveyed his pleasure with people, and sometimes, in my case frequently, his amusement. He raised a hand then, taking the back side of his knuckles and touching them lightly, and very briefly, to my temple.

"Ask me again sometime," he answered.

"Jesus?" James's nervous voice broke in, "are you ready to go?"

Jesus's eyes remained on mine only a second, and then he turned around. He and James walked across the ladder to the courtyard wall, then hopped off the other side of it and down into the alley with the others. The unfamiliar man, whom I took to be the owner of the house, pulled back the ladder and set it in place again. As per custom he said nothing to me, but his reproval was evident in his glare as he gestured emphatically in the direction of the other women.

I ignored him.

I walked to the edge of the roof and looked out. The disciples were heading down the alley covertly, moving away from the crowd that waited in vain by the courtyard gate. The men walked in silence, with a minimum of torches.

I would never see Jesus again.

Never mind that I hadn't expected to see him in the first place. Never mind that I had wasted so much time in his company puzzling over the physics and fretting over the theology — the very nonsense that had driven me from organized religion in the first place. In the end, I had gotten the message. It was all so simple, when you stripped away the trappings. At least he made it seem so.

Which is why I was fighting so hard, right now, not to cry. Not because he was off to settle some celestial score for the sake of all humanity. But just because I would miss him.

I picked out the back of his head in the glow of the torches. Every step the men took pierced me like a knife, and I was overwhelmed with an emotion I vowed never to hide again. I knew now that it, too, was a strength. Never, ever, a weakness.

My lips moved, barely making a sound. "I love you."

The owner of the house didn't hear me. He was only three feet away, gesticulating wildly now, no doubt contemplating the consequences of grabbing a respectable widow by the arm and shoving her bodily off his roof.

Mr. BullyMan hadn't heard me. But far down the alley, the head I had been watching so keenly turned around, and the light of the torch Peter carried shone fully on Jesus's face. He looked back at me.

He smiled.

*Commentary for Chapter 21 begins on page 285.*

# Chapter 22

My eyes opened, but I couldn't see anything. Something was covering my face. I reached up a hand and pulled away the soft, fluffy fabric of a T-shirt. I blinked. Late afternoon sun filtered around the edges of my window shades. My body lay enveloped in the familiar, cushioned comfort of the twenty-eight hundred dollar mattress.

I blinked again. Then I smiled.

I was home.

For a long moment I lay still, afraid to break the spell. But with each second that passed, I grew more confident. And more excited.

*I was home.*

Sounds drifted up from the family room below: the swell of canned crowd noises from one of Ryan's sports games, the swooshing noise from Rachel's phone as she blitzed inane text messages to her friends.

The kids were safe. They were fine.

All was well.

I stood up. I half-expected my legs to be shaky, but they weren't. I felt good. Remarkably good.

I had never felt better.

I padded across carpet as soft as a pillow to stand at the door to my bathroom and stare. White porcelain. It was a thing of beauty. I looked into the open medicine cabinet, feasting my eyes. Pain reliever. Toothbrush and toothpaste. Deodorant. Shampoo. Feminine hygiene products... oh my. I could kiss the box.

It was all here, just as I had left it. I had missed nothing. Nothing had changed.

I moved toward the door, anxious to see the kids and confirm with my own eyes that they really were okay, but as I passed the entrance to my walk-in closet I stopped. Then I stared.

There were enough clothes in my closet for fifty people. I stepped inside, dazed, reaching out to touch them, to verify their bizarre existence. Why had I bought them all? Most I hadn't worn in years. "Thin clothes" I would never get my thighs in again. Why were they still here? And the *shoes!* The shoes must be breeding in their trees at night. Even an octopus couldn't make use of them all.

I stepped out and slammed the door behind me.

Maybe everything wasn't the same.

My heart beat fast.

It must have been a dream. How it could have seemed so real and lasted so long was beyond me. But I was here, in the twenty-first century, and I had never been anywhere else. The people weren't real. The places weren't real. I hadn't accomplished any of the things I thought I had accomplished. All I had done was take a nap.

My euphoria disappeared.

It wasn't real.

None of it.

I stood still in the dim room. I felt cold.

Empty.

The sunlight that peeked around the shades cast a pattern of warm yellow lines across my bedspread. I raised my eyes to the window. I crossed to it and rolled up the shade with a snap.

My big, beautiful backyard was filled with trees. Lush green grass. Bushes. Spring flowers. Sunlight streamed in long, slanted rays through the branches of the oaks, dappling the fertile ground with shafts of brightness. Only one sun had ever shone on the earth. This same one had shone on Galilee.

My body began to warm.

It could too have been real. Who was to say? It had happened to me, no one else. Everything that had happened was between me, myself, and the preternatural. And with everything in me, I *wanted* it to be real.

A wave of heat crept through my veins. I could make it so, couldn't I?

All I had to do was believe.

The warmth spread through my limbs, causing every fingertip and toe to tingle. A smile lit up my face.

*I had the power.*

All those weeks — or was it months? — I had not only felt lost, I had felt powerless. Powerless to change an outcome that had already been determined, that had already charted the course of future history. But now I was back in my element. My own world. My own time. Its future hadn't been written yet.

Its future was *me*, baby.

I whirled from the window and headed downstairs towards the

family room with a grin. Where to begin? There were so many options...

I passed Ryan's door. He had soft carpet too, but I couldn't see it. The floor was completely obscured. I moved on and shot a glance through Bekka's door. Patches of carpet were visible in places, but I couldn't see her walls, and she hadn't been able to close her closet doors since she was ten.

*Stuff.* It was everywhere, and it was in the way. The *stuff* would be the first thing to go. I tripped down the stairs at a gallop, humming to myself. Our first task, clearly, would be a garage sale. We could color-code the kid's contributions; they could keep their profits separate. With a bonus, perhaps, to the one who sells the most. They could spend their earnings any way they wanted, with one proviso, of course. They couldn't spend it on themselves.

It was diabolical. I loved it.

I put both hands on the newel post, pushed off, and leapt over the last three steps. I landed on the tile floor of the foyer with a bang, shaking the china cabinet in the dining room so hard the glassware tinkled.

*Crystal cake plate.* It had been a wedding gift from some friends of my parents I'd never liked. I'd used it once in twenty years. *Sold.*

*The good silver.* Who used silver? If it couldn't go in the dishwasher, screw it. I never had dinner parties anyway. *Sold.*

*The gold-rimmed china.* Ditto the part about the dishwasher. *Sold.*

I looked over my shoulder into the living room. I would hate to deprive Joe of the six-foot television screen he loved so much, but all the DVDs we owned were a joke. Had we watched any of them more than twice? Just because we liked something didn't mean we had to possess it. *Sold.*

How much money was that? I would need more, of course. Much more. It wouldn't be nearly so much fun otherwise.

*The basement!* Heavens, yes. The basement was like manna. Everything down there was essentially useless. Particularly the stair-stepping machine I had to have three years ago, the one I had cajoled Joe into getting me for Christmas by promising him a wife with perfectly toned thighs and buttocks, the machine I had loathed with an intense passion ever since the succeeding February. Like the house didn't have enough stairs to climb? The cost of it could vaccinate a village. *Sold.*

I turned and floated down the hall. *Extra coats.* Gone. Antique hat stand? The only one in the family who ever even wore a hat was Ryan, and if he put one of those greasy beasts on my antique hat stand, he'd be in trouble. *Sold.*

I put a hand on the doorframe and swung into the family room.

"Hello! How's everybody doing?"

Bekka, who was lounging on the couch, slid her eyes warily in my direction.

Ryan didn't look up.

"I'm fine, Mom," Bekka said slowly, staring at me. "What's up with you? I thought you had a migraine."

I released the doorframe and stood up straight. *Migraine?*

My hand flew to my temple. I had forgotten all about it. I ran my fingertips over the spot where the pain had been centered. The place where, in the last few moments of my dream, Jesus the Nazarene had touched me.

I laughed.

Bekka's brow wrinkled in confusion.

"The migraine's gone, Honey," I answered cheerfully. "I feel great."

Ryan was looking at me now, too. His batter missed a pitch. The fake crowd booed.

"Mom," Bekka said slowly, carefully. "What medicine did you take for it?"

I laughed again. "Nothing, I promise. I just took a little nap. It was very refreshing." My eyes scanned the room. It was packed to the gills. Stuff was everywhere. How could I ever have thought I needed it all?

It was so simple to live simply. Not that I had any desire to live as simply as Bernice — mess with my flush toilet, and I would scratch your eyes out — but simpler than this. *This* was ridiculous. This was a millstone around my neck.

And Joe's.

"Did your dad call?" I asked, looking into Bekka's still-worried face. She shook her head. Ryan, who had paused his game, shook his head, too.

They were good kids. If they weren't, they wouldn't care so much — and they wouldn't be looking at me now as if they were afraid I had been abducted by aliens. All because I was in an unusually good mood.

Made me wonder what I was like ordinarily.

It wasn't their fault they were self-absorbed, poor things. Part of that was just being a teenager. The other part was my fault. How could

I expect them *not* to be completely wrapped up in their own lives — when I was?

"You did get a call from that friend of yours who does the soup kitchen," Bekka offered. Her phone made a cuckoo noise. She glanced at it a second, tapped the screen, then returned her attention to me. "She said she was desperate for help tonight, but don't worry. I told her you had a migraine."

*Ask me again sometime.*

The sun was still shining outside, trying desperately to seep through the slats of the Venetian blinds that covered our picture window. Ryan liked the family room dark. He said he could see his games better.

I crossed to the window and opened the blinds. Sunlight streamed in. The kids winced.

"Mom!" Ryan protested. "How come your headache went away so fast? I thought light made it worse."

"It used to," I answered. "Shut everything down, guys. We're going out."

The light illuminated the room's dusty corners. The mini-fridge, bought to avoid extra trips to the kitchen for beer and pop. *Sold.* The recliner with the built-in audio system that no one ever sat in because the cushions were too hard. *Gone.* Singing deer head. *SO gone.*

I rubbed my hands together. I could hardly decide where to start. I could change so much. For the better. For all of us.

"Out where?" Bekka inquired. I figured she must still be worried about me. Her tone wasn't nearly petulant enough.

"I want pizza," Ryan voted, switching off his game obligingly. "Or maybe chicken. But I've had burgers at school every day and last night, too. Should I get my uniform on now?"

"Bri can't make it tonight anyway," Bekka cut in, "so we're making it an after-prom thing instead. I'll eat with you guys if we go somewhere with salads."

I hummed a little. "We're not eating out," I informed them, moving into the kitchen and collecting my keys. "We're not going to be eating out nearly as often, from now on. We have to cut back on expenses."

Bekka was on my heels in a flash. "Why? Did Dad get laid off?"

"Well, no," I answered calmly, "but he is going to quit."

"No way!" Ryan interjected from the door. "What gives?"

"He works too hard," I explained, moving around to turn off all the lights. "Too many hours, too much travel. That's no kind of life for anybody. Your father's worked hard his whole life; he needs to take it easy, spend more time at home, relax a little."

"But what other kind of job can he get?" Bekka asked, her voice near a squeak. Her friend Claire's father had been out of work for over a year, wreaking havoc with his daughter's shopping budget. Bekka had only been a bystander and she had been traumatized.

"One that pays a lot less, no doubt," I said confidently. "But don't worry, we'll make do."

And we would make do. I would see to that. I was good with budgets, and I was up for a challenge. There was no reason I couldn't go back to work myself, part-time, during school hours. The kids could pick up some of the household chores. We could work it out, together.

I wasn't worried about it. I opened the door to the steps and headed down toward the garage.

"Mom!" Bekka demanded from the top step. "If we're not going out to eat, where are we going?"

"Yeah!" Ryan added, from behind her. "Do I need my uniform or what?"

"Just follow me," I instructed, hopping down the steps and out the basement door. I passed the monster riding mower with a grin. If I could dig a latrine, I could push a lawn mower around the yard, couldn't I? More savings would mean more money to give to charity. Researching a few new ones would be fun.

So much to do. Plenty of time.

I was *made* of time.

The kids didn't appear. I laid on the horn.

They spilled out through the basement door and into the garage. "Mom," Bekka insisted as she slid into the front passenger seat, her lovely dark eyes filled with angst. "I'm serious. Whatever you took for that migraine, you took too much of it. I really think you should let me drive."

For a split second I saw Tamar there — sweet, strong, and caring.

My Bekka would make a good mother too, someday. Someday a very, *very* long time away.

"I told you, sweetheart," I said patiently. "I didn't take any drugs. I'm fine. I'm just happy to be pain-free and alive, and to have so many choices ahead of me."

"Are we getting take-out, then?" Ryan said hopefully, plopping into the back. "I mean, I thought you already went to the grocery store."

I hit the button to open the garage door, turned on the ignition, and backed out. Once we were safely moving with the doors locked, I dropped the bomb.

"We," I announced gleefully, "are going to do something really fun this evening. We're going to work at a soup kitchen!"

The barking of the neighbor's dog drifted through the car windows. If there had been crickets, we could have heard those too.

"All of us?" Ryan asked incredulously.

I stole a glance at Bekka. She was horror-stricken. "Mom," she began finally, her voice slow and deliberate, as if she were talking to a small child, "Just pull over now and let me drive. Okay?"

I tried hard not to laugh again. "Bekka, Love," I reiterated. "There is nothing wrong with me. I've been meaning to help out Julie at this soup kitchen for months now, and I've stood her up at least three times already. This time, I'm following through. And I think it would be good for the two of you to help. Have you ever even seen how an inner-city mission works?"

"Um, *no,*" Bekka answered, her ordinary petulance returning. "Why would I? It's not like I have any reason to go down there."

*No reason.*

Only that that's where the need was. A need that was easy to ignore when you prevented yourself from seeing it.

"Well, we're going," I asserted. "It will be good for you. For all of us."

"Um, Mom?" Ryan said pedantically, "Baseball game? Remember?"

I hadn't. But I wasn't stopping now.

"There will be other baseball games, Ryan," I answered. "But right now, this is more important."

Bekka's mouth hung open. "Mom!" she protested again, "You're letting him skip a game? What about all those lectures you gave me about *responsibility?*"

I lifted my chin. Was I a woman, or a mouse? "Responsibility is important," I explained. "But sometimes, you have a take a step back and think about what you're being responsible *to.*"

Under ordinary circumstances, the icy vibes wending their way toward me would have caused an uncomfortable chill of guilt. But not now. Not today. I was entirely too warm inside.

I was back at home. I was still me. But I was back to the *real* me now, the one who, like Mary the Magdalene, had wanted so desperately to do something meaningful with her life. I had gotten waylaid, distracted, discombobulated. I had been trying so hard to make every aspect of my life and my kids' lives perfect that I had lost sight of what it was that made me happy in the first place.

Now I understood. I was brave. And bold. And compassionate. And until I used those strengths to make some small measure of difference in the world, I would never feel fulfilled.

Being a wife and a mother was great. But I needed to be more. For *me.*

I needed to *be* me.

And here in my own time, I could. I had the power to do whatever I wanted, change the future however I wanted. The possibilities were endless.

"Um... Mom?" Ryan called from the rear seat, his voice deadpan. "Why are you, like, *smiling* so much? I've got to tell you, it's creeping me out."

My smile broadened.

*Good job, Rachel.*

In my mind, I saw the eyes again. Not the vibrant blue ones in the portraits, but the more ordinary dark ones I had come to know and love. They were twinkling at me. I could feel it.

"Get used to it, kid," I fired back warmly. "Get used to it."

# Epilogue

Tomorrow is Joe's last day at work. When I suggested he look for something else I expected to have a major battle on my hands. I never expected him to be relieved. I felt bad that I hadn't seen it before — how unhappy he was. I guess I had been seeing what I wanted to see.

He took his time about it, thought it through for a couple months, but finally he made the decision. He'll be off for two weeks before starting his new job, and for the first time in more years than I care to count, he and I are going away together for a week — just the two of us. We will be relaxing with fishing poles, books, and board games in a rustic cabin in the mountains; the kids will be at home, managing on their own. Now granted, they won't be completely alone. I've made plans to install their seventy-five-year-old great aunt in the spare room, for the express purpose of enforcing a zero-tolerance policy on houseguests. Other than that, Nana will be sitting with her feet up reading romance novels. Bekka will be doing the cooking. Ryan will be cleaning the house.

They'll be fine.

My children believe that I popped an artery. Whenever I impose some bizarre new dictum on them, they roll their eyes and tell me I'm "PMing" again. PM means "post migraine." Thinking of my new outlook as a disease seems to amuse them. But I don't let their moans and groans get to me. I know they're happier now, too.

They're growing up.

And me? I'm still happy. Happier than I've ever been. Every now and then I do get melancholy, thinking of the people who meant so much to me, missing them, wondering what happened to them all.

Judas did take his own life. I haven't the slightest doubt about that; I wouldn't even if there was no record of it. Realizing that his machinations had actually hastened his friend's fate, even if that fate was ultimately unavoidable, would create an unbearable burden of guilt for him. But I understood that he meant well. And I was confident that Jesus understood, too.

I still wonder often about Tamar, and whether she and James ever had children. I wonder what kind of woman Leah grew to be, and whether Naomi ever came out of her shell. I wonder if Bernice ever stopped worrying, if Joanna ever converted her husband Chuza to the cause, and whether Susanna ever went back to her birding business. But especially, I wonder about Mary. There are so blasted many legends about her, based on so many questionable sources, it's impossible to know for sure. But of one thing, I have no doubt. Whatever she determined her mission to be after Jesus was gone, she carried it through with flying colors.

I'm talking about them all as if they were real people. My husband doesn't think they were. He believes I created my own, idealized version of the historic Jesus: the way I most wanted him to be, the way I could best relate to him. The personalities I ascribed to the different characters, he thinks I borrowed from friends or relatives, or spawned from my own fertile imagination. He could be right. It would be perfectly logical.

But I don't really care.

The result of my dream is the same, regardless. It's changed me. It's changed the way I look at life in general and religion in particular. I still can't stand dogmatic thinking or mindless ritual, and the hypocrites — who will always be among us — drive me even more nuts than they did before. But I do miss the camaraderie I felt with the disciples: the joy and the excitement of sharing a purpose with people who understand.

Maybe someday I'll find a group of friends like that again. Perhaps even at a church. I'm skeptical, but I might give it a try.

Otherwise, I'm happy. Happy doing things that mean something. Happy just to be alive. And not because I'm wearing rose-colored glasses, either. All the glasses, of any shade, are off. I *want* to see the suffering I used to ignore. I know exactly how vast, frightening, cruel, difficult, painful, and downright horrifying a world this can be. But as Jesus seemed intent on demonstrating, that's all the more reason to celebrate the good things.

Love, friendship, laughter — even the little comforts bear rejoicing. So long as one never forgets those without. So long as one is willing to share.

It seems to me now that I could never forget the look in Jesus's eyes, the way he smiled, the sound of his laughter. But I recognize that this indescribable sense of happiness the dream has left me with is very likely to wear off. The minutiae of life will rise up to choke me, the euphoria will slowly start to lessen, and in time, I will slip right back into being the same floundering, discontent, blindly driven perfectionist I became once before.

But I hope not.

*Commentary for Epilogue begins on page 288.*

# Commentary

Rev. Peter C. de Vries, Ph. D.

# Introduction

Ten years ago, during a migraine, my friend Rachel had an inspiration for the novel you're about to read. She wanted to consider how modern women would experience not just a face-to-face encounter with Jesus, but months of living with him during his earthly ministry. After she had written her first draft, she asked for my help. As a pastor with a Ph.D. in Biblical interpretation, I'm able to offer some historical and Biblical background for her story and provide comments to help you reflect on what she went through and to develop your own understanding of life and faith. Because of the beauty of ebooks, you can read my comments at the end of each chapter or consider them after you've finished reading her whole story.

As your companion on this trip Rachel has prepared for you, I'd like to introduce myself. I've been the pastor of smallish Presbyterian churches in western Pennsylvania for twenty-seven years. In addition to the more typical duties of a pastor, I enjoy volunteering at summer church camp, leading mission trips to parts of our country devastated by natural disasters, and training student pastors. I'm a leader in my denomination at the regional level, helping with the relationships between churches and pastors. Along the way, I've earned a Ph.D. in New Testament interpretation and have taught at Pittsburgh Theological Seminary as an adjunct professor. For the past eighteen years I've made regular trips to the west African nation of Ghana, where I do my part to train leaders for a rapidly growing church. When I have a chance I like to hike, ski, bicycle, and kayak. Technically, I am a tattooed biker. But enough about me...

If you know your Bible well, you'll notice that Rachel's tale doesn't line up perfectly with what we read in Matthew, Mark, Luke, and John, the books in the New Testament that describe Jesus's ministry. This novel is different from what you may have been taught over the years as you learned the Bible stories, in three ways.

First, she tells the stories of Jesus's ministry in a different order from what you'll find in the four books of the Bible known as the Gospels (Matthew, Mark, Luke, and John), which also describe Jesus's life on earth. The first three of these books (Matthew, Mark, and Luke) tell the story in pretty much the same order. Bible scholars call them the "synoptic" gospels, meaning that they look at Jesus from the same angle. But John's gospel comes at Jesus from a whole other direction. For example, John describes Jesus's cleansing of the temple at the beginning of the story, instead of during the last week before his crucifixion. Does that mean he got it wrong, and the other three gospels got it right? Not necessarily. The four people who wrote the Biblical accounts of Jesus's life did so for their own reasons. They organize the events differently in order to make their point. Rachel does the same thing, and it's something we do all the time. When we describe an event, we organize the episodes into a story. We tell our stories for a reason, and we tell them in a way that highlights that reason.

Second, you'll also notice that Rachel doesn't mention some of the familiar Bible stories, and she describes things you won't find anywhere in Scripture, such as the woman she meets in Chapter Thirteen. You'll find the same differences among the four gospels in the Bible. For example, Luke is the only one to tell us the story of the Prodigal Son, and no one other than John talks about Jesus turning water into wine. The Bible writers never claim to provide a blow-by-blow account of everything Jesus said and did. In fact, at the end of his gospel John says the exact opposite: "There are also many other things that Jesus did; if every one of them were written down, I suppose that the world itself could not contain the books that would be written" (21:25). Every time we tell a story, we decide what to include and what isn't worth bringing up. It's another part of how we tell stories to get our point across.

For example, if you spend the evening out with friends and then tell your family about it the next morning, you select details that contribute to what the evening meant for you. Would you tell your family what your waiter's name was? Perhaps, if it was an unusual name that happens to be your brother's name, and it started a conversation between you and your server. Would you tell them what song the band played, or where you parked the car? It all depends upon whether or not these details are a significant part of what the evening was like for you.

Let's take this scenario one step farther. One of your friends also describes the evening, and her account is very different from yours. You may describe the same significant events of the night, but you'll each have a different spin on them. That doesn't necessarily mean that one of you is lying or trying to conceal something. You're two different people, and what is important for one of you may not matter to the other one. For example, your friend may be a tightwad and talk about what a good bargain the food and entertainment were. You may be a fashion-conscious person who noticed a new style people were wearing. The character Rachel presents here is different from the Bible authors, so it makes sense for her story to be different.

That leads to the third reason why the story you're about to read is different from what you'll find in the Bible. The Bible was written by men of the ancient world. Rachel lives in the twenty-first and not the first century. She knows about microwaves, airplanes, and cell phones. She knows that many diseases are caused by miniscule critters called bacteria and viruses; the gospel writers had no clue. We believe that the earth is a giant ball in space, whirling around other giant balls like the sun, moon, and other planets. The ancients thought the earth was a flat surface with a giant blue bowl on top of it and a strange underworld beneath. Things that they took for granted are bizarre to us. As Rachel brings her modern sensibilities to the first century, she brings her twenty-first century knowledge and values with her.

On top of that, Rachel is a woman. The gospel writers of the Bible were men. Even today, men and women tend to see things differently. The differences were even greater back then, as you'll find out while reading Rachel's story. Because virtually all ancient authors were men, it's hard for us to grasp what life was like for women in those days. The contributions of some powerful and influential women were overlooked or belittled. The hardships that women faced were overlooked or explained away. Rachel, as a woman, describes things that the Bible's male authors had no clue about.

Rachel helps us rethink the familiar old Bible stories in another way as well. Have you ever thought about what happened to the people in the stories when the story is finished? It's easy to imagine them as actors who disappear from the stage when the play is over. But life continued for them. What happened to the rich young man after Jesus told him to give all his wealth away and follow him (Luke 18:18-23)? What was life like for the woman caught in adultery when Jesus forgave her and sent her on her way (John 8:1-11)? Rachel tries to answer some of these questions. In so doing, she reminds us that they are real people, not simply props for a neat story.

1. When have you and someone else described something that happened to you both, but described it in very different ways? Why

were your stories different?

2. Write down the story of how Jesus was born, as you remember it. Then read Matthew 1:18-2:12 and Luke 2-1-20. How many details in your story are from the Bible, and how many are not?

*The first chapter of the novel begins on page 6.*

# Chapter 1

## Reflection

Rachel has everything, but she has nothing. To look at her, you'd think that she is living the American Dream: college education, big house in the suburbs, fancy SUV, two healthy, well-adjusted children, a happy (or at least satisfactory) marriage, comfortable lifestyle... even a $2800 mattress! But the emptiness within her seems to get larger and larger with every new thing she crams into her life, or allows others to stuff into it. It's a state of affairs that far too many of us can relate to. Like Rachel, the more things that we juggle in our lives, the less meaning we seem to find. We take on new projects and join new activities, hoping that the next one will be the source of contentment and purpose for us. But none of them are. We're like children in December, eager for the shiny new Christmas gifts that will be exactly what we wanted and that will make us happier than we can imagine. For a day or two, they do. But by the time the groundhog looks for his shadow, half of the presents are broken and the other half are forgotten. The empty pit of nothingness within us grows bigger and bigger, and we try to fill it by getting more stuff, doing more things. But that hollow space is never filled, and we hope that the frenetic pace of our lives will distract us from it.

Rachel used to have a vision for herself. She imagined being well-grounded, enjoying where she was, following a purpose that brought meaning to her life. But then life took over. She is too busy with the chores and expectations that fill her days even to remember what that vision had been. As former President Dwight D. Eisenhower put it,

"What is important is seldom urgent and what is urgent is seldom important." The urgency of life overwhelms the important things that fulfill us and touch the heart of who we are.

The frenzied pace of Rachel's schedule blocks her relationship with the most important people in her life. The very activities that are devoted to her daughter and son's welfare simply become part of the cloud that obscures them from her. Any sense of emotional intimacy with her husband has been washed away by his workload and her commitments. She lives in a household of four lonely people.

Rachel lost the sense of who she really is. As physically painful as her migraine may be, her struggle with her identity gnaws more deeply at her spirit. She knows there is more to her than doing what everyone expects of her, what she expects of herself. Her identity cannot be found in who she used to be, nor in her aspirations for who she wants to be. It is in these times of internal struggle that God finds us. When we see the futility of our everyday lives and realize there has to be something more, God can break through the shells that we build around ourselves and reveal something new to us. He surprises us by cutting through the clutter and the void that fills our lives, and by showing us who we really are in his grand plan for the world. You have a place in what God is doing. When you find it and live it, it brings a satisfaction that fills the empty pit that has been eating away your insides. Finding our place in God's plan is not simply another expectation dumped upon us, or yet one more thing we have to do. It is the focus that brings order and meaning to all that we do.

1. What do you look to in order to find significance and purpose for your life?

2. In what ways have you lost a sense of the person you believe yourself to be?

3. What messages do you receive (from friends and family, media and advertising, or other sources) about how you can fill the void in your life?

4. What are the most important relationships in your life? How do you nurture them?

*The next chapter of the novel begins on page 11.*

# Chapter 2

## Background

Welcome to the first century! Rachel has arrived in a strange new environment. Sometimes we forget how differently people lived in other times, and how different life can be in other parts of our world today. We'll get to that topic in a moment. But first, a bit of explanation for what Rachel describes for us.

Rachel wakes up in the courtyard of a family's home totally different from houses you'll typically find in the US. Like many traditional societies today, people in first century Palestine didn't live in single-family homes made up of mom, dad, and the kids. The household consisted of several related families, such as parents, their adult children, and extended family members, each of whom had separate living spaces that opened onto a common courtyard, like the one where Rachel landed. Children, parents, grandparents, aunts, uncles, cousins, and various hangers-on all lived under one roof... or around the same courtyard. Extended family members weren't people you saw during the holidays or at family reunions; they were people who ate with you, did chores beside you, and had to wait until you were done in the bathroom.

In 1968, archaeologists from the Franciscan Biblical School discovered the remains of a house at the site of the Galilean town of Capernaum, dating back to the time of Jesus. It was buried under the remains of a fourth century synagogue, and many people believe it was the home of the apostle Peter. Like the house where Rachel has found herself, this house consisted of a courtyard with a cobblestone and beaten-earth floor, and several rooms that opened onto it. Some were storerooms, some were sleeping areas, and others were spaces where daily chores took place. The house the archaeologists found had a second courtyard, connected to the first by open passageways. It also included a room that opened directly onto the street; this was probably a business that the family ran, perhaps selling things like bread, fabric, or fish. As Rachel has discovered, the rooms of the house tend to be dark and stuffy, so family members spent a lot of time in courtyard, which often was shaded by canopies. They would also go up to the house's flat roof where the air was cooler and less stinky. In Acts 10:9, that's where Peter went to pray while supper was being made. Mark 13:5 also talks about people out on the roofs of their homes.

In the first century, the household was more than a group of relatives who lived together. It was an economic and legal foundation for society: our word "economy" comes from the Greek word for house: oikos. Today's family businesses and family farms are about as close as we get to this family style today. Nobody worked "outside the home," because there were no jobs other than the ones you had as part of your household. Nepotism was not merely acceptable; it was standard practice. Your identity in the community was based upon the household to which you belonged. Servants were considered to be members of the household, even though they weren't blood relatives. If you couldn't claim membership in a household, you were left out in the cold and life could be difficult, dangerous, and meager.

The head of the household was in charge of everything that took place, and he was responsible for everyone under his care. Invariably, the head of the household was a "him." Women had no legal rights and were considered to be the property of their fathers or husbands. We still have a hint of that in traditional wedding services when the father of the bride "gives her away" to the groom. Now, it's a heartwarming moment for father and daughter. Back then, it was a legal transfer of property, like signing the title for a car that you've just bought. In the household where Rachel finds herself, Zebedee is the head of the household. Each of the men and women are members of the household, attached to it in various ways.

## Reflection

Rachel's initial reaction to her strange surroundings is fear. She's terrified of the men, appalled by her clothing and the lack of hygiene, and mystified by the way everyone acts around her. As Rachel continues to tell us her tale, her uneasiness doesn't diminish. Every new experience or sight is another reason for adrenalin to start pumping through her system. Many of us react similarly to the unfamiliar. When we don't understand something, we assume the worst. When someone who doesn't fit into our expectations shows up in our lives, we guard ourselves against her, believing that she may cause us harm. When circumstances aren't what we're used to, we worry that something bad might happen. At such times, we're more likely to notice what's unusual, rather than seeing the similarities. It makes us even more wary.

When I visited Jerusalem back in 1992 I found myself on the Palestinian side of town early one evening. These were the days just after the intifada, when the media was full of images of angry young Palestinians throwing rocks and damaging property. As I walked down the street hoping to find a taxi driver willing to risk a trip to my hotel on the Israeli part of the city, I saw a group of a half dozen Palestinian teenagers coming toward me. My stomach tightened, and so did my grip on my backpack. What were they going to do to me? But when we met, they greeted me with smiles and friendly waves. They were just like teenagers back home, out for a good time with their friends. All I could see was how different Palestinians are, instead of noticing what all adolescents have in common.

There can be dramatic variations between the ways that people live, and Rachel is experiencing a whole bunch of them. When we are in such situations, we have a choice to make: we can focus our attention on the strange and unfamiliar, or we can recognize the universal aspects of human experience that every member of our species faces. We can be like anthropologists, who study the variations between different cultures, or we can be like sociologists, who examine the universal elements of every society. Like Rachel, many of us notice what makes people different, and we frequently respond to those differences with fear and hatred. Imagine what life would be like if our first impulse instead was to recognize what we have in common.

1. How do you normally respond when you see someone whose life is different from yours?

2. When have others distrusted you because you were different? How did you feel at the time?

3. Are you more like an anthropologist or a sociologist?

*The next chapter of the novel begins on page 19.*

# Chapter 3

## Background

The birth of Leah's baby boy was cause for celebration for more than one reason. First of all, the mother and baby survived the delivery. Childbirth was dangerous business in those days. According to the World Health Organization, there is less than a one percent chance even in the least developed nations on Earth that a mother will die in giving birth, and less than one baby in a thousand dies coming into the world. In the United States, less than three mothers in ten thousand and less than one baby in ten thousand die. But according to Australian researcher Donald Todman, one in forty women in ancient Rome died in childbirth. One baby out of three didn't make it. A healthy mother and baby were nothing to take for granted in first century Palestine.

But the Zebedee household was celebrating for another reason: the baby was a boy. Today we may ask expectant parents if they want a boy or a girl, but back then the answer was so obvious that no one bothered to ask. The family needed a male heir to continue into the next generation. Without a baby boy, the family would die off. Remember the importance of the family household in those days. Baby girls were familial dead-ends, because they couldn't pass along the family name or property.

The Old Testament Law has some rather disconcerting regulations that are rooted in the concern for a male heir. According to Deuteronomy 25, if a man died without having a son, his brother was required to marry his widow to "help" her have a baby boy. If she did, that child was considered to be the heir of her first husband. Think about your brother- or sister-in-law: is that something you'd want to face? In Numbers 36, the enterprising daughters of Zelophahad, who died without having any sons, successfully convinced Moses to grant them an exception so that the family name and property could be passed along through them.

By now, Rachel has figured out that she is in a town called Capernaum. It was a community of about 1500 people along the Sea of Galilee (also called Lake Genneserat) that straddled an important trade route. Bible scholars don't agree on much, but they all believe Capernaum was home base for Jesus during his ministry. Nazareth may have been his hometown, but he lived as an adult in Capernaum. When he wasn't traveling all over the countryside, that is.

We read about Rachel's two companions in Luke 8:1-3, which tells us about the women who traveled with Jesus: "The twelve were with him, as well as some women who had been cured of evil spirits and infirmities: Mary, called Magdalene, from whom seven demons had gone out, and Joanna, the wife of Herod's steward Chuza, and Susanna, and many others, who provided for them out of their resources." We meet Joanna again as one of the women at the empty tomb on Easter morning (Luke 24:10), but Mary Magdalene is Jesus's only female companion that we remember. We'll talk more about Mary later on, as Rachel continues her story and you get to know her better. Not many of us remember that Jesus and his traveling companions had expenses to cover, and even fewer of us realize that it was the women who took care of it. Because Joanna's husband Chuza was the manager of King Herod's household, it makes perfect sense for her to have the wherewithal to bankroll Jesus's enterprise. We can only speculate how the others got their deep pockets.

## Reflection

According to Luke 8:2 and Mark 16:9, Jesus cast out "seven demons" from Mary Magdalene. The concept of demon possession is something that those of us who live in the modern world don't take very seriously. We may enjoy scaring the bejeebers out of ourselves by watching horror movies like Carrie and The Exorcist, but we're pretty confident things like this just don't happen. People back in Jesus's time, who didn't have the scientific and psychological knowledge that we do, blamed demons for human behavior and actions that they didn't understand, but we know better. Or do we?

Until the last generation or so, we thought of ourselves as a collection of little boxes: one box is our body, one box is our mind, and one box is our spirit. If something is ailing you physically, your body needs to be healed. If your mind is troubled, see a psychologist. The two have nothing to do with each other. Increasingly, however, we are becoming aware of the interconnectedness of the mind, body, and spirit. Have you ever noticed that you tend to get a cold when you're stressed out? Or that a long recovery from an injury can put you into a funk? Depression brings physical symptoms. Medicines that affect brain chemistry can change your mood. I wouldn't be surprised if Rachel's migraine headaches have something to do with all the pressure she puts on herself to be the perfect mother, or that nagging sense that there has to be something more to her life.

These are examples of how our minds and bodies work together. But human beings are also spiritual beings. We've lost sight of that. For us, something is only worth caring about if you can measure it, weigh it, observe it, and analyze it. Since that doesn't apply to the spiritual dimension of life, we ignore it and doubt that it even exists. My friends in the west African nation of Ghana are very aware of the active spiritual dimension of reality. They see the influence of spiritual beings around them every day, and they're aware of how they can affect us. This is not just what simple, superstitious people believe; highly educated church leaders share this perspective. Spending time with my Ghanaian friends helped me realize that while our lives are affected by physical causes that science can explain, there is also a spiritual source for the blessings and struggles that we face. We short-change ourselves when we think it has to be one or the other. Mary Magdalene may have been a mean-spirited, nasty woman because of life experiences she endured, or because of psychological issues she struggled with. These would be the causes of the personality that scientific, rational thinking can consider. But there is also a spiritual element to her life. We don't have to choose among physical, psychological, and spiritual factors. They are all part of the same reality. Jesus made the change in her life not just because he was a gifted psychotherapist; he healed the brokenness of her spirit.

1. When have you experienced a relationship among your spiritual, physical, and emotional health?

2. Read Mark 2:1-12. Did Jesus bring physical or spiritual healing to the man?

3. How do you want Jesus to heal your spirit, as he did for Mary Magdalene?

*The next chapter of the novel begins on page 29.*

# Chapter 4

## Background

Rachel is confused by Mary Magdalene, and perhaps you are, too. Even those of us who don't know much about the Bible have heard about her. But what we think we know about Mary Magdalene has more to do with a sermon preached by a pope in the sixth century than anything we'll find in the Bible or in the historical record. So let's separate fact from fancy.

We call her "Magdalene" because she came from the town of Magdala, a village on the western shores of the Sea of Galilee. As I've already discussed, the Bible tells us that Jesus cast seven demons out of her. And she was one of the women who traveled with Jesus and the Twelve. Because Luke 8:3 tells us that these women covered the costs for Jesus's work, it's reasonable to think of her as a woman of means. All four gospels tell us that Mary was the first witness to Jesus's resurrection when she visited the empty tomb on Easter morning: according to John she was the only one who did so. There's a very good chance Mary was a prominent leader in the early church, partly because of the time she spent with Jesus during his ministry, and partly because she was an eyewitness to the resurrection. She is mentioned twelve times in the Bible: more often than most of the apostles. She was so well known that about a hundred years after her death someone wrote an account of Jesus's ministry and claimed that Mary had been the original author. If you want to make up a fake author, especially in those days, you pick someone famous that everyone knows. In the fourth century, the prominent theologian Augustine even called Mary "apostle to the apostles" in his commentary on the gospel of John. An apostle is someone who bears witness to a personal experience with Jesus, and that's exactly what Mary did when she ran back from the empty tomb to tell the disciples "I have seen the Lord!"

But as Rachel is discovering, the ancient world was a man's world. The Powers That Be simply couldn't permit a woman to have a place of prominence, could they? Beginning in the fourth century church authorities worked to suppress women leaders, and that's when the picture of Mary Magdalene started to change. The campaign began to discredit her as a respected hero of the faith. Fast forward a couple hundred years, and in 597 Pope Gregory the Great preached that Mary Magdalene was the anonymous prostitute who anointed Jesus's feet in Luke 7. For good measure, he also claimed that she was the woman caught in adultery in John 8. If you want to discredit a woman, calling her a prostitute and a home-wrecker will do the job quite nicely. By the time we get to the twentieth century, Andrew Lloyd Webber and Tim Rice's rock opera *Jesus Christ Superstar*, Martin Scorsese's movie *The Last Temptation of Christ*, and Dan Brown's book *The Da Vinci Code* each show a romantic love interest between Mary and Jesus, and Mary's transformation is complete. She has gone from a prominent church leader to some cheap trash trying to sully Jesus himself. Instead of going along with the myth, it's probably a good idea to stick with the facts.

## Reflection

Whether Mary Magdalene was a reformed prostitute, someone who had demons exorcised from her, or an ornery tightwad who changed her ways, she had become a completely different person. Jesus has a way of doing that to people. That's why many people talk about being "born again." The phase has negative connotations for many people who have encountered the misguided zeal of some Christians who use this term, but it testifies to the new way of life that we can experience when we're touched by Jesus's love. As Jesus says in John 10:10, "I came that they may have life, and have it abundantly." Before Jesus did whatever he did to Mary, she was technically alive. She ate, slept, ran a business, and complained about the weather. But her spirit was empty and lifeless. She lived the way she did because it was the only way she knew how to get through life. Many of us today are just like Mary had been.

Each of us are unique, so the touch of God's grace upon us is never the same for two people. Mary can tell you what she experienced, I can tell you what Jesus means to me, and friendly people who knock on your door on Saturday mornings can do the same. Your encounter with Jesus, and the change that it brings, will be yours alone.

I'm not a Christian because I want to get to heaven when I die. That's just some exceptionally good icing on the cake. I follow Jesus because it's the best kind of life you can ever have. I've seen him change too many people's lives, as he did for Mary, for me to doubt that he can transform anyone and turn their life right-side-up.

1. What does it mean for you to have an "abundant" life? When have you experienced it?

2. In what ways do you feel "dead" in your own spirit?

3. Has there been a time when you've felt the transforming work of Jesus for yourself?

*The next chapter of the novel begins on page 37.*

# Chapter 5

## Background

The 1500 or so people who called Capernaum home made their living for the most part by fishing and farming. They lived, worked, and did their business in buildings made of stone block without mortar, plastered with mud. Dung was sometimes mixed into the mud to reinforce it, adding its own special odor to the town, especially when it rained. The houses had wooden roofs covered with thatch. Rats and other vermin love to live in thatch. Capernaum didn't have a department of public works. No one hauled away the garbage once a week, filled the potholes in the streets, or maintained a sewer system. The streets were nothing but muddy, dusty ruts, filled with the litter that people threw outside their houses. Fortunately, as Rachel discovers to her dismay, there's no paper or plastic trash. The street is one giant compost heap, and it smells like one.

The town is packed with people who came to see Jesus. Rachel must have arrived after he began to attract a following, and everyone wanted to hear him for themselves. In addition to the Jesus groupies, the marketplace is busy with farmers from the surrounding area who have come into town to sell their produce and to buy supplies. It took about twenty donkey loads of food every day to sustain the population of the town, with supplies like rope, pots, and cloth loaded onto even more donkeys. The food wouldn't cook itself, so charcoal had to be hauled in for the cooking fires. It's no wonder that Rachel feels overwhelmed by the activity in the town.

Our standards of health and hygiene were unheard of in the first century, even among the wealthy elite. It's not simply that people had no access to medical care; there was no medical care to which anyone could have access. Together with a lack of balanced nutrition, it's obvious why Rachel sees so many sick and disabled people relying on the handouts of others to survive. Even the healthy are in pretty bad shape by our standards.

## Reflection

We are very good at protecting ourselves from the unpleasantries of life. If you live a comfortable life, you can go for weeks, months, and even years without seeing the struggling people all around you. Churches in nice neighborhoods are at a loss for how to "care for the sick and feed the poor" because they don't see any in their zip code. They are there: the addicts, the disabled, the abused, the poverty-stricken, the castoffs of society. But we have all gotten very good at finding ways to hide them so they don't make us uneasy. Rachel is experiencing the reality of life that is all around us. The only difference is that it's out for all to see in Capernaum.

We shield and protect ourselves from other unpleasantries as well. We find a way to mask the very presence of anything distasteful or disturbing so that we can live the delusion that all is well with the world. We sweep the homeless off our streets and send them "somewhere else." Where exactly is this "somewhere else?" We don't care, as long as we don't have to look at them in our neighborhoods, or on our way to work and to shop. We don't want to face disease and injury, so we take dying people to fancy buildings with limited visiting hours and leave it to the medical professionals to take care of them. Death is the ugliest, most unpleasant thing we ever face, so we avoid it most of all. Very few people die at home anymore; we send them to hospice facilities, specialty care homes, and hospital beds. Everything is neat, clean, and antiseptic. Death happens far away from our everyday lives. We pay the funeral industry a mint to ensure that our deceased loved ones look good when we pay our final respects to them. As a pastor, I'm often with families when they see the funeral director's work on their dearly departed for the first time. I struggle to maintain the solemnity of the moment when I hear the typical comment, "She looks so good!" Part of me wants to quip, "But she's not; she's dead!" We don't want to face it, so we do whatever it takes to maintain our self-delusion that death is a distant concept, not a present reality.

We shudder to think of living in filthy, smelly, unsanitary conditions like those where Rachel has found herself. So we cut ourselves off from the earthy reality that is human life. We eat chicken and roast beef with no clue about what it takes for that beautifully packaged meat to show up on the grocery shelves. We hide from the sun, protect ourselves from allergens, and make our homes smell like jasmine, vanilla, or a spring rain. We prefer an antiseptic sterile environment protected by disinfectants that kill 99.9% of all germs. Germs are bad, aren't they? We don't want anything bad around us. Not germs. Not death. Not "those kind of people." They make us uncomfortable.

God did not promise to keep us comfortable. His vision for the world, for your life, is unsettling. You can't remain comfortable if you want to change. He wants so much more for your life than what it is now. That is part of what's making Rachel so nervous.

1. What people or things do you try to ignore or get rid of?

2. How do you try to avoid them?

3. When has following God been unsettling for you?

*The next chapter of the novel begins on page 43.*

# Chapter 6

## Background

Rachel has found herself in first century Palestine, when men were men and women were women. We continue to face issues of gender discrimination today, in issues such as wage inequity and the sometimes-not-so-subtle patronizing attitudes that men have toward women. But in the days of Jesus, there was nothing subtle about it. Men had their place, and women had theirs.

In some situations, the separation of men and women was fairly innocuous. The men in Jesus's entourage gathered together around one campfire, and the women gathered around another. In some traditional African societies today, this separation continues. It's common for the men to eat their meals in one room, while the women eat theirs in another. The two genders simply keep company and socialize apart from one another. The man farms and hunts; the woman does the buying and selling and handles the family finances. In the time and place where Rachel finds herself, however, the divide is more severe. The closest modern parallel we have today are Islamic societies that enforce sharia law, a code of conduct developed from the lifestyle of Mohammed and his companions in the seventh century. Men and women have no contact with each other outside of the home.

As Rachel is learning, however, there is no such thing as "separate but equal," the legal justification for racial discrimination in the U.S. before the civil rights movement. Similarly, apartheid South Africa tried to convince its black citizens and the world that whites and blacks thrived in separate territories and that the quality of life was the same in every "homeland." It was nothing but propaganda, of course, and nobody bought it. When people are separated from each other, those who have power will ensure that they are "more equal than others," as George Orwell put it in his book *Animal Farm*.

Rachel is in a world where men have the power. Women live separately, and they are not equal. We saw the first hint of this in Chapter Three, when Mary and Joanna were shocked that Rachel was traveling without a man. Their surprise was not merely a concern about her safety, but also the impropriety of a woman on her own. In this society, women have to be attached to a household (headed by a man, of course) in order to have any sort of a chance in the world. Typically, that man is the woman's father or husband. Unmarried women, widows and divorcees have to rely on the mercy of some other male relative or they are out on the street with no legal standing, trying to keep body and soul together. Strong, independent women like Mary Magdalene are the exception that proves the rule. Even when a woman is part of a household, she is still a notch or two below her male counterparts. A woman's value in the household depends on the work she can do or the children she can bear. The "bride price" that a groom pays is compensation to the woman's father for the household laborer that he is losing.

Jesus challenged this separation between man and woman, just as he challenges all the ways that we like to divide ourselves from each other. Particularly by the standards of the culture within which he lived, Jesus's willingness to interact with women, to take them seriously, and to entrust them with authority was nothing short of scandalous. As Paul described Jesus's program to the Galatians, "There is no longer Jew or Greek, there is no longer slave or free, there is no longer male and female; for all of you are one in Christ Jesus" (3:28). Ephesians 2:11-22 also reminds us that the work of Jesus Christ removes the "dividing wall of hostility" that separates people from each other. It's a shame that our human tendency to separate and discriminate is so strong that even the most loyal followers of Jesus continue to rebuild these dividing walls, frequently claiming they are acting according to God's will when they do so.

## Reflection

Jesus isn't what Rachel expected. He never is. Physically, she expects him to have a commanding presence, instead of seeming to be perfectly ordinary. As Isaiah 53's prophecy puts it, "He had no form or majesty that we should look at him, nothing in his appearance that we should desire him." His appearance just didn't match what she, and many of us, learned growing up in the church. Sure, we know that he lived in a part of the world where almost everyone has brown eyes, black hair, and a swarthy complexion. The image of a blond haired, blue-eyed Jesus developed while Christianity was practiced almost exclusively in Europe for more than a thousand years. German Biblical scholars in the 1930's and 40's went so far as to pervert historical facts to argue that Jesus was an "Aryan," so they could fit him into Nazi racial schemes. God forbid that anyone ever does so again.

We are naturally and powerfully motivated to imagine Jesus as "one of us." Isn't that what the incarnation is all about? Jesus could only be incarnate within one particular ethnic and cultural setting, but because we sense his presence in our own places and times as well, we portray him as one of us. Frederick Buechner's book *The Faces Of Jesus* offers a wonderful sample of how Christians from around the globe have represented Jesus as a member of their own culture. My wife and I treasure our collection we've accumulated of images of Jesus by artists around the world. He is a child from Uruguay on his mother's lap, a Japanese boy learning from his father how to be a carpenter, a "black power" leader, and an African man hanging on the cross. Because Jesus was incarnate to share human life with us, we imagine him as someone like us, no matter what kind of somebody we may be.

Jesus shatters our expectations not only with his appearance, but also with his words and deeds. Our efforts to portray Jesus frequently lead to a description that says more about ourselves than about him. It's a tendency that has plagued Bible scholars for decades. As one author puts it, when we try to see the face of the historical Jesus, all we find is our own reflection at the bottom of a well. This is partly because we don't have that much historical evidence beyond the New Testament to work with, and partly because we don't want Jesus to challenge us. We'd much rather have him approve of us just the way we are. So we suppose that he is just like us.

1. When have you been on the losing side of a division that people make? When have you been on the "winning" side? What did you do?

2. What image of Jesus do you have in your mind? How accurate, historically, do you think it is?

3. What does Jesus have in common with you? What makes him different from you?

4. Is there a challenge Jesus is presenting to you that you'd rather ignore?

*The next chapter of the novel begins on page 51.*

# Chapter 7

## Background

Rachel's account of the centurion asking Jesus to heal his servant is spot-on with Luke's version (7:1-10). Interestingly, however, when Matthew recounts the same episode (8:5-13), he tells us that the centurion approached Jesus directly, instead of asking someone else to do the asking because he didn't think he was worthy to ask Jesus himself. This is one example of how the Bible's gospel-writers don't always tell the same story with the same details. Like any other storyteller, they selected the details that mattered the most to them. Luke, in this case, wants to put a spotlight on the centurion's humility. Since Matthew isn't as concerned about that part of the story, he smooths over this detail so we can focus on the point he cares about more. Mark and John don't mention the event at all, probably because it wasn't as important to them as they present their overall description of Jesus.

One detail that Rachel, Matthew, and Luke all agree upon is that the officer was a "centurion." The name literally means that he was an officer commanding 100 soldiers (the Latin word for 100 is the root for some of our other English words, like century and cent). Since the title comes from Latin, the language of the Romans, we naturally assume that the officer was a Roman, the way that Rachel describes him. However, historians consider it to be very unlikely that there was a Roman garrison in Capernaum at the time of Jesus. Galilee, the region where Capernaum is found, was under the control of Herod Antipas, one of the puppet rulers that the Romans propped up to run this particular corner of their empire. The Romans left it up to him to maintain order in Galilee. It was only after the Romans crushed the Jewish rebellion in 70 that they stationed their own soldiers in Galilee. It's most likely that the centurion who sought Jesus's help was an officer in Antipas's army and not a Roman.

Herod Antipas's soldiers weren't loved any more than the Romans would have been. In fact, Jewish patriots probably would have resented Herod and his ilk even more than the Romans. Rome was the enemy: you might hate them, but at least you can understand that they're working for their country's best interests. Herod and the other Jewish stoolies were traitors, collaborating with the enemy in order to stick it to their own kind. An enemy is one thing; a turncoat is even worse.

Herod Antipas may have been Jewish, but his soldiers weren't. Jews were exempt from the military draft, so Herod would have had to bring in Gentile conscripts to serve in his army. The centurion was most likely the only professional soldier in the lot. Most centurions were regarded by ordinary folk as cruel, violent, and self-serving. The centurion in Capernaum must have been a rare exception.

That distinction didn't matter to a group of Jews known as the Zealots. These fierce Jewish patriots held a venomous hatred for the Roman occupation and the Herodian family that cooperated with them. If they lived in our time, we would call them revolutionaries, or insurgents, or freedom fighters, or the Jewish underground. They did whatever they could to undermine and resist Roman rule. About ten years after Jesus's birth, the Zealots led a revolt against Rome under the leadership of a man named Judas the Galilean. It didn't end very nicely for them. Barabbas, the man who received clemency from Pontius Pilate instead of Jesus at his trial, was a Zealot leader. The guerrilla war that the Zealots led against Rome erupted into a full-blown war in 66, leading to the destruction of the temple in Jerusalem and the imposition of direct Roman rule. At least one of Jesus's disciples, Simon the Zealot, was a member of this party. As Rachel tells us, it would be quite natural for him to resent Jesus's act of mercy for the centurion.

As I said before, Jesus is all about tearing down the divisions that we build between each other. The twelve men that he chose to be his inner circle included both Simon the Zealot and Matthew the tax collector. Tax collectors were simply civilian members of the occupying force and their local collaborators. They were the ones who took money from their countrymen to finance the Roman occupation that the Zealots resisted so passionately. Rachel didn't hear all of the conversations among the men at their campfire or along the road, but I suspect Simon and Matthew had some spirited debates. Imagine what it took for both of them to lay down their fiercely held ideologies in order to follow Jesus.

## Reflection

COMMENTARY

It's no wonder that Rachel, like many of us, has the image of Jesus that she does. He's God, after all, and God is perfect and pure and holy. On top of that, he's all-knowing and pretty doggone powerful. If you do something that is less than pure and perfect and holy, he'll know about it and punish you for it. I've been conducting an experiment throughout my career, asking people if they've ever done something they know God doesn't like. I have yet to meet anyone who thinks they've lived the perfect life that would be pleasing to God. I suppose some church leaders feel the need to point out people's sins to them, but I don't. Everyone has done wrong, and they know it. In fact, an awful lot of us have at least one dark shameful deed in our past that fills us with such guilt that we don't want anyone to know about it. For me to belabor the point would only make them feel more guilty and miserable, and imprint on their hearts even more firmly the notion that Jesus is a stern overseer, watching for any slight misstep before he sends down a lightning bolt with your name on it. He's like an evil Santa Claus: he knows if you've been good or bad. If you're bad, you get something a lot worse than a lump of coal. And if you're good... . Well, that doesn't matter. His standards are so high that none of us could ever make it onto the "nice" list.

Rachel has discovered that this is not the real Jesus. In fact, she's had to unlearn a lot of things about him. He doesn't stand ten feet tall with a brilliant halo floating over his head and a voice that would make James Earl Jones sound like a wimp. He is so utterly ordinary, so much like any other person, that you'd have no clue there might be something divine about him. You catch a glimpse of his divinity, not because he floats six inches off the ground and always sounds like he's quoting Scripture, but in the way he treats people. He is unlike any of the rest of us. When it comes to anyone else, we try to gain their favor. If Bekka wants to get on her mother's good side, she needs to do something like clean her room or unload the dishwasher. If Ryan wants to win his coach's respect, he needs to block more kicks, buckle down harder at practice, and score the game-winning goal. If Joe wants to impress his boss, he needs to land the big contract and find a way to cut some fat off the bottom line. If Rachel wants Jesus to approve of her, she needs to... . Well, she doesn't need to do anything. That's what sets Jesus apart from the rest of us, not sprinkling fairy dust on the ground before him.

Because we beat ourselves up over the awful things we've done, we assume that Jesus will, too. No one else accepts us unless we measure up to their standards, so we assume that Jesus won't either. Instead, we experience what Rachel did when she meets Jesus for the first time. No schoolmarm gaze because you didn't do your homework. No police officer at your car window asking if you know what you did wrong. No letter from HR because you showed up late for work six times this quarter. Simply a smile and look of acceptance. Not because you earned it or did anything to deserve it. Just because you're you. That's exactly what Jesus loves about you.

Far too often, we can be like Simon, not wanting Jesus to be kind to the people that are unkind to us, the ones we think should be held accountable for what they've done. Our sense of justice demands that they pay for what they've done. That's Jesus's job. Or so we think. His gospel is so good we just can't believe it's for real. We refuse to accept that Jesus accepts them. And we can't wrap our minds around the fact that he accepts us. Just the way we are.

1. What do you imagine that God thinks of you?

2. Whom do you have trouble believing that Jesus would accept?

3. What is it about you that makes it difficult to receive Jesus's love?

*The next chapter of the novel begins on page 61.*

# Chapter 8

## Background

Rachel is now on the road with Jesus, which is where he typically is. Each of the four gospel books in the Bible gives the impression that Jesus was an itinerant preacher. Capernaum may have been his home base, but he moved from place to place an awful lot. As Mark puts it, "Jesus came to Galilee, proclaiming the good news of God, and saying, 'The time is fulfilled, and the kingdom of God has come near; repent, and believe in the good news'" (1:14-15).

Rachel has barely gotten used to the primitive living conditions in town, but now she's traveling with Jesus and living in even more challenging circumstances. Despite the insistence of some Christian leaders that following Jesus will lead to a life of luxury and riches, Rachel's experience is much more typical. Jesus himself lived a tough life that many people were reluctant to share. Luke records an incident in which one of Jesus's admirers wants to follow him the way that Rachel and the rest of the group are. Jesus responds by saying, "Foxes have holes, and birds of the air have nests; but the Son of Man [that's the way Jesus referred to himself] has nowhere to lay his head" (9:58). In a society where everyone lived as part of a household, Jesus had none. If he had a wife and kids, the Bible tells us nothing about them. Mark tells that his mother and brothers wanted to bring Jesus back into their household, where he had grown up. He would have nothing to do with it, and offered a completely different definition of family (3:20-34).

In a sense, the wandering band that Rachel has joined is a household of its own, with Jesus as its head. We don't exactly know big this "family" was. Many people assume the total group size was thirteen: Jesus plus twelve disciples. They miss Luke's comment (8:1-3) that Mary and Joanna and "many other" women had also come along to follow Jesus. We also know from Acts 1:21-26 that other men in addition to the Twelve were part of Jesus's traveling band. In seeking for a replacement for Judas after his death, Peter proposed that it should be "one of the men who have accompanied us during all the time that the Lord Jesus went in and out among us." They seemed to have had a whole group of candidates to choose from. These were the people who had a more intimate connection with Jesus than the crowds that followed him, and whom Jesus taught more deeply (Mark 3:34).

## Reflection

Why do Rachel's companions enjoy doing the dreary chores that it took to keep the group going? It's one thing for a woman like Bernice, who is in her own element when managing a kitchen and the other household duties. But what about Mary and Joanna, who would never otherwise stoop to perform such tasks? And why do people today still take on menial, demanding, even dangerous tasks for the cause of Jesus with a smile on their faces? I'm nobody's handyman; why do I look forward to a week every summer of climbing into a van to travel a couple states away so I can hang drywall, shovel muck, or lay block? I'm just like all those other crazy lunatics.

Some people think we do it out of guilt: we're doing penance to try to make up for all the terrible things in our lives. Others may suppose that we're doing it out of obligation or duty: we have to do what Jesus tells us to do, whether we like it or not. Still others assume that we're trying to earn our way into heaven: getting a few extra stars in our crowns by performing thankless tasks. I suppose that there are people who act in service to God for reasons like this. I've heard of US Christians going to Africa to run an orphanage and hating every minute of it. They only did it because they thought they had to, in order to be obedient to God.

I certainly can't speak for everyone who calls themselves a Christian, but I find joy in doing things that no one in their right mind would volunteer for. I do it because I want to do it. Part of it is out of gratitude: when I consider everything that God has done and continues to do for me, it's a way of showing my appreciation. Acting out of thankfulness is not like the thank-you card that your mother makes you write to Aunt Mildred for the sweater she gave you for your birthday. It's more like the exuberant joy that fills a teenager being given the latest gaming system, or the excitement that explodes within a sports fanatic getting season tickets for his favorite team, or the breath-taking wonder that floods a fashion-conscious woman receiving an incredibly beautiful piece of jewelry.

I also do it because Jesus has turned me into a different kind of person. The things that bring me pleasure are different from what they would be without him in my life. This is what Paul talks about in Romans 8:5-17: we focus our lives in a completely different direction because of the effect that God has upon us. Do we always get it right? Of course not! But there's something different going on inside of us when we choose what we want to do.

It's not about pretending to be someone that we're not, or putting burdens on ourselves because we believe that's what God wants from us. It's not about feeling even worse about ourselves when we don't experience the joy of gratitude or when we simply don't want to do good and noble things. It's about being exactly who we are, exactly whom God made us to be. Relax. Enjoy yourself. Watch what God is doing inside of you and around you.

1. When have you found pleasure in doing things to help others or to serve God, instead of acting out of your own self-interest?

2. Why do you do what you believe God wants you to do?

3. In what ways has God's presence in your life changed who you are?

*The next chapter of the novel begins on page 71.*

# Chapter 9

## Background

We don't know exactly how large or prosperous Nain was. Archeological excavations indicate that the community was once of considerable size, but it didn't have a wall or gate, as most substantial towns would have had. Nain was situated on the lower slopes of Mount Moreh, with a beautiful view across the valley to Mount Tabor, about five miles to the north.

According to Luke 7:11-50, Jesus had a full schedule while he was in town. As Rachel tells us, Jesus encountered a funeral procession headed to the graveyard as he entered town, and he restored life to a widow's son. Not surprisingly, this caused quite a stir. Luke goes on to tell us that some followers of John the Baptist came to speak with Jesus while he was in Nain. Before he left Nain, Jesus received a precious gift of devotion from a prostitute while he was eating in the home of a Pharisee named Simon: tears and expensive perfume. As you'll see in Chapter Ten, Rachel describes the incident with the prostitute happening in a different town. Matthew and Mark tell us that Jesus met this woman in Bethany, a town just outside of Jerusalem far to the south.

Like other major events in the life of a person or community, each culture has its own customs and rituals surrounding death. In the Ancient Near East, custom required that a death be mourned properly, beginning at the moment of the person's death. Mourning typically included shrill cries and wails, tearing your clothes, beating yourself on the chest, and wearing uncomfortable garments made out of sackcloth or itchy cloth made out of goat's hair. In some situations, you might throw ashes over yourself. The ritual of mourning typically was more important than the actual expression of your grief. If you didn't mourn for your family member in the right way, people would look down their noses at you, just as they might today if your wedding reception doesn't have personalized napkins and satin chair covers.

To ensure that their loved one was mourned properly, families often hired professional mourners. Professional mourners were usually women who made their living not only from perfecting a wail of grief (often accompanied by flutes), but also by composing and performing odes to honor the deceased. The more important you were, the longer and more impressive your funeral ode would be. Some people even believed that "mourning women" had special knowledge or even magical abilities that were passed down through the generations. A widow with no family other than her young son would probably have to borrow money to make sure she gave him a proper send-off, and she'd likely be able to afford only the bare minimum. His funeral ode was probably nothing more than "He was such a good boy!"

Rachel considered the grilling that Jesus received from Pharisees and other religious leaders to be a hostile confrontation, trying to discredit him. That's certainly what it turned into as time went on, but at first their questions were more benign. Pharisees considered themselves to be self-appointed guardians of proper Jewish belief and practice. It was therefore up to them to vet any up-and-coming rabbi and to ensure that he was kosher (in more ways than one). In the Presbyterian church, pastoral candidates must pass examination at a regional meeting of pastors and elders before they can become ordained. I've seen some pretty nit-picky examinations that make the candidates sweat bullets as they try to get through them. It's not that the members of the assembly don't like the candidate or want to trip them up; they just want to make sure that he or she measures up to their standards before they'll give their approval. That's what the Pharisees are doing with Jesus. Being examined or vetted may feel hostile, even when it's not. It was only after Jesus kept violating their standards and presenting a new perspective on their beliefs that the Pharisees started to turn on him.

## Reflection

Imagine you have the opportunity to ask or say something to Jesus. Even if you're convinced that Jesus is no more than an important historical figure who presents an interesting perspective on life, I expect that you'd put some thought into what you'd say. That's what I'd do if I had the chance to talk with Aristotle, Mohammed, or George Washington. Now along come these two brothers, trying to get Jesus's attention. It's bad enough that they pushed their way through a mob that was all stirred up by a miracle. As Luke tells the story (12:13-21), they were even more obnoxious than that. Jesus was in the middle of preaching to a crowd of thousands of people, speaking about things like how closely God watches over us and the importance of honoring him. Right in the middle of Jesus's speech, one of the brothers interrupts him with a shout. He wasn't listening to what Jesus was saying, and he didn't care about all the people around him who wanted to hear it. He saw his chance to talk with Jesus, and he seized it. And what was the earth-shattering topic? The struggle of his soul that he wanted Jesus's insight on? The wisdom about the human experience that he sought? "Tell my brother to give me my share of the inheritance!"

1. If you could ask Jesus anything, what would it be?

2. When have you been so preoccupied or obsessed over something that you've missed the chance for a once-in-a-lifetime experience?

*The next chapter of the novel begins on page 83.*

# Chapter 10

## Background

For us freedom-loving Americans, "the law" is unpleasant. Whether it's God's law or federal, state, or local regulations, we don't like them. The law says "no" to whatever we want to do, and it commands us to do what we don't want. But for the Pharisees, "the Law" is an expression of God's will. It provides a detailed, meticulous description of how God wants us to live. For them, the Law is a description of what we can do to bring God pleasure. When your life honors God, you receive blessings from his hand. These blessings aren't simply payment for services rendered unto the Lord; they are inherent to lives lived under the Law. Lives are blessed by the Law because it is a gift from God.

That's why the Pharisees took the Law seriously. They studied it carefully and came up with hundreds of regulations: what to do and what not to do. The Law was so important that it deserved careful scrutiny to get every possible benefit out of it. It doesn't matter if some of the commands were limiting or constricting, or even if they made no sense at all, because the Law is an expression of God's will. It's better to submit to what we don't understand, trusting that the God who is beyond our comprehension knows what he's talking about.

The Pharisees were meticulous about identifying every aspect of the Law, and how it could be applied properly to life. They ended up with 613 regulations: 365 negative rules ("thou shalt not") to correspond with every day of the year, and 248 positive commands to correspond with what they understood to be the number of parts of the human body. They took it upon themselves to work out every aspect of faithful obedience to the law. For example, Leviticus (19:9-10 and again in 23:22) commands that when you reap your harvest, you must leave the edges for the poor to gather. That seems straightforward, but it was too vague for the precise Pharisees. How big is the edge that you don't harvest? Who qualifies as the poor who get to gather the leftovers? These things have to be specified if you want to follow the Law properly.

Obedience to the Law was so important that the Pharisees didn't even want to get close to breaking it. They engaged in a practice called "Fencing the Law." In order to be faithful to the dictates of the Law, they avoided things that might lead them to disobeying the Law. These things might be perfectly permissible under the Law, but if they put you at risk of breaking the Law, the Pharisees forbade it. There's nothing wrong with a recovering alcoholic going into a bar, but it might tempt him to start drinking. Your gallon of milk is still good for a week after the expiration date, but stores won't sell it after that just to be safe.

Pharisees may have acted "holier than thou," but they actually were. In Jesus's time, Pharisees were honored and revered. They committed themselves to lives of devotion and discipline far beyond what the average person could handle. Parents hoped their sons would grow up to be Pharisees, and they hoped their daughters would marry one. As he did with just about everything else, Jesus saw the Pharisees in a different way. They were so caught up in the intricacies of the Law that they lost the spirit behind it. Instead of inspiring others to follow their lead in obeying God's will by following the Law, they instilled guilt by condemning those who fell short of their exacting standards.

## Reflection

We all have a little Pharisee living inside of us. We set up standards for what we consider to be the right way to live our lives, and then we look down our noses on those who don't measure up. But we don't all have the same code of conduct we're trying to follow like the Pharisees did. We each have our own little version of the Law. If you don't follow my take on what's right and wrong, I'll come down on you like a ton of bricks. It doesn't matter what you think about it.

If you challenge my version of right and wrong, I'm likely to respond the same way Bernice did when Jesus forgave the prostitute. Because you don't live up to my standards, I don't want anything to do with you. The situation is a bit more complex for us because we live in a society that values freedom and tolerance. Or at least, we say that we do. I have no right to impose my standards upon you, as long as you're not breaking the law or hurting someone else. But we have entire groups of people in our nation who condemn each other because their codes of ethics are different. Homophobes and gay rights activists. Pro-choice and pro-life. Red state and blue state. We can't make "them" agree with "us," so we choose to speak ill of them and decide to have nothing to do with them.

We're also much less patient and thoughtful than these Pharisees we think so poorly of. They spent decades sorting through every nuance of the Law, debating and considering each command from every angle. We, on the other hand, tend to prefer the knee-jerk reaction. Consider, for example, our political landscape in which the sound bite is king. If candidates can't explain their position in five words or less, we get bored and tune them out. We live in an increasingly complex world, but we don't have the stomach for extended consideration of whether or not what we think is right actually is the way to go.

Our preference for simplistic thinking finds its way into our churches as well. Some churches welcome and encourage critical thought, as congregation members delve into the complicated matters of faith and feel free to disagree with each other. But many people would rather go to a church where church leaders provide clear-cut, black-and-white instruction for how to live and how to believe.

1. Why do you think people tend to prefer the simple and clear-cut over the ambiguous and nuanced?

2. Under what circumstances are you more likely to make judgments quickly, and when are you more likely to investigate the subtleties of the situation?

3. How does Jesus's refusal to treat us according to a set of standards affect our penchant to assert our own version of right and wrong?

*The next chapter of the novel begins on page 92.*

# Chapter 11

## Background

I've mentioned before that storytellers weave the events of their tale together in a certain way in order to make their point. You may accuse them of playing fast and loose with the facts, just as politicians seem to be able to cherry-pick statistics and take quotes out of context to support their positions. At other times, however, you bring different episodes together, when perhaps they happened at different times, not to obfuscate but to shed some light on the subject. Rachel describes two events together which the gospel writers kept separate. She combined the events of Jesus teaching just offshore in a boat to avoid the crush of the crowd with his healing of a sick woman and a dying girl. Matthew and Mark didn't (9:18-26 and 13:1-3 for Matthew, and

4:1-2 and 5:21-43 for Mark). She wants us to realize how large and excited the crowd was, how eager the people were to be with Jesus, to give us a sense of how bizarre it was that Jesus noticed the touch of one woman in the streets.

Mark combined the story of the woman who had been suffering from chronic hemorrhaging (probably a "female problem," as some people politely call it) with the story of a little girl on death's doorstep. Because Matthew used Mark as one of his sources of inspiration, he followed suit. Were the two miracles intertwined as Mark describes them? Perhaps. Or, just as Rachel brought together the offshore preaching and the healings to make her point, Mark may have done so to make a point of his own.

Mark liked to combine two stories and tell them together. The fancy word for this practice is "intercalation:" interrupting one story to tell a second one, then finishing your first story. One purpose for intercalation is to add suspense, as you're left hanging to see how the first story will end. Even more importantly, intercalation is the storyteller's way of helping us see similarities in the two stories. Those similarities are the point the narrator wants to make. Two other examples of intercalation in Mark's gospel are 3:20-35, which highlights similarities between Jesus's family and his detractors, and 11:12-26, to illustrate the fruitlessness of temple rituals.

Let's consider the similarities between the healing of the hemorrhaging woman and dying girl.

Both of the people who were healed were women, who typically were overlooked or pushed into the background. Jesus made time to take each of them seriously.

As Mark tells the story, both Jairus and the woman fell at Jesus's feet: one because of hope, the other because of fear.

Jesus encouraged Jairus to have faith; the woman acted out of faith.

Both the woman and the little girl were healed with a physical touch. What would change if Mark had intertwined either of these stories with the healing of the centurion's servant, whom he didn't touch?

The woman had been suffering from her disease for twelve years, and Jairus's daughter was twelve years old. The woman suffered as long as Jairus had had the joy of his daughter.

The miracles were instantaneous: the woman recovered from her illness as she kneeled before Jesus, and Jairus's daughter had her life restored immediately.

Now let's look at some of the differences between the two miracles.

Jairus was a respected religious leader; the woman was a religious outcast because of her bleeding (Leviticus 15:25).

Jairus asked for a miracle; the woman took one without asking.

The woman was healed out in public; the girl was brought to life in private.

By telling the stories together, Mark shows us that there is no person and no situation beyond Jesus's care, as we trust him. No matter how long it takes, and no matter how hopeless the situation may seem, there is always hope.

## Reflection

Jesus can help us in any situation, but he doesn't. He calmed the storm out on the lake, but he didn't get rid of the rainstorm that soaked their camp one night. He healed the woman on the street and the little girl in the house, but he did nothing for a woman in his own group. Why does God intervene in some situations and not others? A number of years ago, two men in my congregation, with the interesting nicknames of Butch and Boots, developed the same kind of cancer at the same time. They and their wives were good friends, and we all asked for God's healing for both men. One made a full recovery; the other died. Why did God help Boots, and not Butch? Did he like Boots' family better? Did Butch and his family not have enough faith, or not pray hard enough? It's easy to feel guilty when God doesn't come through for us. If only we had done something differently, or if we were different people, God would give us what we want. Seeing someone else getting what we want, as Butch's family and Tamar did, only makes it worse.

If you're expecting me to explain why this happens, I'm sorry to disappoint you. People much wiser than me have spent centuries debating why God allows some people to suffer when he could rescue them. No one has ever come up with an answer that satisfies everyone. Some ideas make sense, while others are just downright offensive. But none resolve the ache we feel.

It's not a final answer, but Rachel brings up one idea that can help.

When she tells us that some of the disciples wanted Jesus to put together an itinerary for his travels, she comments that "Jesus would not be scheduled." It frustrates Judas and Thomas, and it continues to frustrate us today. We want a God whom we can predict, a God who does things according to our schedules, a God who plays by our rules. In other words, we want a God we can control. We want him to do our bidding, instead of the other way around. But God doesn't operate according to our schedules. When he does act, it usually takes him longer to do so than we'd like. I've never met someone who said that God answered their prayers too quickly! The woman with the hemorrhage would have loved to have been healed a decade earlier.

Bible scholars notice two ways in which people of the Bible relate to God. Sometimes they meet the God of the temple, who lays everything out in an orderly fashion. There's a plan, they know what they're supposed to do, and their expectations are met. At other times, they meet the God of the wilderness, who turns their lives and their beliefs topsy-turvy. In these disturbing, confusing times when we encounter the God of the wilderness, he reshapes who we are, the world we live in, and the way we understand him.

1. Have you or someone you care about ever been in a situation that seemed hopeless? Was it ever resolved? Are you still seeking God's help? Have you given up?

2. What answers have you heard to the question of why God sometimes doesn't act? How helpful are they?

3. Remember a time of chaos and uncertainty in your life. How did you meet God during this trip into the "wilderness"?

*The next chapter of the novel begins on page 104.*

# Chapter 12

## Background

Jews and Gentiles had nothing to do with each other beyond what was absolutely necessary. Neither group had much respect for the other.

The Gentiles considered the Jews to be a stubborn bunch that remained in their own little bubble instead of catching up with the times. As Greek culture and Roman power united many ethnicities, the Jews were the exception. Each of the other nationalities found ways to incorporate their local culture into the larger world. They would identify their gods with those of the Romans, and they accepted Greek as their primary language. But not the Jews. A hundred and fifty years before the time of Jesus, a regional emperor tried to drag the Jews into the modern world and incited a bloody rebellion as a result. The Romans were a bit more conciliatory. They granted the Jews special exemptions from what was required of other subjugated peoples, with the hopes that their extra-sensitive necks wouldn't chafe under the Roman yoke. It didn't work. About a generation after Jesus's time, the Roman legions had to come in and crush the Jewish nation in order to maintain their control over it. Everyone else just thought the Jews were weird. They only worshiped one god, while everyone else had a whole collection of them. How can you call yourself religious with only one god? They refused to conduct business or do any work one day of the week, which meant that one seventh of the week's business was lost. They had the strangest requirements about what they could and couldn't eat, which meant that they couldn't buy food in the marketplace like everyone else.

There wasn't much love lost in the other direction either. It's no wonder the women in Jesus's group treated Rachel the way they did when they thought she wasn't one of "them." It's not only that the Gentiles were utterly clueless about the holy and divine, which was bad enough. They just weren't the right kind of people. The Jews were the chosen people of God, plain and simple. If you weren't a Jew, you didn't belong to God. Your impurity and non-Jewishness may contaminate any Jews with whom you associate, so it was better for Jews simply not to have anything to do with you. And none of this even takes into account the mistreatment that the Jews suffered from

Gentiles in the past. Staying away from Gentiles was self-protection, like steering clear of a rattlesnake on the hiking trail. Jews didn't eat with Gentiles or even go into their homes.

The only thing the Jews had going for them in the eyes of everyone else was how ancient their religion was. Unlike today when new means improved, age added value. Any religion that can trace its roots back more than a thousand years deserved to be taken seriously. There were some Gentiles who admired the Jewish religion and wanted to participate in it. A few of them actually converted, a process that involved a rather painful procedure that makes even the most courageous men quiver. For the most part, they would settle for the halfway status of being a "God-fearer." They obeyed the Law and worshiped God as best they could without actually becoming a Jew. There was a special courtyard at the temple in Jerusalem for the God-fearers since they weren't allowed to enter the temple itself. Jewish scholars debated the eternal fate of these devout non-Jews. The centurion in Capernaum was probably one of these God-fearers; he had the respect of the synagogue leaders and had underwritten their building project.

When the early church started, everyone assumed that you needed to be a Jew in order to be a follower of Jesus. Christians were simply one other type of Jew, along with the Pharisees, Sadducees, and Essenes. Even Jesus seemed at times to think this way. While he did make a point of traveling to non-Jewish regions around Galilee and associating with people like the Samaritans, he insulted a Canaanite woman who wanted his help (Matthew 15:21-28), giving in only because she was willing to grovel and demean herself.

Things changed when Paul was convinced that God had selected him to preach the gospel to Gentiles (Acts 9:15), and when Peter got a message through a vision that he was supposed to reach out to a God-fearing Gentile named Cornelius (Acts 10:28). Some Christians began to reach out to include Gentiles in their faith, and it caused quite a ruckus. The church leaders held a conference to debate the issue (Acts 15) and agreed that Jesus's gospel extended to include the Gentiles. But a sizeable number of Christians resisted this move and continued to insist that Gentiles had to become Jews before they could become Christians. Paul's letter to the Galatians is his scathing rebuttal of this position.

# Reflection

Society's expectations can put us in precarious positions. If Tamar does not get pregnant, she risks being tossed out into the street and living a life of poverty and mistreatment. If Rachel's friends realize that she's a Gentile, they're going to disown her. They'll probably reject her even more than the typical Gentile because she has been trying to fool them. The particulars may have changed over the years, but the threat has not. Do something or be someone other than what you're "supposed" to, and even your closest friends and family will turn on you. Ask the teenager who doesn't have a smart phone, or who enjoys classical music. Ask the gay man whose family refuses to have anything to do with him since he came out. Ask the mother who doesn't focus her entire life on her daughter's softball team, attending every game and taking part in every fund-raiser. Ask any of us who are afraid to let others see who we really are, out of fear that we'll be ostracized. If you're bold like Rachel, you may have the courage to stand up for yourself, and perhaps make a difference in doing so. But you'll still end up paying a heavy price for it.

Rachel found courage through the acceptance that Jesus had shown her. Her response to Mary's question about her identity was not simply a rhetorical move to win a debate. It was the foundation for her self-confidence in the face of rejection. When we fear what people will think of us or how they will treat us, we can find confidence of our own from the same source. God takes delight in exactly who you are, because that's how he created you. Even when you want to reject yourself because of the faults you see in yourself, God cannot take his eyes off you. He enjoys everything you do and everything you are. God knows you better than you know yourself, and he thinks you're amazing. If God thinks you're wonderful, who are you to argue with him about it?

Don't worry about conforming to the expectations others have for you. Don't try to squeeze into little boxes of acceptable identity and behavior. Take joy in the unique way that God created you, and find courage in Jesus's acceptance of you to let others see it.

1. Who are the people today that decent folks avoid and reject?

2. Is there anyone who is excluded from the groups you are part of?

3. When have you been afraid to show your true self to others?

4. When have you rejected others because you don't approve of who they are?

5. How do you find the courage in Christ not to hide yourself, and to open yourself up to others?

*The next chapter of the novel begins on page 114.*

# Chapter 13

## Background

Rachel is noticing and experiencing firsthand how Jesus breaks social convention in the way he reaches out to women. Everyone else considers women to be second-rate human beings, but Jesus treats them with respect and appreciation. His willingness to treat them as equals was a breath of fresh air after a lifetime of subjugation.

And the women were not the only ones who received Jesus's welcome. The society of the Roman Empire categorized people into strict classes. There were people who had power and privilege, and those who didn't. You had to "know your place" or there would be trouble. Society was organized into pairings of dominant and subordinate: men and women, parents and children, masters and slaves, patrons and clients, the rich and the poor, the well-bred and the common rabble. The great teachers of the day outlined exactly how each group was to treat the other. We find Christian versions of these codes in places such as Ephesians 5:21-6:9, Colossians 3:18-4:1, and 1 Peter 2:13-3:7. But when we compare the New Testament teachings with other codes of the time, we notice something unusual. The Christian outlines of social interaction focus primarily upon the conduct of the groups who hold the short end of the stick: the slaves, the women, the poor. That's because the early church was made up primarily of the underclass. The gospel of Jesus Christ had a particularly powerful appeal for those who had spent their lives under the boots of their superiors. They found a message of equality in a world based on inequality. They found communities of believers that called one another "brother" and "sister" no matter how well bred they were or to whom they were supposed to bow down. Perhaps the strongest magnet of all was that the Christians took care of those whom everyone else ignored, providing for the widows and the poor and caring for the sick and elderly. This was not just a nice concept for Jesus's early followers: financial records from early churches reveal a staggering level of support for people on the margins of society. No other movement in those days could compare to the church when it came to helping the disadvantaged. Early Christianity was a true grassroots movement, arising from the bottom of society. Things changed about 300 years later by the time Emperor Constantine declared Christianity to be the official religion of the empire. Church leaders became society leaders and began to enforce the very social stratification that Jesus had ignored. But today, the church thrives most strongly in conditions of poverty, crisis, and violence. In comfortable places like Western Europe and North America, Christianity tends to wane in comparison. But in all contexts, the church flourishes when it claims the role it had in those early years.

## Reflection

Jesus can only help us if we let him. You won't find the story of Susanna in the New Testament (only a mention of her name in Luke 8:3), but she epitomizes a common human trait. Susanna fiercely resisted assistance of any kind, most likely because she had spent years protecting herself from the attack and scorn of others. Receiving help is a sign of weakness, and she needed to be strong. She could trust no one, because people had hurt her so much in the past. When we allow our pride and fear to dominate, we isolate ourselves from the transformation that Jesus offers. This is Susanna's hurdle to overcome.

Our challenge is not only is to take the risk of trusting that Jesus can make a positive difference in our lives, but also to believe that he is able to. This is Rachel's obstacle. That little word "if" betrayed her heart as she asked Jesus to help her new friend. "If" is a great word to use when you want to hedge your bets. To Rachel's credit, she is at least open to the possibility that maybe Jesus could do something. But she wasn't convinced. By asking with an "if" she was casting her fishing line into a lake, hoping that maybe a bass would take the bait, but not putting the frying pan on the fire until she actually reeled one in.

Rachel isn't the only person who "if'd" Jesus. Mark (9:17-27) tells us about a man who brought his son to Jesus to be healed. The disciples tried to help him but couldn't. When the man got Jesus's attention, he said, "If you are able to do anything, have pity on us and help us." Jesus picked up on the "if" in a heartbeat and challenged the father about it. The poor man, desperate to find relief for his son, exclaimed one of the most honest and powerful expressions of faith that we'll find in the Bible: "I believe; help my unbelief!" He had at least a little bit of faith, and he wanted to believe even more. By asking Jesus to help his unbelief, the man acknowledged his need for Jesus to enable him even to bring his needs before him. The story ended well for the father and his son, just as it did for Rachel and Susanna.

At times, when someone is struggling with the delay or apparent absence of God's response to their prayers for help, a well-meaning companion may say, "You just have to believe strongly enough, and God will do it for you," or "Maybe you're not praying hard enough." What may be intended as friendly words of encouragement can become fodder for a massive guilt trip. They give the message that God's failure to come through for us is our own fault. We come to believe that we didn't measure up to what God required from us, so he refused to give us the help we wanted.

Jesus offers us a word of grace and hope in the midst of it all. When the disciples had their own awareness of the shortcomings of their faith, they echoed the words of the distraught father: "Increase our faith!" Jesus replied that all they needed was a tiny amount of faith: only the size of a mustard seed, smaller than a grain of sand (Luke 17:5-6). If we have even the smallest spark of hope that Jesus might be able to make a difference in our lives, he's happy to work with it and surprise us with his grace.

1. Why do you think people are more drawn to Jesus in times of oppression rather than in times of prosperity?

2. If you are part of a church, how well does it support people in need? Do people from the margins of society find welcome and acceptance?

3. When does your fear or pride interfere with your willingness to ask God for help?

4. Have you ever felt, or been told, that your faith wasn't strong enough? What emotions did you feel at the time?

*The next chapter of the novel begins on page 126.*

# Chapter 14

## Background

Ask someone today what the first word is that pops into their mind when you say the word "Samaritan," and most likely they'll respond with "good." But ask the same question of a first century Jew, and they may respond with "traitor," "half-breed," "blasphemer," or simply with a snarl. As we've considered already, our opinion of Pharisees is the opposite of what it was back then. The same is true of the Samaritans.

Starting about 900 years before the time of Jesus, the Hebrew people were divided into two kingdoms: Israel in the north, and Judah in the south. If Facebook had existed back then, they would have posted their relationship status as "it's complicated." The people of the two nations were kin and they worshiped the same God, but there was very little love lost between them. When the Assyrian Empire rolled through the region about two centuries later, Israel was overtaken and Judah barely escaped by the skin of its teeth. In order to consolidate their empire, the Assyrians forced ethnic groups to move out of their homelands to other parts of the empire. It was a bit like what the United States did with the Cherokees and what the Soviets did with the Tatars. The people of the northern kingdom endured the same fate. The Assyrians dispersed them throughout the other parts of the empire, and they lost their identity as a people. This is what people refer to when they mention the "ten lost tribes of Israel." Then the Assyrians shipped people from other parts of the empire to Israel and told them that it was their new home. The newcomers intermingled with the few Israelites that remained, adopted a hybrid version of their religion, and became known as Samaritans. They weren't "really" Jews, but they were related and worshiped God in a roughly similar way. The two biggest religious differences between Samaritans and Jews were that Samaritans only accepted the first five books of the Old Testament to be Scripture and that they worshiped God at Mount Gerizim, near the site of the old northern kingdom's sanctuary at Shechem. The Jews, on the other hand, included the rest of what we call the Old Testament in their Bible and insisted that worship of the Lord had to take place in the temple of Jerusalem.

For the Jews, Samaritans were a mongrel race from their ancient rivals in the northern kingdom who had bastardized their worship of God. But about 200 years before Jesus was born, it got even worse. As I've described in an earlier chapter, the Jews had rebelled against an emperor who had tried to eliminate their distinctive religious practices. As they worked to assert their independence, they took over Samaritan territory and even destroyed their holy sites. The Samaritans, in retaliation, helped the empire in their battle to reconquer the Jews. It's no wonder that in the days of Jesus, Jews would burn down Samaritan villages and Samaritans would harass Jews traveling through their region.

## Reflection

Jesus may be making a point to break down barriers and to bring reconciliation, but his followers have a tough time following in his footsteps. From Bernice and the rest of Rachel's companions to the present day, we're very willing to turn our backs on people who are different from us. Let's face it: there are some people who simply disgust us, whom we are unable to think kind thoughts about. We have plenty of Samaritans to hate. And it goes both ways: there are plenty of people who despise us in return.

Paul once wrote that God "desires everyone to be saved and to come to the knowledge of the truth" (1 Timothy 2:4). He also declared that God has entrusted the "ministry of reconciliation" to us, and that we are "ambassadors for Christ" (2 Corinthians 5:18-20). In other words, it's up to us to get over our qualms about "those people" and share in his work of breaking down barriers and declaring the news of his wonderful love for us all. But we have our limits of acceptance. Consider the way Rachel's friends responded to the prostitute who kissed Jesus's feet, how they were ready to dump her because they thought she was a Gentile, and their refusal to have anything to do with the Samaritans. Remember how Susanna was treated by the people in her village. When we're honest with ourselves, we can each acknowledge that there are those whom we want absolutely nothing to do with. How can we be the agents of reconciliation and the barrier-breakers that Jesus wants us to be?

The best way to tear down a wall is to walk to the other side. What is it like to be on the other side of our barriers of hostility and distrust? Maybe we don't even care what "they" are going through. And if we do, we most likely have a skewed perception of what life is like for them. As a white American, I cannot know for myself the subtle and not-so-subtle forms of discrimination that African-Americans face on a daily basis. I certainly have no right to tell them that "it's not so bad" and they need to quit making a big deal about it. Set a goal to know people on the other side of the fence. It's easy to judge, fear, condemn, and hate others when they're not real people to you, but simply a generic "them." It's a lot harder when they have names, faces, and real lives.

Here's one challenging example. India was gripped with terrible violence and upheaval in 1946 as the nation was being partitioned into Muslim Pakistan and Hindu India. A Hindu man named Souren Bannerji witnessed his wife and children being killed by a Muslim mob and retaliated by joining a Hindu mob that killed a Muslim family. Wracked with guilt, he sought advice from Mahatma Gandhi, who advised him to find an orphan child and raise it as his own. "But first," Gandhi said, "be sure the child is a Muslim." He challenged Souren to cross the barrier and welcome one of "them" into his family. He did, not only adopting a Muslim son but marrying his widowed mother and becoming a family.

1. Who are people that make your blood boil? Why?

2. What makes it difficult to accept people who are different from ourselves?

3. Have you ever gotten to know someone from "the other side of the fence?" What effect, if any, did it have on your understanding about

your differences?

*The next chapter of the novel begins on page 136.*

# Chapter 15

## Background

Rachel's confusion about Jesus's refusal to take credit for his miracles is understandable. Particularly in Mark's account of his ministry, Jesus frequently tells people not to talk about the wonders he performs. As the disciples begin to figure out Jesus's identity as the Messiah, Jesus forbids them to tell anyone. He frequently hides his identity from the public and only lets his disciples in on his special teachings. Put all this together and you'll understand why Bible scholars refer to the "Messianic Secret" that Jesus keeps. It's been the source of a lot of head-scratching over the years. If Jesus wanted to show people the new way of life that he was championing and creating, why wouldn't he want people to know who he was?

Some people suggest that Jesus was humble and modest and simply didn't want to draw attention to himself. Others think that he was avoiding the scrutiny of the authorities who might arrest him if they thought he was getting too big for his britches. People in the crowd might rally around him to rebel against the Romans and the Jewish leadership who collaborated with them. Then there are those who claim that it was all about timing. If Jesus's identity as the Messiah or Son of God got out too quickly, it would ruin the divine plan for redeeming the world through his death and resurrection.

In Mark's telling the tale of Jesus's ministry, there is something deeper going on. People could hazard a guess now and then about who Jesus might be, but it was impossible to recognize and understand his identity as Messiah, the Son of God, until he accomplished the purpose of Messiahship: his atoning death on the cross. Up to that point, no one had a clue: not the crowds following him, not the religious scholars who supposedly knew everything there was to know about God, and not even the disciples. Jesus would explain himself clearly to them, yet they seem like a bunch of lunkheads who couldn't make head or tail out of it. But at the moment of Jesus's death, when the purpose for his coming into the world and for his ministry was fulfilled, Jesus's identity was so obvious that even the Gentile Roman officer in charge of a squad of torturers and executioners could declare "Truly this man was God's Son!" (Mark 15:39). Until then, anything that people said about Jesus was as accurate as the pearls of journalistic integrity that you find in the grocery store check-out line.

Jesus's reluctance to grab the limelight isn't the only baffling subject in the story. Why did Judas betray Jesus to his enemies? No one really knows, but we have a lot of very different ideas. The most common understanding of Judas is that he is history's most notorious traitor. Dazzled by the prospect of a bag of silver coins, he turned against his leader. Maybe he planned all along to set Jesus up. Maybe his greed got the better of him. This is probably the theory John had when he wrote his gospel, struggling to understand how his close companion could have done such a thing. When Judas protested that the money spent to pour perfume on Jesus's feet could have gone to help the poor, John adds the comment, "He said this not because he cared about the poor, but because he was a thief; he kept the common purse and used to steal what was put into it" (12:6). Perhaps over the decades John's 20-20 hindsight convinced him that there were signs all along that Judas was a louse. But you can't be a traitor if people don't trust you. Perhaps Jesus's omniscience enabled him to see how things would turn out between him and Judas, but everyone else would have thought of him as a cherished member of their close-knit group.

Luke saw things differently. As Jesus's enemies were looking for a way to eliminate Jesus, he tells us that Satan entered Judas (22:3). The betrayal was a result of demonic possession. Powerful spiritual forces were at play, and Judas happened to be the one that the powers of evil used to attack Jesus. Judas wasn't a bad guy; the Devil made him do it. We might even pity him for becoming a pawn in the cosmic struggle. Once he realized how he had been used to do something so awful, it's no wonder that he killed himself (Matthew 27:1-10).

Some people understand Judas as the man that Rachel has met: a devoted follower of Jesus who recognized the danger of Jesus's growing popularity. If it got out of hand, or if the Zealots claimed Jesus as their leader, things would get ugly and bloody very fast. In John's telling of the crowd's response to the miraculous meal for a multitude, that's exactly what was starting to happen (6:14 and following). They wanted to make him a king, trusting that he would provide for their every need. This is the Judas we also meet in the rock opera *Jesus Christ Superstar*, who tries in vain to shake the stardust out of Jesus's eyes so he could see the dangerous position he had put himself in. The temple leaders used his concern as a way to manipulate him into serving their cause. Judas was, at worst, a gullible stooge who was chewed up in a political struggle.

Another theory is that Judas's devotion for Jesus was so strong that he wanted to help advance his cause. He believed Jesus was the leader that Israel had been waiting for. Perhaps he was frustrated that the plan was taking so long to unfold, so he tried to force Jesus's hand. He could have been just like Abraham and Sarah in the Old Testament, who had become impatient for God to fulfill his promise to give them a son. They thought they'd speed along the process, and things didn't turn out well for them either (Genesis 16:1-16 and 21:8-20). In Judas's case, the plan was to create a confrontation between Jesus and his enemies. He was convinced that Jesus would seize the opportunity to demonstrate his power. When it didn't happen, Judas was devastated.

Then there's the idea that Jesus and Judas were in cahoots. Jesus wanted things to turn out as they did, and Judas was part of the plan all along. They had planned it out in advance, so when Jesus told Judas at the Last Supper, "Do quickly what you are going to do" (John 13:27), he in effect instructed Judas that it was time for him to get the plan in motion. Some theologians debate the issue: if Judas's betrayal was part of God's plan, should he be held accountable for it? Lots of ink has been spilled trying to answer that question, and I'm not going spill more here. You can ponder the matter yourself.

## Reflection

We're quick to categorize personality traits as good or bad, positive or negative. But when we consider our own temperament we discover that the value of our characteristics has more to do with how we exercise them, and the situations in which we do so. Our virtues and vices typically are opposite sides of the same coin. Someone who is careful with money may be thrifty and know how to find a good bargain to stretch a limited budget, or she may be a tightwad who keeps her family in rags while the bank account gets fatter and fatter.

The obnoxious loudmouth who confronts his co-workers over every perceived offense is the same person who intervenes when punks taunt a senior citizen. It all depends on what you do with your personality traits.

Consider Rachel and her companions. Rachel sees Judas as the kind of detail-oriented person that every team needs, but Mary calls him a fussbudget. Bernice is a highly organized manager, but can become trapped in her own rigidity. Mary is a take-charge kind of a person, but risks steamrolling people in her path. Apparently before she met Jesus she did it quite regularly. Rachel sometimes speaks up when she shouldn't and gets herself in trouble, but she's also the person who championed Susanna's cause in a wonderful way. Are these virtues or vices? It all depends on how they are used.

1. What are some features of your personality that you are sometimes ashamed of or wish you could eliminate? How could they be an asset for you?

2. When have you acted or spoken with good intentions, only to discover later that you only made matters worse?

*The next chapter of the novel begins on page 147.*

# Chapter 16

## Background

Scholars agree that John did not include the story of the woman caught in adultery (John 8:1-11) in his gospel, but that later editors added it to his book. As with the rest of the books of the Bible, we don't have John's original manuscript. But we do have copies as early as the second and third centuries. This passage doesn't begin to show up in copies of the Bible until about eight hundred years after John wrote his gospel. That's a longer period of time than the time between Leonardo da Vinci and us.

Our modern sensibilities may cry "Foul!" over this, offended that someone might actually tamper with Holy Scripture. And yet, every modern English translation of the Bible includes it. Even the scholars' definitive versions of the Bible in the original Greek have it. Granted, they all mark it off in special way and include a note that the story wasn't in John's original gospel. But there it is. It's one of the better-known stories from Jesus's ministry, and the tag line about not throwing the first stone has become a commonplace expression. How seriously should we take this passage? Should it even be in the Bible?

The first thing to keep in mind is that the Bible comes from a time when there were no such things as copyright laws and plagiarism standards. There were no printing presses or photocopiers. It wasn't unusual for scribes to add their comments, or to take out parts they didn't like, as they were making a copy of a manuscript. In those days people would write books and claim that the author was a hero from the ancient past, and no one batted an eye. In the century or so before Jesus, some of the most popular Jewish books were attributed to people like Moses, Enoch, and Elijah, even though they had been dead and gone for many centuries. In the first few centuries of the early church, versions of the gospel supposedly written by Peter, Thomas, and even Mary Magdalene sprouted up. No one today thinks for a moment that these were their authors, but back in the day entire Christian communities focused their faith upon these erstwhile gospels. The addition of a story to John's gospel would simply have been par for the course.

Some scholars speculate that the story of the woman caught in adultery was a story that had been passed down through the generations as an oral rather than written remembrance of Jesus. Eventually someone decided to write it down and put it in John's gospel. Some ancient manuscripts put this story in a different place in John's gospel, and a couple even put it in Luke's gospel. The fact that the story includes historical details that would not have been familiar to people several hundred years after Jesus adds some credibility to this theory. But that's all it is: a theory.

Regardless of how this story comes to us, it's become famous for good reason. We find a compassionate yet commanding presentation of Jesus in it, and it touches us in a deeply personal way as we contemplate our sinfulness in the presence of a mighty, holy God. Maybe those copyists who added the story look at it the same way I do: if it wasn't in the Bible, it should be.

The hypocrisy of the religious elite is obvious. As Susanna points out, you can't catch someone in the act of adultery by themself. If the accusation is correct and they caught her red-handed, there would also be a man with scarlet palms and fingers. The Jewish Law is quite clear: "If a man commits adultery with the wife of his neighbor, both the adulterer and the adulteress shall be put to death" (Leviticus 20:10). The men who confronted Jesus had no interest in justice: they were simply using the woman to put him in a bind.

It was a two-fold bind. First, they wanted to force Jesus to choose between compassion and justice. He had attracted quite a following with his message and lifestyle of acceptance and love. As Rachel noticed back in Chapter Thirteen, a disproportionate number of Jesus's followers were women. If he approved of the brutal infliction of justice, especially upon a woman, his popularity would tank. On the other hand, if he failed to uphold the Law, Jesus would lose his legitimacy as a teacher of Jewish Law.

Jesus faced a second bind as well. As Mary tells Rachel, the Jewish leaders had no right of capital punishment. Only the Romans were permitted to execute criminals, and they only did so according to their law. That's why the temple authorities couldn't put Jesus to death after they had arrested him. They needed Pilate, their Roman governor, to authorize it. If Jesus agreed that the woman should be stoned, the Romans would nab him for refusing to live under their authority. But if he let her off the hook, he'd forfeit his rabbinic authority. The quandary these men set for Jesus was similar to the one he faced when they asked him later if they should pay taxes to Caesar (Matthew 22:15-22, Mark 12:13-17, Luke 20:20-26).

Jesus's response should not be misconstrued as carte blanche for ignoring God's commands and doing whatever we want. And it was more than simply a sly way to dodge a sticky situation. It was an exposure of hypocrisy. It is an unfortunate feature of human nature to see the flaws in other people while overlooking our own. As Jesus said in the Sermon on the Mount, we need to take the log out of own eye before we can say anything about the piece of sawdust in someone else's (Matthew 7:1-5). Jesus stuck a moral mirror in the faces of the accusing men. They didn't like it, but they couldn't ignore it either.

Jesus didn't let the woman off scot-free either. His words to her were not simply an assurance of forgiveness and acceptance. He told the woman not to sin anymore. Had Rachel and Susanna not intervened, it would have been a tough order to follow. When Jesus touches our lives he expects them to change. About twenty years later, this was a point that the church in Corinth didn't catch. They thought that the grace of Jesus was a free pass to do anything they wanted. Things became pretty outrageous and scandalous, until Paul wrote his first letter to them to set things straight.

## Reflection

If you're part of a church or any other religious institution and Rachel's story doesn't make you uncomfortable, you're not paying attention. You're not paying attention to how hypocrisy, pretentiousness, and lack of compassion get in the way of what Jesus is trying to do, both in his own time and in ours. The bumper-sticker makers have captured the sentiment many people have about us church-type people: "I Love Jesus: It's His Fan Club I Can't Stand," and "Jesus, Save Me from Your Followers." We do a miserable job of emulating the One we seek (or at least claim to seek) to follow.

At times we treat people the way Rachel's companions treated the prostitute who snuck into the home of Simon the Pharisee to express her gratitude to him. We don't notice the sometimes-awkward ways that they try to express their devotion. Instead, we comment on the ways that they're not getting it "right." We complain that they don't know the proper way to be a Christian and that they are making a mockery of what we hold dear. We assume that they are not worthy to share Jesus with us. They need to clean up their act before they can associate with us. Or, as Bernice and the others seem to believe, there is some indelible stain upon the person that no amount of religion could ever wash away. Like the men who wanted to stone the poor girl they dragged in front of Jesus, we are blind to our own stains and to how inadequate our devotion to God is.

Usually, we don't even notice "those people." I once had a conversation with the leaders of a prim and proper church about their connection with their community, and they mentioned the addicts who walked past their building every day on the way to the methadone clinic. It was amazing to watch them realize for the first time that their church could have anything to do with them. Even when we do include people in our churches and ensure that they are playing by our rules, we still find ways to turn folks off. Rachel grew up going to church with her parents, but hated every minute of it. The dress, tights, and tight shoes interfered with any chance of feeling comfortable on Sunday morning. Being paraded in front of the congregation for Christmas pageants and hearing more judgmentalism than love certainly didn't help. The form of the institutional church mattered more than the spirit of the fellowship gathered in honor of Jesus.

The mission for those of us who claim Christ's name is to continue his grace in the lives of those around us, especially those whose need for grace is the greatest. God is at work in everyone's lives, whether they realize it or not. When we touch someone's life, it's not the first time that God gets involved. Our calling is to participate in and to build upon the movement of God in that person's life. Jesus counted on Rachel to continue his work of grace in the life of the girl who escaped death. He's counting on us, too.

1. When have you suffered at the hands of those who claimed to be doing Christ's work? How did the experience affect you?

2. Under what circumstances are you likely to forget your own failings and condemn others instead?

3. Are there times when you have ignored or failed to pick up the role that God has given you to continue his work of grace?

4. Who is in your life now that you can touch? How will you do it?

*The next chapter of the novel begins on page 159.*

# Chapter 17

## Background

Sometimes people get a reputation for the most trivial reason. Someone on our work trips once had trouble getting a grip on his hammer, and now he's the butt of our jokes every time he picks one up. It doesn't matter how good of a carpenter he is; the reputation sticks. The usually careful driver gets a speeding ticket, and now her family calls her Speedy Gonzales. Once the reputation takes hold, it can last a lifetime.

Or even longer. My heart goes out to the apostle Thomas, dead these many centuries but still carrying an albatross of a reputation around his neck. Earlier I asked you to play word association with "Samaritan," and I suspect you responded "Good." When I ask you what comes to your mind when I say "Thomas," you might say "Tank Engine." But I imagine it wouldn't take long before you'd come to "Doubting Thomas."

Most of the twelve disciples get only a passing reference in the Bible, or figure in perhaps one or two episodes. Thomas is best known for his response to the other disciples when they tell him they have seen Jesus risen from the dead after his crucifixion (John 20:24-29). He didn't believe them. It wasn't until Jesus came to the group again a week later and Thomas saw him in the flesh before he would believe that Jesus was risen. Jesus doesn't exactly chide Thomas for not believing until he could see it for himself, but he gives a special blessing for those who can. So Thomas gets called the doubter.

Let's get real. Can you really blame a guy for not believing that someone who was tortured to death has come back to life? If Thomas deserves to be called a doubter, I imagine anyone with a sound brain in their skull should be, too. We've taken this perfectly natural response to outrageous news and cast Thomas as the ultimate resident of Missouri, the Show-Me State. We see him as the skeptic who needs cold hard evidence before he'll accept anything.

And that's not fair. It's not even a reasonable assessment of how Thomas is presented in the Bible. He's not as prominent of a figure as Peter, James, and John, but he does get two other mentions. During the Last Supper, when Jesus told the disciples that they knew the place where he was going, Thomas chimed in, "Lord, we do not know where you are going. How can we know the way?" (John 14:5). Is that doubt? Not really. It's a desire to understand and learn. He probably said what was on everyone's mind. And no one disses Philip for his follow-up question a couple verses later.

We get the best insight into Thomas's character through a simple but powerful statement he makes in John 11. By this point in Jesus's ministry, everyone knew that Jerusalem was a death trap for Jesus. The Powers That Be were out to get him, and nothing short of a miracle would save him if he went there. The thought of going to Jerusalem probably gave everyone their own version of Rachel's ulcer that's chewing her up from the inside.

While Jesus was off on the far side of the Jordan River where John had done his baptizing, he got word that his friend Lazarus was dying. Lazarus and his two sisters lived in a suburb of Jerusalem called Bethany. It was natural for Jesus to want to come to the aid of his friend, but it would mean that he would be walking into the lion's den. He delayed for two days before announcing to his disciples that he was going Bethany. Everyone knew that things could get ugly: not just for Jesus, but for anyone remotely associated with him. The disciples had a choice: would they stay on the far side of the river in safety, or would they follow Jesus into the firestorm? At this point Thomas made one of the boldest statements of commitment and devotion you'll find in Scripture, and perhaps anywhere else: "Let us also go, that we may die with him" (John 11:16). As Priscilla told Rachel, he was afraid of what was going to happen in Jerusalem. But he was going to go anyway.

Peter gets all the credit for his declaration of faith when Jesus asked the disciples who they said that he was: "You are the Messiah, the Son of the living God" (Matthew 16:16). Peter gets a marvelous blessing in return, and people still make a big deal about the courage and insight it took for Peter to say that. I certainly don't want to take away from Peter's big moment, but it pales in comparison to what Thomas said. Peter could say whatever he wanted about Jesus, and nothing would happen to him. Thomas put his life on the line.

When I prepare people to join my church, we talk about the difference between belief and faith, and I give the example of airplanes. It's one thing to believe that planes can fly, and go to the airport to watch them take off and land. But it takes faith to get into the giant aluminum tube and strap yourself in, knowing that you're surrounded by about 40,000 gallons of highly explosive jet fuel. If your faith is misplaced and planes don't fly, you're on your way to a fiery death at the end of the runway. Peter may have believed in Jesus, but Thomas put his faith in him.

Doubting Thomas, my eye.

## Reflection

It's hard to keep up with Jesus and all this forgiving stuff. We simply don't have hearts the size of his to release our anger or pain over the offenses that we face. Even if we're not personally affected by someone's crime we still want them to pay for it. When they've done so, we still won't let go of our resentment. Even if your family has not been affected by sexual assault, I doubt you'd be happy to have a violent convicted sex offender as your next-door neighbor. He may have done the time, confessed the crime, and successfully completed treatment to be reformed, but I don't think it would make much of a difference. You may not fear for your safety, but you probably won't invite him over for a backyard barbecue either.

It's even harder to forgive when the offense is personal. Those deep cuts never seem to heal. More than twenty years ago someone who should have known better caused great pain to me and to those I love, and nearly ended my pastoral career. After all these years, thinking of him can make my blood boil. A man in my congregation was wronged by a family member more than fifty years ago. He struggles to forgive him, but it's all he can do to be in the same room with him. Many people are like us. As the saying goes, we may forgive, but we'll never forget.

In other words, we're all a bit like Bernice, Leah, and Naomi. Tell us that Jesus has forgiven someone of a crime that really galls us, and we're not likely to play along nicely. The news of God's incredible grace for us that erases everything that causes guilt and shame is a truth we relish and seek to understand and appreciate for ourselves. But we're much more reluctant to celebrate God's grace in the lives of other people.

Rachel has gotten to know Mahlah and to learn the tragic story that led to her near-fatal accusation of adultery. She had been caught up in affairs beyond her control and desperately sought a way to escape her impending doom. Condemning her for adultery is similar to convicting a man who stole bread to keep his children from starving. It was still bad, but it was perfectly understandable: she was motivated by self-preservation. Rachel could sympathize with Mahlah's plight. But I wonder how easy it would have been for Rachel to accept Mahlah and take her under her wing if the circumstances had been different. What if Mahlah was married to a solid respectable man but had the hots for the beefcake down the lane? What if she had committed adultery for purely selfish or lustful reasons? How understanding would Rachel have been then?

The circumstances might make a difference to us, but they matter not a whit to Jesus. There is nothing so terrible, done for the most disgusting reasons, that is beyond his eagerness to forgive.

1. Is your relationship with Jesus more about belief, like Peter, or about faith, like Thomas?

2. Who is someone from your past who has angered or hurt you deeply? What is your attitude toward this person today?

3. Is it easier for you to accept forgiveness for yourself than to offer it to others? Why?

*The next chapter of the novel begins on page 168.*

# Chapter 18

## Background

Rachel is still trying to figure out who Jesus really is. Who can blame her? People have spent two millennia doing the same thing. It's tough, because on a theological or philosophical level, the best answer we can come up with is incomprehensible. Is Jesus a human being like us, or is he God? Christians know they're supposed to say that he's both, but we each tend to emphasize one over the other. Some of us take our cue from passages like Hebrews 1:1-4, which tells us that Jesus is "the reflection of God's glory and the exact imprint of God's very being, and he sustains all things by his powerful word." In other words, Jesus is God. He is the omniscient One who knew all about Rachel and her story when he met her the first time out at Jackal's Rock. Others of us hone in on Hebrews 2:14-18, which tells us that Jesus shared our flesh and blood and "had to become like his brothers and sisters in every respect." In other words, he's just like us. As Rachel tells us, he laughs at fish jokes and likes his stew heavy on the onion. The fact that the Bible describes Jesus both as the exact imprint of God's being, and then only a chapter later as someone like us in every respect, is enough to make our heads spin. Our brains can only hold one concept or the other. Rachel struggles because she grew up with a Jesus-as-God image, and now she is confronted with his utter, ordinary humanity.

For the first 400 years of church history, Jesus's nature was a major bone of contention. Constantinople, the eastern capital of the Roman Empire, was gripped by riots between rival bands of Christians who disagreed over this issue. When you arrived in Alexandria, the major port city of Egypt, the dockworkers would ask your opinion of Jesus. If you didn't give the answer they wanted, they'd toss you in the harbor. At one end of the spectrum were people like the Docetists, who believe that Jesus was fully completely God but only looked like a human being. He felt no pain and didn't need to eat or sleep. At the other end were groups like the Arians, who considered Jesus to be the ideal human being, the greatest of God's creation. He had some god-like qualities about him, but he wasn't God.

The battles between factions like these were so intense that the Roman emperor was worried they would tear apart the empire. So he gathered all the church leaders together, stuck them in a room, and told them to work it out. It took several tries, but finally in 451 at a gathering in the city of Chalcedon, they were able to hammer out a definition of Jesus's nature that everyone could swallow. They declared that Jesus is "at once complete in Godhead and complete in manhood, truly God and truly man, ... of one substance with the Father as regards his Godhead, and at the same time of one substance with us as regards his manhood; like us in all respects, apart from sin." They explained that Jesus has two natures "without confusion, without change, without division, without separation." He wasn't God part of the time and human part of the time. He was both, completely, at all times.

If that doesn't seem like much of an answer to you, I don't blame you. Perhaps that's the point. If we could wrap our minds around Jesus, he would become predictable. There is power in Jesus's mystery. Because he is beyond our comprehension and control, we can spend our entire lifetimes learning from and being challenged by him.

## Reflection

Whether you're part of AA or not, you probably know the Serenity Prayer that they use at each meeting: "God grant me the serenity to accept the things I cannot change; courage to change the things I can; and wisdom to know the difference." The prayer captures a common dilemma: we see things we can't accept and we want to fix them. Sometimes we can, and sometimes we can't. The cynic within us says that there's no point in trying to change anything, while our inner idealist can't imagine that we'd settle for anything other than the best.

In politics, they call it the art of the possible. Political ideologues at both ends of the spectrum refuse to compromise on their principles and are virtually impossible to work with. A bit of pragmatism is necessary to gain something that may not be perfect, but at least moves things a bit farther in your direction. Over time, your position will hopefully win.

That's fine for politics, but we tell ourselves that faith should never compromise. We admire Daniel for holding unswervingly to his principles, even though it landed him in a lion's den. We look up to his three friends, who were willing to be thrown into a fiery furnace rather than bow down before the emperor's statue. They could easily have rationalized it: what's a small thing like pretending to worship an emperor compared to the lifetime of work in God's name that they could accomplish? But they didn't, and we respect them for it.

There are things that we can change, and there are things we must accept. We need the wisdom to tell the difference. It's not in Rachel's nature to give up on anything. The subservient role of women sticks in her craw. The smug hypocrisy of the religious elite drives her up the wall. She wants to tackle every challenge head-on. She wishes that Jesus would confront the problems in his culture and shake things up. Judas, on the other hand, is very aware of the things you can't change. He sees the powerful forces of the status quo, and he fears what they will do to anyone who challenges them. Better to lurk in the background, keep quiet, and work on the fringes, or they'll eat you for breakfast.

We each face the dilemma in our own ways. When we see an injustice and don't address it, we feel like sell-outs. But when we hit our heads against the brick wall long enough, we scramble our brains and collapse in a bloody mess. Should Jesus have taken up the banner of gender equality? Should he have spoken against the harsh occupation of the Romans? Should the writers of the New Testament letters have condemned slavery instead of instructing slaves how to live faithfully in their positions (Ephesians 6:5-8, Colossians 3:22-25, Titus 2:9-10, 1 Peter 2:18)? Ideally, yes. But perhaps they were wise enough to know the difference between what they could change and what they couldn't. Perhaps, as Rachel's Sunday school teachers taught her, Jesus was sensitive to how much people of that cultural climate could absorb.

Perhaps he worked for incremental change instead of ripping the bandage off.

For some, this may sound like explaining your way out of necessary but tough work. Others may use this argument to avoid changes they can really make. The wisdom is to know the difference.

1. Are you more comfortable with mystery or with certainty? Why?

2. When have you tackled something too big and paid the price for it?

3. When have you avoided an issue and come to regret it?

4. Should Jesus have been more forceful in challenging the culture?

*The next chapter of the novel begins on page 181.*

# Chapter 19

## Background

Tax collectors were scum, no matter how you looked at them. When the Romans began their occupation of the region, they collected their taxes from the citizens directly. Relatively quickly, however, they farmed out the work to local subcontractors. The tax collecting duties for a region were put up for auction; the bidder who offered the highest revenue for the Romans got the job. The winner of the tax-auction had to pay the money up front, and he was then free to recoup that payment, plus expenses and personal profit, however he wanted. All the Romans cared about was getting their money.

These "chief tax collectors" like Zacchaeus typically hired agents to assist in the work of squeezing money out of the populace. Matthew was most likely one of these underlings. There were three primary forms of taxation: a property tax, a poll or head tax, and customs fees at ports and city gates. In Jerusalem, there was an additional tax on houses. The Romans did not set an official tax rate for any of these levies. The chief tax collector charged whatever he wanted. This was not merely a system that allowed for corruption and abuse; it was a system that encouraged such practices. The tax collector could use whatever means he chose to collect as much as he wanted, and if anyone protested, he had the might of the Roman Empire to back him up.

People hated tax collectors for two reasons. First, they were collaborators with the occupation forces. They were traitors to their own people who put the allure of riches ahead of national loyalty. You may hate the foreign army that invades and dominates your land, but there's a special loathing for turncoats who help them do it. Second, tax collectors were engaged in literal robbery. They took whatever they wanted with impunity. Jewish law, as set forth by the rabbis of the time, reflects the level of animosity people had for tax collectors. Rabbinic sources frequently refer to tax collectors as a type of bandit, thief, or robber. They were barred from holding any communal office, and they could not testify in a Jewish court of law.

No one likes to pay taxes under any conditions. But when your money is paying for the brutal domination of your occupiers and is lining the pockets of extortionists, the acrimony is almost unbearable. Of course no one made room for Zacchaeus to see Jesus (Luke 19:1-10); they probably made a point to block his view. Of course people were outraged that Jesus gave him the honor of hosting him while in Jericho. Of course Jesus ruffled feathers throughout his ministry by associating with such scum (Matthew 11:19, 21:31-32; Mark 2:15-16; Luke 7:29-30, 15:1-2). But Jesus recognized that they, perhaps more than anyone else, needed the good news he had to offer.

## Reflection

Zacchaeus's generosity in response to Jesus's acceptance unsettled Mary, and for good reason. She resonated more with the ruler who couldn't bring himself to part with his riches (Luke 18:18-23) than with the tax collector's joyful change of heart. One could respond openly to Jesus's call, but the other could not. His wealth was simply too important to him. And Mary's lucrative business was too important to her to let go. It was her identity. It was what she relied on to take care of her. In other words, it had become an idol. I don't mean that she literally bowed down and prayed to it. But it threatened to overtake the place in her life that belongs to God. An idol is anything that becomes the ultimate source of your hope and happiness. It receives your greatest allegiance, and it's where you turn when the chips are down. It is the foundation for decisions you make, the source of the values you have.

Idols come in all shapes and sizes. Earlier, Rachel recognized that she had focused her entire life upon her children, sacrificing her own goals and dreams to cater to their every whim and need. Children are a blessing from God, but they become idols when they overtake our lives. Rachel also shares Mary's struggle with wealth. Her time in the first century has led her to realize the powerful hold that money and possessions have upon Joe and her. Their marriage is suffering because they "have" to maintain their standard of living, twenty-eight hundred dollar mattresses, top of the line SUVs, and all the rest. Like any other idol, the pursuit of wealth can take over our lives. We train ourselves to believe that we "need" that which we enjoy or desire, but could live perfectly fine without. But it never satisfies. Like the two brothers arguing over their inheritance, we always want more. We all have a bit of Rachel's uncle in us: defining our lives by what we have and believing that this is exactly what God wants for us.

Jesus's simple, direct advice to the ruler is a slap in our faces. Zacchaeus's eagerness to give it all away sets a disquieting example for us. That's what happens any time our idols are threatened. Until we accept the advice and follow the example, we block our ability to respond to Jesus's mindset and way of living. The struggle with idolatry is particularly difficult when it comes to money. It doesn't matter how much you have; it only matters how much you want it. You can be Rachel's fat cat uncle, or you can be struggling to get by on food stamps. If money is the answer to your problems, you're not going to want to get rid of it.

Our unwillingness to let go of the idol motivates us to obscure the plain, simple meaning of Jesus's words: "Sell all that you own and distribute the money to the poor." Over the centuries, Christians have worked very hard to pull the teeth out of the challenge. Surely we need to keep something to keep ourselves going, don't we? Don't we help the poor better when we use our assets to help them, instead of just getting rid of it all? It's not the wealth itself that Jesus is talking about, but the hold it has on us. You can be rich and still devote your life to God. These are the things we say to take the sting out of Jesus's words. But the words are still there. Sell all that you own and distribute the money to the poor. It is easier for a camel to go through the eye of a needle than for someone who is rich to enter the kingdom of God. If you haven't learned how to rationalize away the challenge, God is going to turn your life upside down.

1. When has your desire for financial gain led you to do something you regretted?

2. What are the idols in your life?

3. If you took Jesus's challenge seriously, what would your life look like?

*The next chapter of the novel begins on page 190.*

# Chapter 20

## Background

Rachel and her companions had been dreading it, and now it's happened. Jesus has arrived in Jerusalem. The situation was every bit as bad as Rachel had been worrying it would be.

What Jesus did just before entering the city didn't help. He had heard about his friend Lazarus's illness, and his delay in traveling to see him meant that the man had been dead and buried by the time Jesus arrived. In dramatic fashion, he restored life to someone who had been in the tomb for more than half a week (John 11:1-44). This wasn't the first time that Jesus brought someone back from the dead: remember Jairus's daughter in Capernaum and the widow's son in Nain. But those had been recent deaths. One could argue that they weren't completely dead, or that they were in some sort of a coma. Jesus was nothing more than an extremely gifted first century EMT who resuscitated them. But this is different. Four days is a long time. Lazarus was dead, and his body had even started to rot. Jesus has just taken his wonder-working to a new level.

What Jesus did for Lazarus caused a huge stir for another reason.

He was now on the outskirts of Jerusalem, the epicenter of the Jewish world. When he was up in the boondocks of Galilee exciting the locals, the bigshots down in the capital heard about him, and a few even went up north to investigate. But as long as he kept his spectacles out of the limelight, they could tolerate him. Now things were different. Jesus was at their front gate, exceeding even his own past performances. Not only had he brought along a rabble of fellow Galileans who were sure to cause a scene, but now the residents of Judea were getting on his band wagon. Jesus could no longer be ignored.

Perhaps the religious leaders acted out of jealousy. He received the attention and the devotion they wanted. As a pastor, I can confirm that church leaders can get jealous of each other. Does your choir sound better than mine? Do I have a bigger youth program than you? Did I have more people in my pews than you did last Sunday? If we have these attitudes today, I'm confident they had them in Jesus's time as well. Then again, the religious establishment may have opposed Jesus's message simply because it was new. We find this attitude in churches today. As the old joke goes, the Seven Last Words of the Church are "we've never done it that way before." Innovation is inherently suspicious. Another possibility is that Jesus faced the wrath of the religious elite because his message offended them. How dare he encourage people to think about the Jewish laws and traditions the way he did! Did he really think that forgiveness and love was at the heart of their faith? They were the experts, and they knew better. Maybe Jesus bothered the Powers That Be for a combination of all these reasons, plus several more. Either way, his threat to the establishment had to be dealt with.

That's what the authorities thought about Jesus. But everyone else was catching the Jesus fever. Again, they probably did so for a whole host of reasons. Some people, like Rachel and her companions, were drawn to him because of what he taught, the way he lived, and his very demeanor. He was a breath of fresh air in a stale world that refreshed everything and everyone. For others, it was the miracles. They may have experienced one, or knew about what Jesus had done in the past. Everyone loves a good show. Even though, as Rachel saw for herself, Jesus didn't draw attention to himself with fireworks and brass bands, he astounded thousands with what he had done. Some wanted a miracle for themselves, others simply wanted a front row seat for the next performance. Then there are those who join any crowd that happens to come along. These are the people today who follow celebrities simply because they're celebrities. Jesus was hot stuff, and they wanted to join the fad.

Last, and perhaps most dangerous of all, were the people who had their own plans for Jesus. They saw his charisma and the unprecedented following he had attracted. He had thousands of people who would eagerly do anything he told them to do. That's power. When someone has that kind of power, you expect them to do something about it. Some hailed him as the Messiah: the long-awaited leader who would make Israel a mighty nation and vanquish her foes. The Zealots, desperate for a way to fight the Romans, wanted to take full advantage of the opportunity Jesus presented. With him at the helm, they were convinced the whole nation would rise up and throw off the shackles of oppression. All their hopes for the nation would be fulfilled.

The crowd on Palm Sunday included all these people. It didn't take long until Jesus's entry into Jerusalem took on the air of an ancient king of Israel entering his capital to reclaim it as his own. Even the donkey upon which he rode was reminiscent of the mules that only the king and his family could ride during the glory days of David and Solomon. The chant "Hosanna!" was not an exclamation of praise, but a call for Jesus to help and save them. They saw him as someone who could make everything better for them and fulfill all their hopes. The Zealots and the temple leadership, who agreed on very little, were both convinced that Jesus was ready to announce his kingship and drive away his enemies.

When Rachel noticed Jesus receiving the crowd's adoration with uncharacteristic solemnity, she thought it was because he knew that their devotion wouldn't last. According to Luke 19:41-44, Jesus was more than solemn. He broke down and wept, not for the fate that awaited him, but for the grim future that the people of Jerusalem would face. He knew that the warmongers would have their way, and that the battles and uprisings would go badly. He knew that the world's suffering would continue.

## Reflection

Whom do you trust? What do you rely upon? The answer determines the course you take for your life. Judas has followed Jesus from the very beginning, confident that he was a man who could make a real difference. But his trust had its limits: Jesus was leading them on a path that Judas was sure would end terribly. Proverbs 3:5 tells us "Trust in the Lord with all your heart, and do not rely on your own insight." That's a nice sentiment. But in that critical moment of decision, we typically follow our own instincts instead of the assurance that God will lead us along. Judas believes that he can count on the religious establishment to pull the whole enterprise off the edge of the cliff. Rachel and Mary have been relying on their wealth, but they're struggling to set aside their idol in favor of trust in Jesus. Judas isn't able to do the same thing. He, and many people today, fail to see the distinction between deep faith and blind trust. Instead of quoting Proverbs, they'd much rather focus upon Jesus's words as he sent out the disciples: "Be wise as serpents and innocent as doves" (Matthew 10:16). Trusting in Jesus may be fine, but we've got to use our wits to get through it all.

Rachel doesn't have a conversation with Simon the Zealot, but I suspect his wits are telling him something very different from Judas'. Assuming that he was still a Zealot, he didn't trust the establishment any farther than he could throw the temple. They were all in cahoots with the Romans. Judas hopes "the system" can protect Jesus from his own maniacal delusions. If Simon had been part of Rachel and Judas's conversation, he would have argued that Jesus should act even more boldly against the leadership. This doesn't mean that Simon puts more trust in Jesus; he's also following his own insights. They simply happen to be different from Judas'. Fight and overthrow, and all will be well. Jesus is the perfect person to do it. Come Friday, Simon will be just as disappointed as Judas.

We continue to put our trust in the wrong places. No matter how many times they fail us and disappoint us, we always give them another chance. Our investments and savings will get us through... until the stock market crashes. Our family will always be there for us... until our kids move into another time zone and our spouse dies unexpectedly. Yet we still keep looking for something, someone, to rely upon. We simply can't stand the uncertainty of a life with nothing dependable. Psalm 46 may tell us that God is a "very present help in trouble" when everything else collapses around us. We may even believe it. But it's very difficult to walk off the cliff and trust that God will catch you.

1. Has someone ever disappointed you or let you down? What came of

it?

2. What makes it hard for you to trust God?

*The next chapter of the novel begins on page 201.*

# Chapter 21

## Background

Rachel poked her nose into the famous Last Supper: the meal Jesus shared with his disciples before his arrest, interrogation, torture, crucifixion, and death. When we imagine what it must have looked like, Leonardo da Vinci's iconic painting typically springs to mind. Salvador Dali's more modern rendering may also color the imagination of your mind's eye. But unlike both of these paintings, the Last Supper was more than a dozen men around a table, watching Jesus break the bread and share the cup.

First, this was no ordinary dinner. Jesus and his companions were sharing the Passover Seder, the ritual meal that begins the seven-day observance of God's powerful action to free the Israelites from slavery in Egypt. Even today it is one of Judaism's most important holidays, together with the high holy holidays of Yom Kippur and Rosh Hashanah. The Seder is a meal somewhat akin to our Thanksgiving suppers, but it includes rituals that draw everyone's attention to the spiritual significance of the gathering.

In Jesus's day, people were expected to gather in Jerusalem to celebrate Passover and to ensure that they were ritually pure, in accordance with the requirements of the Old Testament law. Because so many people traveled to Jerusalem for this important occasion, they gathered wherever they could find the space. One house would often host multiple groups, with some families even eating in the courtyard or on the roof. Jesus and his friends gathered in an "upper room" of a house, but they were likely not the only ones in that house.

Although the Seder was originally intended to be shared by families, the prevalent practice today, in Jesus's time people would gather in a group called a haburah, consisting of ten to twenty adults. Usually most members of a haburah were relatives, but non-family members would commonly be included. By these standards, Jesus and his twelve disciples would have formed a typical haburah. Most likely, Rachel and the other women would have been included in the ritual and the meal. While women and children could not make up the majority of the haburah, they certainly gathered with the men at the meal. In fact, part of the Seder ceremony included questions asked by a son to his father about the meaning of the meal. We can thank Leonardo da Vinci for reinforcing our notion that the Last Supper was a male-only club. In telling this tale, Rachel adheres to the traditional portrayal of the Last Supper by having the men (attended perhaps by a few women) meet in the upper room while the women formed their own haburah in the courtyard. If the entire group was too big to be a single haburah, it would make sense for Jesus to be inside where no one could see him. The authorities didn't pay attention to the women, so they could hang around outside the house and no one would suspect a thing.

According to historical sources from the first century, the Seder ceremony began when a servant gave you water to wash your hands as you entered the room. The fact that Jesus, the host for the meal, takes this role upon himself (John 13:1-17) and washes the guests' feet and not their hands, would shock everyone and show how Jesus disrupts Standard Operating Procedure. The meal began with wine, the first of four times that wine is shared. Bible scholars have lots of fun debating which of these four cups was the one that Jesus called his blood. The meal continued with ceremonies such as dipping vegetables in salt to commemorate the tears of enslavement, eating bitter herbs as a reminder the harshness of servitude, and sharing the roast lamb to bring to mind the lambs that were killed and eaten to protect the Israelites from death (Exodus 12:21-23). When the host blessed the bread, he might bestow honor on one member of the gathering by giving them the first piece from the plate. For Jesus to provide this distinction to Judas his betrayer (John 13:26) is at least as convention-shattering as washing everyone's feet.

# Reflection

When Jesus described himself as the Good Shepherd, he said, "the sheep follow him because they know his voice" (John 10:4). It is exceedingly difficult for us to recognize Jesus's voice in the cacophony of noise around us, and the confusion of thoughts, urges, and emotions within our skulls. And it is beyond disappointing when we get it wrong. Since the advent of Christianity, the faithful have engaged in what is now called "spiritual discernment": the practice of discovering how God guides us, and the endeavor to distinguish between his voice and all the others around and within us. History is riddled with destruction caused by those who were convinced that they were following the Lord but were terribly, terribly wrong. This dilemma is not a relic from the past; people continue to act reprehensibly in the name of God.

When Rachel first heard Jesus speak on the hillside outside of Capernaum, she didn't understand how she could recognize a voice she had never heard. We have an innate sense, as those created by God, to understand the voice of our Creator as he speaks to us. However, the obstacles that arise between us and him stifle this awareness. The pressures of life overwhelm us. Messages from our upbringing, cues from our culture, and the desires of our own hearts so easily masquerade as the guidance of God. We sheep may know our Shepherd's voice, but sometimes it is so faint we can barely hear it. Even when we can hear it and recognize it to be his, we often ignore it and go merrily along the path that seems best to us.

Mary and Rachel are lucky as they struggle with the grip that wealth has upon them, and with Jesus's challenge for the rich ruler to give it all up. They could go up to Jesus and ask him to explain what he meant, and how it affects them. According to the Bible, the disciples did it all the time (Mark 4:10-20 and 9:28, for example). I would absolutely love to have the opportunity to walk up to Jesus and hear his unambiguous, clear direction for me. But that's not an option for us. Even if it were, I'm not sure how willing I'd be to exercise it. I'm like Mary, who responded to Rachel's suggestion that she talk with Jesus about her struggle by saying, "I'm too afraid of his answer." We may be kidding ourselves to think that even if we could talk with Jesus face to face, his words to us would be unambiguous. Rachel has been trying for weeks to understand what Jesus meant when he told her, "Out of the overflow of the heart, the mouth speaks."

Rachel's question to Jesus as he left the house is a question for all of us to ask him: "What do you want me to do?" The answer will be a shifting target, never what we expect, and rarely simple and obvious.

But it defines a life of faith. We do not ask it because we are servants looking for orders from a master or soldiers seeking a command from their officer. We don't ask Jesus what he wants us to do because we are obliged to follow him. We ask because like Rachel we are motivated by devotion, love, and a desire to help. When Jesus answers, he tells us the same thing he told Rachel: "Ask me again sometime." Each day is another opportunity to ask Jesus, "What do you want me to do?"

1. When have you been convinced that God wanted you to do something, only to find out you were wrong? Why do you think you misunderstood?

2. In what ways do you seek God's guidance for your life? What works best for you?

*The last chapter of the novel begins on page 208.*

# Epilogue

The woman who went to bed with a migraine is not the same one who turned her family's lives upside down (or maybe, right-side up). In my experience, that's what an encounter with Jesus will do to you. Over the course of my ministry, I've seen it happen far too often and far too dramatically to attribute it to anything as mundane as a change of heart or a psychological re-orientation. I've seen an old man who spent his whole life being a brute to his family and an absolute pain to his neighbors seek reconciliation and do whatever it took to make it happen. I've seen a drug addict discover a joy that no high could ever give him. I've seen a man crippled by past trauma break out of his painful secret and discover his true worth as a human being. I've seen lonely people find fellowship, self-centered people find humility, and cruel people find kindness. As in Rachel's case, I've seen someone trapped in materialism find generosity.

It's dangerous to hang out with Jesus. You never know what he'll do to you.

You can never understand it until you experience it yourself.

Bekka and Ryan were absolutely mystified by Rachel's transformation. We can only imagine how Joe responded when he got home from his business trip. It makes no sense until you go through it yourself. My friend the recovering drug addict went to his parole officer, who was convinced he was high. That was the only way he could comprehend the pure joy and peace that he saw in my friend. When some Christians call themselves "born again," they are using an expression that Jesus coined (John 3:3-8) which is an apt description of how dramatically one's life changes with Jesus's touch. It really is as if you've started to live a new life. It's impossible to describe to someone who hasn't had it happen to them. How do you describe turquoise to someone who's been blind their entire life? How do you describe chocolate mousse to someone who's only ever eaten rice and beans? Some people are fortunate enough never to have known anything other than the life Jesus brings, because they knew him before their earliest memory. Even such people, however, experience Jesus in new and surprising ways that can take them on a roller coaster ride.

There are many ways in which Rachel's time with Jesus could have changed her life. After seeing women's second-class treatment and Jesus's willingness to challenge it, she could have recognized the continuing sexism of our culture and provided a challenge of her own. After discovering her gift of boldness, she could have taken on the bullies at the school bus stop and the PTA meetings. But Rachel's take-away from her experience was a call to simplicity. She became aware that the "stuff" we have constrains our lives, as we work like dogs to buy twenty-eight hundred dollar mattresses so we can get a good night's rest after working like a dog. We provide our children with every convenience and fad to enrich their lives, and we rob them of the opportunity to enrich their own lives, to become more self-confident and capable. Rachel's call to simplicity was reinforced by her conversations with Mary, who was troubled with her own wealth. Will we have the joy of Zacchaeus, who gave it all away, or the sadness of the rich ruler who could not?

When Rachel walked through the streets of Capernaum for the first time, she was struck by the abject poverty and the disease and disability that confronted her. There are people in need in our world today, but we've gotten better at concealing and ignoring them. You can live in any major city in the US and see nothing but tidy neighborhoods and swanky shopping plazas if you want to. Or you can go to the seedier parts of town and see people much like the ones

Rachel saw in Capernaum. The poor and disadvantaged live in their places, and the comfortable and well-to-do live in theirs. Poverty and prosperity don't mingle well. By the time my church's work team arrives to help rebuild after floods, hurricanes, and tornados, the people with resources have already rebuilt their homes and businesses. Nobody thinks about the widow living in a hotel room or in her son's living room for over a year because her house has been condemned. We're very good at forgetting about such people. Rachel's transformation has enabled her to recognize what is so easy to ignore.

The family has been transformed, as they gleefully rid themselves of the possessions that had come to possess them. Bekka and Ryan are taking responsibility for themselves. Joe has gotten out from under a job that was sucking the life out of him. Rachel is discovering the delights of enriching the lives of the impoverished. But there is still so much more for her to understand and integrate into her new life. It will take years – probably the rest of her life.

Give her time. Jesus is.

1. Have you ever had a dramatic faith experience that reshaped your life? In what way?

2. What distorted views of Jesus have you been exposed to? What effect did they have on you?

3. How aware are you of the needs in your community? Are you doing anything about it?

4. What does your life focus upon?

## Summary

Before Rachel had her amazing experience, she had a nagging feeling that something was missing from her life. By all accounts she had it made: a healthy and productive family, an active life, and all the conveniences that suburban America can offer. But she felt an ache within her. As she put it, she felt like life was passing her by and something was slipping away. That intangible "something" was a desire that nothing in her perfect middle-class world could fill.

She was missing a purpose for her life.

An encounter with Jesus can bring joy, peace, healing, forgiveness, dignity, salvation, and so much more. But one of the greatest blessings we can receive is a sense of meaning for our lives. We want a direction toward which we live and a reason for doing what we are doing. Rick Warren made a tremendous name for himself with his book *The Purpose Driven Life* because he scratched an itch that so many people feel. We want a purpose to drive our lives. That's what Rachel ached for. She had gone numb because her life was going nowhere.

Rachel's companion Mary lived without purpose for years before Jesus came into her world. The feather in her cap was a thriving ship-building business, but it turned her into a crafty shrew who made everyone around her miserable. The moment she died, everything she had accomplished would be forgotten. If Rachel hadn't lain down with her migraine and experienced what she did, the same fate may have awaited her.

It can be tricky to recognize God's purpose for your life because it is unique to you. God doesn't use a cookie cutter, making all of us from the same mold for the same reason. He forms each of us with the abilities and desires to find our place in his grand design. You and I are different people, and we have different purposes for our lives. Perhaps Jesus didn't want Mary to sell all her possessions, because she is a different person from the rich ruler. Rachel didn't merrily divest her family of the possessions that possessed them so they could live monkish lives of asceticism and self-deprivation. Maybe that's what he wants for other people, but not for Rachel. The point for her goal of simplicity was to give and to help: to address the deep need that continues to fill our world. If you want to discover the purpose that will bring meaning to your life, don't expect it to be the same as someone else's.

As Rachel played Peeping Tom at the Last Supper, she began to understand God's purpose for her life. To reach that point, she first needed someone like Mary to help her see her gift of boldness. Sometimes we are the worst assessor of our own gifts because we're too close to ourselves to perceive what may be obvious to others. Next, Rachel had to overcome her notion that her boldness was something bad that she had to conceal or overcome. People in my congregation tell me that they want to change who they are because they think it's "wrong." The only way it can be wrong is if they use it in destructive ways and for misguided objectives. We waste time bemoaning our weaknesses when we can be acting on our strengths. They both come from the same part of our being.

Earlier I described Rachel's experience as a transformation, as though she was "born again" into a new life. That's not completely accurate. Jesus didn't turn her into a new person; he simply enabled her to become the person she really was. She had suffered under the nagging dissatisfaction for so long because she wasn't being herself. She wasn't doing what God created her to do. She was a book being used as a doorstop, a spatula used to stir paint. Now her life was being lived for the very reason God had created it in the first place.

When Rachel woke up with a realization of her purpose and an appreciation for the power she had to fulfill it, she could hardly contain herself. Instead of bouncing through life off the pinball bumpers that surrounded her, she could take charge and make the difference she wanted to make: the difference Jesus had awakened and directed within her. Rachel was committed to a life of simplicity and service, not only for herself but for her entire family. Her gift of boldness enabled her to rise above Bekka and Ryan's resistance. It even empowered her to decide Joe would quit his job... without consulting him to find out if he wanted to. She knew it was best for him, and for the whole family. That's all that mattered to her.

God created each of us for a reason, and we all have a part to play in the incredible orchestra that is called the will of God. In Ephesians we read that God "chose us in Christ before the foundation of the world" (1:4), and that "we are what God has made us, created in Christ Jesus for good works, which God prepared beforehand to be our way of life" (2:10). You are not an afterthought. Long before God said "Let there be light!" he chose you. He knew you by name. And he created you for a reason. Thousands of years before your parents met each other and had a baby, God prepared a way of life for you. The more fully we are aware of Jesus's presence and love in our lives, the better we are able to discern what that purpose is. When we do, and when we live for the reason that God created us, all the joy and peace and salvation that everyone talks about will flood our spirits.

Rachel misses her old friends, and what they had together. She doubts that she'll ever find something like that again. Rachel's desire for what she and the rest of Jesus's companions shared should be able to be filled today, and it is an indictment of the church when it is not. What she called camaraderie with a purpose is what churches call fellowship with a mission. Same concept, just churchier sounding words. In theory, that's what church is. But somehow, it rarely seems to work out that way.

When Christians clump themselves together (or more properly, when God clumps Christians together), it's called a church. Those who call themselves Christians identify themselves as today's version of the band that followed Jesus during his earthly ministry. They, like Rachel and her companions, are committed to following Jesus through thick and thin, struggling with and relishing his presence, discovering the way that he changes people's lives, and realizing the part that they have to play in his plans. Short of the Second Coming, none of us are going to see Jesus's face and look into his eyes like Rachel did. But we should be able to see a reflection of those twinkling, unnerving, tender, wise eyes in the people who gather in his name. That's what a church is supposed to be.

Rachel is right: churches and the people in them often get stuck in dogmatism, ritual, and hypocrisy. They lose sight of the purpose, the mission, that God has given them. They obsess over the organizational aspects of being a church, like budgets and buildings. They view people as numbers on a Sunday morning, contributors to the offering, and tools to be used to advance the institution's standing. In other words, they often succumb to the same malady that infects every religious group, just like the Pharisees of Jesus's time. Churches, like people, can spin away from the reason God created them. They can become as empty as Rachel was before her experience: keeping very busy for no reason. When this happens, churches alienate people around them and deaden the spirits of people within them. Rachel has experienced the real thing. The sham that she sees in churches is now even more intolerable, because she knows what they could be, what they should be, what they can be.

The gang that followed Jesus was far from perfect. It would be easy to find fault with each person in the bunch. That's what you'll find even in the churches that get it right. You'll find narrow-minded control freaks like Bernice. You'll find timid wallflowers like Naomi. You'll find people with checkered pasts like Mary. You'll find people whose good intentions lead them astray, like Judas. You'll even find outspoken people whose boldness sometimes offends, like Rachel. If Rachel is looking for a group of perfect people to help her recapture the joy and excitement she found while trekking across Galilee with Jesus, she never will. If you are looking for a church that has no jerks, hypocrites, and faultfinders, you're wasting your time. Jesus does not gather perfect people. He collects people with problems and people who cause problems, so they can discover a new way to live. The church's purpose is not to provide for you. It is a place where you can discover your purpose, as Rachel did during her fantastic adventure.

1. How has your faith helped or hindered your quest for meaning?

2. Have you found a purpose for your life? If so, how has it changed you? What is the next goal Jesus has put in front of you?

3. Have you experienced the church in primarily a positive or negative way? How has it affected your relationship with Jesus?

4. If you are part of a church, how closely does it reflect the fellowship and mission that Jesus shared with his disciples?

# About the Authors

**Rachel Stackhouse** is a former veterinarian, childbirth educator, and mother of three who under another pen name is a USA-Today bestselling author of mystery and romantic fiction. In her own frenetic life, she frequently has to remind herself to slow down, take stock, and simplify in order to remember what matters most.

**Rev. Peter C. de Vries, Ph. D.** has spent more than half of his life as a pastor and teacher, daring Jesus-followers to discover the challenges and joys of having their lives turned upside down. He is married to his best friend and has three children, one grandchild, and a goofy little dog. He blogs at **petercdevries.blogspot.com** and may be reached by email at **rev.dr.devries@gmail.com**.

Made in the USA
Middletown, DE
14 September 2020